The Maltese Crisis

Alexander Kirkwood

To Ian

with every blessing

Alexander R Kirkwood

Raider Publishing International

New York London Swansea

First Printing

ISBN: 0-9790799-5-0
Published By Raider Publishing International

www.RaiderPublishing.com

New York London Swansea

Printed in the United States of America and the United Kingdom

By Lightning Source Ltd.

Dedicated to my recently departed parents. I miss them dearly, especially their jokes about my over active imagination. Alex and Agnes Kirkwood will forever live on in my memories. They were the best parents an author could ever wish to have.

The Maltese Crisis

Alexander Kirkwood

Make a chain, for the land is filled with blood, and the city is full of violence. Therefore I will bring the worst of the gentiles, And they will possess their houses: I will cause the pomp of the strong to cease, And their holy places shall be defiled. Destruction comes; they shall seek peace, but there shall be none. Disaster will come upon disaster, and rumour upon rumour.

Then they will seek a vision from a prophet;

But the law will perish from the priest, and council from the elders.

EZEKIEL. 7: 23 – 26. (Quoted from the New King James Bible)

CHAPTER 311. MALTA-LIBYA TREATY OF FRIENDSHIP AND CO-OPERATION (RATIFICATION) ACT.

To ratify the Treaty of Friendship and Co-operation between Malta and Libya (7th December 1984)

Enacted by ACT XXII of 1984, as amended by ACT XXIII of 1990.

FIRST SCHEDULE

(Section 2)

TREATY OF FRIENDSHIP AND CO-OPERATION BETWEEN THE GOVERNMENT OF THE REPUBLIC OF MALTA AND THE SOCIALIST PEOPLE'S LIBYAN ARAB JAMAHIRIYA.

Article 3

The Socialist People's Libyan Arab Jamahiriya undertakes to respect and support Malta's neutrality and will assist Malta whenever the Government of the Republic of Malta explicitly requests so in cases of threats or acts of aggression against Malta's territorial integrity and sovereignty.

PROTOCOL ON CO-OPERATION IN SECURITY

Having regard to Article 3 of the Treaty of Friendship and co-operation between the Government of the Republic of Malta and the Socialist People's Libyan Arab Jamahiriya, signed in Malta on the 19th November, 1984, the two sides further agree as follows;

1. In order that each side may be fully informed on matters pertaining to this agreement, the two sides

agree that there should be continuous exchange of information on matters of special interest to the mutual security and defense purposes of the other side and

2. In order to enable the Maltese Armed Forces to reach higher standards of military preparedness to be able to withstand threats or acts of aggression against Malta's territorial integrity and sovereignty, the Libyan side shall train Maltese military personnel in Libya or Malta as the two sides may agree from time to time and in the numbers and modalities that may be agreed upon.
3. To meet the requirements of the Maltese Armed Forces which will be identified from time to time by the different sections of the Maltase's forces, the Libyan side agree to study supplying from their armouries and stores any military equipment and armaments which the Maltese side may require for their own use.

Dr. Ali Treiki
Secretary of the People's Bureau
Foreign Liaison of the Socialist People's Libyan Arab Jamahiriya.

Dr. Alex Sciberras Trigona
Minister of Foreign Affairs and Culture for of the Republic of Malta.

Chapter One

As Gaz Seymour leaned over the railing of HMS Edinburgh; the British Naval Destroyer he had found himself on, he was in a reflective mood. He had, a few hours earlier, seen the destruction of the lovely Island of Cyprus, and also the death of his best friend and fellow RAF Intelligence operative Alan; someone he had seen action with in many different parts of the world, which was in Gaz's view becoming a very dangerous place. He was also very angry; angry at the Israeli's for launching their nuclear warhead against Cyprus, and the invading Turkish troops, but he was also angry at the Turks for taking the lives of his friends, some of whom he had only met briefly but would have a lasting impact in his life. If Gaz's whole mood could be summed up, it would be fair to say that he was at this moment angry with the world but most of all, he was angry with himself. Feelings of guilt seemed to hang on to him "*Why am I still alive when so many better people are now dead?*" It was a feeling he couldn't shrug off and it was starting to pull him close to despair.

What was left of Cyprus on the horizon was shrinking fast as the British and American fleets headed east towards Israel. Although the British or the Americans had no idea as to what they would be doing when they arrived; there was a general feeling among the Naval Ranks that they were purely going to do some 'saber rattling' - at least that was what the majority of men and women on the ships hoped for, they had no will to enter into a full blown conflict with Israel especially since they now knew that

Israel wouldn't hesitate to use whatever means it had at it's disposal to defend itself; the atmosphere in the fleet was tense and that didn't help Gaz cope with his own demons.

"Hi ya bud…how you doin?"

Gaz had been so wrapped up in his own thoughts, he hadn't noticed his friend of a few days; Captain James Kirk, come along side of him. James had been rescued with Gaz from Cyprus prior to the nuclear explosion that had put an end to Turkeys desires for the sunshine island - Israel's response to the threat of being surrounded by Muslim states.

"Hi James," Gaz replied, struggling to refocus his thoughts to the present situation. "I'm OK."

"Just OK… that doesn't sound to promising." James replied in his easy American way. He was a 'Top Gun' on F22 – Raptors but had been shot down by Rapiers over the Island of Cyprus during the latter stages of the Turkish invasion.

"It's all this," Gaz turned to face James, holding his arms and shrugging his shoulders. "Why James…I'm lost for any answers…I'm alive and my friends are dead, Alan, Feri, Osman, Forbes, Amanda, Woody….gone….what's going on?"

James held back from saying anything right away, he saw the tears starting to come to Gaz's eyes, but he was an optimist in most areas of life and felt a little uncomfortable. "Eh…look…buddy, I just come to tell you that I'm going over to the USS Theodore Roosevelt, they want me back in the cockpit."

Gaz sensed James's hesitation and wiped his eyes with the back of his hand. "Sorry James, I didn't mean to unsettle you - I'll be fine in a little while."

James moved forward and embraced Gaz tightly. "It was good to serve with you my British friend, who knows maybe our paths will cross again."

"I hope so mate - take care though; those Israeli pilots are hot."

James recognized the laboured attempt at humour so he slapped Gaz on his shoulder. "Hey my man, I'll 'beam up' the first one I meet."

Gaz started to laugh as Captain Kirk headed back along the way he had come; he realized at that moment that he would cope, thanks to James Kirk. "James." Gaz shouted above the sounds of the sea hitting the ship as it sped at top speed towards its destination; James turned but kept walking. "Kick some butt for me and the others."

James put his thumb up and smiled, "You got it babe," then disappeared around one of the ships grey metallic fixtures.

The next time Gaz saw James, he was suspended between HMS Edinburgh his own ship, and a lower deck of the USS Theodore Roosevelt; the second largest Aircraft carrier in the American fleet, in a boson's chair. The whole ship had gathered to watch the transfer and the British had put on a small naval band to play the theme tune for Thunderbirds, which Gaz thought was totally inappropriate for the occasion. At one point it looked as though the chair with James on it might drop into the sea between the two massive ships, but Gaz convinced himself that it was purely an optical illusion and James would soon be safely on board his new ship; but the sea was choppy and Gaz was glad that it was James and not him hanging from the chair; it looked very unsafe. Of course the men were shouting the usual comments like, "Beam me up Scottie," or "It's a chair captain, but not as we know it," and "Boldly going where no man has gone before," but James seemed to take it all in his stride. Gaz knew he would miss his cheery presence. *"I hope we meet again mate."*

*

Chief Petty Officer Betty Williams was very good at her job and also very officious. She had distinct philosophies about rank protocols and ran a very tight 'ship'. Her one aim in life was to make sure that the Missile Interceptor Control Centre she was responsible for ran smoothly and efficiently. Her 'crew' of radar operators secretly called her the 'Ice Maiden' but they also knew that whatever else they thought about her, she was good at what she did. Betty had worked hard to keep her team focused after the nuclear explosion. There was a tense moment as they tracked the missile that 'took out' Cyprus, followed by a period of numbed shock, but whatever else was happening outside, the ship she was guarding would be kept alert and safe if she had anything to do with it: Her team were in effect the 'eyes and ears' of the same destroyer that Gaz had found himself on.

Now as the ship headed towards Israel the MICC were on full alert and many of the operators were starting to suffer from eye strain as they peered nervously at their tracking consoles. Betty had retired for a brief moment into the small room that served as both an engineers work shop and also her office; she was tired and the dulled confines of the MICC were starting to irritate her.

"Chief?" A young man stood at the doorway into her space, and she felt irritated with his presence.

"Can I not even get a minute?" "Yes what is it sailor?" The reply was sharp and the young sailor cringed slightly.

"There's a message from the Admiralty…Chief." He handed the piece of paper over, snapped to attention and turned to leave.

"Excuse me," Betty spoke calmly but with authority. "Did I tell you to leave yet?"

"No Chief."

"Well stay where you are until I do." The young sailor remained at attention as Betty read the brief memo, then, after a moment she looked up at the sailor.

"Yes Chief?"

"You're dismissed."

"Thank you Chief." *"Ice Maiden,"* he said to himself.

"Sailor!"

The young man stopped in his tracks. *"What now?"* "Yes Chief?"

"I've changed my mind find me someone called Gaz, apparently works for RAF Intelligence and is on this ship."

"Is there no rank or second name Chief?"

"No sailor just Gaz."

"With over three hundred crew, how will I find him Chief; it's a big ship?"

Betty frowned, *"Will I have to do this myself?"* "He'll be the one with the 'Brill Cream', now off you go."

"Yes Chief." The young sailor turned and left the MICC, he was muttering to himself but no one paid any attention to him. *"What's Brill Cream?"*

*

Gaz had just returned to his cabin and was stretching out on his bed when he heard the knock on his cabin door.

"Yes, who is it?"

"Excuse me sir, are you the person they call Gaz?"

"Who is asking?"

"Chief Petty Officer Williams wants you to come down to the MICC sir."

"MI what?" Gaz asked, not yet familiar with naval abbreviations.

"MICC sir, that's the Missile Intercept Control Centre."

"Why doesn't she come up here, if she wants to speak to me?"

"Sorry sir, but the Ice Maiden wants you there, and there you will have to go, either now or later; believe me sir it's best to do as she says.

Gaz was intrigued especially with the title 'Ice Maiden'. *"This might be worth the trip after all."* "OK my man you might as well come in while I get ready."

*

The first thing that Gaz noticed about the MICC was the quietness of the room; it was full of people all intent on watching orange glowing radar consoles. The second thing that struck him was the ambient lighting; the ceiling was full of UV lighting and the overall effect was to produce an eerie dark room interspersed by the bright white glow of the various naval uniforms in front of the glowing consoles. It reminded him of some of the Cypriot night clubs where the punters often wore white dresses and shirts so as to shine under the Ultra Violet lighting, to Gaz the memory now seemed surreal and in another life at another time.

Then it happened; Gaz wasn't sure if he had died and gone to heaven and he had to blink to clear his eyes. Coming towards him glowing bright white under the UV was the most attracting woman he had ever seen in his entire life. It seemed as though she was walking towards him in slow motion, her long blonde hair flowing out, and Gaz at once realized that he was, for the first time in his life, captivated by a woman's beauty. He held his breath and then he held out his hand to introduce himself.

"Welcome to the MICC," Betty held out her hand to shake Gaz's offered hand. "You must be the 'Blue Job' everyone is after."

The illusion was shattered: "And you must be the Ice Maiden everyone tries to avoid." Gaz couldn't help it he hated being referred to as a 'blue job' but as soon as he had spoken he noticed the entire room stopped dead, and instantly wished he had hadn't.

However Gaz noticed that the Chief Petty Officer in front of him didn't even flinch so he quickly added, "Nice to meet you," hoping to effect some damage limitation.

"We better go into my office I have a confidential message for you from Air Force intelligence."

The Chief turned without waiting for an answer and walked towards the room at the side of the MICC, Gaz followed still feeling impacted by the woman he had just met, and at the same time noticing that all the operators were watching him in silence. "What are you all looking at;" Gaz said defensively, "Have you 'Scope Dopes' never seen a 'Blue Job' before?"

*

Betty was aware that something had passed between herself and the RAF Intelligence man now sharing her office space. She had instantly regretted using the term 'Blue Job', but felt vindicated when he had called her the Ice maiden. Betty of course new about the nick name and was quite proud of it, it fitted her character nicely; that was until today when suddenly it seemed to strangely cause her concern. *"It's the long hours in this cave; you must be loosing it, get a grip girl."* "Please make yourself at home." As she spoke, Betty was aware that she was trying to avoid eye contact with the stranger in her office.

Gaz looked around the small space and saw a stool next to a work bench scattered with various electronic bits and pieces; he grabbed it and sat down leaning on the cluttered work bench next to him.

"I have a message from your intelligence folk…I think you should read it for yourself!" Betty handed Gaz the computer print out.

RAF INTELLEGENCE MESSAGE TO AGENT GAZ.
ARRANGEMENTS MADE TO FOR YOU TO PROCEED WITH HASTE TO MALTA.
YOU WILL BE MET AT LUQA BY AGENT GEORGE; HE WILL BRIEF YOU ON THE MISSION.
YOU WILL BE ACCOMPANIED BY A NAVAL MISSILES EXPERT.
MESSAGE END.

"Is that it?" Gaz asked, looking puzzled at the memo.

"No…I think you should see this one as well." Betty handed Gaz a second computer print out and his face dropped as he read its contents.

NAVAL INTELLEGENCE MESSAGE TO CHIEF PETTY OFFICER WILLIAMS
ARRANGEMENTS MADE FOR YOU TO ACCOMPANY AGENT CODE NAMED GAZ TO MALTA.
YOU WILL BE MET AT LUQA BY AGENT CODE NAME GEORGE AND HE WILL BRIEF YOU BOTH ON YOUR MISSION.
MESSAGE END.

"You're the missiles expert I have to take to Malta?"

"Looks like it." Betty smiled at Gaz.

"But…. "

"But you were expecting a man, right?" Betty asked sarcastically.

"Well …..yes…but that doesn't mean I'm….."

"I'd quit while you are ahead if I were you." Betty said but at the same time thinking *"RAF Intelligence is obviously a contradiction in terms."* "So, code name Gaz - what's your rank?"

Gaz was puzzled *"My rank, what's that about?"* I'm sorry; I don't quite understand why you need that information!"

"Well if I'm to be working with you, I need to know who's in charge." Betty folded her arms in a defiant gesture.

"I'm in charge." Gaz replied trying to assert himself in what was fast becoming a one sided situation.

"Why?" Betty asked. "Because you're the man; I'm afraid that's not good enough. So what's your rank blue job?"

"That's classified information, and don't call me 'blue job', as far as you are concerned I am a Chief Petty Officer, my official rank has no bearing on the work that I do." Gaz was becoming impatient with the conversation

"Ok then…..'blue job'…..what's next?"

Gaz handed back the second memo to Betty. "Well if arrangements have already been made by my department then its best we pack to go; I wouldn't be surprised if when we get to the top deck there's a great big chopper there already waiting for us." Gaz was speaking deliberately slowly and like a child; he knew it would irritate Chief Williams and wanted to get a lot of mileage out of it; what he didn't know was that there was indeed a helicopter waiting for them on the Edinburgh's heaving deck.

"Ice Maiden!" Gaz thought as he left the MICC to go to his cabin and pack a few light belongings, *"I can see why you got that nick name girl."*

*

Captain James Kirk was glad when the 'Boson's Chair ride was over. He had put on a brave face as he was crossing; waving to everyone as they shouted out their 'star trek' jokes. He was well used to them and had often reflected on the fact that having a name like James Kirk had made him the butt of many jokes, but that very fact had pushed him to achieve more that the average person. As one of America's top pilots flying the staggeringly powerful F22-Raptor he knew he was one of a few who could truly claim they had nothing to prove. That day, however, Raptor pilot or not, James Kirk stood on the third deck of the Theodore Roosevelt, having just stepped off the Boson's chair, and in front of half the six thousand crew men who occupy the large carrier, brought his breakfast up to the loud cheers of the gathered officers and men. James didn't know it but there was an unwritten custom among the men of the Theodore Roosevelt to lay 'bets' on the probability of the very thing James had just done; the cheer had come from the winners.

James was still wiping the mess from his uniform when he was approached by a Naval Officer. "Sorry about the men sir; it's a bit of a custom with the ship."

James looked at the young man who was smiling, "Its ok pal," he said, "I hope a lot of guys won."

"Well actually, only a few sir - a lot of the men didn't think a Raptor trained pilot would have a problem with the Boson's."

"We'll I sure as hell ruined that concept - eh?" It was a rhetorical question.

"Would you follow me sir, the Commander has a message for you."

"What - like this?"

"He did say right away sir; we can pick up a new jacket on the way if you like."

James followed the young man to a lift which took them up to the top deck of the Aircraft carrier. The wind was blowing hard when James and his guide stepped out onto the deck, and as he looked out beyond the carrier he noticed that the HMS Edinburgh was now dipping her bows deep into the sea's swell. *"Glad I got across when I did,"* he thought, and then he saw a highly decorated high ranking officer walking towards him so he quickly came to attention and saluted.

"Welcome on board Captain Kirk your reputation has preceded you."

"I hope it was all good Sir." James said lightheartedly.

"Oh yes", replied the Commander of the Theodore Roosevelt; "Well most of it anyway."

They both laughed and James relaxed as the Commander took him into a small door in the Carriers tower. "Can I offer you something to drink Captain?" They were now inside a small but well furnished cabin.

"Sure sir; a tonic water will do." James watched as the Commander poured his drink; he was now feeling perplexed as to why this Commander would come and meet him personally, and then even pour him a drink.

"No doubt Captain you have questions to ask but we have not got a lot of time, so permit me to do the taking." He gestured for James to take a seat and then he followed suit. "Captain how much do you enjoy flying your F-22's?"

"Very much sir, there's no other buzz quite like it, I'm looking forward to getting back into the cockpit."

"What would you say if I said there would be sometime before that is likely to happen?"

"I'd want to know why sir." James wondered where the conversation was leading

"We need a volunteer to fly two agents to Malta; it requires a pilot with a lot of skill, and your name was forwarded by the Royal Air Force as a possible."

"The Royal Air Force?"

"Yes Captain." The Commander stood up and walked over to a square porthole in the cabin wall. "We have a small Cessna aircraft on board which has been modified to make the journey; extra fuel and such; even as we speak the two agents we are talking about are being prepared to transfer from the Edinburgh.

"The Edinburgh, I've just came from her?"

"I believe you know one of them." The Commander turned and looked at James. "It's a one way flight captain."

"I'll do it," James said standing up; he'd already worked out that it must be Gaz. "When do we go?"

"Now…Captain….right now, even as we speak, the chopper carrying the two agents has landed come - have a look."

James walked over to the square port hole and looked out, sure enough just coming out of a small Lynx helicopter was his friend Gaz followed by the second agent who he didn't know but, instantly knew he wanted to.

Chapter Two

Gaz and Chief Petty Officer Williams had packed quickly and found themselves, without any ceremony, loaded onto the small Lynx chopper that would take them to the USS Theodore Roosevelt. Gaz had noticed that Chief Williams had not said anything since take off and he wondered if she was having 'second thoughts' about the mission. However as they landed on the still deck of the Carrier he noticed that she smiled as the crew of the Theodore Roosevelt gathered to give her their 'wolf whistles'.

"She makes an impact everywhere she goes." Gaz thought as he caught sight of a familiar face heading towards him. "James," he shouted, then dropped his bag and ran to embrace the American.

"It seems we are going to be working together Gaz." James was talking to Gaz, but his eyes were looking beyond Gaz at the British Naval Chief Petty Officer now stepping from the chopper.

"That's Chief Petty Officer Williams; Betty to her friends," said Gaz aware of James's point of focus.

James walked past Gaz and held out his hand to introduce himself to Betty but instead of her hand, she held out her small hold all. "Why thank you, your so very kind."

James looked back at Gaz who was now trying to hide his sniggering. "Looks like I'll have to work at this."

"There's no doubt about that," replied Gaz, in fact I can guarantee it."

*

After a brief stop for a wash and a change of clothing; they had to change into civilian clothes, all three were led down into the heart of the Theodore Roosevelt to an operations briefing room. The walls in this room were soundproofed so that anything discussed inside would not be overheard outside; even in the American Navy trust was rationed. All three sat in silence as the ships security officer told them all the information he had been given.

"Firstly gentlemen….and…um…ladies, let me introduce myself. I am the ships security officer Lieutenant Stanley and what I'm about to tell you is classified information."

Gaz looked at James who was smiling at Betty who in turn was trying hard to ignore him.

Stanley continued. "About the same time that the Israeli's nuked Cyprus a 'may day' distress signal was received from an American AWAC patrolling and monitoring the eastern side of the Med. Seems they ran into some sort of engine trouble, were not really sure, but the up shot is that it crashed into the sea slightly East of Malta with no survivors reported. The exact spot is not yet clear but we need to recover a certain piece of very sensitive equipment from it. That's your job. You will make contact with our man George in Malta, and take it from there. Are there any questions?"

Betty raised her hand. "Why do you need a missiles person?"

"Ah yes," replied the Lieutenant looking at a clip board in his hand. "You must be Petty Officer Williams."

"That's Chief Petty Officer to you Lieutenant."

James – surprised at Betty's reply, looked at Gaz who just shrugged.

Lieutenant Stanley ignored the correction. "The sensitive part that needs recovered is in a fact a missile."

Gaz sat up straight, as did James; they were both wondering if they had heard correct.

"That's right gentlemen…and…um… ladies."

"Cut the crap." Betty was getting irritated with the Lieutenant.

"Ok – um - yes it's a missile and it was on the AWAC, that's all the information I have, anything else will be on a need to know basis."

All three sat quiet and said nothing else, the 'need to know' card was always pulled when no more information was going to be given; and they all knew it.

"Good if there are no more questions then all that leaves is for me to wish you all good hunting: good day gentlemen and……" The Lieutenant decided not to finish the sentence and left.

James turned to Gaz. "Missiles on an AWAC - why would anyone put missiles on an AWAC?"

"You tell me James," said Gaz. "It belongs to you Americans."

Betty stood to leave. "I'm turning in boys; I'll see you in the morning at five hundred hours."

Both James and Gaz stood in response to the CPO's announcement, but they said nothing as they watched her walk out of the room. After a few moments James broke the silence, "Boy Gaz I think I'm in love."

"Forget it James, she is a stunner on the outside, but inside she has a heart of ice."

As they both left the room and headed to the sleeping accommodation, Gaz felt guilty about what he had just said about Betty but he couldn't work out why. That night none of the team slept, each had their own thoughts that troubled them, but it was Betty that was troubling Gaz.

*

James was very talkative the following morning even though it was only five am and Gaz came to an unspoken conclusion that James was always hyper about something, but then assumed that was what made him a very good pilot. As for Gaz and Betty, none of the two of them were 'morning people' so they sat and patiently endured James's cheery tirade of words. Gaz was aware of Betty staring at him at one point, but when he looked up from his coffee and looked her way, she quickly diverted her gaze back to her own coffee; even so Gaz couldn't help notice how attractive she looked and he frowned into himself. *"Get a grip."* It was a typical American breakfast; sausages, beans, fried eggs, waffles and other normally delightfully unhealthy foods and normally Gaz would have 'wolfed' it down with enthusiasm, but this morning he had no appetite. He looked at his watch; it was almost six.

"Almost time," he said lightly flinging his table napkin down.

"You two haven't eaten much." James said standing up from the long breakfast table typical of naval ward rooms.

Gaz looked at Betty and noticed that she too hadn't ate her breakfast; "Were not hungry mate." As he spoke he glanced at Betty but she was turning away from the table to pick up a small hand bag she had with her.

James looked at Gaz and then Betty, he could feel the tension from both of them and he guessed it was not just pre mission nerves. *"Chemistry and stubbornness are not good combinations."* "Eh...lets get to the off then guys," he said as they made their way to the lifts that would take them onto the upper flight deck of the Theodore Roosevelt Carrier.

*

Sitting at the end of the take off point of the runway, the small Cessna seemed unimpressive, almost ridicules against the huge forms of the F-22's parked at various angles along the flight decks edge.

"Is that it?" Betty asked, suddenly feeling slightly nauseous at the thought of flying for four hours in such a flimsy looking aircraft.

"That's the babe…isn't she a beauty?" James replied sarcastically.

"She'll do the job though, so let's get started." Gaz said, already opening the aircraft's door to fling his small hold-all in.

Betty wasn't convinced but said nothing as she climbed into the back of the Cessna.

"I was hoping you would sit beside me at the front!" James smiled at Betty and joked lightheartedly.

"In your dreams fly boy."

"*Ouch,*" James thought to himself, *"No sense of humour."*

Gaz looked at James as he made himself comfortable in the front seat beside him; "Guess you'll just have to do with me gorgeous." The effeminate way he said it broke the ice; they all laughed, and then set their thoughts finally to the work ahead.

James revved the Cessna engines high before letting it charge off down the length of the Theodore Roosevelt and just as it flew of the end he pulled on the 'stick'. For a gut retching moment the aircraft dropped towards the sea, then started to climb slowly into the sky. Gaz wasn't sure; he was concentrating on his hand grips on the side of his seat, and keeping his stomach where it should be, but he thought he heard James shout "Geronimo" as they left the aircraft's carrier's runway edge. *"He's totally insane."* Gaz thought, but said nothing, he was too busy concentrating on his white knuckle grip.

*

'George' was a 'sleeper'; he had been receiving a 'very nice' retainer from the British government since 1979 when the British Forces had withdrawn out of Malta. He was at that time employed by RAFM, the Maltese branch of the RAF, but had suddenly found himself redundant with no prospects of finding any work. When he was approached by the British, who quite simply asked him to remain on the Island, do nothing and receive a wage for it, the only provision being that he should, if needed give information about Libyan troop movements, he couldn't believe his luck.

He had almost forgotten about the commitment when suddenly, out of the blue, he received a message that he was being 'activated'. George panicked at first, he had never dreamed he would be needed after all this time, but as he looked around his sea view villa in Marsaskala, he was aware that he had always known that sooner or later 'pay back' time would come. He was puzzled though, there had been no Libyan troops on the Island since the treaty of 84, at least not officially, so he wondered 'why now'? George had heard a rumour about a downed AWAC off the coast of Gozo, Malta's smaller sister island, but that news had been drowned out in the horror of the event in Cyprus, and he couldn't think what relevance there was to his position in Malta.

"Where are you going?" Maria his wife asked, as George leaned over the bed to kiss her.

"I have to go out for a short time, but I wont be long darling."

George's wife sat up and stretched, in spite if her years, she was still in many ways a young woman, partly due to the easy life they had both had.

"But where….?"

"Please Maria; don't ask…I cannot tell you."

"You have been….called?" Maria asked, suddenly feeling a wave of fear come over her.

"Please Maria… you know I cannot say more, just go back to sleep and I will be back later."

"Be careful, love."

George didn't answer, he turned and left the room, walked out of the house into the morning sunshine, and drove quickly towards Luqa Airport, just as he had been instructed on the message he had just received. *"Look out for a Cessna carrying three British agents…..Why now…..why me….Allah-Madonna?"* George's mind was racing for answers as he negotiated the unevenly surfaced roads that were a characteristic of Maltese driving conditions, and then he saw the Airport bringing the realization that, like it or not, this was really happening.

*

James, Gaz and Betty sat in silence for a while as the Cessna skimmed along the surface of the Mediterranean Sea. It was not because they had nothing to say; the very opposite was in fact true, they had a lot to discuss, but the engine of the Cessna was so loud that taking about the details they would like to have discussed would have been a practical impossibility. Eventually, however, Gaz spoke up in a higher pitched voice than normal. "James?"

"Yeh?" James was concentrating very hard at flying the small airplane literally feet above the sea, skimming so near to the surface they could see the waves rolling and the whites of the breakers underneath them.

"Why you?"

"Why me what?"

Gaz heard a noise from behind him and looked over at Betty who was motioning with her finger, making circular movements and mouthing quietly *"He's bonkers."*

Gaz smiled and went to reply when James asked again. "Gaz - why me what?"

"Sorry James I was distracted for a moment; why did they ask you to come with us?"

"See that sea beneath us its fifty meters to the surface, and for that kind of flying you needed the best there was…and hey…I'm the best."

"Oh please." Betty said from the back seat, motioning with her hand faked nausea.

Gaz just smiled, he knew that James had a huge ego, but he also knew that it was true what he had said.

"Two hours into the flight," James added, "We should see Malta soon."

He had just finished speaking when they all felt a lurch that pulled the aircraft violently to one side.

"What was that?" Gaz consciously renewed his white knuckle grip.

"Don't know!" James was frantically checking the various dials and switches on the Cessna fascia.

Betty was about to say something when the same thing happened again, only this time Gaz noticed part of the wing tip on his left fragmented and fall away.

"Hold on pals;" James was now struggling with the controls of the Cessna as it took a dive to their left and started to spin uncontrollably, "We are going down."

All three watched helplessly as the rolling sea suddenly seemed to hit the Cessna and with several violent jolts it then 'bounced' along the sea's surface. Although none of them were hurt, they were stunned by the series of impacts, and could only watch helplessly, held fast in their seats by the aircraft's seat belts, as the day light around them suddenly changed into a dull green blue: The Cessna had finally jolted to a halt and slowly began to sink.

*

Libyan Naval Officer; Lt. Ishmael Zughaid was not the best officer in the Libyan Navy, but he as very proud of his own personal achievements. Having been born in the slum areas of Tripoli and not of the higher class normally associated with Libyan Naval officers, he worked his way up through the ranks and had, in his own opinion, reached the summit of his career. Ishmael was however, in spite of his self pride, a very fair and gentle young man and most of his crew had to volunteer to get a chance to serve with him; such was the demand among the lower Naval ratings, that many found themselves on a waiting list. He wasn't that perturbed about the recent events in Cyprus, nor the upsurge in Arab national feelings of unity against the western allies and the EU that the nuking of Cyprus had generated, but he did hate Israel, and as far as he was concerned, anything coming from that direction could only be bad; especially if it was unscheduled.

It was early morning, and Ishmael stood in the small bridge of the Russian made Nanuchka-class Corvette he now commanded, surveying the horizon towards the east in the direction of Cyprus. It wasn't the most up- to- date costal patrol boat that the Libyan Navy had, in fact it was one of the oldest, and had turned out to be incredibly unreliable, but it was Ishmael's command and that was good enough for him. He hadn't hesitated in firing one of the Corvette's four on board SA-N-4 SAM's when he saw a Cessna flying deliberately low in order to remain unseen from any radar, but he was relieved to see that the small aircraft had not sank immediately; it gave him a chance to investigate who the occupants were, and why they were trying to avoid detection.

"Turn about and search for survivors." Ishmael always gave his orders officiously, standing fully erect with his hands behind his back.

“Aye aye–sir.” Came the reply from a young Naval Rating who responded by spinning the ‘ship’s wheel’ hard to his left.

The Corvette swung around creating a large wave of foam from it’s bows as it steered in the direction of the now half sunk Cessna, ‘whooping’ and gathering speed.

*

British Navy Captain, Ross M Morgan came from a long line of naval officers and always believed that he had been ‘pressed’ into the Senior Service. His father, his Grandfather and no doubt his Great-grandfather had all been Naval Captains and he had been informed by his father in a manner that made a very important issue perfectly clear. “If you want to inherit the family heritage, then the Navy it will be young man*.*” However Ross had found a way of fulfilling his father’s demands and at the same time serving his own desires for excitement and challenge; he had volunteered to be a submariner.

Unlike his Libyan counterpart, he had been born into position and as a result tried very hard to ‘break the mold’ he had been ‘fashioned into’ by his family and their Navy connections. Most of his crew were also volunteers, many quite simply submariners because of the extra money it merited, but that wasn’t an issue with Ross, he wanted excitement and action, and Submarine service had provided plenty of it.

He was on duty in his Vanguard Class SSBN and was having a snigger into himself as he thought of the Navy’s way of abbreviating things *“SSBN; Ship Submersible Ballistic Nuclear,”* it was a sort of mind game he was playing with himself to pass what he thought would be another routine shift, when suddenly the ship’s tactical weapons system and submarine command system bust into life. The crew went automatically into battle stations and a red hue fell over the entire control room, the memories of Cyprus and the recent use of nuclear weapons fresh on each sailors memories.

"What's the status Chief?" Ross asked, looking across at a row of operators seated in front of an array of various electronic panels and viewers.

"Someone near us has let off a SAM, sir and it looks as though it has hit a small low flying aircraft."

"How far away from here?"

"About twenty miles east."

"Anything in from CNC in Northwood?"

"Nothing since the Cyprus bang; sir."

Ross thought for a moment and then without looking at anyone in particular said, "Turn about, and bring us up to periscope depth…..Chief."

"Aye, aye sir."

"Keep your eye and ears open and focused and let me now the minute we hear from the CNC."

"Aye, aye sir."

Ross turned and left the submarines control centre intending to walk along the narrow passageway to his small cabin, but he had only taken one or two steps when the Chief shouted after him.

"Sir, signal coming in from CNC."

Ross turned back and walked over to where the chief was standing; the computer in front of him was already deciphering and printing the order.

"Read it to me Chief."

The chief looked at his men; this was not part of proper procedure. "Sir I really think that….."

"Just read the signal Chief." Although he didn't elaborate, Ross felt that anymore secrecy would be detrimental to the men's moral. They were isolated from the world and had fretted about their families when the fleet had been ordered to sail to Israel; Ross felt it was better to know than not know, even if the news was bad.

"Aye, aye sir." The chief took a short breath. "Message from Commander-in-Chief Northwood. Stop. Proceed with haste to sector Tango Eight Bravo one six. Stop. Search for three survivors of downed Cessna. Stop. No engagement of foreign naval forces. Repeat. No engagement. Stop."

The control room fell silent, there was, however a tangible sense of 'relief' in Ross's immediate vicinity, and at that moment he knew it had been right to let everyone 'in' on the signal. "Is that it Chief?"

"Aye sir."

"They want to send a Vanguard Class SSBN to pick up survivors of a Cessna crash?"

"Fair play sir they were brought down by a SAM."

"Local Libyans playing cowboys, with some unfortunate tourists." Ross replied rubbing his chin.

"Not with the CNC taking an interest, boss."

Ross liked being called 'boss' it was better that 'sir' and fitted in with Ross's need to be seen as a nonconformist. "Yea your right Chief; OK set a course for the target area and give me a call when we get there, I'll be in my cabin."

Ross saluted the 'deck' spoke briefly to the 'on' duty officer and left, a feeling of weariness suddenly flowing over his mind as he began to unwind.

Chapter Three

The day after the American AWAC crashed of the coast of Malta's sister Island Gozo, The Libyan ambassador in Malta met with the Maltese Foreign Secretary and offered to bring military aid to help with the 'intrusion' of western military forces. He was invoking Chapter three of the 1984 Malta – Libya Treaty of Friendship and had been instructed by his own government not to accept anything other that full compliance. In other words Libya, under the direction of the Arab council, wanted to place its troops on the small island.

The request was refused categorically on the grounds that Malta was now part of the European Union and would not tolerate the presence of any foreign forces on their ground, however in taking this position with the Libyans, Malta now had chosen sides with the EU against the growing Islamic impatience with the West and their failure to strike at Israel after it's attack on Cyprus and Iran.

In a general sense every one had underestimated the strategic importance of the small island of Malta, except the Libyans who, under the present international tensions, saw an opportunity to exploit their desire to spread Islamic Fundamentalism further north; the Treaty was the catalyst of legality.

*

Gaz looked across at James, then back at Betty; they were both looking back at each other as though someone among the three of them must have some idea of what to do next. The Cessna was suspended about three or four meters below the waters surface at an awkward angle but the cabin they were in was only partially filled with sea water. Gaz looked to his right his position was such that he was could see the deep blue depths beneath him and he suddenly felt scared.

James broke the suspense. “I have an idea Guys,” he said turning to look at Betty.

“I hope it’s a good one,” said Betty but she wasn’t smiling, and if it was intended to be some sort of humorous snippet, it was lost on James and Gaz.

“Go on then,” Gaz said impatiently, “We haven’t got a lot of time to be hanging around in this position.”

James couldn’t believe his ears, *“British humour at this time?”* He ignored it though and continued. “There are life jackets under the seats, put them but don’t inflate them.”

Everyone took a few moments to locate and then put on the bright orange life jackets.

“OK fly boy,” said Betty tying up the ‘ties’ that snaked around her waist, “What now?”

“We let the water in.”

“What?” Gaz was taken by surprise, “Is this some sort of joke?”

“Wait guys, keep cool, and just listen.”

Gaz nodded looking at Betty for some sort of support, but there wasn’t any indication of any concern in her face; Gaz noticed her eyes were darting from him to James rapidly.

“We have to equalize the pressure in the cabin before we open the doors, so we will let a little water in through the widows until we are full, then we can open the doors and swim out.”

“Are you sure this will work James?” Gaz was aware that his mind was saying, *“No way!”*

“Have you any better ideas?” James asked looking between Betty and Gaz.

“That’s settled then….let get to it, but remember just before the cabin fills take a deep breath, but don’t inflate your life jackets until you are clear of the aircraft. It would be a shame to get out but get caught in the wreckage.”

All three sat as the cabin slowly filled with sea water, it took some time and Gaz was worried that the Cessna would sink with less buoyancy, but the wings had plenty fuel and that helped keep the plane buoyant just below the surface. Just before the cabin was completely full, all three took a deep breath and held it until the water was well over their heads.

James’s door was jammed so they all had to attempt to escape through the door at Gaz’s side. Gaz went out first and then swam back to help Betty who was climbing out from the rear seat. As Gaz took hold of Betty’s hands to help her out, he noticed that James was also moving out but he couldn’t believe what he was seeing. James had his hands on Betty’s buttocks and was pushing her gently forward. At first he had thought nothing of it until he saw a grin on James’s face. Gaz felt himself starting to grin under the water and a stream of bubbles came out of his mouth which Betty saw as she struggled to get free of the Cessna and James’s hands, even under the water Gaz could see her frowning expression. *“If looks could kill,”* he thought to himself.

When they were sufficiently clear the wreckage, all three pulled their ‘inflate’ cords and almost immediately shot to the surface; as they broke the water gasping for air, they heard the whooping of a Naval ship and soon saw the shape of a Corvette bearing down on their position.

“What now?” Betty shouted above the noise.

"It can't be British," James said, "Not this far west anyway, there aren't any bases near that a small boat can operate from."

"Then they must be…." Gaz never finished the sentence, a stream of bullets broke the sea surface near to them as the Corvette came to a surprisingly quick stop, its powerful marine diesel engines roaring as its propellers reversed their direction, and Gaz, James and Betty automatically raised their hands high shouting, "Don't shoot, don't shoot."

*

George had returned home later in the day; the expected Cessna aircraft had not materialized. He felt a bit foolish when he had asked at the airport terminal if a small Cessna had landed carrying some 'friends'.

"Where have you been hiding?" The young female airport official had asked; "Didn't you know there had been some fighting. Everyone is leaving, not arriving."

It was true of course, since the Cyprus event tourism in the Mediterranean had taken a very big dive most people choosing to be at home somewhere in Europe where they thought they might be safer; no one talked about being safe, only safer.

"None the less," George had been pedantic with the young official, "I am expecting three friends."

"Either mad or very brave," the official had replied.

George thought about it for a moment then answered, "Extreme sports….you know the type…. your right, totally mad." They had both laughed at that and the humour made it easy for George to ask the girl to keep a look out.

Maria was in the kitchen preparing some food and oblivious to the growing worry that George was experiencing. He walked through to see if he could distract his thoughts for a moment, and placed his arms around his wife's waist.

"Hmmm," she said and leaned her head back onto the front of his chest feeling an unusual tension in his arms. "What's up darling, you seem a bit tense?"

"I'm fine Maria, just fine." George loved his wife very much. He let her go and walked back into his lounge; Maria followed him and sat down.

"Right what's really up?" She always knew when George had a problem.

George knew it was time to tell her about the three missing agents, and his promise and commitment to the British Government.

Maria sat and listened until George had finished telling her the whole story, when he concluded she said nothing for a few moments allowing the seriousness of the situation to sink in.

"So that's where the money has been coming from?" Maria asked showing no emotions.

"Yes, the British have been paying me to do nothing but wait 'just in case'."

"And now the 'just in case' has happened?"

"Yes, sweetheart and the three British agents supposedly landing at Luqa haven't turned up."

"You need to let the British know George; this could be serious."

That's just the point, I don't know who to contact or how; all I received was a very cryptic note about meeting these people."

Maria thought it through again in silence while George got up from his seat and walked over to the fridge where they kept the drinks. "Want anything?"

Maria shook her head and frowned, "We must go to Ta'Xbiex and speak with the British High Commission and we must go now."

"What's with the 'we' part?" George replied.

"I'm in now and I'm coming with you - like it or not."

George didn't argue he put his drink down half finished and picked up the keys to his car. "Let's go then." A short time later both of them left for Ta'Xbiex.

*

Ross had only just stretched out on his 'bunk' when the Duty Officer knocked on his door. "Yes?" He said trying to hide the sudden rise in anticipation he felt.

"Sir; contact has been made with the downed Cessna." He was out off breath, but Ross knew the young junior officer and guessed his adrenalin was rising like his own.

"OK, tell the Chief I'll be along in a minute."

"There is something else sir."

"What?"

"We have a Corvette on our tracking as well….we think it could be Libyan….or Russian; Nanuchka –class."

Ross jumped up from his bunk. "Sound battle stations and prepare to surface."

As Ross pulled on his trainers, he heard the battle station's alarm sound and suddenly the whole submarine was buzzing with men running to their various positions. When Ross arrived at the control centre, every one was in position; the Chief nodded towards him as he arrived

"We have the Cessna boss, but there is another ship up there and it's close to the Cessna."

"Get the Spearfish Torpedoes ready and armed and prepare to surface."

"Is that wise sir?" The Duty officer coordinating the ships navigation had been listening to the conversation with the Chief. "These Corvettes carry SAM's sir and SSM's."

"How many SSM's?"

"Not sure sir but one would be enough."

Suddenly Ross was hit with the enormous responsibility that had been thrust upon him; on one hand it seemed unusual for the CNC to take an interest in such a small event, but on the other if they felt the need to invoke a nuclear submarine in a rescue bid, then it must be important enough to take a huge risk. "Thank you lieutenant, I'll note your objection in the ship's log."

"Sir I wasn't objecting I was simply……." He never finished his sentence; Ross had turned and ordered the ship to surface and boarding parties to stand by.

*

Gaz, Betty and James could do nothing except wait for the Libyan boat to drift close to where they were. As they floated on the surface, their buoyancy aids supporting them, they could see several Libyan sailors pointing their weapons at them while others were preparing to launch a small inflatable from the Corvette's side.

"Are we at war with the Libyans?" Gaz wondered as he watched the sailors now lower the inflatable into the water.

"Are you kidding?" James serious, "We've always been at war with Libya."

"This does not look good." Betty said quietly.

Gaz thought he should swim over and offer some sort of comfort, but then thought better of it, so they waited until the inflatable with two Libyan sailors came along side and ordered them to pull themselves into the small craft which was bobbing about on the sea's surface.

"You two go first." Betty, remembering the Cessna, glowered at James, who just smiled cheekily.

"Sure you don't want any help?" James asked sarcastically.

"Lay off her." Gaz, was feeling annoyed with James, but he was not sure why.

Betty looked at Gaz but her expression was unemotional and gave nothing away. *"Ice maiden,"* thought Gaz and he eventually managed to pull himself onboard the rubber inflatable.

*

"I am Lt. Ishmael Zughaid of the Glorious Libyan Navy." Ishmael stood erect as he addressed the three wet prisoners who had just been brought to his 'bridge'. He felt a bit 'false' as the Corvette's bridge was anything but glorious, but he comforted his lack of confidence in his ship with the sure knowledge that whoever these people were, he had defeated them. "You will be treated decently, as is the custom of all Libyan Forces, but first you must answer one or two questions." Ishmael started to pace in front of his three prisoners feeling superior; he liked to where possible, play the part of a superior among infidels.

"Get Stuffed!" James said before Gaz could stop him.

Ishmael stopped in his tracks, he wasn't sure what 'get stuffed' meant but he did recognize the American accent, and concluded very quickly that he had found a very big catch. He asked his first question, pretending to ignore the American's outburst. "Who are you, are you American?"

Gaz spoke up. "We are British tourists Lieutenant, trying to escape from the terrible events in Cyprus."

"British, you say, but why the are you so far out to sea; where were you hoping to land?"

Gaz looked at the others then spoke, "Malta."

Ishmael froze for a moment, and Gaz and James noticed his sudden change. "You are spies, you already know about the plan for Malta?"

"We don't know what you are talking about," interrupted Betty impatiently. "Look Libya, we are tired and cold and wet, if you have any decency you would let us get changed and dried at least before you ask all these totally inappropriate questions."

Ishmael was surprised by the good looking woman's forthright attitude; in his country a woman would never be so bold; he was intrigued. "You are right of course, you have our apologies, my Midshipman will escort you to suitable quarters and then you must dine with me later."

"Get stuffed!" James remarked again, but Ishmael ignored him. He had just turned to give his Midshipman the order when he noticed that something had caught the sailor's attention. Ishmael followed his man's stare and then he too froze in unbelief.

*

James spoke first and broke the now frigid atmosphere, "Geese... it's a sub!"

The Libyan Lieutenant, who had been calm and very courteous, was now shouting out orders ignoring James, Gaz and Betty's presence; "Battle stations....Battle stations."

"Move back slowly." Gaz said quietly, at the same time gently nodding towards the door in the bridge of the Corvette, which was now open. They slowly edged towards the door intending to make a break for the open sea when suddenly the Libyan Midshipman drew his pistol. "I wouldn't try it if I were you." He spoke in perfect English and Gaz and the others froze.

*

Ross stood with two of his men inside the 'sail' of the submarine waiting on the signal to climb into the 'look-out' recess. When it came they scrambled up one at a time and as the hatch was opened, Ross could smell the fresh air of the Mediterranean Sea drift down towards him. At the same time he was taking his commander's place in the 'sail', boarding teams were pouring out onto the black deck of the submarine all armed with SA.80's. The Duty Officer climbed up beside Ross and looked out with him towards the small Corvette which had been caught unawares in the open sea. He had his binoculars lifted to his eyes, "Looks like they intend to fight sir."

"Don't be bloody daft," Ross replied reaching for the Binoculars, "And get these men down there ready to go."

"Aye, Aye, sir."

Ross looked through the binoculars at the small Corvette; he had thought they were a bit over the top at first, *"The boat's only a few hundred yards away."* But then as he looked through them, he saw the shapes of three people being held at gunpoint in the Corvette's bridge. He turned to his Duty Officer. "They have the men we are after...switch on the amp." Ross picked up a microphone and spoke, his voice now carrying loudly across to Ishmael's small but defiant boat. "Lay down your weapons and prepare to be boarded by the British Navy." Ross waited for a few moments but nothing happened; he was about to shout the command again when a buzz came from the Chief in the Tactical Weapons control. "Yes Chief, is it important, were a bit busy at the moment?"

"Sir we have detected two of the Corvettes SSM's have been armed and primed for firing."

"The cheeky..." "Thanks Chief." Ross felt a little irritated at this sudden development *"The Duty Officer was right!"* He spoke once more into the 'amp'.

"This is the commander of the British Nuclear Submarine, I intend to board you, now be a good chap and lay down your weapons." Then he nodded to the boarding teams and they set off in the direction of the Corvette.

Ross knew he was taking a risk with both the ship and his boarding parties, but he also knew that who ever they were, those three people being held captive, now needed to be freed.

As the boarding parties drew near the Libyan Corvette one of the Libyan sailors suddenly fired off a AK-47 spraying a hail of deadly bullets across the rubber bows of the leading boarding party, but a rapid reply from a SA.80 on the second dingy 'dropped him' and the other Libyans lowered their weapons, not wishing to take on a fully armed nuclear subs crew.

Ross watched from the submarine's 'sail' as the crew members slowly gathered on the Corvette's small forward deck; he breathed out a sigh of relief then ordered another dingy party to disembark and pick up the survivors of the first dingy that was shot and was now sinking fast.

*

Ishmael had intended to put up a fight after the initial shock of seeing the huge black submarine suddenly surface directly in front of his Corvette; he had ordered his crews to arm and 'make ready' the four surface to surface missiles he carried. He would only need to hit the sub with one of the deadly 6SS-N-9SSM's he had primed for firing, but he guessed he would be inviting the demise of his career if he caused an act of war with a major world power. When he heard the shots being fired and saw one of his crew men fall dead into the sea, he felt he had no choice but to allow the British Sailors to board his boat. He watched helplessly as the British servicemen climbed on board the Corvette, round up his men and start to search inside the lower deck.

A young naval Chief Petty Officer in charge of the boarding party came into the 'bridge', saluted Ishmael then turned to where Gaz and the others were standing; shivering with the cold wet clothes they still had on.

"CPO Roland at you service; glad to see you are ok, the Boss is waiting for you over at the sub."

"Glad you decided to come." Gaz held out his hand.

Chief Roland then shook James's hand, Betty's hand and then turned and offered his hand to the Libyan Lieutenant, who reluctantly accepted. "Sir, Captain Morgan sends his compliments and invites you over to meet with him."

"I'm afraid that will not be possible." Ishmael stood up straight in his perfect military manner.

Chief Roland raised his SA.80 until it was level with Ishmael's chest. "You don't understand sir…it's a formal request." As he said it he looked over to where Gaz, James and Betty were still standing and winked then smiled. Ensuring that the Libyan Officer was in compliance he turned, "Come on then you lot lets get out of here before anyone sees our lovely black lady of the deep."

It didn't take long for the Corvette's crew to be transferred to the SSBN. The last to leave and cross over were Gaz, James and Betty along with Chief Roland.

"Look…better hang on to something." Roland was pointing to an area of the sea just in front of the stationary Corvette.

The three looked, but before they could take in fully what they were looking at, a Spearfish torpedo slipped towards the Libyan boat. The next thing they knew, there was a huge explosion and a bright flash that filled the air: The Sea seemed to 'boil' around them with bits of wood and metal flying in all directions, and the shock wave threw Betty off her balance; Gaz had to fling himself at her before she fell overboard. When it was all over, except for some still falling debris, the Corvette was already half submerged and on fire but sinking fast.

*

It took an unusually long time for George and Maria to reach the British High Commission in Ta'Xbiex, due to the heavy traffic through Hamrun, most of it seemingly going in the general direction of Fort Manoel.

"It's not usually as busy as this George." Maria commented as they sat in a traffic jam at Msida.

"There seems to be a lot of people trying to get off the island; although they are mainly ex-pats who think they will be safer back in the UK after the Cyprus tragedy."

"What about the airport at Luqa?"

"Chartered flights have been cancelled, there's only one company that's still working and they are charging too much money for normal people to use."

"Who's that?" Maria asked as the car started to move again.

"Air Malta!"

"Typical," Maria thought as they turned into the coastal road that took them to the front of the British High Commissioners Offices.

The huge colonial style building stood erect and imposing reflecting the glories of a bygone empire, and George hesitated for a moment, appearing to have second thoughts, before they both walked into the cool hard tiled, echoing interior.

A young lady was sitting at a large desk looking very official, but it was clear to Maria that the whole set-up, as it was, looked 'temporary'. There were piles of boxes, most marked 'confidential', and workmen were busy moving computers and the like backwards and forwards from the various offices that surrounded the foyer; the area they were now in looked as though it was being prepared for decorating.

As they both walked over to the 'reception' desk; looking around themselves as they went, the young receptionist rose to her feet and politely spoke. “Excuse me….can I help you?”

George was relieved to hear, what sounded like a very friendly way of welcoming them, he was about to speak when Maria said, “We need to speak with the Commissioner.”

“I’m sorry,” the girl replied, “That will not be possible; he is ….um…..unavailable at the present time.”

“And the Assistant Commissioner is he also unavailable?” Maria asked, not deterred by the obvious ‘deceit’.

“I’m sorry he too is very busy.”

“Look you!”

Maria didn’t finish what she was about to call the young girl as George intervened. “I’m sorry about my wife’s enthusiasm,” Maria looked surprised at what George had just said, “She does tend to get carried away.” George gave Maria a strong look from his eyes and she shrugged and muttered under her breath. He continued. “Now I know you are doing your job and by all accounts well, but I think you will find that the Commissioner will want to see us; just tell him George is here.”

The receptionist looked at George for a moment before she picked up her mobile phone and pressed a button. “Sorry sir I….yes I know you didn’t want to be disturbed but…..ok sir…will do sir.”

George could see that the receptionist was being ‘fobbed off’ so he grabbed the phone from her hand and spoke into it. “George is here and I need to speak with you.” There was silence on the other end for a few moments before the Commissioners voice was heard. “Better come up.”

George and Maria were shown to a lift by the now ‘unfriendly’ receptionist and when they were in she leaned over, pushed a button inside the lift and then stepped back. “You will be met when the lift stops.” That was all she said before the doors closed; George and Maria found themselves alone as the lift started to rise.

Chapter Four

With the failure of the Western powers and the EU directed fleet to address the 'Israeli' problem once and for all, the Arab Council secretly instructed Libya to use its Treaty with Malta to establish a 'gate way' into Europe with the intent of establishing an Islamic military presence on Europe's door step. It was felt that using the Treaty of Friendship would give a legal reason to invade the tiny western allied island, which would prevent further 'comeback' on Libya itself.

The Americans and the British now at sea off the coast of Israel found that they were now 'policing' the Near eastern Islamic Nations of Syria, Jordon, Iraq and Egypt; all of whom would have wiped Israel off the face of the planet had it not been for the presence of the fleet. The whole world was tottering on the brink of a cataclysmic confrontation which the Arab Council mistakenly believed would allow their plans for Malta to go unchallenged; Jihad had been declared and Libya grasped it with enthusiasm, mobilizing its forces without giving a second thought for the world wide consequences as a whole.

*

Ishmael had been 'herded' with his men aboard the huge Vanguard Class SSBN, so he didn't see the Torpedo that finished his command and, for that matter, his career. He did however; hear the explosion and felt that a part of him had just been wiped out. They had been pushed down one of the rear hatches that was positioned in front of the sixteen missile tubes holding the now outdated but still effective, Trident D5's. Ishmael couldn't help feel himself shudder un-expectantly at the thought of the amount of destruction sitting malevolently within the black bulk of the submarine; its presence had surprised him until he realized that this ship's position made it perfect to fire at his own country.

Once inside the Submarine Ishmael was separated from his men, although under protest and eventually he found himself in the ship's Officers Mess with a naval rating on guard at the door, but with no other obvious restriction. He couldn't help the feeling that he was being treated like a guest and not a prisoner, which was contrary to all he had been taught about the Western 'devils'.

While he was still assimilating to his surroundings, a young man in a white jacket came into the Mess carrying a silver tray with a tea and coffee set. "Captain Ross sends his compliments sir and will be with you as soon as is possible." Then he left the tray on the table, turned and walked back out.

"*Is this real? Am I dreaming?*" He wasn't sure, but one thing was becoming abundantly clear in his head, he had to escape. He didn't know how, or when, or where to, but he knew he had to warn his Libyan brothers about the sub's presence, or die in the process.

*

"Captain Ross Morgan at your service," Ross was standing at the 'sail' side hatch, holding out his hand to welcome the three bedraggled but happy strangers he had been sent to rescue, "Please come on board and be my guests."

"I'm Gaz Seymour," Gaz said returning the handshake, "RAF Intelligence, Special Duties."

"Now there's a contradiction; RAF Intelligence?" Ross was unable to resist the age old inter services 'banter', Gaz said nothing, he was just too tired to respond.

"And I'm Captain James Kirk USAF." James felt defensive with the submarine Captain.

"Come again?" Ross was not sure he had heard correctly.

"You heard right," Betty was quick to answer, "I wish some one would beam him up…and quickly."

Ross smiled, holding out his hand again. "And you are?"

"CPO. Williams, sir."

Ross smiled and held on to Betty's hand longer that he needed. *"Oh boy, not another one!"* "They call me the 'Ice-Maiden' on the Edinburgh - sir."

Gaz felt himself cringe. *"Why is she so defensive?"*

Ross let go of Betty's hand, still smiling but slightly 'ruffled' by Betty's obvious 'dig', then he turned and said, "Chief Roland will show you your quarters, but we need to de-brief in one hour in the command centre." Ross then tapped a remote mike attached to his ear piece and after a pause said, "Take her down to one hundred meters, maintain battle stations for now."

A distant voice replied, "Aye Aye boss, a hundred meters and battle stations."

Later, Gaz lay down in the bunk he was given, the others were by now either resting, showering or as Gaz was, stretching out on a soft white linen bed. The exhaustion he felt soon crept over him and without him realizing it, drew him into a fitful sleep full of death filled nightmares.

Betty was showering next door to Gaz when she heard him screaming. She grabbed a towel and flung it around herself in a desperate attempt at modesty while wasting no effort to reach Gaz in the quickest possible time. When she ran into His bunk, Gaz was tossing and turning, sweat was pouring from his body. Betty without any thought grabbed him and started to shake Gaz awake not knowing that in the process her towel slipped partially from her still wet body.

Gaz woke with a fright and grabbed Betty not realizing who she was and both of them fell onto the floor struggling.

"Gaz…it's me … Betty! Get a grip you moron." Betty was gasping for her breath in between speaking and fending off the Gaz's wild grabs.

"Wha…..what's…….happening?" Gaz was coming around, at the same time loosing his grip of Betty.

Betty relaxed and they both fell and lay on the floor together. "You were dreaming." Was all she said now lying still and gazing up at the ceiling.

Gaz looked, he couldn't believe what he was seeing, Betty had no cloths on and the towel she had with her had partially fallen off during the struggle. "Betty…your…towel!" He didn't move but in his heart he thought he must have died and gone to heaven - again. "*Here I am with a good looking woman on a submarine full of men.*" Gaz didn't move he had no intention of spoiling the moment.

Betty lay for a moment longer before she turned her head to look at Gaz, then suddenly she sat up, grabbed her towel and turned, "The brief is due in ten minutes, better get ready." She stared into Gaz's eyes, "You've no idea, have you?" Then got up and left Gaz alone.

"Dam you Ice Maiden…." Gaz's head was spinning with unusual thoughts and feelings.

Later, Gaz and James followed Betty towards the control centre of the submarine, she seemed to know where to go and Gaz guessed she had already had a look around a submarine sometime in her naval career. Even in the one piece boiler suit they were all wearing, Gaz noticed that the men still followed her with their eyes; he had to agree she was stunning. He was still fighting his thoughts about Betty when they unlocked a water tight door and found themselves looking into a very high tech room with Captain Ross standing by a desk full of charts.

"Ah welcome to my world," Ross indicated with his hands the various parts of the centre, "I trust you are all refreshed and raring to go." Then, without waiting for an answer, he said something to a junior officer at his side who then handed him a piece of paper. "Well the three of you are seemingly very important, it's not every day that a Vanguard Class SSBN is called to be a taxi service."

"We don't have a clue what you are talking about." Gaz said, glancing at Betty. She hadn't looked at him since his encounter with her in his 'bunk'.

"CNC want us to drop you off at Malta....any idea why?" Ross asked, intrigued by the mystery.

"Need to know." James smiled.

"Captain," Betty asked, "What has happened to the Libyan Officer in charge of the Corvette you sank?"

"Need to know." Ross replied smiling at James.

"What's the game play Ross?" Gaz asked which caught Ross unexpectedly; he was usually called sir or boss or captain and he could see his men looking at him for some sort of response.

"You can call me Captain."

"And you can call me 'over' if you want; but what's the plan?" Gaz repeated his question.

Ross took hold of Gaz's arm and pulled him to the side, speaking softly. "Now look here, I don't know who you think you are but this is **my** ship and on **my** ship I am Captain, do you understand?"

Gaz sighed before he replied, "You know something in the last week I have been shot at, blown up, and half drowned. On top of that I have not had any proper sleep like my colleagues, and I am tired of being pushed around by people who think they are important. I would suggest that you tell us the plan from your CNC and that way we can all get some sleep….Huh?"

Ross stood stunned as Gaz walked over to join the other two; he knew he had no choice but to do as Gaz was saying but he had to look good in front of his men. "Ah that's OK then." He said smiling. "You said boss…I thought you said Ross; well anyway lets get on with it shall we." Ross changed the subject quickly just in case, but Gaz said nothing.

It was a simple brief; take the three agents to Malta and drop them off at the land mark known as St Paul's islands. There was nothing else, and so with that knowledge they left the control room and tried to get a few hours sleep. Gaz didn't sleep though, he kept wondering if Betty would stumble into his bunk again, but when he heard the ships intercom calling for them a few hours later, he knew it wasn't going to happen. *"She is certainly a cool one,"* he thought as he ran with James and Betty towards the hatch that would take them into the Maltese night. They had to be quick, there wasn't supposed to be any British submarines in Maltese coastal waters, and even though the dark shape of the Submarine would be hard to see against the dark night time waters, Ross wasn't taking any chances with his career; at least not for these three strangers.

*

George and Maria felt they had traveled higher up in the lift than the building seemed to go, but eventually the lift stopped and the doors slipped open. They had no idea what floor they were on but as they stepped uncertainly out of the lift they saw before them a complete communication centre with two men and three women sat at computers with slim head sets; all seemed pre-occupied with whatever they were doing and didn't seem to notice the arrival of the

Maltese couple. Not knowing what to expect next, they just stood still feeling uncomfortable for the next few minutes until a door at the far end of the room opened, and a tall slim man in a very expensive looking suit came out and walked towards them with his hand stretched out to greet them.

"Ah…you must be George," the suit said shaking George's hand. Then he turned to Maria, "And who is this young lady?" He asked in an unfriendly manner as he offered Maria his hand.

"This is Maria," George felt uncomfortable, "My wife."

The suit still hadn't said who he was, but he was obviously upset that Maria was in his office. "This was not part of the plan George."

"What plan – sorry I didn't quite get your name?"

"Oh I do apologies, it's the times, there's a lot happening… too much to take in. I'm Pete Lacer Assistant Commissioner at your service; now where were we…oh yes. Your wife George should not have been involved - shame really - still she's here now. You better come into my office, we need to chat."

George and Maria followed the Commissioner into his office and when they were in Pete Lacer pointed to a large leather couch, indicating that they should sit down.

"Would you like some tea," Pete asked, "There's Earl Grange, Blackcurrant Bracer or ordinary breakfast?"

"Ordinary." George and Maria answered together.

Pete clicked a switch on his desk and gave someone the order, then sat down on the couch beside George and Maria.

"The thing is George, its getting very messy, seems your 'pick up' was shot down by a Libyan Corvette - bad luck really, but they were rescued by one of our subs and are now once more on their way to Malta."

A young Maltese girl came in and placed the tea on a coffee table in front of them. George couldn't help notice that Pete said nothing until she had left.

"Can't be too careful, now shall I be mum?"

George tried to say something but it seemed that the Commissioner had other plans.

"Tonight; should be about 3:00am, they are expected to land on St Paul's Islands, so you need to be there to intercept them."

"Are there still three of them?" George asked.

"Two men and woman to be precise, but Maria please drink your tea."

Over the next hour or so Pete gave George and Maria a detailed plan of the 'target' and the time scale they had to complete the task. When he asked if they had any questions, George had only one. "Pete you said it was a shame that Maria was with me…what did you mean?"

"Quite simply that she is now part of what is happening and believe me George the stakes are getting higher by the moment, I would suggest in the strongest sense that you have her with you where ever you go."

The Assistant Commissioner walked over to his desk, but George was puzzled "What exactly do you mean?" He asked.

"I've already said too much George; here you will both need these." Pete held out two Glock pistols and two boxes of bullets.

"What are these for?" Maria asked, her eyes bulging.

"You will thank me one day…George will show you how to use it."

Maria looked at George as he took the weapons, she was in shock; this was something she had never dreamed she would see.

As they both left the Assistants Office they heard him say "I pray God will be with you both." Then the doors were closed and George and Maria found themselves back in the lift that would take them out of the building and back into the hot Maltese sunshine.

*

Ishmael sensed that the submarine he was on had stopped as he felt it surface. He knew he had to make his dash for freedom now or he would never get the chance again, and it was too important to fail. He looked at the guard on his door and felt a tinge of guilt; he had been treated like a guest on the ship and in some ways he felt as though he was about to betray a friend, but then reasoned that the British were using 'brain' techniques to lull him into a false feeling of security, and with this in his head he quietly approached his guard who was half asleep with the boredom of the task, grabbed his head with one hand and as he slipped his arm around the sailor's neck he snapped his hand back and the guard fell still at his feet. Ishmael checked to see if the corridor outside his prison was clear and then ran towards the centre of the submarine. It seemed everyone was too pre-occupied to notice him slip past various 'stations' and eventually Ishmael could smell the fresh sea air coming from near to where he was. Then he saw it, an open hatch and it was unguarded. Ishmael couldn't believe his luck as he quietly slipped off the side of the submarine into the warm night Mediterranean waters, and swam off in the direction of the coastal lights he could see not too far away. By the time the dead guard was discovered the submarine had dived back into the darkness and Ross had no way of alerting the three agents he had dropped off.

Chapter Five

Neither George nor Maria slept very well that evening. George had major concerns over Maria's unplanned involvement and the casual way that Pete had handed over the two Glock pistols. He was now wishing he had never taken the large retainers from the British Government, but he had never dreamed that sooner or later there would be a 'pay back' time.

Maria on the other hand couldn't sleep due to the new wave of excitement and intrigue she suddenly found thrust upon her otherwise boring lifestyle, and she was looking forward with a measure of anticipation towards 3:00 am. She had made a drink for herself and George some moments before when the phone rang; it was by then almost 2:00am.

George jumped and looked at Maria; he had been 'day dreaming' as he sipped the hot chocolate Maria had given him. Maria's eyes were wide, *"This is it,"* she was thinking and at the same time indicted with her hands for George to hurry up and answer.

George was in no hurry to lift the phone up and Maria was getting impatient with him. "Pick it up," she said forcefully. George reluctantly put the hand set to his ear.

"Yes?"

"George is that you?"

"Eh…Yes, who is that?"

"It's Pete…. from the High Commission."

George put his hand over the mouth piece of the hand set and whispered "It's the Assistant High Commissioner." Maria nodded.

"Are you there George?"

"Yes sorry… what's the…." Before George could say any more the Assistant Commissioner went into his usual mode of speaking and not waiting for an answer, George felt it was a way of intimidation but he knew he had little or no choice.

"Just a quickie George, just got a message from CNC.UK, seems some nasty fellow, a Libyan I believe, jumped ship when the British Sub dropped our three friends off. Now the thing is, George, he knows where the sub is now and that's a huge 'no no' for us Brits, so could you be a good chap and head for the Malta Libyan Enterprise Offices, that's where he will probably try to make contact, and…er…you know….remove the problem. Oh and by the way, didn't I tell you we are shutting 'shop' so must dash you know the rest of the stuff…Good luck to both of you."

George tried to say something but he heard a click as Pete put his phone down, he felt alone and troubled, but his thoughts were interrupted by Maria.

"Well…what did he say…are we on for tonight?"

"Seems we have another mission to fulfill first…." George sat Maria down and explained the content of the call from Pete.

Maria sat and listened quietly taking it all in; when George had finished she quite simply said, "Well, in that case you better show me how to use this thing." She lifted up the Glock. "There isn't a lot of time, if we are to meet the Brits as well."

George could not believe how 'cool' Maria was, most women would have panicked by now, as indeed he was on the verge off doing himself, but then he always knew that Maria had that 'special something'; it was this that attracted him to her.

“I’ll explain on the way the Libyan Offices,” he said as he reached for the car keys.

*

The submarine had dropped Gaz, James and Betty off at the sea ward end of St Paul’s islands, which they were glad about, as the other approaches would have meant a serious cliff face climb. Although they were tired and wet from the swim, they knew they had to get up to the monument at the south west facing side of the Islands, they had been told that there was a small chapel there where they could shelter until their contact, the Maltese ‘sleeper’ known as George would meet them. The climb was relatively easy but due to their weariness, the dark, and the very rocky terrain, they stumbled up slowly, occasionally tripping up or slipping on some wet unseen rocks, which this island had its fair share of. In site of the uncomfortable climb, all three kept their voices quiet, all that they could hear where their own panting breaths as they neared the monument that marked St Paul’s ship wreck almost two thousand years previous.

Gaz was the first to reach the huge stone obelisk, and he sat down on one of the steps that surrounded the monument, looking back as the other two, first Betty then James, came into view.

“Over here guys,” he softly shouted.

Betty didn’t respond, but James raised his hand to acknowledge and within minutes they were all resting on the step and looking out towards the early morning light of a new Mediterranean day.

“Gorgeous isn’t it?” James was mesmerized by the morning glow of the early sun rise. “Under any other circumstances it would be perfect.”

Betty turned and looked at Gaz, “What now Gaz?”

Gaz thought he saw a flicker of something in Betty's eyes as she looked at him, but he couldn't be sure; they were all tired, wet and hungry. "We need to get into that small white chapel over there, and rest until George finds us.....come on let's get under cover."

Picking up the few possessions they had between them, they broke into the locked Chapel and stepped inside. There were no benches or chairs inside the Chapel, only a hard rock floor and a few 'religious trinkets' that decorated a simple alter table in the corner, breaking the otherwise mundane white walls.

"Find a space and try to get some sleep." Gaz said, looking around at the bare floor.

"Want to cuddle up with me Betty?" James asked smiling.

"In your dreams fly boy." Betty glanced at Gaz.

When Gaz eventual settled and drifted on the edge of a trance like sleep, he was vaguely aware of Betty coming close up beside him and resting her head on the side of his chest. He didn't move or say anything, afraid once more of spoiling the moment.

*

Ishmael had swam for what seemed like an eternity, he had cramps in his legs, and the usually warm Mediterranean waters now had a feeling of coldness; he was exhausted but knew he had to keep going until he reached the land. He had guessed that Malta was the Island he had seen silhouetted against the dark sky in the early hours as he left the British submarine, but as the morning light began to invade the land with its soft orange hue, he knew for sure that it was indeed Malta.

When Ishmael eventually hit land it was at Qawra Point. He was aware, due to his memory of the Naval charts he had of Malta, that if he had missed this land mark he would have drifted out to sea, so he stopped for a moment and gave thanks to Allah for his miraculous escape, then stumbled along to a nearby Tower where he rested in the early morning warmth.

*

Pete Lacer had been nick named the Cosmic Racer by the High Commissions staff, not only due to the fact that it rhymed so well, but also because he generally worked at a very high speed. Of course he was aware of the nick name and he rather liked it, but it would not have been the right thing if he were to admit to that; he had his position to think about. However, if anyone had thought he was fast then, they would have been astounded by the speed he was working at now. An encrypted confidential email had just arrived at his desk informing him that a Libyan invasion was imminent. It had stressed that the information was 'sketchy', and the source was 'not too reliable', but Pete knew that his government would not have sent the message without good reason. He had told his Maltese 'sleeper' earlier that they were leaving, but that had been a planned orderly event due to diplomatic tensions; now he only had a day or so to destroy all sensitive documents, get home and pack, and catch a flight out of the country. *"Good grief,"* he thought as stood looking at the message, *"There's no way I'm going to get a flight, there's absolute chaos at Luqa Airport."*

Pete looked slowly around his office he wasn't a coward by any sense of the word but he was no hero either. *"I have to prioritize."* He picked up the phone on his desk and called the staff into his office, most were Maltese nationals employed locally but one or two were British subjects. When everyone had arrived he told them the facts as he saw them, and even mentioned the possibility of the Libyan invasion. The responses were mixed, some started to cry, while others left quickly to try to escape the island, or warn loved ones. "I would keep this to your selves," he had counseled. "It will make the job of getting your families to safety easier…I pray God is with you all."

When the staff had all eventually left, and Pete was left alone, he sat down in his leather chair and looked around at the empty office. Papers were now scattered all over the office floor and desks, while the various telephones that operators would have answered, rang out unanswered.

"Well Pete," he said to himself stretching his arms out on top of his desk, *"Time to call it a day."* He reached into a drawer in his desk and pulled out a framed picture that had a woman and two children on it smiling and cuddling up to each other. A tear formed in his eyes as he remembered back to 'happier' days, before the terrible air crash that took his family from him. They had been on a 'once in a lifetime' holiday trip to Israel, a sort of spiritual pilgrimage, when the chartered Israeli airline had exploded without any warning and fell out of the sky with no survivors, as it flew close to Turkey. The circumstances of the air disaster were suspicious, but no one ever really found out why the 747 had crashed. He undid the back of the picture frame, removed the picture and stuffed it roughly into his jacket pocket. *"Breakfast I think would be in order,"* and then he left the building being careful to lock the huge wooden front doors as he did.

*

It hadn't taken George and Maria long to reach the Libyan Offices now based in the commercial part of Sliema, normally the long wide street would be packed with tourists visiting the large amounts of Jewelry and designer clothes shops, but tourism was a thing of the past since the Cyprus event. There was the very odd, more optimistic, one or two taking advantage of the sudden price drops, but the street was by normal standards very quite; which suited George and Maria. Nervously they looked for a suitable place where they could survey the approach to the Libyan Offices and found a small, narrow and covered in ally way just a few meters from the front doors of the offices.

"This will do," George said to Maria, "We can see the approached from both directions."

"How will we know him when we see him?" Maria was leaning against a wall

"I guess we will have to look for something that stands out, we know his name is Ishmael, so we could just call his name, if it's him he will get a surprise we know him."

"I'm scared George."

"Yes….me too."

*

After a short rest and feeling better, although he was feeling the effects of a lack of food and water, Ishmael set off from Qawra Tower as the sun was rising above the Mediterranean Sea behind him. He knew a little about Malta from the military briefs they had all received, but he had two misconceptions about the Maltese; the first was that they were allies and loved the Libyans, and the second was he would be received where ever he went as a hero. Both these misconceptions were soon to be shattered. The other piece of information he had about Malta was the location of the Maltese Enterprise Libyan Offices in Sliema, and the fact that all the orange and white buses ran into and out of Valletta. With this information Ishmael formed a plan to reach the Libyan offices and perceived safety, there was also the knowledge of the three British agents, the reason they were there, and the British

Submarines location, he had a duty to get the information to his Government somehow.

Ishmael continued to walk over rocky ground that led from the Tower, but he hadn't gone far when he saw a lone fisherman standing by the water's edge with the typically long fishing rod used by the Maltese for off the shore leisure fishing. He wondered if he could just walk over and ask for help, but soon realized, as he approached, that his presence was starting to intimidate the elderly Maltese man.

"Hello…can you help…I need help to get to Sliema?" Ishmael spoke cautiously.

The old man was terrified to be confronted by the Libyan and stood unmoving.

Ishmael moved closer. "Do you under stand…I need your help…friend?" He spoke slowly so the old man could under stand that he had no intention of harming him.

"Here, take my money…there's not much…please I'm just an old man." He trembled as he held out an old tattered wallet which fell out of his hand onto the ground.

Ishmael couldn't understand why the old man was afraid of him; they were supposed to be allies. Ishmael picked up the wallet and removed two Maltese Liras from inside the folders. "I'm sorry old man to rob you but I need to get to Sliema, it's very important, if you give me your name I will make sure you are refunded for your help."

"Just take the money, take it all…but don't hurt me please."

"I'm not going to……" Ishmael realized it was not worth trying to persuade the old man that he was safe, so he put the two Liras in his pocket and left the wallet on the ground in front of the old man who he could see was still terrified.

Ishmael didn't have to walk too far to find the main road that came from Buggiba and after a short wait he managed to wave down an orange and white bus that was flagged for Valletta. He got directions from a very friendly Catholic priest who was on the bus and, as instructed, jumped off at Msida to catch the bus to Sliema, only ten minutes away. His spirits were high even though he was hungry and tired, because he knew the exact location of the Libyan offices, and looked forward to a shave, some clean clothes, but most of all a good breakfast.

*

By now it was almost mid day and George and Maria had seen no one who they thought would fill the description they had been given by Pete over the phone. Occasionally George or Maria had stepped out and addressed one or two people as 'Ishmael', to see if they reacted in any way; but they had so far drawn a blank.

As the time past, they were both getting increasingly hotter and more despondent; they had almost given up any hope of finding the Libyan when Maria noticed a young, tall man walking quickly towards them. She dived into the alleyway and told George what she had seen. "I think we have him now."

"Why?" George asked, thinking it could be another false identity.

"It's him George…he has a Libyan naval uniform on, but its soiled and dirty as though he has just been for a swim in it."

George suddenly snapped out of his day dream and looked out of the alley, sure enough he could see the Libyan approaching, but by now he was close and they didn't have enough time to discuss what to do next. George took a deep breath and stepped out in front of the Libyan. "Excuse me are you Ishmael?"

The young Officer stopped dead but smiled and said "Why… yes!"

George raised his Glock pistol and Ishmael stopped smiling. "Get into the alley…quickly." George said, waving the pistol in the direction of Maria.

They both stepped out of the street into the narrow passage way and George indicated to Ishmael to walk towards the far end.

Ishmael could see Maria waiting there and the fact that she also had a pistol pointing at him. "What is this all about?" He asked keeping his composure.

"I'm sorry but you know too much," George replied.

"But we are supposed to be allies…friends… you know we are on the same side."

Maria replied with an amount of conviction that surprised George. "Our government always makes friends with snakes…. do it George…we have to kill him."

George hesitated; he didn't really have the 'stomach' for the job. "What are you waiting for George… he has to die for all our sakes." Maria was shaking and starting to cry as she yelled at George.

"I'm so sorry." George raised his Glock to shoot.

His hesitation however gave Ishmael the opportunity he needed. He grabbed George's wrist with both his hands and the two men began to struggle in the narrow confines of the alley; Ishmael having the advantage of being younger and taller than George. As they struggled for the weapon Maria knew she couldn't get a good shot at the Libyan, and she watched in horror as Ishmael slowly managed to turn the pistol round towards George's face. "Shoot him, Maria….shoot him." George shouted desperately, his lungs panting with the sudden effort.

"Your too close to him, I might….."

George's strength was weakening. "Just shoot him Maria before he gets you as well."

Maria, instead of shooting ran up behind Ishmael and hit him on his head, as hard as she could. Ishmael staggered back with the sudden unbearable pain and let go of George's weapon, but he was strong, and the blow didn't knock him out. Ishmael turned to face Maria with a questioning expression, then staggered out of the alley, his hand against his now bloodied head, and ran off in the direction of Sliema harbour stumbling with the intense pain the wound was causing.

George was slumped on the ground, exhausted with the rush of adrenaline that had flushed through his body. "Why didn't you shoot him Maria?"

Maria kneeled down beside him cupping George's face in her hands. "I might have hit you as well… you were too close."

"That would have been better than him getting away… who knows what will happen to our three 'Brits' now."

"Come on George we have to get to St Paul's Bay and warn them."

They were about to run back to their car when George's mobile rang. "Yes?"

"Ah George Pete here, change of plan, return to your home and stay there, I will be in touch, any joy with the 'Lib?"

"He got away."

"Dashed bad luck…ok, you two go back home…the situation is getting very bad all over…best you stay out of it for a short time… Oh and thanks."

*

The sun was now high in the sky, and the heat was getting unbearable for Gaz and the other two. They were now slumped against the cool walls on the inside of the Chapel and they all felt dehydrated and weak. Gaz had said nothing to Betty about their earlier rest; after the short sleep, she had simply sat up without a word. James was quiet as well and Gaz suspected there was a serious problem brewing; he had never known James to sit and say nothing about anything. He got up and walked to the door of the Chapel, the bright high sun blinding him for a moment as he scanned for any sign of movement or help arriving. Gaz stepped out into the day light and turned, intending to walk to the end of the Chapel wall, when he found himself suddenly facing a black robed man.

"What the!" All Gaz's training and experience came into action automatically and as he grabbed the black robed man he shouted at the top of his voice "Intruder….Intruder." There was light shuffle of movement from the Chapel and then Betty and James appeared at the door.

At first Gaz couldn't understand why James and Betty just stood without making any attempt to intervene, but when he saw James start to smile in a mocking sort of way, he realized something wasn't quite right. As he let go of the black robed man he heard his winded voice say, "Father Dominique Caruana at you service… and you are?"

Gaz let go of the priest feeling a little embarrassed at having panicked in front of Betty, and that annoyed him slightly, however Betty didn't seem to notice.

"How nice to meet you Father." Betty said approaching the priest and offering her hand, ignoring Gaz as she passed him.

"Ice." Gaz thought to himself.

"Unfortunately we had hoped that our presence here would not be discovered," she turned and looked at James and Gaz; "I think we have a problem boys, don't you?"

Before Gaz or James could answer the priest stepped forward and held out his hand. "Please take this and phone the number I give you."

"Who are you?" Gaz asked the Priest as he took the mobile from him.

"Father Dominique Caruana," he replied then gave Gaz a number from his memory.

As Gaz put the number into the phone the priest smiled at the other two. "I have food and water for you all, I hid it in the chapel yesterday when I heard you would be coming."

Betty and James looked at each other puzzled about the priest's obvious knowledge of them, however as Gaz dialed the number he had been given, they meekly followed the priest into the cool dark interior of the Chapel.

The phone rang and Gaz heard an English upper class voice answer. "Hello...."

Gaz wasn't sure what to say so he mentioned the only word that came to his head, "Priest."

"Thank God," the upper class voice said, "You are all safe." There was a pause then, "Stay where you are, your contact has been delayed, seems you had a Libyan with you named Ishmael; he escaped from the submarine and is somewhere on the Island...they will be with you as soon as they can, can't say any more...tracking and all that stuff...enjoy your meal with the priest."

"Who are you?" Gaz asked, but the phone had gone dead and he was unable to call back.

Gaz walked back into the Chapel where the other two were eating with the Priest. He walked deliberately over to the Priest, grabbed him by his collar and lifted him up against the chapel's wall. "Right what is going on?"

"Hey cool it Gaz....what has got into you?" James said jumping to his feet, "Sheesh!"

Gaz let go and looked at James and Betty, "You don't find this strange...how many more people know that we are here?"

"Probably the whole of the Libyan army by now," the priest replied calmly.

"What?" Gaz asked, getting irritated.

“Sit down and eat something Gaz,” Betty said warmly, “Father Dominique has been telling us a lot of stuff…and I think you should listen.”

Chapter Six

As Gaz, Betty and James Listened to Father Dominique and as George and Maria returned to their home to wait on further direction; Libyan invasion forces were preparing to sail against Malta to establish a forward Islamic base in Western Europe. Their whole military machine had been mobilized to hit 'fast and hard', and was only waiting on the order to sail. Advance commando units would initially land at Hal Far; old disused airfields previously converted to a craft village for tourists, and establish an operational base to help capture Luqa, the main airport for the island. Once the Airport was secured, the Libyan Navy would then move into Valletta harbour, and bring with it Libyan troops, tanks and hardware to take control of the small countries capital.

As the sun began to set on Malta, many people living in and around Birzebbuga, the nearest town to Hal Far, were awoke up from their afternoon rest time to the sounds of Russian built Ilyushin IL-76 medium range transport aircraft circling around the area before dropping out of sight. As they attempted precarious landings on the old tarmac at Hal Far airfield; some of them crashed into the small buildings that individual small businesses had set up on the runway edges. The time was four pm and the first Libyan troops to land were specially trained commandos who knew their job, they wasted little time in setting about their planned tasks, once they were safely on the ground.

*

Colonel Ibraham Musfet had none of the preconceived ideas about 'friendship' that Ishmael had been taught. He was a realist and knew that the Libyan decision to invade would not be popular with the Maltese people; Treaty of Friendship or no Treaty of Friendship. Nor was he very happy about the choice of airfields he had been given. He remembered back to the argument he had two days ago with a very week and 'weedy' official from the Libyan government.

"What's wrong with Luqa airfield?" He had argued with the official when he had been shown his 'target'.

"We are landing under the Treaty of Friendship so we cannot use an airfield we are not given permission to."

"Treaty of Friendship?" Retorted Ibraham, "Now there's a load of bollocks, what's friendly about landing unannounced and setting up a military base on a tourist island?"

"The world will not respond to our tactics until they realize we have won... after all Colonel, we are entitled to 'help' Malta in times of any national threat."

"We are the biggest threat." Ibraham countered defiantly

"Quite, now if you would rather someone else commanded your unit... it can be...shall we say....arranged."

Ibraham now stood by a hut that was converted into a temporary command and counted the cost of the Treaty to his men. Three Aircraft had crashed on landing, one had valuable equipment on board, the others carried his beloved commando unit and he estimated that he had lost around thirty percent of his strength. He turned to a young ragged looking communications operator who looked as though he had been through the worst of the crashes. "Are your OK young man?"

"Yes sir," the soldier replied, shaking, and in an uncertain sounding voice.

"Ok send a signal to Command in Libya. Operation Blue Grotto in place. We have sustained some casualties, due to bad landing conditions. Second phase is now in place to go. Stop - I wonder why they called it operation Blue Grotto?" Ibraham commented to the young soldier, who was frantically noting down the signal, not really expecting a reply.

"Probably because the place they call the 'Blue Grotto, sir, is quite near here."

"Oh!" Ibraham replied, not really paying too much attention, as he turned to leave the hut and mobilize his commandos for the second phase of the operation. His mind was focused on his next target; Luqa Airport.

*

Pete, the British Assistant Commissioner, paced the floor of his apartment situated in the popular holiday area of Buggiba. He was feeling frustrated at the utterly hopeless situation he had found himself in, especially since hearing that the Libyan Navy Officer had managed to escape from George and Maria. He hadn't wanted to use the 'sleeper' in the first place, quite simply because he was 'untried' and now, although he felt vindicated in his initial assessment of George, Pete was uncertain what to do next. He had three British service men hiding on St Paul's Islands, hosted by the 'incredulous' Father Caruana and now also a 'sleeper' lying low with his newly involved wife. To top all of this Pete knew that the Libyans were about to invade, and he had no contact with the UK Government department that had initialized the whole affair.

Pete poured himself a sparkling water while he waited on his kettle to boil, a good strong cup of tea always seemed to help him think through a crisis. When it was ready he went out to his apartment's balcony and sat looking out towards the blue green Mediterranean Sea. As he sipped his tea he found it hard to imagine that the world was in the process of destroying itself while he sat in the sunshine sipping his tea. *"Typically British,"* he thought to himself, then, as though he had received some sort of revelation, *"Stick to plan Pete, plan A is always the best."* He got up from his seat, walked into the apartment, and picked up his phone. "George is that you…..ah good.... plan A is back on, only this time as you come up through Buggiba, you can pick me up as well……yes I'll be at the sea front wall in two hours." Pete walked back to his balcony, lifted his cup of tea and saluted the view. "Cheers," he said, then after smashing the cup against the balcony wall, he left his apartment and set off for the sea front wall. As he waited on George and Maria he watched in awe as the sun lowered against the orange horizon casting a fiery path across the sea in front of him.

*

"What are all those aircraft doing?" Betty asked as she lay in the late afternoon sun relaxing.

Gaz looked and felt a deep feeling of familiar dread. "James come out here."

James had been talking with Father Dominique for along time in the shade of the Chapel about the history of St Paul's landing. He stepped out with the priest. "What's up mate?"

Gaz pointed into the distant towards the south and James felt his blood go cold. "Its started mate, they are Russian made transporters, the Libyans use them to move rapid response commandos and their kit:" Father Dominique had told them earlier that the invasion was likely.

“What will we do now?” Betty asked, getting up on her feet.

“Wait,” the Priest replied, “That’s all we can do until your contact arrives.”

“Is that wise?” James asked, “You heard the man earlier if Ishmael has made contact with these commandos,” he nodded in the direction of the circling aircraft, “We will be hunted down for sure.”

Gaz felt once more the weight of leadership hanging over him; his next decision could cost them all their lives. “Ok, we will wait on the ‘contact’ but if he is not here by tonight, we will abandon our mission and find a way out of here, in the meantime we better ‘pray’ that the Libyans will be too busy to bother with us for the moment.”

“The contact will come,” the Priest said, “You have made a good choice – oh, I **will** pray.”

*

Ross had retired to his cabin within the Vanguard Class SSBN; he too was feeling the weight of command hanging over him. He knew that he had ‘bungled’ when Gaz and the others had been dropped off, and it was one of these very big ‘bungles’ that would not only jeopardize the three ‘agent’s chances of completing their task; he had also compromised his subs position, and put all of their lives at risk, including Gaz’s team. *“Dam.”* As Ross lay on his ‘bunk’ looking at a picture of his father neatly hung on the wall adjacent to his bed, he wondered why he was more afraid of what his father would think, than what the CNC would, without any doubt, have to say about the situation. *“Bang goes my career in the Navy dad,”* he said to himself as he tried to come to terms with the ‘stupid*’* mistake of not guarding the Libyan sailor a bit better. *“Why didn’t I just sink him and his stinking crew with his stinking Corvette?”* Ross felt his whole world was starting to fall apart, and there was nothing he could do about it. He sat up and reached over to a small cabinet that held cool soft drinks, he would have liked something stronger but alcohol was not allowed on this particular ship. As he started to pour himself a cola he heard someone outside of his cabin; he waited in dread for the knock that he knew was coming.

"Message from CNC boss."

"Bring it in Chief."

CPO Roland walked into the Captain's cabin and looked over at Ross. "Are you OK boss, you look a bit…..?"

"Just hand over the message Chief."

"Ok Boss." Roland hesitated before he left Ross, and then closed the door behind him, he had been with the sub since its commission, as Ross had, and regarded his captain as more that just his senior commanding Officer.

Ross opened the signal.

'Message from CNC. Maintain present location; security status bikini red. Libyan forces poised to invade Malta. Silo's one to three make ready, possible targets grid references as follows……..'

Ross looked at the grids and recognized at least one of them without looking at his charts, *"Good grief...Tripoli?"* He ran from his room and when he reached the control centre shouted to Roland to check the authenticity of the signal he had just been given.

CPO. Roland looked straight at Ross without moving. "Already have boss…there's no mistake."

Ross felt his adrenaline start to rise, "OK lets do as the man said…looks like we might be going to war. Where are we at present Chief?" Ross asked, looking over the illuminated chart desk.

"Just slightly south of Gozo, boss."

"That's where Gaz and the others were going, isn't it?"

"Eventually," replied the Chief, "Although with all that's happening they may have aborted."

Ross thought for a moment. “I think it would take a lot to put those three off… don’t you?”

“What’s your thinking boss?”

“I want six of our best divers to report to my cabin ASAP, maybe we can help our three Musketeers get off the island…don’t you agree it’s worth the try?”

“I’m on it boss.”

Latter on that evening Ross watched from the sub’s ‘sail’ as six highly trained Navy divers slipped into the warm deep waters off the south coast of Gozo; using the latest re-breather units they were soon out of sight, there were no air bubbles breaking the surface that would give away their presence, and after waiting for a few minutes, Ross spoke into the sub’s ‘comm’ system quietly. “Dive, Dive.” Moments latter all trace of the sub and the divers, had disappeared.

*

By evening Luqa had fallen to Colonel Ibraham Musfet’s commandoes. They had wasted no time in moving from Hal Far into Luqa which was only two kilometers away. The Maltese Forces who had been guarding the International Airport since the Cyprus Event stood no chance against the highly professional and mobile Libyan forces, and Colonel Musfet’s order to take no prisoners whilst the attack was in progress, meant that many Maltese civilians as well as military personnel were systematically butchered. The Libyans were thorough in obeying their Colonel’s order and within an hour the entire airport was well under Libyan control. Ibraham called his operation ‘surgeon’s shock’ which most of his men thought was appropriate; the intention was to shock the Maltese into submission so as to avoid any latter problems with the populace.

As Ibraham had stood to address his men prior to 'operation surgeon's knife' he had said to them, "Hit them hard men and remember no prisoners; we have to sweep through quickly and decisively." Then they went in.....

Now as Ibraham walked through the arrivals area of the airport, followed by his various junior officers and SNCO's, a young Corporal approached him, stopped and stood directly to attention, his weapon held across his chest. "Sir!"

"Your report Corporal!"

The young soldier was about to speak when a young Maltese woman who worked for Air Malta groaned and moved near to where Ibraham was standing; she had been wounded and was leaning over the 'inquiry desk'. Ibraham pulled out his pistol, aimed it at the woman and pulled the trigger, putting a bullet mercilessly through her head.

He then turned to his soldier and repeated his command. "Your report."

The young soldier in spite of the work they had already done had suddenly drained pale; he had not expected this from his Colonel. "Sir.....the eh....."

"Come on get it out." Ibraham was getting irritated by the commandoes obvious distress.

"Sorry ....sir....Eh the area has been cleansed....sir."

Ibraham turned to his junior officers. "Good....well done." Then he turned to his communications man. "Send a message to Tripoli; message to read - second phase complete and the operation is a complete success, awaiting next instructions."

"Now gentlemen we wait, and hopefully not for long." They laughed as they walked out of the airport to continue with their various invasion tasks. As Colonel Musfet walked towards his waiting transport, he could smell the warm air of the Maltese evening and hear the repetitious chirping of mating crickets. He looked up at the evening sky; the stars were already starting to show. Stepping into the vehicle he hesitated to take a deep breath as though he was at peace with life, then after closing the door, they drove off back towards Hal Far where his temporary HQ had been established.

Chapter Seven

The attack on Luqa caused immediate panic among the Maltese people although the heaviest movement came initially from those nearest to the airfields. The Libyans had been especially brutal in their attack on Luqa, working on the principle of terrorism that the population would not want to be anywhere near, after such a violent and merciless take over. These were terrorism tactics taken to the extreme and they had the desired effect. Libya wanted the island turned into a huge military garrison, and there was no room for a civilian population sympathetic to the Western powers. The terror tactics put the whole island into flight; and the only place to flee to was Gozo, which the Libyans had already worked out as well. The EU, and America still had its eyes well and truly fixed on events in the East, so much so, that they failed to see what was happening on their own doorstep, or just failed to see the significance of the developing Maltese crisis. Attempts by the Maltese Government to meet with their Libyan 'friends' was deliberately being delayed and it seemed for the moment that it suited everyone, including the EU, to turn a blind eye on the events now unfolding in Malta. From a military perspective, Malta had a very small and under equipped Army and Police Force; the most they could hope to do was protect their fleeing population. The rout of Malta had started and there was worse to come; a lot worse.

*

When George and Maria left their home in Marsaskala, they had no idea what had happened at Luqa Airport, but when they started to try to get through Msida and take the road up to Buggiba, they realized something was seriously wrong. The traffic on the main road that went straight to Mellieha Bay was in chaos, so they decided to try going up the old coast road; it was normally a longer drive but on this occasion it seemed the best option. The coastal road was still relatively quite although they did notice that it was busier than normal, and most people were driving north as they were.

"What's going on George?" Maria asked as she sat beside George who was struggling to get their car moving quicker through the traffic.

"If I didn't know better Maria, I would say there was some sort of full scale evacuation going on."

"That's impossible, there is no……." Maria didn't finish her sentence; she had seen something in the sky above and sat staring at it in unbelief.

George followed her gaze and when he saw what she was looking at, he slammed the brakes of his car on hard. "Allah Madonna," he said as he looked towards the sky, "There must be loads of them."

"Who are they George?"

"If I'm not mistaken, they are Libyans."

"Libyans?"

"Yes Maria!" George started the car again, crunching the gears in his eagerness to get going. "It's an invasion force, they must have taken Luqa."

"Oh no!" Maria began to feel dread, as they maneuvered their way on towards Buggiba; George with one hand permanently on the car's horn.

When George and Maria eventually reached the sea wall in Buggiba, in was getting dark and Pete was getting frantic. "Where have you two been, it has been four hours since I called?"

"Traffic," said George, "The whole of Malta is on the move…have you not seen the Libyan transports going in and out of Luqa?"

"Yes," Pete replied irritably, "Still - four hours?"

"Its chaos Pete," Maria smiled uncertainly, "There is no way we could have got here any sooner."

Pete looked at the two Maltese; they looked shattered and concerned. "Sorry folks…I'm just a bit on edge. It's really important that we get to the three agents on St Paul's Island; the Libyans would be very interested in their mission."

"Better get into the car then, I have a boat waiting for us just off Rxawn Point. It used to belong to my cousin, but I'm quite sure he will be adding to the chaos by now."

Pete smiled as Maria leaned back to pull the catch that opened the rear door of the car and as he slipped into the back seat, Maria passed him a bottle of sparkling water. "You look like you need it." She turned back to face the front of the car.

*

From where they were waiting, Gaz and the others had seen the smoke rising from Luqa, and in the dulling day light, the flashes of explosions lighting up the horizon with the bright white phosphoric glow preceding the dull 'thump' and 'cracks' of a fire fight. They had stood in silence until it had stopped; except the Priest who was muttering quietly on his knees in front of the Statue of St Paul.

"Still reckon we should stay till midnight Gaz?"

"Plan A is always best James."

"What do you think Betty?" James turned to Betty hoping for some support; he was 'itching' to do something - anything but wait.

"I think we should wait." Betty replied, looking at her feet to avoid anyone's eyes, especially Gaz's.

"I might have known you would choose his side." James replied, with a cheeky smirk.

"What is that supposed to mean?" Betty asked defensively, yet feeling her face redden.

"Ouch…don't be so jumpy." James lifted his hands in a mock feminine gesture.

Betty walked away from both Gaz and James, she wasn't sure why, but she was feeling embarrassed by James's jokes about Gaz. *"What's wrong with you girl, your falling apart, get a grip."* She turned and walked back towards James and Gaz. "Listen fly boy, given the choice I would always go British before I went American, nothing personal you understand?"

As she turned and walked over to see Father Dominique, Gaz was watching her. *"She's cool, but hardly ice."*

As the darkness began to fall over the Island of St Paul, Gaz, Betty, James and Father Dominique stood in silence as they watched the Libyan transport aircraft flying in and out of Luqa continuously. Gaz looked at his watch it was now almost nine in the evening and he was wondering if he had made the correct choice. The priest had sounded so certain that their contact would come but it was getting late, and who knows what had happened since the Libyans invaded. He turned to the Priest. "Where is the contact you promised Dominique…its getting very late?"

"They will come," was all he said in reply.

"Look I don't think we can hold on much longer, this is a very small Island and it will not take the Libyans long to reach here."

"Wait one more hour Gaz, if they are not here by then, we will leave."

"Leave to go exactly where?" Betty interrupted, overhearing the conversation.

"Not south, that's for sure." James interjected flippantly.

"Gozo." Gaz said ignoring James's sarcasm. "That's where we were sent and that seems like a good enough place to start with."

"But without the contact we have no idea where the AWAC is, or even how deep it is; they didn't tell us in case we got captured; remember?" Betty had also ignored James's interruption.

"Who cares," James said flippantly, "Let's just get off this Island."

"Let's just play it one step at a time." Gaz said to Betty

"That's your biggest problem Gaz." Betty replied.

"Meow…hisss," James said as Betty walked away from them both and sat on the step of the monument, "She's really got your number boy."

"What's that supposed to mean?" Gaz was puzzled by James's words.

"She's hot for you Gaz… are you blind or something?"

Gaz was about to reply when suddenly Betty shouted out, but in a quiet cautious manner, "Intruder's coming in a small boat."

"Down!" Gaz said, and they all dived behind the large rocks of the Monument. Then he saw it, a small Maltese fishing boat with its 'shrimp' light shining brightly above the sea's dark surface.

"It's probably just a small fisherman doing his evening shrimping," James whispered as they hid together.

"Maybe!" Gaz replied, still thinking about what James had said about Betty earlier. "Were you serious about.....?"

He didn't finish his question.

Father Dominique suddenly stood up and shouted. "Allah Madonna......Hey...Pete..." Then ran down the sloping end of the Island; his black robes appearing like a silhouetted cartoon figure, to where three people had stepped from the shrimping boat.

"Looks like our contacts." Betty said rising from behind her hiding place. "Come on boys this is not the time to play shy."

*

Master Diver Robbie McMaster and the five other men with him surfaced at the entrance to Xlendi Bay, a rocky inlet that leveled off some distance from Gozo's shore line, which meant they had to paddle for about five hundred yards with their heavy diving equipment still on. It had been a very bad place to come in and Robbie felt 'exposed' even in the dark, but there had been no other option for them, it was the only way in between the high cliff faces they had encountered on this side of Gozo. Robbie had waited in the sea for hours until he thought it was safe enough to bring his men ashore, but that meant they were all exhausted and cold from the dive, and they dragged their feet and equipment as they approached a small piece of sandy beach; the left hand side skirted by a low wall that rose in height as it curved around the bay to their right.

"Right lads get the gear off quickly, we dinni want the locals to get a wee fright dae we?"

Although tired, they soon had their dry suits off to expose a variety of civilian cloths; some had jeans and tee shirts others wore checked shirts and shorts.

"Hurry men." Robbie said, and then he looked at one of the divers. "Hae a quick scout aboot laddie and see if there is ony one around." Then turning around to look at the others, "The rest 'o' ye get doon in the sand and keep yer heeds low."

One of the divers had returned to the deep sea with the diving equipment, his job was to 'sink' it and mark the place so it could be recovered latter. He was just returning through the shallow waters when a voice shouted out.

"You there stop and lift you hands."

He froze without looking in the direction of the other divers.

Robbie could see a Maltese Policeman just near to him and he had drawn his gun. As the diver started to walk slowly towards the Policeman, Robbie signaled two of his men who were lying next to him in the sand. They slowly took out their diver's knifes and moved quietly to the side of the beach and onto the main road behind the Policeman. He was still shouting orders to the returning diver when he was grabbed from behind; a cold sharp metallic feeling slicing into his neck was the last thing he knew.

The still 'suited up' diver now ran to the beach and removed his wet suit hastily. Robbie walked towards the place where the policeman had fallen. "Sorry mate," he said, "Just can't take a chance on the sub being found."

He had just ordered the body to be hidden, when his 'scout' returned. "Chief, there's a load of tourists shops along the road, with lots of food and cold drinks. The main road goes on up a hill and out of this town, and there are plenty hills and rocks to hide and rest."

"Gid work laddie." Robbie turned to his waiting men. "You heard the man…first food…then up the hill for a wee rest…quietly though."

When they eventually moved out from the beach area, it was as though they had never been; the last man, without being ordered to, 'roughed' up the sand so there was not even a foot print to tell the tale.

*

Ishmael had managed to get as far as Birzebbuga just before panic had reached the small town; the driver of the orange and white bus had insisted that all passengers disembark, but as he turned to head back towards Valetta, his bus had been mobbed and many clung to the door and bumpers desperate to get away. Ishmael had seen and heard the fire fight at Luqa from a distance and immediately knew it was his own countrymen who had arrived. He had been surprised by the attempt on his life in Sliema, but now he had learned to be more cautious; he had no more allusions about the so – called 'friendship' between the Maltese and the Libyans. Walking along the crowded sea front on the newly paved pathway, he watched as the evening sun began to set and the endless stream of Russian made transports made their precarious landings just two kilometers from where he now was. From time to time Ishmael had to push against the crush of the crowd, who were generally moving in the opposite direction to him, but when he reached Kalafrana most of the Maltese had already left and Ishmael found himself alone with Hal Far in his sight.

As he approached two Libyan commandos guarding the base, he saw they were dressed in full combats and Ishmael realized that most of his white uniform was stained and unidentifiable; he braced himself as he saw the two guards raise there weapons.

"Halt…Identify yourself."

Ishmael breathed a sign of relief; he had wondered if they were shooting first and asking questions later, which was the general order of events in this type of situation.

"I'm Lieutenant Ishmael Zughaid of the Libyan Navy."

The guards glanced at each other before one replied. "Down on your face…arms stretched out in front of you."

Ishmael did as they said without any hesitation; he knew that it was the standard way of dealing with an unidentifiable intruder. As he lay on the ground the way they had instructed him to, one of the guards approached him and systematically did a body search, frisking first his body and then moving down his legs.

"OK your clean – on your feet – sir." Ishmael was helped to his feet.

"Who is it you need to see?" The second guard now asked still pointing his weapon menacingly towards Ishmael.

"The officer in charge; I have information that he may find very interesting."

As the dark of the evening started to settle, Ishmael was led away towards a craft shop that sat near a crashed Transport aircraft. He thought it quite funny that above this particular shop there was a sign that said "Genuine Malta Knights Armour for sale here, buy one get second free." However the humour was lost when he saw a very tough looking Colonel sitting at a desk just inside the door.

*

Colonel Ibraham Musfet had finished debriefing his officers and making arrangements for the next stage of the offensive, he was now hungry, tired and looking forward to a few hours rest when he was disturbed by one of his beloved commandos.

"Sir…sorry to disturb you but we have a man here who claims to be a Libyan Naval Officer."

Ibraham thought for a moment; he wasn't expecting any Navy ships to arrive yet and when they did eventually get here, he certainly didn't expect them to come to Hal Far.

"Shouldn't he be at Valetta or something?" Ibraham didn't even look up from the paperwork he was working through.

The commando smiled at his CO's triteness. "He says he has information you would like to hear."

"It can wait until morning now, show him to a shop or something…he can get some 'pressies' for the little woman back home."

Before the commando could do anything else. Ishmael stepped forward and pushed the guard to the side. "Colonel," he said standing up straight. "I am Lieutenant Ishmael Zughaid of the Libyan Navy - and I insist you hear what I have to say."

Ibraham stood up sharply; he didn't like Navy Officers and he was quickly starting to dislike this particular one. "You have one minute…and it better be good."

*

Betty had already reached the small 'shrimping' boat when Gaz and James decided to leave the cover of St Paul's statue and follow her down. They could see her silhouette against the moon lit sky as Father Dominique was doing introductions. They saw the three strangers get out of the small boat and start walking towards them and Gaz felt a slight feeling of excitement mixed with relief as they came closer.

"Which one is George?" James asked as he and Gaz reached out their hands to welcome their rescuers.

It was Father Dominique who replied. "Gaz, James, this is Pete, Maria, and of course George who you have been waiting for." He was smiling like a small boy.

They all walked back up to the small chapel, talking briefly about the Libyans and the fleeing Maltese people, but it was Pete who brought the conversation to order when they reached the statue. "OK folks…where do we go from here?"

"Gozo," said Gaz without any hesitation. "Libyans or no Libyans we have an appointment with an American AWAC."

"You're not serious!" James said. "Half of the blooming Libyan Army is landing on this island, we'll be lucky to get off it alive, never mind find the AWAC."

"There is another problem," said George looking sadly at Maria. "The Libyan Naval Officer who was a prisoner on the British Nuclear Submarine, has escaped and has by now probably reached the invading Libyans."

"So the sub has been compromised?" Betty asked showing a genuine concern.

No one answered but the silence was answer enough.

"That's just great!" James flung his hands into the air.

Pete tried to bring some sort of reasoning to the situation. "I think the way things are going, the best thing we can do now is head for Gozo and try to find a way of getting you all off the island…we cannot afford to have any of you fall into Libyan hands and I presume that the Maltese Government will probably take some sort of defensive posture there."

Gaz had noticed that Betty had moved beside him while the discussion was going on and he felt a sense of 'comfort' with her closeness. He wanted to reach out and hold her; not passionately, just hold her, and he was puzzled by this new awareness. *"Get a grip boy."*

"Ok." Gaz responded, pushing his thoughts of Betty aside. "We move to Gozo… but on one condition…we dive if we get the chance."

They all looked at James for approval. "Hey…if the man says we dive…then we dive."

"Then let us go quickly," said Father Dominique. "We can get there by sea in the 'shrimper."

"What in that thing down there?" Betty had her doubts. "No way - I'll swim first."

"That could be arranged." James was smirking as he picked up his 'kit'.

"It would take a better man than you." Betty was now walking away from Gaz towards the slope that led to the small boat.

As Gaz and the others followed her down to the waiting boat, Gaz wondered how a delicate and good looking woman like Betty could be so hard inside. "*Ice Maiden,*" he thought but then felt guilt flood his soul. "*What is the matter with you…get a grip.*" He was finding it harder to focus on the mission; no matter how it turned out Gaz knew in himself that he didn't want to live his life without the 'Ice Maiden'.

Chapter Eight

Colonel Musfet continued to move papers around his desk as Ishmael told his story. He occasionally looked up when he heard a piece of information that interested him, but apart from these short indications of interest, Ishmael felt as though he was talking to a blank 'wall'. However, the Colonel was very interested in what he was being told and a plan was already forming in his mind. He listened patiently until Ishmael had drawn out every salient point, at least those points that Ishmael though were salient, and then started to ask the numerous questions that he needed answers for.

It was a long interview for Ishmael and when it had all finished he felt faint from hunger and exhaustion, *"Is there no concern for anything in this man?"* As he swayed in front of the tough looking Colonel who was now on his feet, Ishmael laboured to remain at attention.

Just when he though he could endure no more questioning the Colonel turned and smiled, rubbing the stubble that had grown on his unshaven face. "You have done very well Lieutenant, you should be proud of your work so far." He turned and sat down at his desk once more, picked up a green field telephone and barked a command. "I want food and a place for the Naval Officer to rest," he paused to glance at Ishmael then spoke again. "Get me twelve good men…we have work to do."

Ishmael felt relief flowing through his whole being; the Colonel had believed his story. As that relief started to take effect, Ishmael saw everything go black; the last thing he heard was the strong commanding voice of the Colonel shouting "Medics," then the darkness completed its hold.

*

The small 'shrimper' was not build to hold seven people and as a result, when Gaz and the others set off towards Gozo, it sat very low in the water. George had set a heading for Dahiet ix – Xiep where the Madonna Statue could just be seen against the moons silver light which was just past Mellieha bay, hoping to run the coast past Ahrax Point, where the famous Dragunara view point was, and then pass Comino to the south, however when they hit the open sea between St Paul's Islands and 'Dahiet' there as a large swell and they started to take in water. They 'bailed' with their bare hands and a small bucket they found on the craft, but the swell was too much; by the time they reached the South Comino Channel they realized that they were sinking in very deep water.

"What do you suggest now?" Pete asked as he wiped sweat from his brow; he was getting tired as were the others.

George, now the unofficial boson, was standing at the front of the small boat next to a large pulley that would have been used for hauling in the shrimp nets. He could see in the distance the silhouetted shape of the Comino coast line, but as he peered into the darkness something caught his eye, *"The tower; Comino Tower."* "Over there!" George shouted to the others above the noise of the boat's diesel engine. "Comino Tower - if we can reach that point we will be able to get onto the Island at the 'Blue Lagoon'."

They all kept 'bailing' with renewed vigor.

Betty stood up to stretch her back and wipe sweat from her face, as she did Gaz watched her, he couldn't help himself, her every move was 'interesting'. Betty noticed and smiled before she started bailing again. *"Dam,"* thought Gaz as he bailed harder.

It wasn't enough though and, although they all worked to the point of exhaustion, the small boat continued to take in water and sink lower. By the time they were off the point at Ras I-Irqieqa, near Comino Tower, they had to abandon the boat and swim for the inland bay near to the Blue Lagoon, in the unsettled sea.

*

Gaz was the first to drag himself, and Betty, onto the sandy beach area of the small island; she had taken cramp shortly after they had jumped into the sea and had almost gone under when Gaz had grabbed her. As she clung onto his shoulder with her arms they collapsed at the waters edge, burying their faces in the sand as they fell. Gaz tried lifted his head slightly to see where they were and whether the others were in sight, but he couldn't fight the overpowering exhaustion and as his head hit the sand once more, he fell into a fitful sleep.

He had no idea how long it had been since they arrived on Gozo when Gaz woke up, but as he refocused his eyes, the sun was low in the morning sky and Betty was sitting in front of him with her legs drawn up to her chest, staring out to sea.

"Betty!" Gaz croaked it, his throat was dry and he was still weak. "Betty!" He shouted a bit louder and Betty moved towards him.

"Shhhh, Gaz…take it easy."

Gaz tried to sit up but felt sore. "Where are the others…did they make it?"

Betty looked away and said nothing.

"Betty….did they make it?"

Betty turned and placed her arms around Gaz's body, drawing herself so close to him that he could feel the comfort of her warmth. As she lay next to him she was weeping, and Gaz knew without any reply, that the others hadn't come out of the sea. He held on to her as she sobbed into his shoulder but said nothing; he was in shock himself, fighting back the rising emotion until he couldn't hold it anymore, for the next thirty minutes they just lay together in the sand weeping and mourning their lost friends.

*

The last time James saw the others, they were drifting away from where he had entered the sea. He tried as much as he could to stay with Gaz and Betty but they had 'jumped' from the opposite side of the boat and had missed the strong current that had grabbed James and the others. He had shouted as much as he could during the dark night and had heard George and Maria shouting too, but soon that had faded out and James found himself alone in the Comino Channel drifting at the mercy of the strong current. James's survival skills from being a pilot kept him afloat for the next few hours, and as the morning sun began to rise on the horizon, he saw that he had drifted towards the smaller island of Gozo. He could see the ferry port at Mgarr, which he recognized from his brief on the carrier Theodore Roosevelt, but it was too far away to reach. However he noticed he was drifting towards a point jutting out from the coast, where the large shape of an old fort dominated the cliff edges; James thought he could, with a little effort, reach it. "*It's that or nothing, Jamesie Babe,*" he said to himself, and then using his remaining strength, he began to swim vigorously towards Mellieha Point where Fort Chambray rested on the cliffs. When he eventually reached the point he found it hid a small rocky bay surrounded by cliffs but flat on one side, and as he pulled himself onto the warms rocks he noticed a narrow track that would take him inland. "*Secure, Rest, then explore...that's what the manual says.*" He looked around for a safe place to rest then fell asleep wondering if the others had 'made it'.

*

Robbie McMaster and the other divers had rested and fed well when the sun rose on the new day. They had found a hidden space in Xlendi valley and had not been seen since the police incident. However Robbie knew that sooner or later the Maltese Police would be looking for the missing policeman, and with that in mind they struck camp and headed inland. The last thing they wanted was to pass through any major place of residence so after searching their maps they headed for Munxar keeping to narrow tracks.

"Chief?" It was one of the younger and more inexperienced of the divers. "How will we manage to find the three agents...we don't even know if they are in Gozo…what if the Libyans have them…or they are stranded in Malta…we don't have much to go on?"

As they marched on towards Robbie kept his eyes forward. "The boss says to find them son, and that's whit we are going ti dae."

"But…sir!"

"The way I see it is, thon blokes…you know…Gaz, the American, and the wee lassie; they know their stuff, they will reach Mgarr eventually and we will be there tae meet them…got that?"

"Aye, aye Chief."

They trudged on as the sun began to rise passing Munxar to the south and on towards the village of Sannat still avoiding the built up areas where the locals were most likely be. They could hear the early morning dogs barking and the cocks crowing and Robbie knew that soon the locals would be moving around about their business, however as they arrived at the main road that left Sannat they were shocked to see that traffic was already moving and it seemed to be badly congested.

"Cover." Robbie said, signaling at the same time to the other divers to go low.

"What's going on?" One of the divers at his side whispered quietly.

"It's a traffic jam, and there all headin fur Victoria by the looks." Robbie answered scratching his head.

"What now?" The diver asked rhetorically.

Robbie turned, "Nip back and tell the lads tae keep their heeds doon…we will wait until it clears…then move out." As the diver passed the message Robbie checked his map again, he was looking for a track that would take them to Mgarr and avoid the population; as he searched he saw a track that led from where they were, all the way to Fort Chambray, south of Mgarr. *"Have to do."* "Right lads on yer feet and move out."

They waited until there seemed to be a lull in the congestion, then started to move east out of Sannat and away from the direction of the traffic flow, towards Xewkija and the track that would take them to the Fort about four kilometers away. A few hours later they were walking along a dirt track in a shallow valley that led them past Xewkija and then further on past the area of Ghajnsielem, where Robbie could see the white walls of Fort Chambray a short distance in front of them. "Well tak a wee rest in that big fort in front of us; we can keep an eye on Mgarr from its walls."

"Sir look!" One of the other divers was pointing towards the Fort. "Someone is moving around the Fort area."

Robbie opened his 'ruck' sack and pulled out a pair of high power binoculars. "Your right son…ok every one spread out…and be careful."

The divers climbed over the hard rocky surface covering the shallow valley and advanced, on Robbie's signal, in a line towards the fort; all of them now carried their divers knifes in their hands and all of them were proficient at using them.

*

When James had rested and felt ready to move, he decided to check out the Fort above him first. There was a path that led from the sheltered rocky bay he was in but it didn't take him directly to the fort, and he found he had to climb up a slight incline off rock to reach his destination. It was while he was doing this that he saw the six men walking towards the castle along a dirt track, and to James's trained eye they looked suspiciously like soldiers. He clambered over the rocky, slippery surface of the cliff face to try to get out of sight but when he eventually reached the small fort, he wasn't sure whether he had been seen by them or not; James held his breath and lay hard against the fort walls overlooking the sea and Comino. That's when he saw the boats, hundreds of them; an armada of fishing boats, motor boats, Jet Ski's in fact anything that could float seemed to be heading towards the island. *"It's begun...the Maltese are fleeing the Libyans."* He was still staring when he heard the sound of gravely rocks being disturbed by human feet and he held his breath again.

James managed to disarm the first man to step round the side of the fort with a quick fist to his neck, but the second came on too quickly and James found himself on the ground wrestling with all his strength. Then another man appeared and James found he was being overwhelmed by the numbers, however he didn't stop struggling until he heard one of his aggressors speak. "Lie still wee man…were no gonna hurt ye."

"Who are you?" James asked pinned under three of the divers.

Robbie eased up on his grip, he recognized the American accent. "Naw it canni be…James Kirk? Captain James Kirk?"

"That's right I'm Kirk?" Now James was puzzled, *"How does this Scot know who I am."*

Robbie stood up and dusted his cloths down. "Let him go lads, he's one of oor targets." Then he held out his hand and offered James a lift up; which he took. "Sorry aboot the wee tickle…sir but we didni ken it wis you."

James smiled at Robbie and grasped his shoulder as he held on to his hand "Boy am I so glad to see you guys."

*

"Gaz come quickly….hurry." Betty was shouting from a short distance in front of Gaz. They had spent a few hours lying in the dry hot sands near the Blue Lagoon, and then had decided to explore their new surroundings. There was a narrow track that led from Comino Tower, across the small island, ending up at a small chapel called St. Marija that overlooked a small rocky bay. As Gaz got near to it, he could see that Betty was excited about something. "What's up Betty?"

"Look Gaz…over there." Betty was pointing towards the looming coastline of Gozo and smiling at the same time. "Boats…hundreds of them and there are all heading for Gozo."

"They must be trying to escape the Libyans."

"Maybe we can catch someone's attention." Betty started to shout and wave her hands "Hey…over here…help us….."

Gaz started to do the same and they both waved and shouted for several minutes until it became apparent that, although they were seen by many of the small boats, no one responded to their shouts for help.

"What's the matter with them?" Betty asked annoyed at the lack of response, "I'm sure they see us here."

"Yes they see us, but they're scared Betty and not willing to take the risk of picking up any strangers."

"What…were not strangers….were British for heaven's sake…who do they think we are, Libyans…do we look like …."

"Whoa…steady on Betty…freeze it."

Betty looked at Gaz with an annoyed glimmer in her eyes; he realized he had used the wrong choice of words. "I'm sorry… I didn't mean to imply…"

"Freeze it?" "How can I get colder than Ice….Gaz?"

"Oops"

Betty walked away from the side of the chapel but as she did she noticed another small bay and it looked to her like, *"a marina!"* "Gaz… quick come with me." Without waiting she began to run along a narrow rocky track. Gaz couldn't believe the change, *"One minute she is growling at me... the next?"* Then he too saw the marina and started to run after Betty.

*

It only took them a few moments to reach the small marina at San Niklaw Bay but in the now growing heat of the summer day, they were panting and sweating heavily.

"Gaz?" Betty was propping her hands against her knees, to try to ease the effort of 'catching' her breath.

"Yes?"

"Look down there." Betty was still bowed over and panting, but her head and eyes were fixed on something in the water by a small rowing boat.

Gaz followed her gaze while trying to regain some control of his own breathing. “What is that…oh no. Quickly we might not be too late.”

They both ran down the small path that took them to the water’s edge and stopped by the object of Betty’s original attention. It was Pete Lacer the Assistant Commissioner and there was no indication that he was still alive. He had been washed partially onto a rocky edge at the marina’s side and his head was clear of the water, but he was still and they both feared the worst.

They leaned over and taking an arm each, they pulled Pete’s limp body from the water and laid him on his back. Betty then stood back as Gaz looked for signs of life; she was biting her knuckles and began pacing uncertainly around in a small figure of eight. “Is he….?”

“No way to tell yet.” Gaz was feeling for a pulse on Pete’s neck. “I can’t feel a pulse.” Gaz put his head on Pete’s chest to see if he could hear a heart beat. *“Yes.”* “There’s a weak heart beat Betty, come help me.”

Betty came over and counted for Gaz as he gave Pete ‘mouth to mouth’. Initially there didn’t seem to be any response but Gaz kept going. *“Come on Pete…come on.”* Then suddenly Pete coughed. “Betty quickly help me turn him onto his side.”

As they moved Pete onto his side, water came rushing from his mouth and Gaz relaxed, *“At least Pete is still alive.”* Then, without any warning, and to Gaz’s surprise, Betty grabbed him and gave his a long full lingering kiss on his lips. “*There’s nothing ice about her lips,”* Gaz thought as he moved his arms around to embrace her, but with some measure of hesitation.

When Pete opened his eyes he squinted to see where he was, he couldn’t remember much, but he did recognize the couple next to him kissing passionately. Pete groaned, he felt rough that was true, but it was an overstated groan, it was the way he believed a drowned man would groan, because being a perfect gentleman, it seemed the best way to get Gaz and Betty's attention.

Chapter Nine

The European council of war was still staggering from the events in Cyprus and the pre-emptive strike of Israel against Iran and Cyprus, when the initial invasion force from Libya attacked Malta. They had determined that the Arab nations would have rallied together in an attempt to remove the 'Israeli problem' once and for all; but they now realized that they had seriously misjudged the tactical competence of the mainly Muslim nations. It seemed that while Europe and America tried to close the front door, the enemy was sneaking through the back door. International protests were launched against the Libyan government, but they claimed to acting within International law using the 'Treaty of Friendship' as the catalyst for their invasion. As the diatribe continued between Libya and Europe, it emerged that the presence of the downed American AWAC north of Gozo constituted the presence of a foreign force and as such Libya had the right, by Treaty, to 'defend' Malta. With Syria, Lebanon, Jordan and Egypt pouring its land forces up to the Israeli borders, it seemed that removing the combined British and American fleet away from the Israeli coast was an option that would have to be thought through very carefully. For the moment Europe and America were paralyzed to move against Libya and looked on helplessly as the Libyan Socialist Government continued its invasion plans of Malta unhindered. As a last ditch resort, Europe ordered it's multi nation 'Rapid Reaction' forces into Sicily; If the Libyan's had further expansion plans they would need to invade Sicily, and they had no treaty there.

*

Euro MP. Antony Davidson OBE, or Tony as he preferred to be called, found his esteem among his peers had rocketed. When he had arrived back from Cyprus his reputation as 'gung ho' or as he had often been called, 'a loose canon', had been picked up by the media and he had to fight his way past the waiting crowds outside the European Offices in Brussels. When he eventually pushed his way through the buildings front doors, he was met by the other EMP's who seemed eager to shake his hand. As he walked into the main foyer he felt his peers pat his back, while others were clapping their hands and shouting "Bravo…Bravo." *"This must be how it feels to be a famous pop star,"* he thought as he made his way to his office on the fifth floor. Now standing in a lift, alone for the first time since arriving back from Cyprus, he was reflecting on the events that led to his seeming popularity. "*It is all too much really. All I did was fly around in a chopper and pick up a few stragglers."* He thought of James Kirk, *"A brave pilot,"* and of Gaz and the others. *"They are the real hero's, chips off the old blocks; I wonder what they are doing now?"*

His memories, however, were interrupted by an electronic voice that brought him back to the immediate presence. "Fifth floor, doors opening."

As Tony walked out of the lift he noticed that everything was the same as he had left it when he went to Cyprus, it shouldn't have been any other way of course, but after all that had happened in the Mediterranean, and indeed was still happening, he was momentarily surprised. All the typing pools and the communications operators were working as normal, and as if cued, his secretary walked towards him with a pile of files, just as she would normally do each day, *"Just another day at the office,"* but somehow Tony knew he would never be the same again; the Cyprus event had changed him.

As he took the files from his secretary's hands he asked, as he always asked, "Any calls while I've been out?"

The secretary smiled. "Hundreds sir….literally."

Then walking to his office; a glass partitioned corner within the larger area that composed the fifth floor, he heard someone start to clap slowly, then another joined in and then everybody; they were all smiling at Tony. Eventually, behind the glass partition, he sat down at his desk and looked at the paperwork that had piled up; Tony pushed it to the side, and then pressed a button on his phone.

"Yes sir?" His secretary was prompt as ever.

"Get me a cup of tea Jennifer, and the PM, there's a good lass"

"Yes sir."

"Oh - and Jennifer."

"Yes sir?"

"In that order please."

"Yes sir, of course sir….Sir?"

"Yes…?"

"It's great to have you back."

"Thank you Jennifer."

*

When Ishmael eventually woke up he found himself alone in a small room that had obviously been used as a shop at one time with shelves full of tourist gifts and a Wembley Ice Cream dispenser in one corner. There was no guard on the door, but Ishmael could hear the noise of military movements from outside. He sat up and put his hands on his head; everything had begun to 'spin' momentarily but after a few moments his head started to clear. There was a set of 'combats' on the floor beside the bed and Ishmael rightly assumed they were there for his benefit.

After washing in a sink that barely hung from the wall at the back of the small shop, and dressing in the clean uniform, he stepped out into the bright morning Maltese sunshine.

"Ah Lieutenant Zughaid glad to see you decided to grace us with your company."

Ishmael couldn't see who was talking to him as his eyes hadn't yet adjusted to the very bright sunshine; but he did recognize the voice. "Sorry Sir…I'm not sure what happened to me."

"You fainted….probably too much sun and stress…it's not every day someone tries to kill you."

"No sir."

"Well we've waited long enough." The Colonel turned and barked out a command and twelve commandos nearby suddenly stood rigidly to attention. "Right let's get going Sergeant."

Ishmael noticed one of the men step out from the others and do very smart military turn left. "Right you lot…Right turn." As the Sergeant continued to give a few other orders, Colonel Musfet started to walk away from Ishmael towards a Russian made BTR.60, an old amphibious APC that was waiting a short distance away. "Are you coming?" Ibraham Musfet asked turning to look back at Ishmael.

"Er….yes Sir." Ishmael had not expected this to happen. "Can I ask where we are going Colonel?"

"Yes, of course….we have to find your friends, do we not? After all they may know the location of a British Nuclear Sub which our government now wants, and of course they are spies who we are going to catch."

Ishmael climbed into the eight wheeled vehicle, it was well armed with a 14.5 mm Machine gun on it's small turret, but the heat inside was oppressive and when the other commando's eventually piled in; Ishmael felt claustrophobic and very uncomfortable. He prayed under his breath that the Colonel would not try to float the machine even though in theory it should be able to.

"Don't worry Lieutenant - we do not intend to remain in here for too long." Colonel Musfet spoke in a mocking tone for the benefit of his men who, in response, quietly laughed at Ishmael. "Part of the Libyan Invasion fleet has arrived in Valetta and lucky for you there has been no resistance."

"What do you mean sir…lucky for me?"

Colonel Musfet was now sniggering, he intended to get some sort of mileage out of the situation; it was amusement for his men. "Well Lieutenant we were going to ask you to 'liberate' a Maltese Naval Corvette… but you can simply sign for one now."

The men all laughed as the APC headed for Valletta along the main road past Paola, then towards Hamrun. There was very little traffic on the roads as most of the Maltese had headed to the north of the Island, what there was the BTR.60 simply pushed aside with little effort.

It took twenty minutes for Ishmael and the others to reach the docks at Valetta and when the APC doors were opened, Ishmael felt the coolness of the sea blowing against his sweating face. He followed the Colonel down some steps that took them to the edge of 'Grand Harbour' and its concrete landings. There were a few Libyan ships docked within the harbour, but Ishmael noticed that there were no troop carriers or frigates most, as it turned out, were mine sweepers and such.

Ishmael now ran to keep up with the huge strides of Colonel Musfet, he was panting to keep his breath. "Colonel, where is the Navy you said was here?"

“Pass on that one Lieutenant…there is supposed to be a large naval contingent here.”

“What are you going to do then, there’s no sign of any Corvette’s Maltese or any other?”

“Lieutenant, you are getting on my nerves. I can see that for myself.”

They eventually stopped in front of a dock side office, there was a man with gold Naval braiding on his hat sitting at a desk behind the glass window that Ishmael and Ibraham could see through. Colonel Musfet took out his personal weapon from his shoulder holster and began to hammer at the closed door with the weapons metal butt. “Open this door,” he shouted, and Ishmael saw the braided hat turn and look out of the window at him.

Whether it was because Ishmael had no rank markings on his uniform, or whether the ‘braided hat’ was just being pig headed, Ishmael could not be sure, but his failure to jump when Ibraham commanded it almost cost him his life. After waiting for a minute, enough time for anyone to respond, Ibraham started firing his pistol at the door’s lock, and as Ishmael watched through the window he saw the ‘braided hat’ dive for the floor. Several shots later Ibraham raised his boot and gave a huge kick which knocked the door off its hinges; then he stepped over the splintered door and into the office as though he owed it.

“Who’s in charge here?” Ibraham bellowed his smoking pistol still in his hand.

The braided hat rose slowly from the floor, and then noticed the Colonel flashes. “Colonel I must protest at your manners.” The braided hat was now standing up dusting himself down; though now minus the hat.

“Your protest has been noted, now who are you?”

“I am the commander of this…”

“This nothing!” Ibraham interrupted. “Where’s the fleet?”

"Who wants to know?" The commander obstinately demanded.

"Colonel Ibraham Musfet at your service." Ibraham clicked his heels in the customary way.

Ishmael noticed that the Commander was now looking worried. "I've heard of you Colonel…my apologies for not opening the door quicker."

"Apology accepted…now I need a Corvette for this young man to pilot," Ibraham pointed to Ishmael, "He's Navy."

"Colonel where am I to get a Corvette?"

"Well we need a fast boat for me and my twelve men...we have something important to attend to."

"Twelve men you say?" The commander thought for a moment. "We have a commandeered Maltese Police powerboat that is serviceable Colonel; an EW 265cc Law Enforcement, it has twin mercury engines and is very fast, I believe it was used to chase drug smugglers when the tourists were here."

"That will have to do then." Ibraham turned to Ishmael. "Can you drive it?"

"Sir I can drive anything if it floats in water."

"Then get to it, the Commander here will show you where it is. Meet us by the APC where we parked."

"Aye, aye Sir."

"Come on then," said the Commander "Let's get you sea borne young man."

As the Colonel went to get his commandos, Ishmael followed the Commander down to where a small rowing boat was waiting; on its keel there was a small outboard.

"Sir?" Ishmael asked, "I thought you said it had two Mercury engines?"

The Commander laughed. "This isn't it…we have to go across to Fort St.Angelo, the Police boat is moored there… come on get in, it should only take twenty minutes tops."

*

Gaz wasn't sure what to do next, it felt good to hold Betty in his arms; there was a feeling of 'rightness' which he had never felt in the past but, in a confusing way, it also made him feel very vulnerable. He was, in a sense, relieved when he heard Pete groan, and not only because Pete had survived the sea, it had removed his need to think or talk about what they had just done; at least for the moment anyway. However, Gaz was puzzled and at the same time disappointed when Betty moved towards Pete without even a glance back at him. *"...What is going on?"*

By the time Gaz turned to the more important issue of 'seeing to' Pete, Betty was already bending down on one knee to help raise Pete's head from the hard rocky edge of the marina.

Gaz kneeled down and helped Betty raise Pete into a sitting position.

"Are you OK?" He asked Pete, as Betty gently wiped sweat and bits of sea weed from his face. Pete had a large bruise on his head and Gaz guessed he must have hit something that knocked him unconscious.

"Sorry to interrupt your mutual comforting plans," Pete said with a wavering voice, just managing to show a smile as he spoke, "I've got a bit of a head but other than that I feel fine."

Gaz glanced at Betty, she hadn't even flinched at Pete's comment. "Just rest for a time mate you must have hit your head, the bruise is massive."

"What now?" Betty was standing up and turning to look at the large shape of Gozo only half a kilometer across the channel.

"I think we need to take it easy." Gaz replied now standing beside her. "I'm not sure about starting a relationship with all this stuff going on around us."

"What?" Betty turned to look at Gaz, her eyes wide. "You don't think that I…?"

"Forget it." Gaz was now feeling embarrassed. "I obviously misread the signs."

"You obviously did." Betty turned once more to help Pete get up on his feet.

Gaz grabbed one of her arms violently and pulled her towards him, "What is your problem?"

"Where do you want me to start?" Betty was annoyed about something which Gaz couldn't work out. "Your like all the others, you think one kiss makes me your possession… what about my choices, who said anything about a relationship?"

Gaz raised his arms to indicate he had no intention of arguing any more. "Just stay away from me…do you understand?"

"That suits me."

"And me." Gaz started walking a short way around the marina.

"Ice Maiden." He thought

"Ice Man." Thought Betty.

Pete was staring at both Betty and Gaz, then looking up to the sky and raising his arms as though talking to God, "Of all the people that could have saved me; why did it have to be these two?" At that Betty's shoulders started to shake as she tried to hold back a growing giggle. Gaz, although he stubbornly resisted it initially, finally gave in and when he did it triggered all three to bust out into fits of laughter that released all the tension of the last few hours.

"What now?" Pete was still laughing as he walked up to Gaz.

"I don't think I'm ready for a relationship yet." Gaz answered causing the three of them to laugh more. As the laughing died out, Gaz apologies for his flippancy to Pete, who shrugged it off.

"Seriously though Gaz…what is our next step?"

"We still need to get to Gozo and try to find out what has happened to the others."

"Have you tried waving down any of those boats that are heading to Mgarr." Pete pointed to the many small boats that formed the refugee armada escaping from Malta.

"They are afraid to pick us up, and I can't say I blame them…all they want to do is get out of Malta, away from the Libyans."

"Then we may have to swim."

"You're not serious?" Betty was shocked at this suggestion.

"Have you any other suggestions then?" Pete was looking at both of them.

"You are serious!" Betty was beginning to feel uncomfortable. "I don't know if …."

"Let's just take this one step at a time." Gaz said. "None of us are fit to swim half a kilometer; we need to rest and think about this. Come sunset if nothing else turns up I don't suppose we will have much choice but to swim."

"Meanwhile," Pete said, "Let's keep trying to get help from these passing boats, we should take turns each at trying to get their attention…work a shift system, as it were."

"OK I'll go first." Betty turned to walk away. "You two try to get some rest."

*

Although James was genuinely glad to see the divers, in spite of the initial misunderstanding, he was even more impressed with the food rations they carried. He hadn't eaten anything since the day before, and it took all the patience he could muster to wait on it getting cooked on the small ration stoves that one of the divers had lit up. While the rations were being prepared, the other divers took to doing point watches in order to keep the small party secure. Robbie McMaster was standing next to the stoves and studiously staring at the contents of several 'mess tins'. "Are ye hungry kid?"

"You bet," James replied, his eyes fixed on the bubbling contents of the tins.

"Aye it'll nay be long; just a wee minute mare and it'll be fine."

James's mouth was watering with anticipation when one of the divers came over and said something to Robbie that James couldn't make out.

"I'll no be a minute, kid just help yerself tae some of the stew."

As Robbie left with the other diver, James needed no second invite, and helped himself to bread and 'compo' stew; putting as much as he could in his mouth with each bite. The other divers started to come around the cooking area as word got out that lunch was ready, and they watched with interest, some of them making comments that caused them to laugh, as James continued to hungrily 'pig out'.

"Ok lads that's enough get something doon yer gullets and get back on point." Robbie had now returned. "If you've had enough, Captain Kirk….we could do wi your help"

"How can I be of assistance?" James was wiping his mouth with the back of his hand.

"Come up here wi me and tak a wee look."

James was intrigued as he followed the Master Diver to a high point on the cliffs facing Comino. He was watching the boats crowding into Mgarr harbour when one of the divers handed him a pair of binoculars. "Here sir, have a look towards the middle of the Island."

James lifted the binoculars and setting the focus, scanned the edge of Comino. "It can't be…" James refocused the binoculars in an attempt to get a better view. "Well I never…."

"Any one you know?" Robbie was standing by his side.

"I know? I would say so…."

James took the binoculars down and smiled at Robbie "Your mission is almost accomplished Robbie, that's your other two missing 'targets."

"You said two, but there are three people on the Island."

"I wouldn't worry about that, Gaz has a habit of picking up people as he goes along. Quick we need to get to them."

"There lies the heart of the wee problem, we don't hae ony way of getting tae them."

"What about one of the boats that are coming in at Mgarr, there must be lots of them being abandoned."

"Gid thinking," Robbie said, "But we canni get involved wi the locals; nae body needs ti ken aboot the sub…We'll go when it's dark tonight."

"Is there any way to send a signal to them just to let them know we are here?"

"Aye we hae torches wi us, we'll flash until we get their attention. Noo lets get some rest, its going to be a long night by the looks of it."

"Robbie?"

"Whit?"

"Thanks."

"Away wi ye laddie."

*

Ishmael was surprised when he took the helm of the Police boat. It was sleek, fast, and responded well to the 'wheel', he felt very much at home and soon mastered the concept of steering a smaller craft than he had been used to. It was exhilarating crossing the harbour back to where the Colonel was waiting, and Ishmael couldn't wait to try it out on the open sea. He could see the commandos waiting by the harbour opposite him and he also noted that Colonel Musfet was pacing the area in front of his erect men. Ishmael guessed that he was in for some sort of 'brow beating' even though he hadn't taken that long to return. *"Must come with commando territory,"* he thought as he neared the waiting men.

"Where have you been? We have better things to do than stand here in the sun - waiting for you to decide to saunter over." The Colonel was visibly red in the face.

"Sorry sir, but I had to go across the bay to pick this up."

Ibraham ignored Ishmael's excuse, he had already ordered the commandos into the boat and as they started to load, Ishmael noticed that one or two of them gave him decidedly unfriendly looks. *"He must have given his men a good 'pasting' while they were waiting on me."*

"Ok Navy boy lets go."

"Go where Colonel?"

"Up the coast to St Paul's Island of course."

"I don't think they…"

"That's right Navy boy," interjected the Colonel "You don't think from no on, just drive."

Ishmael noticed the other commandos were sniggering at him, but decided to ignore it, he was, after all, the only person there who was qualified to drive the powerboat, and it made him feel superior to the, *"cretins."* As he piloted the craft towards St. Paul's Island, racing hard against the low, gentle waves, he felt tempted to swing the wheel hard to starboard, and when he did, the Colonel and some of the commandos who were standing, fell over onto the others who were sitting; the Colonel was furious.

"What are you playing at?" He screamed in Ishmael's ear above the drone of the Mercury engines which at full power were producing a staggering five hundred HP.

"Sorry sir" Ishmael had a satisfied smile on his face. "I thought I saw an under water rock."

"Be more careful in future." Colonel Musfet replied, "And wipe that satisfied grin from your face…I'm not as stupid as I look….Navy boy."

The assault boat was everything Ishmael thought it would be in the open sea. He was able to fully open the throttle and skim the sea's surface, bouncing on the odd 'out of sync' wave. In what seemed like an impossibly short time, they had reached the North sloping face of the Island of St. Paul, and Ishmael throttled the engines back causing the boat to fall into the calm sea. The commandos had obviously enjoyed the ride and were congratulating each other with the fashionable knuckle to knuckle hand shake, accompanied by expressions of "Cool" and "Yea, alright."

"Right, when the Navy brings us into the rocks I want everyone of you out and up that slope." Ibraham was wasting not time. "Lieutenant Zughaid…good work…You stay with the boat, but keep it running."

"Aye aye sir."

"What?"

"Navy sir…sorry sir."

As Ibraham followed his men up the slope towards St Paul's statue, he was muttering to himself in an uncomplimentary manner. *"Aye aye sir….Navy sir…sorry sir."* Ibraham normally had no time for anything or anyone other than his commandos, so he was struggling to come to terms with the 'bottle' the young Navy man was showing. It took a gutsy person to do what Ishmael had done when he pulled the 'wheel' to starboard on the way up, that was something he was sure none of his men would have dared to do.

Chapter Ten

By the time Ibraham Musfet had reached the top end of St Paul's Island, his men had already done a 'sweep' of the area and they were now waiting on his next command. Ibraham looked at the evidence that his men had uncovered. There were definite signs of a recent presence on the small island and Ibraham had no doubt in his mind that the people that Ishmael had spoken to him about could not be very far away. He took hold of an pair of binoculars that one of his men were scanning the horizon with, wiped the sweat from his eyes, and then looked out towards Comino; it was a hunch but it paid off. As he looked out through the binoculars he could clearly see three people on the small uninhabited island. *"Got you British."* He was about to give the order to move out when something else caught his eye. It was moving fast through the water well clear of the armada of small boats containing Maltese refugees, and in Ibraham's general direction. *"By Allah...what is?"* He refocused his binoculars and looked again. *"They wouldn't dare,"* he thought, but then he remembered the bravery shown by the ill equipped Maltese police and soldiers at the airport. "Quickly," Ibraham yelled the command with an urgency that the men recognized, "Back to the boat."

His men didn't need to be told twice and without any hesitation, they all ran as fast as they could back to the waiting powerboat where Ishmael was.

Ishmael could see the commandos running towards him and he could hear the Colonel shouting but the idle drone of the Mercury engines made it impossible for him to make out what the Colonel was saying. However, it didn't take a trained eye to note that something was very wrong and Ishmael automatically prepared to cast off.

The Colonel was the last to arrive back into the powerboat. "Lieutenant…get out of here quickly, the Maltese police are on their way here."

As the commandos took up their 'stand to' positions in the boat, Ishmael revved the two, powerful marine engines and the boat in an instance raised it's front bow and started to slice through the Maltese waters, as he cleared the island, Ishmael saw the blue and white Police boat barring down on them.

"Get us out of here Lieutenant." Ibraham shouted as he organized his men for a possible fight.

"Sir…I'm not sure we can outrun them… they have the same boat."

"Is that your professional opinion?" The Colonel asked as the powerboat cut and bounced its way through the low sea swell, flinging up a continual spray that soaked every one.

Ishmael wiped his face, some of the spray was stinging his eyes and making it hard to see. "Yes sir…they had the advantage of already being at speed sir."

"In that case turn about."

"What?"

"Turn about lieutenant."

"But sir!"

Ibraham grabbed Ishmael by his shoulder and pulled him towards himself.

"I don't know what they do in the Navy Lieutenant but in the commandos they obey orders…is that clear enough for you."

"Aye, aye…sir."

"Turn about Lieutenant."

"Aye, aye ….sir."

Ishmael swung the powerboat round in a huge wave of churned, and foamed up water and when he straightened it out again he was heading straight towards the on - coming police boat.

"Get ready to fire." Ibraham yelled above the noise of the powerboats screaming engines; the commandos moved like clockwork as they readied their weapons.

As the two boats headed towards each other on a collision course, Ishmael could see a Maltese policeman behind an LMG mounted on the bows of their boat, and others with their weapons at the ready. *"By Allah...they mean to fight us."* Ishmael felt as though he was in a dream, everything seemed to slow down and become unreal, he was sure he heard Colonel Musfet give the order "Fire at will," then Ishmael's world exploded around him.

*

Tony listened intently as the British Prime Minister brought him up to date with the Maltese crisis. As the PM told him of the move and intent of the Libyans with the subsequent support by the Arab nations, a question was starting to form in Tony's mind. He listened patiently to all that was happening; the agents sent and now lost, the closure of the British commission, and the misuse of the Treaty of Friendship; alarm bells were starting to ring but he said nothing until the PM asked him if he had any questions.

"Sir...Pete Lacer, does anyone know what has happened to him?"

"I'm afraid not Tony..." The answer was short but precise.

"What about the agents?"

"There are three missing, two low profile agents and an American, I believe."

Tony knew that the term 'low profile' meant 'ordinary servicemen who were used so as not to implicate a deliberate intervention by the more highly skilled but controversial SBS or SAS.

"Do you have any names sir?"

"Yes we do as a matter of fact, fellow called Gaz Seymour, the American is James Kirk; bet that causes problems eh?" Tony heard the PM laugh briefly. "The other is a girl, Betty Williams apparently a Navy missiles expert."

Tony froze *"Pete, Gaz and James all together in Malta...how could that happen?"* The silence seemed to last for a while and was eventually interrupted by the PM. "Are you still there Tony?"

Tony didn't answer, he could hear the PM's voice but he was lost in his own thoughts; as he put down the phone and cut off the PM his mind was swimming. *"Pete, Gaz and James together in Malta...how could this happen?"* He buzzed his secretary.

"Yes Sir?"

"No calls, no interruptions, nothing…is that clear?"

"Yes sir…anything else sir?"

Tony reflected on his secretary's commitment. "Some tea please."

"Of course sir."

"Oh and get me RAF Operations in Sicily."

"Right away sir…are you planning to be out of your office again sir?"

"That's a need to know…young lady."

"Good luck sir."

"Thank you."

*

It was Betty who first saw the two Police boats heading for each other at what appeared to be a top speed collision course. She had been sitting on a rocky outcrop just above the marina to give her the best advantage view of the North side of the Island and was day dreaming about how, not so very long ago, divers probably came from all over Europe on diving holidays and 'played' in the deep blue waters surrounding the little Island. She could also see the abandoned Comino Bay Hotel towards the south and dreamed of cool nights surrounded by friends and music; it was while she was contemplating sitting on a balcony of the hotel with a long cool lager that she first became aware of the two police boats. Betty ran down the short slope to where Pete and Gaz where resting, slipping as she did on the smooth rock face of the marina. She was about to shout on the two men when she heard the unmistakable 'chatter' of an LMG followed by a cacophony of automatic weapons fire.

"Gaz....Pete...wake up."

Gaz and Pete, however, were already awake, in fact neither of the two of them had slept; it was impossible on the burning hot rocks.

"What's the matter Betty?" Pete was the first to respond

"Automatic weapons fire...that's what the matter is." Gaz could see the worry on Betty's face.

All three ran to the vantage point where Betty had been day dreaming moments earlier, just in time to see the two Police boats almost collide. However it was an optical illusion and as they continued to watch the fight, both boats turned on a wave of foam and began a second run at each other with their weapons firing wildly and seemingly indiscriminately.

"They're Maltese Police," Pete said. "But who are the others?"

"Libyan Commandos by the look of their BD's," Gaz replied. "And it wouldn't surprise me if they were looking for us."

"What can we do?" Betty was transfixed by the unfolding violence.

"Pray," Pete replied. "Pray the Maltese kick their Libyan butts into the sea."

*

Robbie, the other divers and James were settling into resting until they felt it would be the right time to move for a small boat. For the first time in several days James felt relaxed and safe and he too was reflecting on better days when Gozo would have been filled with luxury tourist coaches, probably even visiting the fort they were now resting at, when he thought he heard the sounds of weapons fire. At first he ignored it, refusing to acknowledge the possibility of more trouble, but he realized he would have to accept that something was up when one of the divers doing 'point' came running.

"Chief, I think we have trouble."

"Whit's up laddie?"

"I think you should look sir."

"This better be gid… wee man."

"Oh its gid, - I mean good sir….really good." Robbie detected a bit of sarcasm in the diver's voice. He stood up and took a look in the direction that the young navy diver was pointing, then after looking for a moment he raised his binoculars sharply, and at the same time indicated for James to come beside him.

"Tak a wee look at that James." Robbie handed him the binoculars.

James watched the two Police boats heading towards each other for an obvious second run; at the same time he heard Robbie barking out orders that had urgency about them.

"Right lads change of plan…We go for the boat noo…Get ready to move out in ten."

There was a flurry of activity as the small detachment of divers went about their business as though it were an everyday event, and within ten minutes they were lined up and ready to move out, the site cleared of any evidence that anyone had been there.

"I'm impressed Robbie." James was still getting himself ready to move.

"Aye these are gid lads…canni beat Navy divers."

"You very proud of your men aren't you?"

"Yea…every single one of them is trained to look after his 'buddy' its how divers work; we're a wee faemily."

They started to walk in twos down towards Mgarr harbour making sure they kept to the dirt tracks that led down from the fort. From the moment they left, James noticed that no one spoke. Robbie just gave a series of hand signals and his men instantly obeyed; he was with a very efficient team of men and James knew it. He felt his respect growing for Robbie and his team of navy divers.

*

It took Tony a lot of effort to persuade RAF Operations in Sicily that it would be 'expedient' to allow him to join them during this phase of their deployment. "After all I am one of the only Euro MP's to have 'hands on' experience" in the Med," he told the voice one the other end of the phone.

"That may be so…sir, but I have been specifically told that civilians are not to travel into the forward zone."

Tony was starting to get frustrated by the conversation he was having with what he imagined was a 'snotty' nosed admin clerk, and it didn't help when he heard the clink of a tea cup being put down. "Look young man, you haven't in all this time told me who you are, but that is neither here nor there, I insist you allow me to speak to your commanding Officer"

"I am not allowed to divulge my rank….sir, and the CO is not taking calls…sir."

"Why not?" Tony was flabbergasted "He's supposed to be running the operation in Sicily, how can he do that if he is not taking calls?"

"Sorry sir…I can't answer that question, its need to know."

Tony was getting nowhere fast; this man would not shift no matter how he tried. "What about your Wing Commander?" Tony knew he was now clutching at straws.

There was a long pause and Tony thought he had been cut off; however as he was about to shout at the top of his voice and give the young 'whoever' a piece of his mind, he heard the quiet rustle of a hand taking up the handset.

"Yes can I help you?"

The voice had changed and Tony noticed that it was more authoritative and mature than the previous faceless voice.

"Yes, I hope so. My name is Antony Davidson and ….."

"Well sir this is a privilege."

"What?"

"Your reputation has preceded you sir, its good to speak with you, what can we do to help?"

Tony was speechless for a moment.

"Sir are you still there?"

"Er….yes, just a bit surprised, old bean you caught me unawares, who am I talking to, or are you not allowed say?"

"Sorry sir…Wing Commander Jeremy Shotts at your service, now what can we do for you?"

Tony briefly told the Wing Commander about his talk with the Prime Minister and the presence of his friends on Malta. "I need to get there Wing Co, somehow."

"We are not authorized to take you to Malta, apparently the orders we have are to hold this place and that's it." There was a pause on the line and Tony could hear the Wing Commander talking very quietly to someone near to him.

"Mr Davidson?"

"Call me Tony every body else does."

"How fast can you get to Brize Norton?"

"How fast do I need to?"

"Six hours?"

"Is there any chance of delaying that?"

"Not a chance we have a Hercules ready to come here, he can't wait any longer, at least not officially anyway."

"Wing Co?"

"Call me Jerry."

"I'll be there…oh and Jerry, thanks old boy"

"You're more than welcome Tony."

Tony put the phone down and sipped from a cold cup of tea screwing up his face as the bland taste took its effect on his taste buds, *"Yuck."* He buzzed his secretary one more time.

"Yes sir?"

"Get me a Heli-taxi young lady from here to Brize."

"Brize - as in UK Brize, sir?"

"The very same."

"I don't think that accounts will authorize it sir….a private helicopter sir…I don't…."

"Don't tell them then."

"But sir I need to get autho….."

"Jennifer?" She was a good secretary but Tony felt she was sometimes overtly officious. "Be a doll and get me the chopper."

"Yes sir…by the way sir."

"What?"

"Sicily can be very nice this time of year."

"Thank you for that piece of advice Jennifer."

"Your welcome."

Tony thought he detected a trace of affection in Jennifer's voice but he pushed the thought away; there was no time to delay and he didn't want to miss the flight waiting at Brize for him.

He stepped out of his office in time to hear Jennifer arguing with the Heli-taxi controller about payment for the flight. "Of course it's an official duty flight… what else would it be - number? - Half the world is falling apart and you want a consignment number, where do you get off?"

Tony watched as Jennifer continued to 'negotiate' the chopper, he hadn't realized how dedicated to her work she was; like most bosses, he just took it for granted that the secretary would – well - sort things, however seeing her in action made Tony appreciate the real gift Jennifer was to his admin.

"OK…that's fine….thirty minutes…yes….of course…I'm sure he will….good bye." Jennifer put the phone down. "The Heli-taxi will be thirty minutes sir outside on the flag area."

"Cheers Jennifer, what was all that about?"

"They just wanted to know who was paying."

"And?" Tony waited for the answer.

"I suggested that the Prime Minister would authorize such a flight."

"Jennifer, the PM will never sanction it."

"I know sir, but by the time the invoice arrives on his desk, you will be sunning in Sicily." She gave Tony gave a wiry smile as she spoke.

"You're a darling young lady; I could kiss you."

"About time," said Jennifer under her breath.

"What?"

"Watch your time…sir…and be careful."

Tony ran down the stairs of the Euro Parliament buildings and out into the flag square where the flags of all the member nations flew loosely in the bright day sun. He didn't have to wait for long when he heard the familiar sound of an approaching chopper; *"There was,"* he thought, *"A good chance of making the time."* As the chopper lifted off and turned, heading for the UK, Tony looked back towards the Parliament buildings, he thought he saw Jennifer at one of the windows waving him off, but he was too far away to be certain; but rather than think about what she might or might not be feeling, he changed his thoughts to what ever situations were waiting in the days to come.

*

Ishmael had felt he was in a bad dream, after the initial impact of the automatic weapons fire suddenly busting into life as the boats met just a few feet between them, he felt as though he had taken the boat into a solid wall, but now as his mind began to clear he was aware of open sea in front of him. He could hear Ibraham still screaming commands at his men above the continued noise of 'gun chatter', but there was a low droning going on in his head that was getting steadily louder. Suddenly he felt a solid force hit his face and the droning disappeared instantly bringing Ishmael back into a conscious awareness that hadn't been there a moment earlier.

"Turn this boat about."

Ishmael realized that the force he felt a moment earlier had been the Colonel striking his face to bring him out of the shock induced by the confrontation. As he turned the steering to bring the boat around for another run he could taste blood in his mouth and one of his eyes was blurring. He lifted his hand to his head, it felt wet and sticky; he had been grazed by a bullet and the blood was congealing just above his left eye. However, he felt a rise of nausea when he looked at the boat; many of the commandos had been hit and their wounds looked horrific, a lot of the blood was flowing into the boat itself and Ishmael noticed that he was standing in several inches of it.

"Allah help us." He had noticed the Maltese Police boat had also turned and was heading for a second pass.

"Steady men…mark your targets….Fire."

Ishmael saw Ibraham standing fully erect as the two boats met again in a hails of bullets and foamed water. The Colonel didn't even flinch as Ishmael held the boat on its deadly course with as much will power as he could get together. He closed his eyes and held his breath, fully expecting to feel the terrible force of red hot gun metal slicing through his altogether too vulnerable body, but it never came, in moments he could hear the relative calm of having passed the other boat successfully.

"Good work Lieutenant, well make a commando of you yet."

Ishmael wasn't sure what the Colonel meant but he did know that the other commandos, that is those still alive, were smiling at him and giving him the 'thumbs up'.

"Turn about Lieutenant, lets finish the job." The Colonel was smiling.

As the boat came around again in a huge wave of foam from its bows, Ishmael could now see the reason for the Colonel's smile and the happy faces of the commandos; the Maltese boat lay still in the low swell, and there was no sign of any movement.

"Sir, looks like they're beat." One of the Commandos said.

Ibraham didn't answer he was too busy looking at a new unpredictable threat. He waved for Ishmael to slow down and then signaled his men to get down low.

"What in the name of Allah is going on?" Ibraham was turning to look at Ishmael.

As Ishmael looked he didn't feel the need to reply to his Colonel's question, it was very clear what was happening; all the Maltese refugee boats that had watched the terrible fight were now forming a barrier between the Libyans and their heroic police.

"What now sir?" Asked one of the Commandos whom Ishmael noticed was covered in blood from a wound to his shoulder.

Colonel Ibraham looked frustrated by the result of the fight, he stood and stared at the Maltese boats bobbing silently in front of the Police craft; then he turned and looked at the cost to his beloved commando.

"Lieutenant, we have six dead and three wounded seriously… I think we lost this fight…don't you?" Ishmael didn't answer. "Take us back to Valletta, and go easy we can fight another time."

"What about the agents and the submarine…sir?"

"What do you suggest Lieutenant?"

Ishmael said nothing, he knew it was a no win situation, the Colonel was right, submarine or no submarine; it would have to wait.

Chapter Eleven

Half way through the planned Libyan invasion of Malta there was a change of plan; senior military Officers decided that it would be better to continue to fly in the needed men and equipment using Luqa Airport as a base of operations. It was quicker, and as the Maltese started to organize their own defense plans it became expedient. While the main part of the Libyan Navy was held in inactivity at their bases, troops and materials were diverted to Tripoli and every aircraft that could be utilized was put into the air. Soon the sky over Malta was filled with every conceivable type of air transport and by the third day, thousands of troops were billeted or tented and prepared for the overrunning of the Islands.

At the same time as this was happening the Maltese Army, or what was left of it, was conducting a hit and run fight against the Libyans, but they were badly coordinated and were no match for the well 'oiled' military machine they were fighting against; it was a one sided fight and the Maltese casualties were bitterly high.

*

Chief Superintendent Edward Sophia paced back and forth in his office, he was dressed in his summer uniform but still wore the one piece leather belt and shoulder strap that marked his high position within 'the force'. He also carried a personal Smith and Weston revolver on his left hand side in a holster with a short piece of leather that held the weapon in place and studded to the front. As he continued to pace the floor of his office he nervously 'did' and 'undid' the stud with his left hand causing an audible and regular 'click' that broke the otherwise silence of the room. Edward was aware of the resistance of the Maltese police against the highly trained Libyan soldiers on the mainland, and he wondered if his own police would show the same bravery if and when the Libyan soldiers decided to move against Gozo where he was at present stationed. Now in his office in Victoria, the central 'capital' of Gozo, Edward felt helpless to do any more. His police men were all armed now and stationed along the coastline that formed Mgarr Harbour; he wasn't expecting the Libyans to come any other way since Mgarr was the only place where heavy army materials could disembark easily. Still he had also decided to send regular patrols along the main roads that 'fanned' out from Victoria to Dwejra Point, Xlendi, and Marsalforn. He was still questioning the wisdom of these patrols, especially since he had, due to manpower shortages, sent them out with only one man in each vehicle, when a young police woman burst into his office.

"Sir, we have had no report from the Xlendi patrol, he has now missed two of his scheduled 'check ins."

Edward, normally a cautious man, had ordered that each patrol member should radio in every four hours; his operations staff had explicit orders to alert him personally if a policeman failed to report for his second check.

"Was there anything in his last report, before we lost contact?" Edward had now stopped pacing the floor and clicking the stud of his leather holster.

"No sir….except, he did say he thought he had seen some sort of movement out to sea but only a few moments later said it was nothing."

Edward grabbed his peaked cap. "Get me driver and a car and make sure he is armed; we better check it out."

Then he walked out of his office into the busy streets of Victoria to wait on the transport to take him to Xlendi Bay.

*

"Sorry for the hold up sir." The policeman said, sitting behind the wheel of the white Audi that was used to transport Men like Chief Constable Sophia about in a modicum of style. "There are so many refugees filling into Victoria, its getting harder to move around; we should be alright though when we get out into the countryside."

They made very slow progress through the narrow and crowed streets of Victoria, there were people everywhere, mostly refugees, and even when Edward lifted out the magnetic 'blue' light and placed it on the Audi's roof, there was nowhere for people to go to allow the car passage. *"This is a human disaster."* Edward tried remaining patient as his driver tried to negotiate a passage through the swell of humanity. Occasionally the driver found himself in heated conversations through the car's window bordering on what would normally be classed as 'road rage', but these were not normal times and tensions were running high. It was only when they eventually managed to reach the suburbs of Victoria, and had passed St. George's Chapel, that the crowds thinned out and Edward and his driver started to make better progress.

"Looks like the refugees are spilling into Victoria sir." It was the first time that the driver had spoke to Edward since picking him up. "I'm sorry sir if I 'lost it' with some of them earlier."

"I understand completely, lets just get to Xlendi as quick as we can now."

When they arrived at Xlendi Bay the small tourist village was deserted, it seemed that even the residents had gone to Victoria; nobody wanted to be near the coast if the Libyans came. They stopped the white Audi at the sea front and sat looking for a moment to see if there was anything obvious, but all they saw was an empty beach area and abandoned gift shops and café's to their right.

Edward stepped out of the air conditioned car into the warm summer day's heat; he took his peaked cap off and wiped the quickly forming sweat from his brow. "You check out the tea rooms and things and I will check along the road up towards the cliffs to the right." The Policeman saluted Edward and then headed towards the tourist side of the Bay.

Edward then started to walk up the steep road that would eventually lead to Xlendi Tower, it was hot work even though there was a heavy breeze coming of the sea; by the time he reached the top of the slope, he was panting for his breath. He removed his cap once more and wiped his brow, and the inside of his cap with a crumpled hanky he drew from his pocket, then looking up through the haze of the heat, he saw the abandoned Police car, with its driver side door wide open, sitting at the edge of the track that led from the main road to the Tower.

*

"This place is crawling with cops, not to mention the hundreds of people trying to get into the harbour." Whispered James as he and the team of divers hid behind a harbour side warehouse at the edge of Mgarr Harbour. "How the heck do you expect to steal a boat with all this happening?"

"I'm not sure yet." Robbie was standing with his back pressed against the laminated steel walls of the warehouse. "But I widdne worry aboot the Po'lice, they're too busy to bother wi us." Robbie dropped to his hunches and signaled two of his divers to him; they too hunched down to keep out of sight. "Right lads, you two hae a wee job to dae, I want you to mingle among the refugees there and see if you canni find a boat that naebody wants….you know whit I mean?"

"Aye, aye Chief…leave it to us."

"Right then off yi go."

"What now?" James asked looking nervously around.

"We wait," Robbie replied, putting down his haversack, then making himself comfortable by sitting down and resting against it.

James noticed that the other divers followed suit and feeling he had no choice but to do the same, he reluctantly sat down beside Robbie.

"Dinne worry," Robbie said closing his eyes and enjoying the sun against his face, "If I ken those two, they'll be back before you can say Rabbie Burns."

Sure enough as Robbie had promised, about half an hour later, the two divers turned up at the harbour with a small, powered boat.

"It's a bit of a 'chugger' but it would have to do." Robbie signaled for them to go back towards Mellieha Point where they would be out of sight.

They didn't have to go very far before they found a narrow dirt track that led down to the waters edge by Teffal cliffs and Robbie signaled for the boat to be brought in to the ragged and rocky shore line where they could board safely.

"Gid work lads." Robbie shouted as the small open boat bobbed along side of the rocky inlet and the divers unsteadily boarded the unstable craft. "You next James...in you go." Robbie offered his hand for support. James took the offer and as he stepped into the boat he noticed a blood stain on the side of the boats keel; however he decided not to ask the question that was suddenly forced on his mind.

"Sharks blood probably," Robbie said, as he stepped of the rocks into the boat; he had noticed James's sudden concerned look. "Right lads lets go rescue oor friends on Comino."

*

Pete, Gaz and Betty watched in silence as the Maltese Police boat came to a sudden stop in the water. They had known all along that the battle being fought in front of them would end with the defeat of the Police; they stood no chance against the battle hardened Libyan commandos, but when it happened it was none the less a shock to them. Without saying anything they stood and watched as the Maltese refugees formed a barrier to the Libyan craft, but all three were roused from their trance like shock by seeing the Libyan boat turn around and head away from Comino but more importantly; away from them.

"Thank God." Pete fell to his knees with his hands on his face.

Betty flung her arms around Gaz and held him close, she was crying with the release of tension and Gaz responded by holding her close, *"Safe for the moment,"* thought Gaz. He looked at Pete as he held Betty; Pete was rocking backwards and forwards muttering away to himself and now had his hands raised into the air. *"Strange!"* Gaz thought, but then he closed his eyes and held Betty close; he was determined that this time he would not let her go. He gently kissed her on her exposed neck and felt her respond; he was just lifting her hair from her neck to kiss her again when he felt a tap on his shoulder.

"Sorry to interrupt Gaz and Betty, but we might not be out of the woods yet."

Gaz let go of Betty to see what Pete was looking at but as he did, he noticed that Betty had shied away from them both, momentarily. *"She is more sensitive than she lets on."*

The glare from the sun on the sea surface, at first made it hard to see what Pete was so concerned about but as Gaz's eyes adapted to the intense light he saw it; while most of the boats were heading towards Gozo, there was one heading towards Comino and them.

"What do you make of it?" Gaz was now standing next to Pete; they had moved to the side of the St. Marija Chapel to get a better view but at the same time gain some cover.

"I can see six possibly seven men all in civvies by the look."

"We need to hide and hope they haven't seen us."

"The Hotel!" Betty was already running towards the large building at the bottom end of the Island.

Pete shrugged, "Good a place as any."

"Yep," Gaz said. "Let's go."

All three ran as fast as they could over the rocky barren Island towards the Comino Hotel.

*

Ishmael felt a wave of relief and tiredness flood over his being as they approached Dragutt Point from there he knew it was only a matter of moments until they saw the ancient harbour and walls of Valletta. The Colonel had said that there were hospital facilities at a place called Floriana so the plan was to sail up the stretch of water known as Port Ta' Marsamxett and off load the dead and injured at the first possible place along Valletta's sea wall; where, if they needed to, they could 'commandeer' transport. It wasn't as easy as they had predicted, however, and in the end they had to settle for a Water Polo pitch next to the St. Salvatore's Bastion. One of the commandos found an abandoned Orange and white service bus and after a lot of struggle they were on their way to Floriana with their dead and wounded.

It didn't take long for the bus to get through the main part of Valletta and then head down Triq Nelson past the City bus terminus. However as they entered Triq Sant' Anna, they saw a Libyan road block a short distance to their front.

"Well," Ibraham stood up from his seat "There's maybe no Navy here yet, but there seems to be a lot of soldiers around. Look Lieutenant these guards are infantry, they must have flown in."

The check point guard signaled for the bus to stop and when it did, a young private soldier carrying an AK stepped up into the shaded interior and met the stern face of a Commando Colonel.

"Get off my bus young man and open that check point, I have commandos injured here."

The soldier said nothing, knowing better he stepped back off the bus and waved for the barrier to be lifted; then he watched impassionedly, "*Military cabbages,*" as the orange and white bus noisily revved and drove off in the direction of the hospital.

"Well sir, what next?" Ishmael was sitting in the waiting room of the small clinic when Colonel Musfet came through after making sure his men were being treated properly; two other commandos were with him, they were all that was left, the only survivors of the Police encounter earlier.

"We are going after your friends Lieutenant; are you with us?"

"Do I have a choice?"

"Not really, you're the only person who could recognize them." The Colonel sat down beside Ishmael, with sigh.

"The boats really damaged bad sir; I doubt it will make the journey again."

"Were not taking the boat; come on men lets go."

As Colonel Musfet stood up with the other two commandos, Ishmael grabbed his arm. "What do you mean… your not taking the boat?"

Ibraham looked at Ishmael's hand and then slowly raised his raging eyes, "Don't ever touch me again, Lieutenant."

Ishmael let go. "I…."

"The bus Lt. Zughaid, we are going by bus, after all your friends will be long gone from Comino by now."

"They are not my Fr……" However Ishmael's words were lost in the laughter of the Colonel and his two men as they walked out of the door.

*

.It took another hour for Chief Sophia to get together a team of policemen down to Xlendi to start a search for the missing policeman. Although he didn't have the luxury of trained divers, he had the forethought to ask for police who have amateur diving experience; his thoughts being that there was always the possibility that the missing man had quite simply fell fowl of the deep water at the edge of the bay. However he couldn't shift the uneasy feeling he had about the whole situation. "*Maybe the Libyans have already landed here in Gozo,*" he thought. *"But why would they land secretly if indeed they did?"* Edward was still lost in his thoughts when one of the policemen searching the beach area of the bay waved for his attention; as Edward hurried down from the abandoned Police Car he noted that whatever had been found, there seemed to be a lot of interest by the others; they had formed a group around something in the sand.

"I think we've found him sir," one of the policemen said as Edward arrived at the beach.

Edward pushed his way into the group, and stopped when he saw the body of his missing colleague. He knelt down and started to examine the dead man. "Looks like he has had his throat cut…..professional too." He was about to give another command to look for a possible weapon when he heard one of his 'divers' shouting from the rocky ledge that led to the open sea. As he stood and watched, the Maltese policeman was now dragging what seemed like very sophisticated diving equipment; at least nothing like the average tourist would wear.

"These are Re-breathers sir," the amateur police diver explained as he waded onto the sandy beach. "The same type the military would use so as not to be traced by the bubble stream."

" Have you any ideas who they could be?" Edward knew it was probably a long shot question.

"No doubt sir this stuff belongs to British military divers."

"How do you know?" Edward was surprised at the confidence of his man.

"The Libyans would be using Russian or American made gear sir and not as good as this…most of this is British made and very high tech sir."

"Why would the British come here secretly and why would they need to kill one of my men?" The question would need to hang in the air for the mean time. "Ok good work men, recover the body…has anyone found the weapon yet?"

The same policeman who had found the equipment kneeled down to examine the corpse. "Sir… this is a diver's knife work?"

"Are you sure?"

"Yes sir…you can see the….."

"Ok, ok…so we are looking for a team of British divers who are still carrying their knives?"

"Not just any divers' sir - highly trained military divers; they are generally used in covert work sir and will be hard to find."

"Dam it…I really don't need this right now."

"There's something else sir you should know?"

"What?"

"They wouldn't have just appeared….there will be a British submarine in the area."

"And?"

"That means they will need to come back here sir to be picked up."

"Right – that makes sense." Edward replaced his peaked cap on his head. "Lets get back to Victoria, from now on you men will dedicate your time and efforts into finding these British Divers…I want them found quickly…is that clear?"

The Policeman looked at each other nervously before answering in a staggered unsure manner. "Yes sir."

"Sir?"

Edward turned to look at the diver again.

"Would it not be wise to put a permanent guard here at Xlendi; they will need to come back?"

"You've got the job."

Edward, as he turned away and headed back towards his waiting Audi, was satisfied with the choice of guards; he hated his police to be too smart.

*

The trip across to Comino took longer than James or the others had thought it might. What ever the small boat would have been used for, it was doubtful if its original owners would have taken it out to the open sea. It was hard to maneuver, and the small, weak outboard engine that was screaming with the constant high revs was in danger of overheating, but they eventually made it into Comino's 'Blue Lagoon'. James was mesmerized by the blue clarity of the sea here and had a strong impulse to dive off the boat into the cooling water, but he resisted it.

“Aye its sare tempting eh?” Robbie was looking at James as the small boat bounced off the edge of the small sandy beach that skirted the Lagoon. He turned to face the front of the now ‘beached’ boat. “Right lads lets get going.”

As the divers picked up their rucksacks and other personal belongings, James was already running up to the shallow rocky summit of the Island and shouting loudly. “Gaz, Betty where are you both?” He looked around but there was no sign of any movement, and was about to shout again when he heard the noise of the others coming up beside him.

“Ony sign of your mates?” Robbie asked as he took in the view of the island’s dry lifeless landscape.

“Can’t see anything,” James replied, “But they must be here.”

“Aye they’re here alright; but they probably thought we were Libyans or something…they’ll be hiding in that Chapel…it’s either there or the Hotel.” Robbie turned and signaled for his men to spread out and search. “Let’s go then James, my bonny lads will find them, before ye kin say…..

“I know, Rabbie Burns.” James interrupted smiling.

Robbie clapped James on the back as they followed the other divers across the dry arid surface, “Aye yer awe right ye ken.”

It didn’t take the divers too long to establish that the North West side of the island was deserted. After checking out the Chapel and Marina they moved South East in a line towards the only other refuge of the island - Comino Hotel.

*

Gaz, Betty and Pete were hiding behind the hotel reception desk; it seemed a futile waste of time to Gaz as he had reasoned that it was only a matter of time until you were found on such a small place, but inside he knew that he had to try for Betty's sake. They were waiting for the inevitable sound of someone entering the hotel, when Gaz saw a large kitchen knife; he grabbed it purposely and at the same time he noticed Betty glancing at him and then lowered her eyes, Pete firmed his mouth. Then it came. It was a slight shuffling sound but Gaz knew that it was just the sound of sand on someone's shoes on the polished tiled floors; it would soon go quiet. *"This mans a pro,"* thought Gaz as he waited, trying to sense where he might be heading. Gaz signaled for Betty and Pete to keep perfectly still, and then moved out towards the edge of the hotel desk; the sand had given the intruder's position away again.

As the intruder slowly and stealthily made his way through the hotel foyer, Gaz readied himself for the attack.

When he judged the time was right, his head began to spin from the adrenaline rush, and from the moment he grabbed the stranger, Gaz's world went into slow motion. He had the intruder in a neck lock as he felt for the knife he had picked up earlier: Should he drive it into the man's back or draw it across his neck? It was a moment of reluctant choice when all his training seemed to go out the window; he heard his combat training instructor's voice in his head, *"Don't hesitate; you only get a second...he-si-tate and you are meat."* Gaz reluctantly concluded he was 'meat', he **had** hesitated, he felt his opponent twist and turn, but then his mind went into confusion, *"Is that Betty screaming...Gaz no - What's going on?"* The next thing that Gaz felt was a solid and painful knock to his head, as his world went black he could have sworn he heard James's voice shout, "Gaz...watch;" and then mercifully his mind switched off.

*

In the time it took the heli-taxi to reach Brize Norton, the RAF Hercules Transport Aircraft had already taxed along to it's take off point on runway 01, and was sitting waiting for Tony's arrival. As Tony grabbed his bag and ran towards the waiting aircraft, he could hear the powerful twin engines revving noisily as though they were eager to get going. A door near the front of the 'Herc' was open and a young Airload Master was waving frantically for Tony to get a move on. As he ran into the engine 'slipstream' and felt the heat blast against his face, it struck Tony that the aircraft was straining against its brakes, so with a bit effort he flung himself forward and the Airload Master grabbed his hands and pulled him aboard.

"Glad you could make it sir," shouted the Air Load Master as he secured the aircraft's door.

Tony hadn't even managed to find a seat when he felt the huge aircraft start it's take off run; there didn't seem to be anywhere to sit. Facing him as he had stepped inside were two huge Harrier aircraft engines that seemed to take up the whole of the inner fuselage. However, he wasn't left wondering for long when the Airload Master appeared smiling at Tony's dilemma.

"Here sir, put this on and sit down where you can in any of the canvas strap seats to the sides; sorry it's not 'Club Class." He was shouting above the roar of the engines as they lifted the heavy cargo plane off the ground and into the skies above England.

Tony took the green coloured helmet and placed it on his head, the first thing he noticed was that the noise was instantly cut to almost half, the second was that he could now hear the Air Load Master clearly without any need to shout. He returned a 'thumbs up' that the ALM gave him and then settled down the three hour flight to Sicily. The only other time he saw the ALM was when he came, smiling as usual, with a boxed lunch which Tony appreciated very much.

*

He wasn't sure how long he had dozed, but when he heard the cheery voice of the Air Load Master welcome him to Sicily, Tony turned to look out of one of the small round windows that lined the fuselage and sure enough, just at the edge of the blue horizon, he could see Mount Etna surrounded by a haze of clouds around it's summit.

"Beautiful isn't she?" The voice in Tony's helmet called and he turned back to see the ALM standing next to him and leaning forward to see the sight out of the same window Tony was using.

"You startled me." Tony deliberately ignored the young Load Master's comment.

"Sorry sir, didn't mean to, but I have a bit of fine tuning to do on one of the landing gear housings to your side." As he spoke he smiled and raised a hammer to show Tony.

"I'm intrigued old boy." Tony was looking at the hammer.

"Then watch a 'Master' at work, er…sorry for the pun."

"Apology accepted." Tony was smiling uncertainly.

The ALM opened a panel where the landing gear was housed and then spoke to the other flight crew. "Ready sir."

Tony could hear the noise of the landing gear extending but noticed that the side he was on sounded a bit different to the rest of the extending machinery. However, before he could ask what was happening, the ALM took his hammer and hit the machinery inside several times as hard as he could. Tony's was about to intervene and grab the hammer from the ALM who in Tony's opinion had totally 'lost the plot', when he noticed that the noise was now smoother; a 'safer' sound, more like the other side of the aircraft.

The ALM turned with his now familiar smile. “That’s it now sir, soon have you down in one piece.”

Tony didn’t reply, he sat down and strapped himself into the canvas strapped seat. *“Why are Aircrew always so cheerful?”* A question for another time maybe, all he wanted to do now was put his feet firmly on solid ground, even if it was ‘Fortress Sicily’ as it was now becoming known.

Chapter Twelve

Ishmael was now thoroughly convinced that Colonel Musfet was loosing his grip on reality. As they sped along the road that took them through the centre of Malta, past Mellieha and on up to Mtarfa Point where the ferry crossed over to Gozo, he watched the commando Colonel pace back and forward along the middle walk way in the bus, Ishmael could have sworn there was a 'detached' look in his Colonel's eyes, as though he wasn't really inside his body at all, however that illusion was soon shattered by the Colonel himself.

"What are you gaping at Navy boy?"

Ishmael turned his head away from the Colonel's strong, malevolent eyes and as he did so he noticed that the other two commandos were sniggering. *"Maybe they are all madmen,"* Ishmael thought as he glance back at the Colonel who he now saw had a strange grin on his face as well. He had hoped that the commandos would have accepted him after all they had been through as a team, but Ishmael was learning very quickly that commandos only respect their own, and that began to cause him some concern; there was more going on here than inter forces rivalry.

"How long till we get to Mtarfa lad?" Colonel Musfet asked, as he leaned over the commando who was driving the bus rather erratically.

"About forty minutes sir."

"Is there any chance of more speed from this old bag of nails?"

“Sorry sir but the peddle is now flat to the floor, these buckets are governed; thirty’s the limit.”

“These are strange people the Maltese eh?” Ibraham spoke casually and relaxed to his driver; unlike the manner he addressed Ishmael in.

“Why’s that sir?”

“Look at the position of the steering wheel it’s out of line with the driver’s seat.” Ibraham gave a chuckle as he pointed it out, turning to put the point across to the other commando and Ishmael.

“It’s something to do with their patron saint sir; seems they believe he, or even she, will keep the bus safe, that’s why they have all these icons and saints pictures on the drivers front paneling, especially in these older crates.”

The Colonel walked away from the driver and back towards Ishmael where he sat down. “Don’t you think Lieutenant Zughaid that people so naive deserve all they get?”

It was a provocation and Ishmael knew it, he glanced at one of the commandos and noticed he was looking straight at him, his face curious.

The Colonel leaned over and picked up an AK and cocked the weapon looking inside the breech as though he were inspecting it for cleanliness.

“I’m waiting for your answer Lieutenant!” Ibraham aimed the weapon and pulled the trigger to release the mechanism, there was no magazine fixed but Ishmael jumped when he heard the click: It was a game and he was ‘it’.

“They are supposed to be our allies.” Ishmael spoke quietly so as not to be overheard by the two commandos.

“What was that Lieutenant….I didn’t hear you.”

Ishmael spoke louder this time knowing that he would become once more the subject of derision by the commandos. “We are supposed to be a friendly power…I understood we were allies.”

All three burst into loud laughter; Colonel Ibraham stood up and placed the AK back on the floor. "And I suppose that was a loving hug that the Maltese Police wanted to give us off the coast of Comino." They all laughed again but it only lasted for a moment, the 'fun' was interrupted by the driver. "Mtarfa Ridge ahead sir, but it looks like we have company."

Ibraham ran down to the front of the bus and looked out of the front window at the driver's side. "The Maltese army has set up a road block. There's some police there as well sir, but none of them look too well armed."

"OK keep driving but slow down as though you are going to stop but don't...have you got that?"

"Sir."

Ibraham turned and picked up one of the AK's lying on the floor, he cocked the weapon and then placed a magazine into it. "Here catch," he said as he flung the weapon towards the other commando. "You too Navy", he said as he repeated the action. "When I say fire...you fire and don't stop until I say stop....you got that Lieutenant?"

Ishmael could feel the bus slowing down and he could see on his side a young Maltese soldier signal for the bus to stop. At the same time he heard the word 'Fire'. The next thing he saw was the Maltese soldier drop to his knees as his chest burst open with the spray from Ibraham's AK; he died instantly, a look of surprise on his face, and with no warning. The next few moments were a blur of noise, flying glass, blood and body parts. Ishmael could hear the Colonel shouting commands but he had no idea what they were, he just fired his own weapon, holding onto the trigger, and emptying the magazine without aiming in any particular direction. Just as his AK ran out of ammo and went silent, an eerie stillness had fallen over the area as suddenly as the shooting had started. Then Ishmael heard the occasional single shot as the Colonel jumped off the bus and 'finished' the job.

"Quick, get out of here…head straight for the ferry." Ibraham was stepping back onto the bus replacing a spent magazine, but he kept himself on the step at the doorway; his AK held in readiness for any other intrusions.

As the bus lurched over a Maltese's dead body then drove on towards the ferry, Ishmael was starting to feel he had gone 'too far', he a shaking and nauseated by the Colonel's cold and business like manner in dealing with the road block, and was now wishing he could be back on his Corvette patrolling the Mediterranean where life seemed so simple and calm.

"There's the ferry sir…but it looks very busy."

All four now looked out of the front windows of the bus, the glass had been shattered by the gun fire moments earlier and the hot Maltese air and dust was getting into their eyes, but they could see the ferry and it was very busy with many cars, other buses and hundreds of people, all trying to escape to Gozo.

"What will we do sir?" The young commando who was driving was feeling nervous.

"Do?" Replied the Colonel. "Do? - Drive through them soldier and if anyone tries to stop you, run them over."

"You can't do that!" Interrupted Ishmael. "That would be murder…I'm not going to sit back and allow this to continu….."

Ishmael never finished his protest; it was interrupted by a sharp, painful blow to his face. As he staggered under the blow he was aware of being grabbed from the front and pushed down onto the floor, when his vision cleared the Colonel's face was only inches away. "That's mutiny Navy boy, your lucky I didn't shoot you."

Leaving him on the floor, Ibraham stood up and turned back towards the front of the bus, Ishmael noticed this time that no one was laughing at him; as he lay without moving on the floor of the Maltese bus Ishmael knew that within moments their bus would hit the crowds of people clambering to get onto the ferry, and he felt helpless to stop it.

*

As Tony Davidson stepped out onto the hard surface of the Aircraft pan; the Sicily heat hit him, and for a moment took his breath away. Tony had momentarily forgotten that airports were generally very hot places in that part of the world and it took him a few moments to adjust to his new environment. The Air Load Master who had so cheerily looked after him on the flight over from Brize now patted him on the back as he passed. "You alright sir, do you know where to go from here?"

"I'm fine old boy, just fine. Wing Commander Jerry Shotts is supposed to be meeting me."

"Ah, 'Mousy' Shotts…he's a good man sir, but if I were you I would get out of this sun until he comes."

"Yes - quite." Tony replied. "Tell me young man, if you were me where would you go."

"I'd follow the Air Load Master; he's bound to know where the nearest NAAFI is." The Air Load Master replied in his never ending Joviality.

"Then that's exactly what I am about to do…lead me on Gungadin."

As they walked towards numerous sets of porta-cabins all joined and set up to accommodate the large influx of European military personnel, Tony found out why the Wing Commandeer was called 'Mousey', it was apparently due to his unfortunate first name; a throw back to those old cartoon characters, 'Tom and Jerry'

"Does he not object to being known as 'Mousey'? Tony asked as they entered the cool air conditioned interior of a NAAFI canteen.

"No, not at all we all have nick names here, to be honest it's a sort of unofficial code that seems to have 'kicked 'in…don't know why though." They approached the bar. "What will it be…mate?" The ALM asked.

"Cola for me thanks."

"Make that two," said the ALM catching the attention of the bar man.

"So?" Tony asked they sat down at a small round table, "What do they call you old man?"

"H and D."

"What?"

"Hump and Dump, you know…Air Load Master…hump and dump!"

"Ah." Tony was beginning to get the picture as the drinks arrived at the table.

"Well …er…H and D, cheers."

They had just started to sip their ice cold drinks when, without any notice, 'H and D' suddenly stood up rigidly to attention along with a number of other people in the small canteen. Tony was about to ask what was going on when he saw that a tall slim man had just walked into the room dressed in the light summer uniform popular with the RAF, but obviously a man of some rank; although Tony wasn't too familiar with the rank bands worn by the officers, there was no doubt that this particular officer had quite a few 'bands' on his shoulder.

"At ease." He said as he walked deliberately towards Tony who now stood up to meet him.

"Mr. Anthony Davidson sir… how good to meet you."

Tony took the offered hand and they shook. "I presume you are Wing Commander Shotts?"

"You presumed correctly, can I join you for a drink."

"Off course sir." H and D shouted towards the bar, "Another Cola here."

"So Mr. Davidson, you want to get to Malta?" It was more a rhetorical statement than a question. "That will be very difficult."

"Why is that Wing Commander?"

"Please call me Jerry."

Tony looked at H and D, who smiled and shrugged his shoulders guiltily.

"Why is that then.... Jerry?"

The bar man brought the other Cola over and placed it in front of the Wing Commander who said nothing until he had left.

"It's crawling with Libyan soldiers...seems they want to turn it into a very large military base." He took a sip from his Cola then continued. "However, reports are coming in of disturbances in the Gozo, Comino area and...." He paused to look around and signaled for Tony and H and D to draw closer. "There are reports that a team of British naval divers are at present on Gozo looking for your friends."

"How do you know all this?" Tony was feeling hopeful at the mention of the divers.

The submarine they came from, a Vanguard Class, sends regular updates to their CNC, the last one gave us the information."

"Any thing been heard since?"

"Er....no...that was the last we heard sir: The problem is that the submarine may be compromised, were not sure, but any further communications have been stopped for the moment."

"Where does that leave our divers and the people they went to find?"

"On their own I'm afraid. There own mission to get the missiles from the AWAC is now really 'old hat', purely an academic consideration. Nobody cares about it any more; there is now a threat from Islamic/ Arab forces pushing into Europe. As far as your friends are concerned it's every man for himself."

Tony sat for a moment in silence as the three sat and sipped their cold drinks. *"Its getting way out of control."* He could see the seriousness of the Wing CO's expression.

"So Wing Comm….Jerry, what are you orders?"

"Hold this Island, and 'worry' the Libyans."

"Worry?" Tony was unsure of the terms usage.

"Yes sir, worry. We haven't yet fired on any Libyan aircraft or shipping but we are patrolling the skies south of Sicily in a kind of show of strength; you know, 'saber rattling', just in case they get some funny ideas."

"Seems to me that they have already got the funny ideas, old bean."

"Mmm." Jerry took another drink from his glass.

*

To Gaz it seemed as though he had been in blackness for only an instance; although in reality the blow to his head had knocked him out for the best part of thirty minutes, so when he came round he was surprised to find himself lying on one of the reception couches that lined the Comino Hotel foyer. His first reaction was to try to sit up and continue the struggle with the anonymous stranger who had 'coshed' him, but when he did he found he was being gently restrained by a soft warm hand on his head and a gentle soothing voice.

"Shsss…Gaz try not to move."

He lay back down and stared at the high ceiling for a moment trying to gather his thoughts together when Betty's familiar face came into view and filled his present universe. She lowered her head and Gaz felt the warmth of her lips gently brush against his forehead and he surrendered to the safety of her kiss.

He was aware of talking in the background and he couldn't see where it was originating but, he could have sworn it was a Scottish voice he was hearing.

"You didni have to hit him so hard."

"But Chief he was……."

"Nae buts, I'll deal wi you later… How is he Betty?"

Gaz saw Betty raise her head and look over in the direction of the mysterious Scottish voice; he noticed she had the 'ice' look on her face as she replied. "He looks ok; no thanks to your brutish henchmen."

"What's going on?" Gaz asked as he struggled to sit up; his head throbbing audibly in waves of pain.

"No Gaz you must rest a bit longer." Betty tried once more to restrain him but without success.

"Just like old times kiddo."

Gaz refocused his vision and saw, standing near to Betty, his old friend James Kirk.

"James, you're alive!" Gaz felt like getting on his feet and embracing James, but knew the instant he tried, he couldn't. "It's….great to see you; what happened? Where have you been?"

"Long story bud, but hey takes more than a Maltese fishing boat to finish us off aye."

"More's the pity," Betty hissed under her voice, but James heard her.

"The feelings mutual babe." He said it with a smile that infuriated Betty.

"I thought you lot would be pleased to see each other," Robbie interrupted.

Pete walked over to where Gaz could see him. "That would seem to be the Majority opinion," he said smiling at Gaz and giving him a wink. "But there is a minority opinion that differs."

Betty responded by walking away and standing on her own, but just within Gaz's view.

*

It took just under an hour for James to elaborate on the events that brought them all together on Comino. Although Betty said nothing all the time James was explaining how he came to be with six Navy Divers, he noticed that she stood close to Gaz as often as she could. His assumption that Gaz and Betty were now an 'item' was confirmed when she took Gaz's hand as soon as he mentioned that George, Maria and Father Dominique were presumed dead. Robbie then took over and explained that they had a mandate to search for James, Betty and Gaz and ensure their safety, although he believed that their Captain, Ross Morgan, had sent them without instructions from CNC, therefore putting himself in some considerable risk of a court marshal should the Sub's position be compromised.

"We have another problem." Pete said as soon as Robbie had finished his appraisal. "The Libyan Naval Officer who was a prisoner on your sub is still alive, our agents here failed to catch him, your submarine has already been compromised Master Diver. The group of Libyans we saw earlier fighting with the Maltese Police are probably looking for us and your submarine."

Robbie nodded. "Yea; the Boss thought that might be the case."

"Well!" Betty straightened herself up and swept strands of her hair back from her mouth. "Now that you boys have all agreed we have a massive problem on our hands - has anyone got any suggestions what to do next?"

Gaz noticed the divers looking intently at Betty, "*Was she aware of it?*" He decided that even in these deprived conditions, where a man or a woman looked a long way from her best, Betty still caught men's eyes; he felt a pang of jealousy rise inside him, and knew that from here to where ever they were eventually going to end up, he would always have to cope with it.

No one responded to Betty's challenge for a few moments; she had placed them all in a difficult situation. James was the Ranking Officer among them but although no one said it, the general feeling was that he was just a fly boy, and not a real officer. Robbie was to all intensive purposes the ideal choice of leadership but Betty would probably contend that choice since she was of equal rank. It was Gaz who broke the silence.

"Look," he said standing up; although his head still hurt, he was otherwise alright. "James, myself and Betty here have a mission to complete, and I would like to get on with it."

"Ah!" Robbie was rubbing his chin in thought. "We ken awe aboot your mission, but I dinni think that is a priority ony mare."

Gaz looked at Betty who was obviously as shocked as he was, "What do you mean?"

"The issues are noo bigger than before, you will be awfy lucky to get off these islands alive, never mind the AWAC 'thing'." Robbie was now feeling uncomfortable and it showed in his voice. "The boss on the sub has been advised to prepare for a strike on Tripoli, that's how we were able to come here, the sub is sitting off the coast of Gozo waiting on the 'go' from CNC…I'm afraid your wee mission is now irrelevant Gaz."

"Your mission now is to survive and escape if you can," James said, interrupting Gaz's shocked silence, "We have to get to Gozo and safety."

"I'm afraid that even Gozo will not have a sanctuary for us, if the Libyans want the sub, they will be after us as well," said Pete. "We will have to be careful, what ever we decide - remember, the Libyan Naval Officer knows about us and the sub."

“I don’t believe you lot,” asserted Betty with an obvious level of indignity. “None of you could organize a picnic for teddy bears…I’m going to Gozo to find that AWAC, even if I have to swim down to it myself.” She turned to Gaz. “Are you up for it Gaz?”

“Were all up for it.” Gaz was challenging James with a questioning look; he shrugged and nodded at Robbie.

“Lead on Chief Petty Officer Williams.” Robbie responded sarcastically, but it was lost on Betty who was now heading towards the main entrance of the hotel, followed closely by Gaz and Pete.

*

Chief Superintendent Edward Sophia paced the floor of his office in utter frustration; one of his officers had reported a stolen boat from Mgarr harbour. The report he had was that there had been a struggle between two British men and the owner of the boat, who was now in hospital recovering from a blow to his head: Apparently he had slipped and knocked his head on the side of the boat and was now unconscious. Edward wasn’t yet sure why British divers were on his small island ‘patch’, or even how many, but on top of everything else that was happening, they were proving to be a major irritation to him. There were now so many mainland refugees coming in from Malta to escape the Libyans take over that his men now found it impossible to police the small port harbour, which meant that finding the British would be almost impossible….unless!

Edward turned to a map on his wall; it was a standard tourist map but he found it better than the official police map of the islands. *“Where did that American AWAC come down?”* He turned to his desk and pressed an intercom on his phone. “Who’s around?”

There was a pause before he received an answer, "Constable Bolini here sir."

"Get yourself into my office Bolini."

Edward didn't wait for the reply before turning once more to his map of the Maltese Islands. Within moments a young Maltese Policeman entered and stood to attention.

"Ah Bolini, could you come and point to the supposed crash site of the downed American Aircraft?"

Bolini stepped reluctantly beside the Chief Constable. "No one knows for sure the exact location sir, but rumour has it that it fell into the shallow waters just off Ramla Bay." Bolini pointed to a spot just beyond the rocky outcrop at a ridge known as Rdum Il-Kbir.

Edward thought for a moment. "Hmmm.....If I remember there is only one road in and out of that area."

"Yes Sir." Bolini had now stepped back and drawn himself to attention again.

"Right get me a dozen men…we are off to Ramla Bay to catch us some British Navy Divers, that's if the Blessed Madonna is with us Bolini."

"Sir?"

"Get on with it Bolini."

"Right away sir…yes sir." Bolini saluted and left the Chief Superintendants office as quickly as he could.

"Oh and Bolini?" Bolini stopped dead. "Get some extra ammo from the armoury…we may need it."

Chapter Thirteen

Small pockets of resistance continued to harass the Libyan invasion forces, especially around Rabat and Mosta. These were mostly police or army who had become separated from any organized force and so were ineffective in stopping the advance of the Libyans. With the arrival of the Libyan fleet at Senglea and Vittoriosa, troops and heavy equipment started to move from the ports through Cospicua with orders to secure the Free Port at Birzebbuga and the main towns of Hamrun, and Birkirkara, including the Presidential Palace at San Anton. They had virtually no opposition from the Maltese army who had, neither the equipment or the motivation to put up a serious fight. A small skirmish had been reported at Dingli Cliffs when the Libyans tried to take over the Radar and Transmitter site there, but from all accounts, it only lasted for a short time, ending with the men involved being mercilessly flung over the cliffs by the victorious Libyan engineers.

Admiral Ahmad, the new self appointed governor of Malta issued a decree asking 'all the good people of Malta' not to abandon their homes and places of work, but to 'work hand in hand with the glorious Libyan Liberators,' who had come to the islands to deliver them from the exploitation of their European aggressors. His real motive was, however, more sinister; with the Maltese mixing with the Libyan forces he believed that no foreign powers would attack them, and he was of course right.

Europe had no choice but to wait and see what would happen next.

*

“Sir…the ferry….I think it’s started to leave.”

Colonel Musfet was still standing at the door of the bus when he heard his driver. “What do you mean - it’s leaving?”

The other commando stood up from the seat he was on near where Ishmael still lay on the floor. “Allah be merciful….he’s right, the ferry’s leaving, we’ve missed it.”

“Slow down, slow down.” Ibraham shouted.

“But sir the……”

“Do as I tell you, jackass.”

As the bus slowed down the Colonel stepped off and looked towards Marfa Point a few hundred meters away. The ferry had indeed slipped from its mooring and was already heading towards Comino in the South Comino Channel.

He was about to shout at his driver again for not moving quickly enough, when he noticed the crowds of Maltese starting to edge towards the bus, led by one or two armed police and soldiers. Sensing the danger, Ibraham leaped onto the bus and started to shout. “Reverse, reverse….get us out of here…quickly!”

However, the young commando had also seen the approaching crowds and had also guessed their intent. As he panicked and tried, without success, to get the bus into reverse, Ibraham lost patience. “Let me try,” he said pulling the young commando from the driver’s seat. As Ibraham tried repeatedly to get the reverse gear he heard the first shots as his men started to empty their magazines into the approaching Maltese. A number of people fell to the ground as the white hot AK bullets tore into them, but there were too many and as the screams of the dying or wounded increased, the determination of the crowd grew.

Ishmael lay still on the floor of the bus, he was experiencing the highest level of terror he had ever known and it had paralyzed him. He watched helplessly as the two young commandos, who had by now run out of ammo, were dragged off the bus by the wild crowd, their agony of screams eventually mercifully drowned out by the loud cheers of the Maltese. Ibraham was luckier, as he struggled to get the bus moving, one of the Maltese police walked up to the window side of the driver's seat and calmly fired two shots from his pistol into the Colonel's head. As Ishmael watched in horror, he saw the Colonel quietly slump over the steering wheel instantly dead.

The crowds were now ecstatic and Ishmael wondered what would happen next, as he lay perfectly still he hoped he hadn't been seen. Suddenly he felt the bus rocking and heard the concerted straining of a large group of men as they rocked the bus backward and forward, as it began to go over Ishmael strained himself for wherever it would end up: Then it went, over and over, he held on as best he could but it seemed as though it would never stop tumbling; when it did, the sudden lurch was so violent that Ishmael was flung against the roof of the bus and knocked unconscious. As the bus lay partially covered by the sea in which it now lay, the policeman who had shot the Colonel thought he had seen someone else in the bus, but after watching and seeing no more movement, he shrugged and walked back to the Point to await the next ferry run.

*

Admiral Ahmad turned towards the other officers convened in his plush new offices at San Anton. He had thought the Presidential Palace a fitting place for a man of his rank and privilege so when the Maltese sent an ambassador from the government to complain about the 'misuse of the premises' he quite simply had the ambassador locked up along with the President and resident staff, informing them that any more complaints would be dealt with a little bit more harshly in the future. The Prime Minister of the Maltese Government had accused him of taking hostages, but he only replied with, "What an amusing thought," and dismissed the suggestion as, "Utter nonsense."

Now with a selection of hand picked officers from each of the three services he prepared to address them. "Gentle men please come and relax, make yourselves at home."

There was a low murmur as the officers drew up seats in various places around the room. A young Libyan soldier circulated offering tea and other cool drinks for refreshment which the convened officers took gladly.

Ahmad allowed some time for his officers to settle in before he continued. "Well done gentlemen, I have a signal from Tripoli praising the quick and successful invasion of this small but beautiful Island."

The officers around the room congratulated each other with smiles and acknowledgements.

"However," Ahmed waited until the room fell quiet again before he continued. "There is the issue of Gozo." He waited for effect, and then continued. "We need to take Gozo as well."

As the Admiral looked around the room no one stirred, the silence said it all; then one of the Navy officers spoke everyone's thoughts. "Sir with the deepest respect, we were led to believe that Gozo was now an internationally recognized refugee state, Europe will not be pleased about Libyan troops in Gozo."

The Admiral stared for a moment at the officer then looked around the room. "I want troops from the army, landing craft from the Navy, and the Air Force will patrol the skies to prevent any infidels trying to prevent our liberation of Gozo, any questions?"

Again he looked around the room pausing only for a moment at the young officer who had spoken a moment earlier. "Good gentlemen.... That's all, you have forty eight hours to initiate."

*

Wing Commander Shotts returned to his office after making sure EMP Antony Davidson was accommodated in the Officer's Mess, it wasn't the Ritz of course; Portacabins had a limit to their functional ability, but they were slightly better than most of the crammed quarters the enlisted men had to endure; in reality, however, the summer heat was making it hard for anywhere to be classed as comfortable. After ordering a cool cup of Iced Tea, he sat down at his desk to try to motivate himself to work through the piles of admin that seemed to be accumulating as the days passed by, when he saw, by chance, a satellite picture of Malta sticking out from a pile of recently delivered documents. At first he looked at it purely out of a casual interest and was about to put it down again when he noticed something odd. "*They can't be.....dear God they wouldn't.*" At first he doubted his own interpretation of the visual evidence, but a closer look seemed to confirm the truth of what he was looking at. Jerry quickly rose from his chair and walked sharply to his office door which was still open. Immediately in front of him was another desk were his personal assistant sat; Sergeant Mike Trotter, a chubby man who was renown among the other men on the station for his constant good humour. His unfortunate name and build earned him the nickname of 'chops' but he was happy enough with that.

"Chops!"

"Yes sir?" Mike had not expected the sharpness of his Wing Co's intrusion to his space, as he stood to attention he knocked his coffee over all the papers on his desk.

Jerry smiled at his PA and his sudden 'fright'. "Sorry Chops, I didn't mean to startle you."

"Don't mention it sir, all in a days…er…work. What up?"

Jerry put the satellite picture down on the Sergeants soggy desk. "When did this arrive?"

"Just before you came back sir…is there a problem?"

"I'll say there's a problem chops… a huge bloody problem."

Jerry took a moment to show his PA what had caught his eye on the picture, it was more by way of a confirmation that he shared his find with Chops; he had hoped to be proved wrong.

"What do you think?" Jerry asked looking at Chops.

"Looks to me like an invasion force sir… too much hardware and troops for a sentry change."

"That's what I thought… get the other officers together at my conference room, one senior from each nation on the station…oh and better let the Euro MP in on it as well."

"Time sir?"

"What?"

"What time would you like the meeting for sir."

"Now chops…Now!"

*

Although the general consensus was to head for Gozo and try to locate the fallen AWAC, Pete and James argued that it would be better to stay on the island of Comino until they rested and Gaz was fully recovered from his head injury. Gaz, of course protested that he was fine, but he also recognized that by involving his 'injuries' in the discussion, Betty would be more amenable to cooperate. James had gone to great lengths to point out that it wasn't often anyone had the chance to stay in a five star hotel for free, to which Robbie gave his whole hearted support. Slowly but surely they won Betty over with their arguments and it was unanimously agreed in the end that one night' stay for R and R would be the best thing.

That evening, as the bright orange sun started to settle against the blue horizon, Gaz sat alone on one of the white plastic seats that were scattered around the hotel patio looking at the water gentle lapping against the hotel's small marina. To the left of where he was sitting, he noticed a small bridge that led across to a very small sandy beach; the lure for a swim in the crystal clear blue waters was overwhelming. Once on the sandy beach and feeling no real need for modesty Gaz stripped of his cloths and flung himself into the cool refreshing waters. He had been swimming for what seemed only a few minutes when he noticed movement on the small beach now behind him; when he turned to see what is was he saw Betty playing in the sand with her hands.

"What's she up to now?" Gaz thought as he made his way back to the shore line. The sun was already going down and Gaz had forgotten how quickly the dark comes in on the Islands. As he drew near to the edge he kept himself low in the water.

"Betty, what do you want?"

"Oh…nothing really, just thought I would come and see how you are doing."

"We'll it's a bit awkward, you see I haven't anything on, and I need to get out of the water."

"I'm not stopping you."

Gaz noticed a cheeky smirk on her face and realized he would have no choice; she was not going to move. "OK Betty you asked for it." Gaz felt his adrenalin levels rise as he drew himself out of the water. *"Why am I so scared of this woman?"*

Betty said nothing, at least not right away, but Gaz noticed she didn't even have a blush on her face; she just stood smiling at him. He started to look around for his cloths but they were not where he had left them. *"The oldest trick in the book, and I have fallen for it."* "OK Betty the jokes over, where are my cloths?"

"Oh are you looking for these?" Betty held up Gaz's trousers. "You'll have to catch me first"

Gaz thought he detected a girlish giggle but without waiting for a second invitation, he flung himself at Betty, who, taken by surprise at his quickness didn't have a chance to run.

"Gotcha!"

"So you have Gaz, but what are you going to do about it?"

There was a challenge in her voice that Gaz found irresistible; as they fell onto the sand in the drawing darkness, he felt her surrender fill his whole being with raptures of passion and love. That night in the sands of Comino Betty experienced a passionate, and gentle love that demanded nothing but gave everything, she was fulfilled and contented for the first time in her life.

*

When morning came as Gaz and Betty were both sitting on the Hotel's patio drinking some orange juice they had found in the bar, James walked out stretching his arms to greet the new morning sun rise.

"Could get used to this you know," James said pulling up another white plastic chair to join them. "Gees Gaz, you look like you spent the night on a beach somewhere."

Betty got up and walked back towards the hotel main entrance, she turned to face James just before she disappeared into the dark interior. "I had you down for lots of things, but voyeurism wasn't one of them."

James looked in shock at Gaz. "Sheesh Gaz, what did I say wrong?"

Gaz said nothing for a moment, before he too went to get up from his chair.

"Come on guys, what did I say?" As James grabbed Gaz's arms, the truth suddenly dawned on him. "Oh no….Gaz I swear, it was only a jest, I wasn't watching you and…. You gotta believe me…I wouldn't do…"

Gaz sat down again. "It's OK James, you know Betty by now she's can be sensitive."

"You're telling me. Hey did you really?"

"Don't go there James."

"Ok mate…ok."

*

Shortly after the misunderstanding with James, Betty returned, and although she had 'daggers' for James, she softened when Gaz explained what happened. All three were talking as friends when Pete, Robbie and the other divers appeared.

"The sea's like a swimming pool this morning," said Robbie taking in a deep breath of the morning air, "Perfect for the crossing in oor wee boat."

"Yes," Pete agreed. "Although we would be well advised to move now, before the morning mists burn off."

"If we really must," said James in a gentle protesting voice.

"We must." Betty spoke in her normal cold manner, already starting to stand up.

*

The journey across the Comino Channel was pleasant enough; the sea was very still and if the circumstances had been different they could have actually enjoyed it, but the need to continually be on the look out for Libyan and Maltese Police boats, was enough to keep them all on edge. Even though the boat was cramped and small, they made good time, soon entering into Mgarr Harbour along with other small boats containing the now lessening amounts of people fleeing Malta. They needed to keep a low profile, there were Police and Army everywhere, so they kept to the edge of the rocky inlet that served as part of the ferries route and eventually moored the small boat against the fenced area originally used to direct and separate the fare paid ferry passengers. Once landed the divers grabbed their black shoulder bags then ran for the fencing and soon cut a gap in the wiring big enough for them all to pass through safely and out of sight of the port defense teams.

"That's my boys." Robbie sounded proud as he looked in satisfaction at their handy work.

They all decided to break up into one's and two's and follow the main procession of refugees but promised to keep each other in sight as they walked up the steep road that led out of Mgarr and on to Victoria. It was hot and they were tired but they kept moving inwards towards the Island's centre, all the time looking for opportunities to slip away unnoticed into the country side. The opportunity would come sooner than they thought.

*

Admiral Ahmad stood on the highest point on Marfa Ridge looking across to Gozo. From where he was standing he could see Victoria's Citadel; smiling, he turned to a Libyan Infantry Major and placed his arm around his shoulder; the Major went rigid.

“Well done Major Zammud the men are all in place and right on schedule… well done.”

Zammud visibly relaxed, he wasn’t expecting a compliment from a naval senior officer, especially this particular one. “Thank you sir; now with your permission we will commence our advance on Gozo.”

“At your leisure Major.” The Admiral was still holding onto Zammud’s shoulder. He had sensed the Major’s body relax and was now enjoying the feeling of control he had over him. “One thing though Major.”

“Yes sir?”

“Why are you still here…haven’t you got work to do?”

The Major smartly straightened to attention. “Yes sir.”

“Good we understand each other then.” Admiral Ahmad let go of his Major’s shoulder.

Major Zammud took the opportunity to remove himself from the vicinity of the Admiral as quickly as he could go. *“I would rather attack a thousand Gozo’s than hang about here,”* he thought to himself as he scrambled down towards his waiting troops.

Ahmed stood on the ridge watching and waiting, occasionally glancing up at the clear blue sky’s as though he were expecting something; and he looked troubled.

*

As Ishmael slowly regained consciousness he felt as though he was sinking in a bath of water, it felt unreal like a dream and it took some moments to realize that he was really sinking. The first levels of awareness struck him when he took his first breath of sea water. He felt a sudden surge of panic rise within him and although he tried to fight it, he found himself shouting and splashing within the sinking bus. It took him a few minutes to ‘get hold’ of his senses and when he did he discovered that the bus had only sunk partially into the sea. Ishmael was glad no one had seen him panic; he now felt stupid as he stood in a meter of water that touched his knees. He started to laugh; only slightly at first, but it soon spilled over into a full blown hysterical, uncontrollable tirade.

That was when he heard the unmistakable double click of an automatic weapon and then he froze.

*

"You … put your hands slowly on your head and come out."

Ishmael heard the command and he immediately relaxed; it was unmistakably Libyan. His first reaction was to do the opposite, after all they were on his side, but when the command came again with a threat to shoot, he obeyed without any other arguments.

Initially the Libyan soldier who found Ishmael was reluctant to agree to his requests to be taken to the senior officer in charge; however he relented, although with a degree of uncertainty, when Ishmael explained who he was and information he had of a British Vanguard Class Submarine in the area.

With his head still reeling from the trauma of the bus crash, Ishmael was escorted to the command vehicle where Major Zammud was preparing to launch his invasion of Gozo.

"Please… Lieutenant who?"

"Zughaid, Ishmael Zughaid."

"Please Lt. Zughaid take a seat and relax, you are with friends now."

On the surface of it Zammud seemed like a decent sort of man, so Ishmael sat down on the chair offered. "Thank you, sir."

“You are most welcome Lieutenant.” Zammud sat down next to Ishmael. “Can I get you anything, you look terrible.”

“I’m fine sir, but I have information that is of great strategic importance.”

“You can tell me Lieutenant.” Zammud stood for a moment and called for a medic, then sat down again. “Go on.”

Ishmael began to tell his whole story from the shooting down of the Cessna, right up to how he managed to be found in the crashed bus. While he spoke, the Major said nothing or made any show of surprise, sympathy or interest. When Ishmael had finished, Zammud stood up and walked out of the command vehicle and onto the road that faced the sea looking out towards Comino and Gozo in the distance. For a moment he looked undecided as to what he should do next, then without any warning he turned to face Ishmael. “We cannot go until the Admiral hears your story.”

Ishmael wanted to know who the Admiral was but as he was about to ask, the medic that Major Zammud had sent for arrived. He suddenly felt strangely cold and was aware of the medic suddenly reaching out towards him; as Ishmael’s day turned into darkness he thought he heard the Major’s voice say “Lieutenant are you…..?” Then the dark took over and Ishmael heard nothing else.

Chapter Fourteen

Captain Chris Vella, one of the few Maltese Army Officers left, had fought and lost a running war that had taken him and his few men from their Army barracks in Hamrun, through Birkirkara, Naxxar, across the Victoria Lines and then on up to San Pawl, Mellieha and to his present location in Nadur in Gozo. Chris was well known for his fortitude in his duties as a soldier, and his flight across the mainland had cost him dearly in terms of his men. Each town, village or scrap of land had been fought for and although his men knew that it was really a futile fight, they had none the less resisted the Libyan advance as best they could taking the example of their captains courage, who they all admired. Now as Chris looked across the green valley that lay before him at the edge of Nadur, he wondered if he had made the right decision to resist such a massive force. He pondered the cost, "*Only twenty men left out of a force of one hundred and fifty, and six of those seriously injured.*" It was while he was counting the cost that he saw a black figure trying to walk along the deep valley below him. The mysterious man was staggering and heading away from Ramla bay. Chris was about to call down when the figure collapsed and then went still.

Chris turned quickly. "Two men with me, and bring water;" then without waiting for the response, he leaped over the small wall that lined the edge of the road to Ramla Bay and ran, stumbling, down the side of the valley with two of his men following moments later. When they arrived at the still black clothed person they all crossed themselves in the manner of their Catholic faith.

"Al' Madonna," one of the soldiers explained, "It's a priest!"

Chris kneeled down and turned the priest over to see if he was still alive. He put his head near to the priest's mouth and felt a faint breath. "He's alive, but only just; quickly your water bottle." Chris reached out with one hand for the bottle one of his men gave him, and with the other he carefully raised the priest's head, and gently poured some water over his face. "Padre….can you hear me?" There was no response at first but then suddenly the priest started to move his mouth.

"I think he is trying to say something Captain," said one of the soldiers, leaning forward in an attempt to listen.

Chris moved closer. "Who are you Padre and why are you here?"

The priest whispered weakly, "The others are they safe?"

"There are no others here Padre, just me Captain Chris Vella of the Maltese Army and two of my men."

The priest grabbed Chris's combat jacket and pulled him close. "You must find the others Captain."

"What others Padre?"

One of the soldiers made a sign suggesting that the priest had gone mad, "Sun stroke I reckon sir."

Chris ignored his soldier's comment. "Padre….who are you?"

"My name is Father Dominique Caruana and - I am not mad as your men suggest; you must help me find my friends."

Chris was about to reply when the priest once more passed out of consciousness; the other two soldiers crossed themselves again just to make sure.

*

No one could have guessed for a moment that Major Zammud's decision to hold off his invasion of Gozo, until Admiral Ahmad had heard about the presence of a British Vanguard Class submarine in the area, would have far reaching repercussions on the whole of the Malta Crisis; neither the Libyans nor the European forces packing themselves into the small island of Sicily, but in the wider scale of events now taking place, time was crucial.

Wg.Com. Shotts had finished briefing the other commanders in the linked Porto-cabins that doubled as the COC as well as the officers mess, when Tony Davidson approached him.

"Jerry, can I have a word old boy?"

"Sure Tony, how can I help you?" He poured himself bottled water without looking up; Tony did likewise.

"I have to get to Gozo."

Jerry stopped what he was doing and turned to face the Euro MP. "Absolutely not....no chance." He went to walk away but Tony stopped him.

"Jerry, I know it sounds crazy but two of the British agents over there....well we go back to Cyprus; if there is a way of getting them out of Gozo before the invasion....I need to try."

"Good God man," said Jerry with a suddenness that startled Tony and made other in the room turn. "There could be an invasion, a bloody invasion! Follow me Tony....something's wrong and I cannot put my finger on it...yet."

They both left the temporary COC and rushed back to the Wing Commander's office. Chops was just finishing another cream donut when the two rushed towards his desk.

The sergeant made an attempt to apologies for his gluttony, but the Wg.Co. had other things that were more pressing, on his mind.

"The satellite picture Chops, where is it ?"

Chops nervously rustled among the many scattered papers on his desk, while Tony stood back in utter amazement that the PA could ever find anything on his desk.

Jerry saw the look on Tony face, "He's a good PA Tony, just a little bit untidy."

At that the Sergeant handed over the photograph and Jerry laid in down on his desk.

"Here Tony, what do you see?"

Tony looked at the picture, shocked to see so many troops, but he knew that the Wg.Co. had already seen the picture and was looking for something not so obvious. "Sorry old man apart from the build up of the Libyans at Marfa Ridge, I can't see anything out of sync."

"Forget the picture…dam why didn't I see it before…look at the top of the picture, on the right hand side." Jerry pointed to make it easier.

"Nope…still can't see what you can see Jerry."

Jerry put his finger heavily to the picture. "The time Tony, look at the time this was taken."

"My word," said Tony with a spreading smile, "And they haven't moved."

"They've delayed the invasion for some reason…and in a world where even an hour can make a difference; this is a very bad move."

"What are you going to do?" Tony was moving to sit on the sergeant's desk, but then change his mind as several loose papers fall of the edge; Chops quietly muttered an apology.

"Do Tony?" Jerry replied smiling. "I'm going to put a stop to this silly farce once and for all 'old man'." He turned to the sergeant who now had a look of dread on his face. "Chops tell the chaps in Brussels; were starting a war."

"Wha……?" The sergeant was startled.

“Tell you what,” said Tony lifting the phone on the sergeant’s desk. “I’ll tell them.”

The Wg.Com. slapped Tony lightly on is shoulder. “For that my parliamentary friend, I will fly you to Gozo myself; I have a plan forming in my mind and you are just what I need.”

As Jerry walked into his office to start the mobilization of his forces, he heard Tony on the phone say “Hello Jennifer…yes its me Tony…..yes yes, I’m ok…..look stop fussing I…….” Then he closed his door; he knew that if anyone could get the support from the EU that he needed, it would be a Euro MP; and this one had the necessary ‘bottle’.

*

Admiral Ahmed had decided not to reprimand Major Zammud for the delay in moving to Gozo, even though he felt that the Major had overstepped his position; the news of the Libyan sailor could change the whole scenario, so he paced across the hard tiled floor of the presidential office at San Anton Palace waiting on the arrival of the two officers. He looked a his watch impatiently, muttered something to himself about the need for stricter discipline among his officers then turned to face the huge office doors when he heard the approaching feet on the hard floor outside.

“Enter!” Ahmed shouted as he heard a gentle knock on the other side.

A young Maltese girl entered, she was one of the presidential staff forced to remain when the palace was commandeered.

“Two gentlemen here to see you sir.” She lowered her head so as not to make eye contact.

“Send them in young lady.” He clapped his hands. “Quickly!”

Leaving the door open she turned and ran down the long corridor to the waiting Libyan officers. Then bowing again, without making eye contact she simply said, "The Admiral will see you now." Then she turned and quietly left.

"Friendly lot wouldn't you say?" Zammud spoke sarcastically as they headed towards the presidential Office, but Ishmael kept quiet, he was starting to have doubts about the legality of what they were doing in Malta.

They walked quickly along the long corridor adorned with pictures of past Maltese presidents and the occasional suit of armour until they could see the imposing figure of the Admiral waiting patiently in his spacious presidential office. When they eventually arrived they were welcomed with a suspicious smile and directed to two seats which the Admiral had placed in front of his huge mahogany desk.

"Gentlemen please take a seat and relax. Would either of you like refreshment before we start?"

Major Zammud refused politely without any thought and Ishmael decided to follow suit; he wasn't sure if it was some sort of test, but the first impression he had of the Admiral suggested caution.

"Good, then let's get started; I have little time for formalities."

As the Admiral sat on the edge of his desk Ishmael was glad he had followed the Major's lead.

"Sir, my men were preparing to fulfill your orders to move into Gozo, when they stumbled across Lt. Zughaid here." The Major pointed to Ishmael. "The lieutenant claims that he has news of a British Vanguard Nuclear Submarine in the area; it would be suicide for us to move further if this is true."

The Admiral looked at Ishmael. "And, is this true?"

Ishmael now felt intimidated by Ahmad's focused attention. At first his nervousness made him stutter, but once he got into the story about the British agents and the capture of his crew, he started to relax; the Admiral sat in silence without interrupting until Ishmael had finished.

The three sat in silence for a moment or two while the Admiral took in the enormity of what Ishmael had told him. "So Lieutenant, do you believe this British submarine is still in the area?"

"I don't know sir, but with the build up of European forces in Sicily; if I were in charge that's exactly what I would like to have around; a sort of insurance, if you know what I mean sir."

"Dam that's the last thing we needed to hear….however Major," Ahmad turned his attention to Major Zammud, "The last thing the Europeans will do is use a nuclear submarine, especially to defend this languishing piece of refuge…..I think Major we should continue with our plans."

Major Zammud got up to salute the Admiral and Ishmael followed suit. He was disgusted by the Admirals description of the Maltese Islands; he still had the naive impression that they were allies but the growing evidential truth was now causing him concern. As he saluted the Admiral he felt a conflict growing inside his conscious that he knew would have to be resolved and he feared for the personal outcome.

As Ishmael 'about turned' in as smart a manner as he could, another shock was about to hit them; a Libyan soldier was running towards them with a piece of paper flying in his hand, and he wasn't standing on ceremony as he ran into the Admiral's office.

"Soldier…what is the meaning of this undisciplined intrusion…you better have a very good reason for your insubordination?"

The soldier was clearly worried about his task but stood smartly to attention. "Sir…sorry sir….message from Naval Signals Command sir….I was ordered sir to make sure you got this message without delay sir.....personally sir."

"I wish all my men were so enthusiastic," he said as he took the paper from the soldier looking at Major Zammud with a sinister smile. He glanced at the message, glanced again, then without saying anything, he handed the message to Major Zammud, the smile suddenly gone from his features.

"Merciful Allah," Zammud said, handing Ishmael the same note.

Message from Libyan Naval Signals Command. Stop
British Euro-fighters scrambled from Sicily.
Predicted course Gozo.
Advise. Stop

"It seems gentlemen I have underestimated the British resolve." Ahmad said as he once more began to pace his office floor. Then he suddenly stopped as though coming to a decision. "Major you will return to Marfa Ridge and form a line of defense between us and Gozo; Lt, Zughaid you will stay here, I have something else in mind for you."

As the Major left the office Ahmad continued to talk to Ishmael. "You say you know these British agents who were on the submarine?"

"Yes sir." Ishmael stood still at attention.

"You think there is a good chance they know where it is?"

"I'm not sure sir, but they were heading for Gozo to recover a missile from a crashed AWAC there."

"The chances are that 'they' will need recovering....You will take six men undercover and find these British spies - we must know where that sub is - do you understand?"

"Yes sir."

"Off you go then, you have two days."

Ishmael turned again to leave when he heard the Admiral once more. “Lieutenant.”

“Sir?”

“This is important….with the British submarine’s location known we can bargain for its safety and ultimately prevent an attack on Malta.”

“I’ll do my best sir.”

“Make sure you do sailor….make sure you do.”

*

Gaz and Betty were still wearily walking up the steep slope that lead out of Mgarr when they noticed that Robbie was trying to get theirs and the others attention. He was pointing forward excitedly and Gaz soon saw what he was trying highlight. Several hundred yards ahead of them the Gozo police had set up a check point and were checking each passport coming through thoroughly.

Gaz quickly looked around and saw a narrow road leading from the main road they were on that was signposted for Nadur. “Betty head for that road there, I’ll get the others but wait by that Church.” Gaz pointed to a large Church dome in the not too far distance that belonged to the Church of ‘Our Lady at Lourdes.’

“Don’t be too long Gaz.”

Gaz kissed her and then went looking in the crowds for Pete and James; Robbie had seen Gaz pointing to the Nadur road and had quickly signaled his divers to head that way through the pushing crowds; Pete and James, however, were nowhere to be seen. As Gaz made his way forward he eventually linked with Robbie. “Have you got all you men Robbie?”

“Och aye were fine laddie, but wit aboot the others?”

“Can’t see them…dam I told them to keep in sight.”

"I'll stay wi you Gaz, the other divers can catch up wi Betty."

They both searched as far towards the front of the large cue but the sheer numbers of people trying to reach inland seemed to make the task impossible. Then Robbie noticed a commotion at the check points.

"Gaz…we've found them." Robbie pointed and Gaz's heart sank, there in front of them was Pete and James being arrested and taken away by the Gozo Police. James was arguing and struggling against his captures, but he was too firmly held between the officers to have any effect.

"We've got to help them," but when Gaz surged forward, but he felt the restraining of Robbie's hand on his shoulder.

"No Gaz, we canna help them just yet, we need to get to the others…come on mate, we can think of something later."

Reluctantly Gaz agreed and both he and Robbie were soon running up the quiet Nadur road towards the rest of the team waiting by the Church.

*

Ch.Sup. Sophia was elated to hear of a breakthrough in his search for the British divers. The news that he had received about two men being picked up, an American and a British, was in it's self no great thing, but the fact that they were together and unable to identify themselves or substantiate their story's as to why they were on Gozo, set the Superintendent's instincts on alert; he had a feeling these two men were in some way associated. After ensuring that his men knew exactly what to do should the divers appear at Ramla Bay, he raced back towards Victoria, aware that his adrenalin levels were starting to rise.

When he burst into the Police station he saw two of his men at a desk playing a game of cards; they stood to attention the moment they were aware of his proximity.

"Where are they?" Edward barked at the two men. He desperately wanted to charge them with inappropriate behaviour on duty but he had more important things to attend to at this particular time.

"Secured in the cells sir."

"Take me to them."

"Yes sir." The police officer who was doing the replying lifted a set of keys from the table where the cards where and started to walk through a door behind them. "This way sir."

Edwards turned to the other policeman on is way through the door. "Bring three cold cola's to the cells."

"Right away sir."

*

James and Pete were sitting on the hard cell bed discussing what to do next, when Ch.Sup. Sophia walked in; they both stood to meet him.

Edward offered his hand in a friendly gesture. "Welcome to Gozo gentlemen, I do hope you have been treated well by my officers. Please sit down."

James and Pete sat slowly down without saying anything.

The Chief Superintendent continued. "You may or may not be aware that there are some British divers running amok on my territory; they have killed one of my officers, stole a boat and I have a feeling that in some way the two of you may be connected." He was about to say more when the officer arrived with the cola's.

"Ah! Drinks gentlemen, as you see we are very civilized in Gozo; all these rumours of police brutality are, what shall we say, hearsay…..please drink and be refreshed."

James and Pete gladly took the cola's but still said nothing; they were both feeling dehydrated even though the cells were cool.

Edward continued. "Now where was I? Yes….I was thinking that maybe you could tell me why British naval divers would want to be here in the first place….could it be something to do with an American AWAC near Ramla Bay?"

James was the first to respond. "Captain James Kirk. United States Air force Service number C……."

Edward interrupted. "Oh come, come now Captain James Kirk? Do you think we are simple?"

Pete then spoke "It's true, that's his name."

"And you are?"

"Peter Lacer; assistant to the British High Commission."

Edward was unsure whether to believe these two strangers; there was however one way to find out; he called his men and then smiled at James. "You will tell my two officers your real name and why you are here."

"Go to hell." James spat the words out.

"I must protest at this barbarism." Pete stood as he protested, however the Ch.Sup turned and waved his two police officers into the cell, they in turn lifted and dragged James from the cell and out into the corridor; Pete found himself alone and frightened.

*

When Father Dominique came out of his deep and exhausted sleep, he needed a few moments to re-orientate his mind. The last thing he could recall with clarity was being washed ashore at Ramla Bay, after that everything was a blur of unreality. He looked around where he was but could only make out the dull uninteresting ceiling of what was probably someone's home, however, the bed was soft and comfortable so he decided to lie a few moments before attempting to get up on his feet.

"Ah you are awake Padre?" The sudden voice startled Dominique, he went to sit up but felt a gentle restraint against his chest.

"Take it easy Padre, you are in safe hands."

"And whose hands would they be?" Dominique, voice betrayed his inner fear; even though he had asked in an assertive manner.

"Let me introduce myself Padre."

Dominique felt his head being raised gently and a pillow being adjusted so he could see who was talking.

"Capt. Chris Vella at you service of the now almost defunct Maltese army."

Father Dominique breathed a sign of relief. "God works in mysterious ways Captain; I thought I was finished."

"Not yet Padre, there's a lot of life in the old goat yet." Chris smiled at the priest.

"Would you like to tell me why you were staggering around in the Ta' Sardina, you gave us a scare for a moment." Chris pulled up a chair and sat by Dominique's side as, over the next hour, the priest explained all that had happened to him and the others in their search for the AWAC. When he had finished Chris responded by explaining why they were now in hiding at Nadur, beginning with their withdrawal from Birkirkara barracks and the fight through Malta ending with their present location.

"So you see Padre, there are only a few of us left; there isn't much more to tell."

Dominique sat up on his elbows; he could feel his head swimming but held his position. "You must help me find my friends Captain."

"Your friends will, I have not doubt, take care of themselves Padre, I have my men to think about now......come you need to eat and drink."

Dominique fell back onto the bed exhausted; there was nothing more he could do for now.

*

Gaz and Robbie soon caught up with Betty and the divers who were waiting as ordered by the Church of Our Lady of Lourdes; as soon as they found them they headed inland towards Nadur. They had walked in silence for a few moments when Betty spoke. "Gaz, what will happen to them?"

"They will be identified and deported I guess." Gaz walked on without lifting his gaze from the ground.

"That's good.... right?" Betty's voice betrayed her uncertainty.

Gaz looked at Robbie who firmed his mouth but said nothing.

"That depends Betty."

"On what Gaz?"

"The identification process."

Betty walked on up the steep hill for a few moments before she realized what Gaz was trying to say in a gentle way. "You don't mean - they wouldn't - would they?" She turned and kept walking, the look on Gaz and Robbie's face told her everything and from then, she, like the rest of the men she was with, walked in silence towards Nadur.

*

The heat and the overwhelming despair of their situation meant that Gaz, Betty, Robbie and the other divers normal levels of alertness had dropped to a dangerous level of stupor, and as they entered Nadur they failed to take proper precautions; walking straight into a small Maltese army patrol. The first moment of awareness was when they heard the shout of "Halt," and then the sound of weapons being prepared for firing. Gaz and the others slowly raised their hands and Robbie cursed under his breath for being so careless, as their captures came out from their places of hiding, pointing their guns menacingly at the team.

Gaz looked over at Betty; she had a look of defiance on her face. "Stay close Betty," he whispered. Robbie and the others put down their bags and waited.

One of the Maltese came over and spoke to them. "Who are you and what are you doing here?"

Robbie spoke first. "I'm Master Diver Robbie McMaster of the British Navy and these are my men.

"And who are the other two?" The same man asked, pointing at Gaz and Betty.

"Gaz Seymour Royal Air Force, Special Duties and this is Chief Petty Officer Betty Williams Royal Navy weapons specialist."

"Al Madonna!" The soldier said lowering his weapon and at the same time signaling the others to do the same. "This is turning out to be a very strange day." He walked forward to Robbie with a smile and his arms open. "Welcome friend you are all welcome." The others soon joined in and Gaz smiled at Betty as the Maltese soldiers took it in turns to embrace her and welcome her personally.

They were escorted through the small town until they came to the edge of the road to Ramla Bay; there they were met by the other Maltese soldiers and Captain Chris Vella. However the greatest surprise for Gaz and Betty was seeing Father Caruana safe and well and the three stood for a moment embracing like long lost family.

"Come," Father Dominique said, "And you too Captain, there is much to talk about and more to do."

Chapter Fifteen

Shortly after receiving permission to defend Gozo from further advances of the Libyans, the British contingent based in Sicily scrambled three of its Euro – Fighters with orders to fire on any Libyan military seen crossing the South Comino Channel. Unfortunately the other countries now involved in the military build up in the south of Europe refused to commit there own military hardware but Britain felt that it had a duty due to it's historical connections with Malta. No decision was taken however to land any European forces anywhere on the islands; there was concern that full scale fighting would be too costly in terms of the Maltese civilian population. For the moment it appeared as though there was an impasse, with both sides wondering what would happen next. In the whole scheme of events now unfolding, the AWAC search and recovery was now forgotten under a pile of higher priorities and goals.

*

It hadn't taken Ishmael long to put together a team of six volunteers and a few appropriate light weight weapons for his mission to Gozo and in a very short time, he found himself on the flat sandy shores of Ramla Bay. He had picked this as a landing site because of it's secluded yet easily accessed road to Victoria and after burying the inflatable they had came in under the golden sands, they set off cautiously along the road to Victoria that passed through the edge of Nadur. Although they had initially a lot of cover from the long green bamboo shoots that grow at Ramla; this didn't last long and soon, as they walked up the hill out of the Bay, Ishmael realized that they were now dangerously exposed even though the light of the day was dimming. They kept to as near to the wall as possible that ran along side the road to Nadur but Ishmael's best hope was that there would be no one around to see them; it was a high risk assumption that didn't pay off.

*

Chris, Gaz, Robbie and the others were sitting in a house that had been temporarily confiscated to serve as Chris's resistance HQ. The atmosphere was relaxed and friendly, so much so that Gaz and Betty felt they had known Chris for a lifetime rather than just a few hours. Father Dominique was busy telling one of his many funny stories, as they enjoyed the cool of the evening after the heat of the day, when one of Chris's men ran in.

"Captain the guard has reported movement on the Ramla Road towards the bay."

Christ stood up and straightened his army tunic. "Moving from us or to us?"

"To us sir….there are about six or seven men."

"Any way of identifying who they are?"

"No sir but they are moving in a military manner."

Chris turned to Gaz and the others. "Expecting anyone?" He asked now clipping his pistol belt on.

"No." Gaz replied now standing with the others.

"Here," Chris said picking up an old SLR and flinging it towards Gaz, "You may need this."

While the other divers started to dig into their bags and produce various small arms Betty shouted, looking indignant, "Hey what about me?"

“Here you are lassie,” Robbie said tossing her one of his Smith and Weston revolvers with a smile. “That should dae ye, I widni’ like to see you miss oot on onything.”

She caught the pistol expertly, released the barrel, snapped it shut again, and then ran outside following the others.

*

Major Zammud had relocated himself to the Red Tower on Marfa Ridge so he could get a better view of the invasion hardware now sitting along the coast opposite Gozo. He had a feeling of pride as he looked at the Libyan army stretched before him but he also felt relieved that the Admiral had decided to hold the push for the moment. I was while he was looking through his binoculars at the Comino tower that he was sure something had passed by; he was still pondering the mystery when the sound wave hit him. The lone Euro-Fighter that had passed through his line of sight at supersonic speed now climbed vertically up into the clear blue sky above him. Zammud was mesmerized initially by the speed and grace of the warplane as it banked and turned to make another pass, but when another Euro-Fighter came thundering past him, he was shocked out of his daze.

As he looked down at his defenses he saw the Libyan Rapier lines follow the aircraft as they passed overhead, first one then two and finally a third. *“It’s only a display of bravado,”* he thought as he made his way down the tower and out to the top of the ridge itself; *“Nothing more.”* He was about to jump in his ‘Land Rover’ to return to the lines along Marfa coast when he saw something that chilled his blood; one of the Rapier Missiles had been fired at the swooping Euro-Fighters. From that point on everything seemed to be in slow motion. As he tried to call the Rapier installation on his old Watchman Radio, he watched as the released Rapier missile found its target and suddenly bust into a huge ball of white and orange flame. Parts of the aircraft were still falling out of the sky when the sound of the explosion reached him and he flung himself to the ground.

"The idiot's - by Allah - were finished," he thought to himself as he tried once more to call the Rapiers

"Who gave the order to fire?" Zammud shouted down his radio but no-one was responding, all he could do was watch in horror as the remaining two Euro-Fighters leveled for an attack run.

What happened next was almost predicable and Zammud stood watching brazing himself for the destruction that was about to happen, but it was far worse than he could have imagined when it came moments later.

The first missiles to be released from the Euro's were Meteor Missiles, Zammud counted eight in all before the force of the destruction forced him to fling himself behind the Red Tower for shelter. He had never known such an amount of violence smashing around him and he felt helpless to do anything except hide. As he looked to the sky above him he could see the two Euro-Fighters climbing into the heights rolling there wings in a sign of victory. Zammud felt loathing for the arrogant display of the flyers and was about to stand and shake his fist when he saw, with absolute horror, the two aircraft swoop down for another pass, this time with their controversial Mauser cannons dealing out random death to the defeated Libyan troops below. The noise of the strafing was unbearable for the Major as he sat with his hands over his ears trying to shake off the nightmare vision his imagination was producing. A short time latter, as he sat rocking backward and forward Zammud realized that it was all over; the aircraft had spent their weaponry and were heading back north towards Sicily. He looked at his watch; the whole episode had taken only six minutes. Shaking he stood up on his feet and turned to face the chaos below him on the coastline of Marfa. *"No – no – Allah - .no!"* The scene was like hell itself; nothing stirred, flames and black smoke filled the entire area, and in the redness of the setting sun the scene before him took on the hideous red glow of a hellish inferno. Zammud fell to his knees and wept, his entire command had been wiped out.

*

As Betty, Gaz and the others crouched behind the small wall that lines the road from Ramla Bay as it passes by Nadur to the east, they could see the small troop of Libyans making their way up the hill towards them. They were armed, moved cautiously and were obviously well trained in what they were doing.

Chris turned to look at Gaz and Betty who were crouching low beside him. "The men are right my friends, the way they are coming suggests they are well trained military; possibly Libyans."

"Why would they be coming here?" Gaz asked Chris.

"Maybe looking for resistance fighters - like us," Chris replied with a wiry smile, "If so we will let them find us….eh?"

However, before Gaz could say another word, Betty grabbed his arm. "I think I know why they are here," she pointed to the lead Libyan, "That, lover is Ishmael."

Gaz wasn't fully thinking and couldn't quite work out who she meant. "Ishmael?"

"Remember, the Captain of the Corvette that rescued us from the air crash?"

"Gees…Betty, I think you are right, but why would he be here?"

"I can answer that one," Robbie interrupted. "He escaped when you lot were dropped off at St Paul's Island, and there was no way of catching him."

"Then," Gaz pondered. "He can only be here for one reason - us."

"Or the subs location Gaz." Betty was now looking concerned.

"I'd say the subs location is a higher agenda." Robbie spoke while at the same time signaling his men to be ready to engage. "Either way, there no getting whit they came fur withoot a fight."

Chris signaled his men to hold until they were told to fire and then they waited as the Libyans walked unaware into trouble.

*

Ishmael sensed that he and his men were walking into a trap, but his reasoning told him that it wouldn't be the sort of thing to expect in Gozo, and he got careless. His first feelings of regret were when the first bullets from the hidden enemy cut through two of his men. "Hit the deck," he shouted as the road in front suddenly became alive with bits of tarmac and dust flying into the air around him. As he and his men crawled about for any safe place they could find, Ishmael tried to see who was firing at them and where from. Lying against the side of the low road side wall he looked at his men, it wasn't good; two dead and another bleeding heavily from a leg wound. He wasn't sure what to do next, but when he saw the determined look on the faces of the Libyan soldiers with him, he knew they would never even contemplate surrender. They all checked their weapons and on Ishmael's signal ran forward bent low swerving as they ran to avoid being hit. The next part of the evening reverberated to the noise of fierce automatic fire with white hot and deadly bullets flying in every direction. Ishmael, like his men ducked and swerved firing and yelling; he knew in himself that it was a suicide run but like his men he was determined his death would count for something. He was aware of his men falling at his side; one had twisted his body as the bullets found their mark before he fell, still, on the warm tarmac road. Another was hit several times but ran on firing, even as he faltered and fell to his knees, he fired on until the shower of bullets that was continually racking his body put an end to his resistance.

Ishmael heard himself screaming in madness as he ran, for some unexplained reason he had not been hit and now he began to feel invincible. He had almost reached the wall where Betty was firing from when he saw her and remembered her face. He stopped and looked at her and Betty froze. "You!" Ishmael screamed angrily, "You are the cause of all of this." He raised his pistol and took aim; Betty was still in a state of shock at meeting the Naval Officer face to face, she could do nothing but freeze as she looked at the pointed weapon.

Ishmael felt his finger squeeze the trigger, but he never finished the operation. Nor did he feel the single shot to his forehead, he only got a glimpse of a Maltese Army Captain smiling with a pistol still in his hand, Ishmael wondered for a brief moment, *"Allies?"* Then there was nothing.

*

"Sir," Chops shouted knocking over his entire desk in a flurry of sudden excitement, and sending his coffee and 'must have' cream Sicilian cakes flying about the Wg.Co's outer office. "Sir….quickly," he shouted again, ignoring the clatter of the recently printed "RAF Sicily' mug, as it shattered on the hard tiled floor, and ran unannounced into

Jerry Shott's office. He was waving a piece of printed paper in front of him as he ran in.

Jerry was sitting at his desk wading through the usual reams of paperwork that seemed to always double when they were overseas and looked up at his now floundering PA. "Chops, you must learn to be a bit more self-controlled."

Chops stood for a moment getting his breathe back as his large chest pumped like bellows. "I think you should read this sir." He held out the paper to Jerry Shotts who took it without a seconds thought; he knew that his rather large and bulbous Sgt would have a good reason for his outburst. Jerry glanced quickly at first and then re-read the message slowly as though trying to take in his worst nightmare.

"Its bad sir!" Chops explained almost unnecessarily, but felt he needed to say something defensive.

Jerry said nothing; instead he nodded his head slowly in agreement. Chops watched in silence as his Wg.Co stood up and turned slowly in thought towards the office window.

"What do you suggest sir…..er… I think we should do…..something?"

Jerry turned to face his Sgt, "A cup of tea would be nice."

"Sir?"

"A cup of tea Sgt…you know that brown stuff that comes from a small square bag"

"Sir?"

"Tea Chops, there's a good fellow."

"But sir….we….need…." Chops didn't manage to finish his sentence.

"A mug of tea Chops."

Chops turned and left the office muttering to himself, *"Gone totally loopy must be the stress,"* and went to fetch a cup of tea.

As soon as Chops left the office, Jerry dived to his phone and punched in an internal number, it seemed to ring for an unacceptable length of time before it was answered; then just as he was about to 'hang up' he heard a familiar voice.

"Tony here."

"Tony, where have you been?"

Tony sensed desperation in the Wg.Co's voice. "In the shower old boy; what's up?"

"Tony it's bad - really bad. You know these Euro-Fighters we sent over to Gozo?"

"Yea?" Tony answered guardedly.

"They have annihilated an entire Libyan regiment off the Ridge at Marfa."

"You mean Marfa as in Malta?"

"Tony?"

"I'm on my way Jerry."

*

Tony ran into Jerry's office ignoring the quizzical looks from Chops and the other personnel who where now congregating around the Sgt's untidy desk. He noticed that most had expressions of deep worry on their faces, but Tony had no time to analyze the situation; like them he only knew that something had gone very badly wrong with the plan to dissuade an attack on Gozo. On entering the Wg.Co's office, the first thing that Tony noticed was the still form of Jerry Shotts sitting with his back to the door. "Jerry, old boy.....what has gone wrong?"

Jerry swung round on his chair and pointed to a chair next to the desk. "Tony, bad news I'm afraid, were still trying to get a debrief from the pilots, but it seems that they were fired on by Libyan Rapier's as they flew past Marfa Ridge…..however we should get full details shortly."

"By heaven Jerry," Tony said taking the seat offered, "That's a stroke of bad luck…any damages?"

"One pilot and a Euro-Fighter lost – it was the other two that did the 'messy' bit."

They both sat in silence for several moments before Tony spoke once more. "What about Command…have you heard anything…I mean Jerry what's going to happen next?"

The Wg.Co shrugged his shoulders in a manner of defeated resignation but said nothing and Tony knew at that moment there was nothing anyone could except wait and see how the Libyans respond. "Dear God," Tony said standing up and turning to lookout of the Wg.Co's window, "Dear God."

They, nor the waiting staff outside in Chop's office, had to wait too long to find out how the Libyans would respond. Tony had just reached Jerry's window and was looking out at the various porta-cabins that served as temporary accommodation for the various servicemen of differing nationalities, when the first of three Libyan Scud Missiles hit the base. The only warning was a momentary 'whump' type noise that arrived a fraction of a second ahead of a massive and violent explosion that flung Tony and Jerry across the office against the opposite wall from the now shattering window. When Tony cleared his head from the blast he thought he detected the same strange sound again, and as he shouted, "Get down," flinging himself against the dazed Wg.Co, he heard another two very loud explosions somewhere outside on the airfield; then everything went still and quiet. As Tony and Jerry sat in shock looking at the ruined walls of the office, they began to hear the first sounds of injured and dying men and women. Initially it was faint and only occasional but as the moments passed into minutes the sounds began to increase not only in number but also in intensity

*

James had expected to be beaten by the two Maltese Policemen when they dragged him from the cell that he had been sharing with Pete, and he had determined that come what may, he would not divulge the reason or nature of their presence on the Island, however, he was both shocked and relieved when he was taken to a cold room in the Station and shown the body of a dead Policeman and six sets of navy diving equipment. Once in the room he was let go and Ch.Sup. Edward came and stood by his side.

"All I am after are the men, who killed my policeman Capt. Kirk, but I do find it strange that while searching for divers, I come across an American pilot accompanied by someone claiming to be the Assistant to the British High Commission; do you not think that as strange?"

James looked at the body of the young Maltese man and realized that this must be the work of Robbie and the other divers; he shuddered inwardly at the lengths these men would go to keep the sub a secret, and at the same time wondered whether he could trust this high ranking policeman with the truth, in the end James decided he had no choice. "Chief Superintendent I may have the answers you are looking for but first I must speak with my friend Pete Lacer."

Edward was about to say something when one of his men came into the room and whispered something to him. James strained to hear what was said but he had no need because as soon as the policeman left Edward smiled at James. "It would appear that your friend is indeed the Assistant High Commissioner; you will both join me in my office for a cool drink and please accept my sincerest apologies for your treatment. However, there is still the question of why you are here?"

"Just give me a moment with Pete," James said now feeling more at ease with the new development.

When Pete and James finally arrived in the Ch.Supt's office they had both come to the decision that they had to take a chance on the Chief Policeman's integrity, so after a refreshing drink and some lighthearted conversation Pete went into detail about the AWAC and the three agent's job to recover a missile. He also explained that the divers from the sub were not part of the original plan but with the escape of the Libyan naval officer, the subs location may have been compromised and it was necessary to keep its position secret, for obvious reasons.

Edward sat in silence as he listened to the report without any attempt to interrupt until Pete had finished. Now as they sat together he wasn't sure what he should do next. "But Mr. Lacer, that does not explain my policeman's murder; he was a good man with a family and I would never have expected the British to do such a thing."

"Well boss, he must have stumbled on them when they arrived at - where was it?"

"Xlendi Bay," Edward replied irritated at being referred to as 'boss'.

"Yes....there...and they would have had to act very quickly; you must understand that the situation in Malta and Gozo in very serious."

"So," Edward was leaning back on his seat as the scenario was starting to make some sense, "Where is your team now?"

"That's just it," Pete said, "We don't know."

Edward stood and straightened his summer dress tunic, reached to his desk and lifted his silver braided cap and placed it under his arm. "Come with me my friends, I have an idea that may answer all our questions."

As he turned to leave the office Pete looked at James who shrugged and said casually, "Do we have a choice?"

"No…not that I can see." Pete replied patting James's shoulder as they turned to follow the Police Chief out of his office and into the busy streets of Victoria.

*

Major Zammud staggered in unbelievable shock as he walked among the ruin of his regiment at Marfa. From where he was, he could see the ragged coast of Comino and the high citadel dome in Victoria, further away yet still clear in the evenings orange glow. He knew he should be angry at the utter destruction all around him but it wouldn't manifest itself within him, all he felt were strange feelings of defeat and despair. Turning to look eastward he fell to his knees and started to pray, *"Allah have mercy,"* but he still felt an isolation and despair he couldn't fully understand. All around him was the wreckage of Libya's military machine but Zammud's mind was focused on something else; it was the sounds of the dying, he couldn't de-focus his mind from the screams and the groans of his men. He heard a scream in the distance as he forced his hands to cover his ears but when he did it seemed to get louder; it was his own scream and he was trapped for the moment within a nightmare of agony that numbed his normality and forced him to see and experience the full horror of death.

"Pull yourself together…you're an officer of the Imperial Libyan Infantry." He thought the words, but his body refused to follow his traumatized mind. *"Get on your feet Zammud; officers need to be better than this."* Still no response - he felt paralyzed; then, out of the hot haze of burning smoke and darkness, he saw a man walking towards him. He didn't recognize who he was but it was

clear to Zammud that he was not a Libyan. The stranger smiled as he reached forward to help Zammud onto his feet.

"Who are you?" Zammud heard his voice as though in a dream.

The stranger didn't answer but simply lifted Major Zammud up and walked him away from the carnage around him. Zammud's mind was exploding with grief, fear and dismay so when he felt a needle go into his arm and the spread of darkness covering his mind, he was relieved to be released from the nightmare. Just before he passed into a welcome unconsciousness he caught sight of his rescuer's arm flash, 'ST JOHNS. MALTA' but he had no time to wonder as the drug took hold and gave him rest.

*

Chief Petty Officer Roland was the first to notice the anomaly on his tracer screen within the vanguard Class submarine's control centre. He had counted three blips on his consol and heard the sonic wave generated by the Scuds as they thundered from their transportable platforms now based in Malta. He had also detected the three Euro-Fighters and the resultant short battle that had followed, but was unsure of what could be going on; that is until the three blips appeared.

He ran from the Control Centre at the heart of the sub towards the front where the Officers mess was located and forgetting all protocol shouted as he ran, "Where's the Captain....I need to find the Captain."

Captain Morgan was relaxing in his 'cabin', a luxury reserved only for the highest of ranks within the submarines cramped space, when the Chief finally found him. Still ignoring all protocol he bust into his Captain's cabin and, panting from the run, gasped. "Sir....you need...to....."

"Chief Petty Officer Roland are you in a habit of bursting into a Commissioned officer's quarters, because if you are it's a very bad practice, now go outside and knock."

"But Sir you ......?"

"Go outside Chief Petty Officer and knock."

Roland incredulous, none the less stepped out side of the small room, closed the door behind him, gritted his teeth, and knocked.

"Yes Chief, come in." Captain Morgan responded from inside.

Roland was inwardly fuming as he opened the door and smartly stood to attention before his Captain, who was casually lying on his back on the small narrow bunk. "Sir we have picked up three anomalies on the missile detectors, and we think there may also have been a skirmish off Marfa Point sir. Three Euro-Fighters from Sicily sir....one down.....we think."

"Were they British Fighters Chief?"

"That, we can't tell without contacting CNC sir."

"What about the blips?"

"Looks like three missiles have been fired from Malta sir heading north towards Sicily."

"Has any word from Master Diver McMaster been received?"

"Nothing sir."

Ross flung his legs from the bed as though it was a great effort, and then sat on the edge deep in thought. "When are we due to contact CNC."

Roland looked at his watch. "Another two hours yet sir."

Ross stood up and stretched his legs. "Let's go Chief, we have work to do; sound the alert for battle stations and get ready to surface."

"Sir...that's a bit risky, is it not?"

“Firstly Chief you may have forgotten that I am in charge of this vessel, and secondly I am not prepared to sit here and do nothing when a fighter pilot may be injured and floating about our heads.”

“Yes sir I understand….er….both your points, but we may get compromised and surfacing without CNC permission is, well….. mutiny sir”

Ross pushed his chief out of the cabin and into the corridor following behind him. “Chief your observations have been noted now go and do as I have told you before you are sighted with …..mutiny.”

Roland didn’t reply, he quickly walked ahead of Ross towards the control centre and when he arrived put the Captain’s orders into effect.

Ten minutes later the submarine surfaced just of Marfa Point. It was now dusk and if anyone had been looking in that direction they would only have seen the vague outline of the submarine against the backdrop of Gozo’s coastline. As the search and rescue teams from the submarine searched the dark waters for the missing pilot, Captain Ross, Chief Roland and the Duty officer looked in stunned disbelief from their viewpoint on the ‘Sail’ at the now glowing remains of the Libyan regiment.

“Geees…what a mess,” Roland said summing up his thoughts on the sight laid out before them.

Ross ignored the Chief's comment; he had his own thoughts to deal with. “What’s the update from the search and rescue teams?”

The duty officer who was standing by the communications answered, “Nothing yet sir.”

“OK keep looking.”

“They are being hampered by floating Libyan bodies Sir.”

Ross was about to make a suggestion to his duty officer when Chief Roland interrupted him.

"Sir message from CNC; they want to know why you are on the surface."

"Dam...they were quick." "Reply to CNC Chief....er.....investigating possible disturbance of Marfa point....that should do."

He turned to his Duty officer, "That gives you ten minutes...find that man, if he is alive he will have activated his homing device...find him."

It only took three minutes for CNC to reply and it was simple and straight to the point and Ross bit his lip as he read the message out to the Chief and the Duty Officer.

MASSAGE FROM CNC. STOP
SUBMERGE IMMEDIATELY STOP
CNC NORFOLK STOP

"What's your orders sir?" The Duty Officer enquired.

"I gave you ten minutes young man....you have seven left....find him."

"Yes sir."

Chief Roland looked at his Captain and shook his head slowly from side to side.

"Have you something to say Chief?" Ross was feeling irritated with the Chief.

"No sir...absolutely not sir."

"Then get on with your duties Chief."

"Aye Aye, sir....by the way sir can I say something?"

"Go ahead Chief."

"If you go down for this sir - well me and the lads - were going down with you sir."

Ross was about to reply to his Chief's gesture of support when the Duty officer interrupted them, "Sir, they have found the pilot."

"Is he alive?" Ross asked now feeling justified for his disobedience to orders.

"Yes sir, he is badly burned but alive sir."

Ross turned to Chief Roland, "Chief send a message to CNC; 'will comply immediately' ok?"

"Aye, aye sir"

"Now let's get this beast back into the murky depths of the Med.....as soon as the pilot is safely on board emergency dive, but no audible warning is that clear?" Ross left the Sail and disappeared into the control centre below; the Duty Officer could control the descent. *"He'll enjoy that,"* Ross was feeling pleased with himself; *"Sod's, at least I've done **something**."* "Have we any further word from CNC Chief?"

"No - nothing sir."

Captain Ross Morgan smiled in self contentment as he felt the submarine quietly slip beneath the surface of the sea. "Maintain periscope depth," Ross ordered as the Duty Officer appeared from the direction of the 'sail's hatch.

"Aye, aye sir."

Chapter Sixteen

The European Parliament and Council for War were going frantic; questions needed to be answered but it seemed as though there was no time to get the relevant people together to give the answers. Prior to launching the three Scuds, Libya had sent a message warning against any attempt at military intervention in the main land of Malta; they were quite willing to confront any military action around Gozo, but Malta as afar as they were concerned was to be left in their hands alone. Unfortunately the message was never received by the European Parliament; no one knows why and if they did they were not saying; it remained one of many unanswered questions. Once the attack on Marfa Point had started it seemed as though both sides, British and Libyan, were blaming each other for the escalation on violence. It was during this 'passing the blame' phase that Libya ordered the Scuds to be fired at the European Military Airbase on Sicily calling it a 'legitimate target' and claiming it was for the further protection of their interests in Malta. Strangely, they also sent an apology for any casualties suffered in this attack, claiming that they were only interested in damaging the airfield's runways in order to prevent further illegal attacks by British Euro-Fighters. This perverse 'tit for tat' seemed to calm the situation down, with both sides feeling vindicated and an uneasy 'acceptance' came into force causing the Libyans and the Europeans to stand still for the moment and take stock of the situation.

With the Americans still tied up in the Near East keeping the peace off the shores of Israel however, there was a general feeling among the Arab Nations supporting Libya's invasion of Malta, that time was running short to establish a proper military base on the Island and pressure was exerted on Tripoli to re-assert their hold on Malta as a credible threat to Europe. Tripoli however resisted any pressure to do any more 'saber rattling' for the moment.

*

"Tony here - is that you Jennifer?" Tony had, only a moment earlier struggled to get himself up from the floor of the Wg.Co's damaged office, when the phone had rang.

"Yes, are you alright…I was worried about you when we heard of the attacks."

Tony thought about his secretary; she was always 'fussing' about him, and always took her work beyond the normal levels of concern, especially where Tony was concerned; a warm feeling came over him as he wondered how much Jennifer really cared about him. He was speculating about her to the point of fantasizing when his thoughts were interrupted.

"Tony, are you still there?" Jennifer sounded disturbed as Tony was snapped back to reality by her voice.

"Yes, old girl, still here…why are you phoning…not just for me I suspect?"

"Well as a matter of fact I **was** worried about you and I would have phoned anyway." She sounded defensive. "But the PM wants a word with you."

"The PM - is he there?"

"Here he is….Tony, I…..oh it doesn't matter, you better speak to your boss."

Tony wished he could tell her to hold on and speak some more; he was comforted by the sound of her voice.

"What was she going to say?" However he resisted the temptation and waited on the PM to speak.

"Tony, glad your fit and well, how's the show going over there?"

"You mean apart from the Scuds and the other inconveniences…well fine."

"Good old fellow, between you and me there is a general opinion that these Scuds need removing before we can get this situation sorted."

"Your not suggesting we attack again old man….that would be disastrous?"

"Are you in touch with your friends from Cyprus yet?"

"Well we know they are in Gozo at the moment and we suspect probably near Ramla Bay, the satellite picked up a fire fight there a short time ago, I assume it could be them, the area is right."

"The war council here feel it would prudent if the Maltese themselves put an end to these Scud 'thingimies', and we were wondering if you could make contact and encourage them to contact the resistance on the Main land."

"There is such a thing?" Tony asked.

"Oh yes we have reports of small groups of the Maltese Army still resisting, although they are getting less as time goes on."

"So," Tony now indicated that Jerry should listen in on an extension that had miraculously survived the blast from outside; he was standing dusting down his cloths from the dust that had settled everywhere, "You want me to go to Gozo and find Gaz and James, tell them to go to Malta and encourage the resistance - if it's still there - to attack and destroy the Scud launchers."

"That's it in one; old boy," said the PM. "Oh by the way did I not say, it's an order….Jennifer wants a word now…bye."

Tony was stunned, it wasn't even open for debate he looked at Jerry who had heard the later part of the conversation, but before he could say anything to Jerry, Jennifer was back on line.

"Tony - be careful - I - miss you."

"You too old girl," replied Tony before the phone went dead.

Jerry, now fully aware of what was required took the telephone handset from Tony and redialed an internal number. "Wing Commander Shotts here, I need a chopper to be ready in thirty minutes fully armed……no…..I wont need a pilot, just the chopper….yes the Gazelle is perfect; oh on that subject check out the Magnifying Aid; I want it fully operational."

Jerry was putting the phone down when Tony asked, "What good is the chopper without a pilot, Jerry."

"You don't think I would let you loose with one of my young impressionable airmen do you?" Jerry smiled. "I'm your pilot 'old bean'."

"You fly choppers?" Tony sounded surprised, and a bit dubious.

"Well Tornadoes are my expertise really, but what can be difficult about a little Gazelle eh?"

"Here we go again." Tony was remembering back to the Cyprus Event when Chief Tech Hewlett's claim to being a chopper pilot, which as it turned out was not quite true, almost got them both killed.

"What did you say Tony?" Jerry asked, walking from the office to see if Chop's was ok

"Nothing, old man - nothing that won't come out in the wash, as they say."

*

Chris Vella had wanted to leave the bodies of the fallen Libyan fighters to rot in the valley below Nadur, but

Father Dominique had argued against the 'barbarity' of such an atrocity and had won his case. As the sun set over Gozo and the now peaceful countryside, all that could be heard was the gentle clatter of the spades that Chris's men were using on the slopes above the valley basin.

"Make sure the graves are facing to the East," the priest shouted down to the men digging, "That's very important."

Chris shook his head, turned and walked back towards the house where Gaz, Betty a Robbie were resting; the other divers were now spread out along the Nadur road keeping watch for any more attempts to catch them unaware.

He stepped into the cool darkness of the living room. "Priests; who can understand them?" Then he sat on the floor guarding the open road in front of the door.

"How is Betty?" He asked still looking outside as though to look away for a moment might mean disaster.

"I can speak for myself Captain."

Chris smiled as he detected a stubborn streak manifesting in Betty; that was, in his opinion, a good sign. "I'm sure you can," he replied. "Well?"

"Well what?" Betty asked abruptly.

"How are you?"

"As well as anyone else," Betty replied. "Why?"

"I just thought……."Chris was interrupted.

"You thought Captain that because I am a woman I would be falling apart," countered Betty aggressively.

"Hey take it easy." Chris turned to face Betty for the first time, and noticed how close she was sitting to Gaz; he decided not to take the point any further. "Robbie," He said trying now to change the subject, "What do you think about the situation?"

"Aye," Robbie replied in his broad Scottish accent. "It's a difficult question, we still have to find James and

Pete, I dinni suppose ony of you hae a plan?" He looked over at Gaz and Betty.

"We wait," said Gaz, "At least until the morning, what we all need to do now is rest."

"Whit aboot the guards and my bonny lads, they will need to rest as well, ye ken?"

"Call them in Robbie, we'll do shifts in pairs two on and four off until the sun rises again."

"Works for me," Chris said smiling cheekily, "I'll do my stint with Betty."

"In your dreams, Tree boy."

"Only joking, my fair lady, there's no need to ask who you will be…er…'guarding' us with."

As Chris and Robbie got up to call in his men, Betty looked at Gaz and noticed he was blushing.

For a while Gaz and Betty were left alone with no one interrupting valuable 'space', and during that time, they spoke intimately about how they felt about each other. Gaz learned why Betty was so hard and defensive and what is was that made him attractive to her, by the time Father Dominique arrived back from the burial duty, they had come to a decision about each other.

"Father," Gaz said, looking at the tired face of the old priest, "Would you do something for us?"

Dominique looked at the two people before him and he knew right away what was coming, but waited on the question anyway.

"We would like you to marry us."

As Gaz verbalized the climax off their quiet time together, Betty looked at him with admiration. There was a tear in his eye and Betty knew that this was why she loved him; he was the first men she had ever met who was sensitive enough to be moved with open displays of emotion, yet tough enough to take the 'blows'.

"I would consider it a privilege and a pleasure," replied the Priest. "When do you want me to do it?"

"Now!" Betty said without any hesitation and still looking at Gaz, "Before the others return."

"As you wish." Dominique was smiling in spite of his weariness. "It will be a short blessing only of course, but we can 'formalize' the whole thing later....lets pray."

When Betty and Gaz went out to do their stint on guard, no one knew that they were now married, and neither they nor the Priest told anyone for now.

*

Admiral Ahmad was not very happy when the news about the attack at Marfa reached him: He now realized that Major Zammud's delay in launching his invasion of Gozo was the first of a series of blunders that had led to the unpopular decision to launch the Scuds. After almost pleading with the Libyan defense Minister at Tripoli for a re-think about the possible consequences of such an action, he had been told categorically to obey his orders or allow another to take his place that would. Reluctantly and under immense pressure, Ahmad had given the order to fire the Scuds. He had expected an immediate retaliation from the European Forces in Sicily but when it didn't manifest, his initial surprise turned into personal anger; particularly with Major Zammud.

Ahmad was now pacing the floor of his presidential office when the young Maltese secretary who had been forced into being his PA arrived timidly at the huge office doors.

"Well?" Ahmad turned to face the young secretary; he had little or no respect for these 'westernized' women; if Ahmad had his way they would all be wearing the proper Muslim coverings, but his orders had been very specific on these issues; the invasion had to wear all the signs of an invited ally. "Have you found our missing Major yet?"

The young girl stood her ground; she was scared of this man's power and she also knew that it showed, even though she tried her best to remain 'brave'. "No sir, at least not yet his last reported position was at Marfa Point."

The Admiral thought for a moment, rubbing his hand across his chin while continuing to stare at the secretary. *"She is very tempting,"* he thought to himself. "Come closer to me." He continued to rub his chin in thought.

"Sir…I'd rather not I have many things to see to……" She felt her adrenalin levels suddenly raise, and a deep sickly feeling come over her causing her to stutter as she spoke.

Ahmed reached out his arm in a welcome gesture. "Nonsense, come closer, what is your name?" He realized that he had never bothered to find out.

"Agnes, sir….but I would rather not…" She stopped talking when Ahmed moved to close the office doors behind her.

She struggled at first, but as her strength failed, she realized it was futile. In the far distance she could hear crying and screams as though a sudden nightmare of unreality had invaded her day time reality; she chose to hide in the nightmare where someone else was being violated, and within her soul a burning, obsessive hatred took hold of her life.

*

Major Zammud felt warm and comfortable when he regained consciousness. At first all he could see as he opened his eyes were blurred movements around him and muffled voices speaking quietly, but as the moments went on, his sight cleared and the voices became audible; he was in a hospital, that he assumed very quickly, but it wasn't a military hospital; they were all speaking Maltese and as he noticed the familiar blue cross on the nurses uniforms, his mind went back to the vision of the man who had rescued him from the massacre of his regiment at Marfa.

Zammud tried to sit up, but felt a gentle restraining hand on his shoulder. "No Major, you must rest."

He turned to see a Maltese nurse smiling as she lifted his arm to connect him to a blood pressure monitor. "You have been through much Major, but physically you are fine; just a few minor burns and scratches, however, you'll live."

While the nurse continued to do her various routine checks, Zammud put his head back on the white pillow cases and considered his situation. "*A whole regiment lost forever through a blunder that I am ultimately responsible for; the Admiral will court marshal me for sure.*" Zammud knew that for him everything was over. *"Yes I'll live…at least long enough to be stoned."*

The nurse was starting to place her equipment on a small trolley beside the bed to move on to her next patient, when Zammud grabbed her arm.

"Yes Major?" She said making no attempt to break free from his grip.

"Tell me Nurse, has anyone been looking for me?"

"Not that I'm aware of Major, but I can check ….if you let me go."

Zammud released his grip. "Sorry nurse, but it's important….my regiment was wiped out at Marfa and I'm here with hardly a scratch…it doesn't look too good, does it?"

"Put like that Major; probably not. What will you do?" The nurse now moved back to his bed and Zammud saw a genuine concern of her face which puzzled him.

"I'm not sure yet but I need to know if Admiral Ahmed has send out a search party; he is sure to use me as his scapegoat."

"Then Major how can I help you?"

"Why would you want to help **me**…I'm a Libyan?"

The nurse smiled. "Put it this way Major, I wouldn't want to see all my skills wasted so they can 'stone' you for whatever it is they will blame you for."

Zammud smiled uneasily, *"These Maltese are really nice people…what am I doing here, like this?"*

"You can relax Major, I will do as you ask, give me a few minutes and I will be back."

Zammud watched as the Nurse walked down the ward and stopped by a male nurse who was busy with another patient. She spoke for a moment and then turned and pointed towards his bed. He couldn't make out what was said, but noticed that the talking seemed intense, then without any warning the male nurse walked quickly out of the ward and Zammud's nurse turned back towards his bed smiling; in moments she was beside him again.

"Well Major, you will be pleased to know that for the time being at least, no one has come for you."

"Thank you, Nurse?"

"Bonnici , Major, Staff Nurse Angelina Bonnici."

"You are indeed an angel, how can I thank you?"

Angelina seemed slightly flirtatious when she answered, "Oh I wouldn't worry about that Major, I'm sure we can think of something."

As she left, Zammud watched her walk slowly back down the ward and out through the swing doors at the bottom, he felt a warmth that was foreign to him as he thought of Angelina for a moment, then he once more re-focused on what his next move might be; he knew in his heart that he was finished as a Major in the Libyan Infantry and had no intention of facing the Admiral; that could prove fatal.

*

Pete and James were relieved to be sitting inside the Chief Superintendents staff car. The Audi's air-conditioning system soon cooled the interior of the vehicle down to an acceptable level of temperature comfort, and as the car slowly maneuvered its way out of the busy streets of Victoria and take a left turn down towards the village of Xaghra; Pete and James relaxed quietly looking out at the passing countryside. Once they reached Xaghra the driver took them through the narrow claustrophobic streets characteristic of Gozo villages, and on down a narrow rough road that twisted uncomfortably through the countryside towards Ramla Bay. When they eventually arrived, Pete and James could see several Policemen lining the Bay road next to the tall Bamboo plants that led to the golden sands and a closed deserted Tourist Shop.

The Chief Inspector turned to face Pete and James; he had been sitting in the front passenger seat of the Audi. "This, gentlemen is where the AWAC crashed, just of the point towards your right; I suspect your friends will arrive here sooner or later."

"What will you do when that happens?" James feigned a lack of interest.

"Arrest them of course."

"Why?" Pete asked. "Have you failed to realize that Malta is under the invasion forces of Libya…it's very important that this AWAC is found."

"Important for whom?" Replied the Chief Inspector " Certainly not for us here in Gozo, the Libyan's at present are allowing all Maltese to return to the Mainland and it would appear that you are now the invaders."

"This is rubbish." Pete spoke angrily. "I must protest at this ludicrous and treacherous ….."

"Your protest will be noted officially, however for the present you are my guests; that is until your friends arrive; then you will all be handed over to the Libyans. Would you like a Cola?"

James reached for the car door and opened it to step outside. "I think I need some fresh air," his tone of voice betraying a hint of sarcasm.

"I'll join you." Pete opened the other rear door to step into the hot gentle breeze blowing from the sea.

They both walked together in silence towards the edge of the blue waters gently lapping against the rough golden coloured sands on the Bay, leaving Edward to look after his few men posted by the Bamboo.

"What do you think?" James was kicking some of the sand with his feet.

"I think our Police Chief is crazy." Pete was looking out to sea beyond the small rocky point to his right.

"What about the Libyan's allowing the Maltese to return to their homes as if everything is now normal?"

"I'm not sure James, but my immediate thoughts are 'human shields'.

"What do you mean?"

"Think about it," said Pete turning to face James, "If the Maltese are working and living as normal, the Libyans can build whatever military bases they want, with no fear of anyone attacking them; there is no Government in the world would risk an attack with such a densely populated civilian presence."

James thought for moment, and then spoke. "Pete prison in Libya doesn't work for me."

"Nor me James; got a plan?"

"Nope; but I ain't going to prison…at any cost."

"That's a great plan James, and I'm with you."

Chapter Seventeen

Major Zammud was not sure if he was dreaming at first, but something had disturbed him. When he opened his eyes and knew he should be able to see something, even in the night, realization came on him like an explosion; he had been hooded or blindfolded. He tried to struggle as he became aware of his body being manhandled and lifted from the bed, but the men who were restraining him were far too strong. His next thoughts were that Ahmed had found him and that he was being carted off for interrogation but, *"Why blindfold."* Then he noticed a familiar smell; perfume, a woman's perfume but as he struggled and tried to remember why the perfume was familiar, he just couldn't reach the memory. Then he felt himself being strapped to a medical trolley. Zammud felt panic starting to rise up within himself, he tried to contain it but his thoughts were now racing. *"Is this one of the Admiral's sick jokes?"* Just on the verge of total panic taking over, Zammud sensed a closeness of the source of the perfume; the voice was gentle and reassuring.

"Sorry Major, we need to sedate you but I will stay with you."

As he felt the needle prick the skin of his arm, Zammud relaxed. *"Angel,"* he thought as the sedation took effect.

*

Tony was very relieved to see that Jerry did indeed know how to fly the Gazelle, although it was early morning, and the sun had just began to rise, it was still dark and this had worried him initially. "You fly choppers like an expert Wing Commander," he said through the choppers internal comm.'s helmet they were wearing along with the appropriate flying overalls that the 'health and safety' conscious flight controller had insisted they wear.

"I did tell you I could fly one of these; comes in handy when you want to visit the wife for the week-end."

"You don't…." but he didn't finish when he saw Jerry smiling at him.

"Only kidding Tony - 'old bean'."

"I nearly fell for it….old bean… how long before we make Gozo?"

"Well she does around 233kph so we should see Gozo within the hour; we'll keep low over the water so we don't get picked up by Libyan defenses."

As Jerry took the Gazelle to almost sea level, Tony felt a surge of excitement as the sea below them seemed to pass them at a breath taking speed in the primal light of the rising dawn.

They passed a few small Maltese shrimpers on their way back from the nights fishing, but apart from that, the flight seemed to go unnoticed by any of the Libyan coast guards or radar, and soon they could see ahead of them the silhouette of Gozo and its predominant Citadel in Victoria.

"Beautiful sight, eh Tony?"

"Yes Jerry staggering really, it's hard to imagine we are having all this trouble, when you see everything so peaceful in a morning dawn."

Jerry pointed to his right. "Over there Tony that's Ramla Bay, and Nadur, where we detected the disturbance on satellite, that's straight ahead, we'll fly over a few times then, if we can, we will land."

*

Gaz and Betty were doing their stint when the sun was rising over the Mediterranean Sea in the distance. They were both watching the road from Ramla but sitting next to each other discussing their lover's plans for the future, "After it's all over," when they first heard the sound of the approaching helicopter. They stood to their feet and peered into the rising sun holding their hands up to their eyes to protect them from the burning brightness, but they could not see the aircraft in the sun's blindness.

Chris and Robbie also heard the noise of the Choppers engines and alerted their men who ran out of where they were resting and pointed their weapons at the oncoming Gazelle.

"Hold your fire lads." Robbie was now standing next to Chris. "We dinni yet ken if they are friendly or not."

Chris spoke quietly to Robbie. "Allah-Madonna, if it's Libyan he'll already be radioing our position to his control; are you expecting a chopper from your submarine?"

"Dinni be daft, we dinni hae a chopper in oor boat."

Chris said no more, turning to his men he shouted above the now loud chopper engines, "Fire, bring that machine down."

Without any hesitation Robbie and Chris's men fired their weapons in a deadly shower of bullets into the path of the oncoming Gazelle.

It was Betty who first noticed the small blue Euro flag on the fuselage of the Gazelle as it banked to avoid the hail of bullets it was flying into. "Gaz," she screamed above the deafening noises, "Its…one of ours!"

"Are you sure Betty, because if it's not, we are done for if it gets away."

Betty didn't answer she ran towards the shooting as fast as she could waving and shouting at the top of her voice. "Don't shoot; don't shoot - its one of ours."

"Look that's Betty," said Robbie. "What's she doing?"

"She'll get herself killed one day." Chris continued to fire ignoring Betty's signals.

However Robbie suddenly realized what she was doing. "Cease fire…Cease fire!"

As the firing stopped, Chris came up beside Robbie, "I hope you know what your doing my friend."

So did Robbie!

Moments later Gaz and Betty arrived, and they all watched as the chopper banked as though it was about to make another run.

*

It was Jerry who first realized that the men he could see on the ground at Nadur where firing at them. "Tony, we are under attack, mostly small arms but lethal none the less." As he spoke he pulled the 'stick' back towards himself, and then lurched the Gazelle to the right. As it banked steeply Tony, holding tightly on to his seat, could see two people running towards the group that were firing; waiving their hands. "I don't believe it," said Tony now pointing excitedly to the two runners. "It's Gaz, I don't know who the others are Jerry, but that's defiantly Gaz, and he is trying to stop them shooting at us."

A bullet suddenly ripped through the Gazelle's floor missing Jerry by inches, and moments later a warning sound was emitted from the choppers fuel warning system. "Dam!" Jerry was now trying to correct an over-compensation of the Gazelles flying ability; he had panicked and put the chopper into an almost impossible angle of turning and feared it would cause the aircraft to loose its lift. "That bullet hit the fuel line Tony, I'm afraid we are going down, friends or not; I suggest you hold on very tightly."

Jerry, fighting to keep airborne, turned the machine back towards the people on the ground, he was hoping that Tony was right, but after weighing up the odds of finding the agents so quickly, he began to wonder. He could see the large group of men closer now as he expertly brought the aircraft safely down on the widest part of the road just outside of Nadur's village limits.

"Right Tony;" Jerry was not, waiting for the rotors to stop, or go through the usual post-flight schedules. "Get out…I think I smell aviation fuel…lots of it."

They both climbed out of the chopper's cabin at panic speed, and then ran, stumbling in the effort, towards the waiting strangers shouting and waiving at the same time, "Get back…get back it's going to…." However they didn't finish the warning, even as they ran, the leaking fuel ignited and a huge explosion with a blinding orange fire ball suddenly lit the morning sky, the impacted force of the explosion tossing Jerry and Tony awkwardly to the ground.

*

Pete and James had spent the entire night fighting off mosquitoes as they tried to get some sort of sleep at Ramla. Chief Sup. Sophia had insisted in staying at the beach that night and it soon became obvious to James and Pete that Edward Sophia was a much focused and determined man, especially when it came to his work. They had argued about the necessity of sleeping rough but in the end it seemed they had no choice. Now as the sun started to rise, James, while scratching the numerous bites of the night, was commenting on the peacefulness of the Bay when they heard the fearful explosion from just behind them.

They both turned to see the source of the disruption to their meditations and saw, at the top of the road to Nadur, a huge ball of flame filled smoke rising into the other wise perfect clear blue sky.

Edward Sophia had heard it too and came running from where he had been resting still rubbing the nights sleep from his eyes. "What was that?" He asked arriving beside James.

James said nothing but replied by nodding in the direction of Nadur.

Edward started to shout at his men to get up and get going, and then he came back to James and Pete. "I was sure I heard a helicopter a moment ago quite near and some shots as well, although I wasn't sure about the shots with the noise of the helicopter, does this mean anything to you?"

James and Pete shook their heads.

"Nope," James said almost casually; he suspected it might.

"Then you won't mind coming with us while we check it out?"

"Is there a choice?" Pete asked.

"No…none at all…. my friends."

"Then lead the way Geronimo," James said politely but with a touch of sarcasm that was lost on Edward.

*

"In the name 'o' the wee man," said Robbie. "Did ye see that?" He had automatically flung himself to the ground as had the other divers. Now as he straightened himself he felt a little bit embarrassed especially when he noted that Betty was still standing. *"She's made of ice that yin,"* he said to himself as he now stood next to Chris.

“Are they friends of yours Betty?” Chris was once more getting ready to shoot should the strangers prove to be Libyan.

“The Helicopter was European; Rambo – what is this ‘shoot first ask later’ policy you have anyway?”

Chris was about to defend his actions when he was interrupted by Gaz who now stood, eyes wide open in shock.

“Tony? - Is that you Tony?” As he spoke he started to run towards the two men still lying on the road in front of the burning Gazelle. “Betty, Robbie give me a hand….I know this man.”

Betty and Robbie started to run with Gaz to where the two helicopter flyers lay; they were just starting to pick themselves up when Gaz and the other two arrived.

“Gaz…. old man.” Tony was weakened by the blast but otherwise unhurt.

Gaz kneeled down and helped his friend from Cyprus to his feet. “Tony…..what on earth are you doing here? You nearly got shot down.”

“We **did** get shot down,” said Jerry now on his feet and offering his had to Robbie. “Wing Commander Shotts at your service.”

“A real live Wing Commander?” Robbie came to attention. “Master Diver Robbie McMaster and these others are Gaz Seymour – Special Duties, CPO Betty Williams, and the ‘Malt’ behind us is Capt. Chris Vella.”

“What about James?” Tony enquired, still holding onto Gaz’s hand. “Wasn’t he with you as well?”

“We lost him when we arrived in Gozo, he and Pete were arrested by the police; apparently they are after Robbie and his men.”

“Who might Pete be?”

“It’s a long story Tony but he is the Assistant to the British High Commissioner in Malta….anyway come and meet the others and then you can explain what on earth you are doing here?"

*

Admiral Ahmed put on his navy white tunic, fastened his leather gun belt and holster around his waist and then walked from his office. As he went through the large wooden doors he looked back to see the cowering and trembling form of Agnes, she was squeezing herself into a corner as though hoping the very walls would swallow her up. Ahmed felt disgusted with himself but he wasn't sure why, he was after all the commander of Malta and as such he was entitled to do as he pleased, however, the feeling wouldn't shift and it began to trouble him.

He walked a short distance to another room in the Palace and flung the doors wide open to expose the temporary communications centre that had been set up to co-ordinate the invasion; as he entered the room, a dozen or so naval operatives stood to their feet in surprise.

"Have we heard from Major Zammud yet?" His voice was strong and firm but the operatives were afraid to answer.

Ahmed pointed to an individual who had the rank markings of a Lieutenant on his shoulder flashes. "You, what about the 'whereabouts' of Major Zammud….I asked a question sailor and I want an answer."

The Lieutenant was still reluctant to answer; they had grown used to Agnes passing on questions or instructions from the Admiral, and so they had all been unprepared for the unfolding scenario now taking place.

"Sir….there is…still no sign of him."

"What is being done to find him Lieutenant?"

"Everything possible sir….he seems to have vanished into thin air…it's a puzzle sir."

"Why do you say that Lieutenant?"

The young lieutenant looked around for moral support, he knew that the missing Major was one of the Admirals more favoured officers; but that didn't amount to very much when it came down to actual loyalties within the Libyan Navy. "Sir we are of the opinion that if the Major wanted to be found, he would have made contact with us by now."

Admiral Ahmed thought for a moment about what the young officer had just implied. "By Allah," he suddenly blurted out causing the Lieutenant to cringe. "You think he has deserted?"

"Sir only that he could have contacted us by now."

"Find him," commanded Ahmed in an aggressive voice, before he turned and walked back to his office. He paused at the doors for a second and, turning his head slightly, shouted back along the corridor. "Get me Tripoli on the line." Then he walked through to his office once more. In the short time he had taken to visit the communications centre, Agnes had managed to run and was now missing. "And get me a new PA," he shouted before slamming his office doors to make his call to the naval command in Tripoli.

*

When Major Zammud came round from his drug induced sleep, it didn't take him long to work out that he was sitting in an upright chair with his hands firmly tied behind his back. He was able to look around but the light was very dim and the cave like room he was in was strangely shaped. He noticed several dark crevices and ledges that surrounded him, but apart from that everything was quiet and unfamiliar.

"Major Zammud." The sudden sound of a voice from the dark reassesses of the strange room made Zammud jump. He tried to see where it had come from but the room echoed too much making it hard to give the disembodied voice direction.

"Major Zammud do you understand me?" Zammud noted that the voice was Maltese.

"Yes," he said guardedly trying to stop his mind from going into a wild panic.

"Major Zammud, if you will answer our questions we will not harm you."

"And if I don't?"

"Major you are very lucky to still be alive, I have many comrades who would have had it, shall we say; otherwise. I suggest in the strongest terms possible that you co-operate."

"Who are these people that talk so calmly of killing me?" Zammud hesitated before he answered. "My name is Major Zammud of the Libyan infantry, service number L2235671."

"That is a very good start Major, now who ordered the attack on the Euro – Fighters at Marfa?"

"That was an error of judgment; it wasn't supposed to happen."

"But you were the commanding Officer?"

"Yes, but I didn't give the order."

The voice asked many more questions about Zammud's background and his involvement in the decision to invade Gozo and he did his best to answer honestly; by now he realized that this was some sort of partisan group holding him as a prisoner.

After a time the questions became more pointed and sensitive. "Major, where are the Scuds located?"

"Only Admiral Ahmed knows that information, he alone has that authority."

"Who ordered them to be fired?"

Zammud was now shocked by this question. "What?"

"Three missiles were fired at Sicily, Major; who gave the order."

Zammud started to struggle from his chair but could not get free. "He's a madman, he has to be stopped."

"Who Major?"

"Ahmed dam it; he will get us all annihilated."

Zammud heard some whispering from the dark corners as though a disagreement was taking place, then the voice spoke calmly once more. "You were trying to avoid being found by your people; why was that Major?"

"I'll be court marshaled and probably deported and stoned for what happened at Marfa."

"You are on the run?"

"I am loyal to my country but with the Admiral in charge, I have no choice?"

There was some more whispering in the darkness but then Zammud caught the scent of a familiar aroma and knew who it was right away. "Angelina, is that you?"

The darkness seemed to come in on Zammud as the room went quiet. The lack of questions now gave him a feeling of isolation and he knew that who ever was with Angelina was now faced with a dilemma; what to do with the man who can identify one of the partisans? The muffled arguments started again and as Zammud waited helplessly they seemed to go on for a long time. Eventually they did stop, however, and then he looked uncertainly as several people came out from the shade of the recesses into the dim lit area; Angelina was among them.

*

Edward Sophia walked almost casually behind his men as they made their way up the road from Ramla to Nadur. They didn't follow the same military procedures as Ishmael's men had done earlier but the route was identical. As they drew near to the burning Gazelle, Edward's quick detective mind spotted the signs of a recent gun fight around the area, and he ordered his men to be, "Cautious." He could now see the groups of divers and others who looked as though they might be Maltese army surrounding the downed Helicopter crew so he signaled his men to crouch down and surround the group.

He turned to Pete and James. "Soon all your 'friends' including the helicopter crew will be in my prison cells, this will make a good bargaining focus for the Libyans, if they want to move into Gozo."

"You must be realistic Chief Superintendent," Pete pleaded. "The Libyans will be glad of your offer, but it will not stop them invading if they decide to."

"Still it gives us a good start to the negotiations, a sort of friendship gesture."

James grabbed Pete's shoulder. "It's no good mate he isn't going to listen."

Edward turned and followed his men around the low wall that led up the side of the road.

"Pete," James said. "Remember what we said about not wanting to go to prison in Libya."

"Yes?" Pete was straining to see beyond the wavering heat of the Gazelle.

"If this Policeman has his way, that's exactly what will happen."

"What do you suggest?"

"The way I see it Pete, if I was there and Gaz was here, he would warn me."

"I'm with you James; what do you think on the count of three?"

"Works for me Pete."

"Ok," Pete said getting to his feet nervously "One….two…..three."

On 'three', they both jumped out from behind the burning Gazelle and started to shout and wave their hands franticly. "Gaz. Betty, Robbie, it's a trap…get out of here."

Edward watched in dismay as the scene unfolded in front of him and his officers. "*They are both crazy,*" he thought as he turned to a police corporal at his side and ordered, "Shoot them down, they've betrayed us."

As Gaz and the others turned in surprise to see their missing friends, surprise turned to horror as a hail of small arms fire began to riddle Pete and James's bodies, they watched frozen on the spot as the two men dropped first onto their knees and then fell forward lifeless, the two dead bodies twitching as the bullets continued to be fired unmercifully into them.

Chapter Eighteen

Europe fell into a state of uneasy stillness as the European Union took steps to prevent further escalation of the situation in Sicily, in the aftermath of the three Scuds. There was a general acceptance that there was nothing that could be done about the presence of Libyan forces in Malta without endangering the civilian population, but there were frantic discussions between the European countries about the need to remove the threat of Libyan missiles. The British Prime Minister's report to the EU that a competent agent had been put in place to contact the Maltese Resistance, or what was left of it, with a view of sabotaging the Scud launchers, was received with applause by the European Union war council, formed when Turkey invaded Cyprus. No one thought to ask how it had been so quickly managed, and if they had they kept quiet; everyone knew that the missiles were a big threat to Europe and there didn't seem to be any other course of action available to them. Hopes for peace in Europe now hinged on a handful of men and a woman who still had no idea that the safety of Europe lay firmly in their hands.

*

"You are free to go, Major Zammud." Angelina said stepping backwards from Zammud's chair after cutting the tie wraps from his wrists that had secured him to the chair; her peculiar perfume wafting past Zammud as she did, she then joined the others in the darkness of the place they were in.

Zammud felt the imprint of the tie wraps that had been used to secure him, so he gently rubbed his wrists to ease some of the discomfort and at the same time rose to his feet; this action set of a series of clicks which Zammud recognized as weapons being armed. He had half expected his captors to take such a precaution, but had been taken unaware by the offer of freedom. *"There has to be a catch, maybe they plan to shoot me as leave and claim I was an escaping prisoner…yet Angelina?"* "What's the catch?" Zammud peered hard into the darkness to try to work out who these people were.

"There is no catch Major." Once more the disembodied voice that had been doing the interrogation spoke from the darkness. "Angelina…or rather we…may have a proposition for you."

"What proposition?" Zammud asked guardedly, still rubbing his wrists but more out of nervousness than necessity.

"Angelina seems to think that you would be happy to join us in our fight for freedom."

"So they are resistance, and I thought we had destroyed them all." "Why would I want to do that, I am a Libyan Officer my allegiance is to my country?"

Zammud heard some more whispering only this time he managed to pick up some of the conversation.

"I told you this was a waste of time," said the first voice angrily.

"We should kill him now and be done with it," said another.

Then as Zammud tried to prepare himself mentally for the worst, he heard the reassuring voice of the nurse who intrigued him so much. "No, please; I will try again."

He watched the darkness as Angelina approached him again from the shadows, and once more he could smell the aroma of her sweet perfume. *"Death has such a sweet fragrance,"* he thought.

"Major Zammud, we have been open and honest with you but we need your help; you say you are a Libyan soldier but surely you cannot agree with the way your country is violating ours?"

"No," Zammud spoke quietly. "But what you are suggesting is treason."

"Major, you are, as far as I can make out, already a traitor to your country; it is they who have betrayed your loyalty."

Zammud knew Angelina was speaking the truth so he took a moment to reflect on the choices. *"Angelina is right, at the present time I have no country; and the choices I have seem clear. I could give himself up to the Admiral, in which case I would probably be shot on the spot; 'Ahmed's fall guy', or run with these 'freedom fighters' and especially Angelina until the whole thing is sorted out; it can't go on forever, the Admiral will eventually be replaced and by then...I will have spent a lot more time with Angelina."*

"Ok" Zammud responded with a measure of resignation in his voice. "I'm with you."

Angelina smiled, "You will not regret your decision Major." As she spoke Zammud heard the various weapons being secured to the 'safe' position, and they all breathed easier.

Angelina welcomed Zammud with a hand shake that lingered just long enough to indicate to Zammud that she felt the same intriguing interest in him as he had for her; when the others came out of the darkness and welcomed him with hand shakes and smiles, there was an atmosphere of released tension surrounding Zammud, and he could almost taste it.

*

As far as Edward Sophia was concerned, the death of the American Pilot and the Assistant British Commissioner was unfortunate, but a worthwhile price to pay for the capture of the divers and whoever else was in the group of people now standing looking shocked with their hands reaching into the air. He had noticed that one of the group had tried to run to help the two who had fallen but was restrained by a very tall and attractive woman, he also noted that they all had weapons of various types, which he assumed were from the Maltese soldiers he had just noticed were there as well. Edward felt elated; it had so far turned out to be a very good day for police work, however what he didn't know was that two of Robbie's divers and a Maltese's soldier had responded to a 'call to nature', and were now considering their options as they slipped away unnoticed towards Kenuno Tower a short distance to the south of where their comrades now stood helpless.

The Chief Superintendent straightened his tunic awkwardly as he stood up to his fullest height; he considered it important to look his best for the coming arrests. Followed by his men he walked slowly and deliberately casual over to where Gaz and Betty were standing; Edward couldn't help noticing the look of defiance on both their faces as he drew near to them. When he stopped next to Gaz and Betty, he looked at the others but didn't see the same anger on their faces as he saw on the two people next to him; he came to the conclusion that these two must have known his dead prisoners personally, and took a mental note to 'interrogate' them first.

"You are all under arrest and will surrender your arms to my men." Even as he spoke the other policemen were already grabbing weapons from their captives. "Now you are guests of the Gozo Police shortly transport will arrive to take you to Victoria; where your fate will be decided by the Libyan governor in Malta, please do not try to escape, we wouldn't want to see more of this." Edward nodded towards the bullet mutilated bodies of Pete and James.

"You......murderer." Gaz shook himself free from Betty's grip and flung himself at the Chief Superintendent. "I'll kill you........." Even as he spoke Gaz grabbed at Edwards neck and started to apply pressure to his jugular veins.

"No Gaz!" Betty was screaming.

Edward felt his sight starting to blur, the blood flow to his brain dropping instantly to a trickle. He tried to grapple with Gaz's hands and shout for help to his policemen but the words wouldn't form; instead, fear started to enter into the equation as he thought for the first time in his life he was about to die. Then, as suddenly as the attack had come, Edward felt the pressure from Gaz's lethal grip ease. Choking to regain his breath and clear his mind he saw the form of his assailant lying still at his feet with the woman kneeling over him; he noticed she was now crying. "Get them out of here," stammered Edward angrily as he leaned against another policeman; Edward was relieved to be alive but his biggest concern now was how foolish he must have looked panicking under the death grip he had been in.

"Sir," one of his men was trying to get his attention. "The transport has not yet arrived...but it is on its way, I checked they said about ten minutes."

"Then they can start to walk," Edward croaked, still not fully recovered.

"Sir?"

"You heard me copper, get going."

As Betty and Robbie helped Gaz to his feet, the policemen started to surround them, shoving and pushing until they were formed into a tight group, heading south towards Victoria.

*

Admiral Ahmed was working quietly through his large pile of military bureaucracy when a young naval officer burst into his office. Normally he would have sprung to his feet and released a long line of threats at such an intrusion, but he was glad to be distracted from the mundane paperwork. He lifted his head slowly feigning a lack of interest, and noticed it was the lieutenant he had spoke to earlier from the communications room.

"Yes Lieutenant?"

"Sir…sorry to interrupt sir…but I have a message you might be interested in."

"Ah, you have found our Major Zammud?"

"No sir….but…."

"I gave you an order Lieutenant…. to find him, and I expect you to do that."

"Yes sir but this may be important."

"More important than your commission sailor?"

The young Libyan paused for a brief moment as though considering the risk to his future, then spoke once more. "Sir I think you will find this **is** very important."

"OK sailor I'm listening."

"Sir, we have just had a call from the Chief Superintendent in Victoria in Gozo; he says he has in his custody a team of British Navy divers, some Maltese Army defectors, but more importantly a British Euro MP and, he thinks, two military special duties personnel; one who is a woman."

Admiral Ahmed looked at his young Lieutenant as the message hit home: *"Ibraham's spies…it must be; and the divers, that means there* ***is*** *a submarine in these waters after all."* Ahmed sprang to his feet. "Get together a team of naval Marines, lieutenant and a chopper that is big enough to carry about twenty people; you and I are going to Gozo.

The young Lieutenant stood smartly to attention, this was his chance to impress his superiors, in particular the Admiral. “Count it done Sir.”

“Lets hope you do better with this assignment that the last.” He was referring to the still missing Major Zammud.

*

Tony sat on a chair in front of Edward Sophia’s desk; he was casually looking around himself, everything looked to him like a typical policeman’s office, with posters depicting various crimes and how to avoid them pinned up at various intervals along the walls. Edward was trying to look intimidating but he guessed that the European MP in front of him would not be easily scared, so he changed his tactic. “Would you like a drink of Cola or maybe something hot like tea or coffee?”

Tony continued to look around as if he had no interest in Edward at all.

“My friend we can sit here all day; it matters not to me.” Edward felt a growing impatience.

“I’ll have a cup of tea Old bean; breakfast if you can.”

Edward felt irritated by the heavily accented British man in front of him but decided not to let it overpower him. He got up from his desk and walked out of the office; a few moments later he re-appeared with a tray of tea for two. “Sugar….er?”

“Tony! ….And yes I take two lumps please.”

Edward put the cups down in front of Tony and sat down again taking a sip from his hot cup.

Tony lifted his cup and saucer and sipped his tea politely. “Thanks chum.”

Edward leaned forward and was about to say something when he heard a slight muffled sound from outside of his office that caught his attention. "Excuse me....Tony, I won't be a moment."

"Carry on old man, absolutely no problem." Tony's reply irritated Edward more.

When Edward stepped out of his office he should have been met by one of his men who should have been manning the public desk. *"He was here a moment ago,"* Edward thought as he looked around the outer office public area. He shouted for anyone to answer but there was no reply. *"Where are my officers?"* Edward stepped outside to the busy streets of Victoria, everything looked normal but there was no sign of his men anywhere. He walked back into the station and decided to look in the cells where his prisoners were, but when he arrived he got the shock of his life; the cells were all empty, there was no sign of anyone not even his officers. Edward started to feel his senses rise in a moment of panic. He took a short breath. *"This is not possible,"* then turned and ran back to his office. *"That smug British MP...I'll bet he's behind this...but how is this possible?"*

"Ah Chief Superintendent, I see you are back." Tony was now standing with Gaz, Robbie, Chris, Jerry and Betty.

Edward was about to say something when he felt the cold hard touch of a gun muzzle press into his side; he raised his hands slowly.

"Tch Tch Superintendent, you really should learn to count 'old man', you left two of us at Nadur and my colleagues behind you felt left out; they just had to come along and join us." Tony removed Edward's weapon from its leather holster as he spoke.

"What have you done with my men?" Edward was trying to keep his sense of dignity in the light if what looked like a complete and utter mess

“Unlike you we don’t shoot our prisoners.” Gaz was still angry with the Chief Policeman.

“They are safe Chief; locked up in cells and you will now be joining them,” Tony said nodding to the men behind Edward; they pushed their weapons into his side forcing him to oblige with their wishes.

“Right!” Robbie said, smiling at the others. “Let’s get oot ‘o’ this place its gee-in me the heebi jeebi’s”

“Where to now?” Betty asked.

“Malta,” Tony replied. “Didn’t I tell you….sorry….your mission young lady has changed, but all will be revealed soon?”

They borrowed a Gozo bus that was trying to negotiate the large groups of refugees still looking for a place to rest; the passengers and driver offered no argument as the two divers who had rescued the team produced their small arms as an encouragement to disembark. As Robbie drove them towards Mgarr, Tony and Jerry did their best to explain how the whole scenario had changed with the threat of the Scuds; they sat in silence as their new mission was outlined and when they were finished the weight of the task was only lifted when they heard Robbie’s broad Scottish, voice.

“Mgarr straight ahead ma bony wee bairns!”

*

Admiral Ahmed and his small troop of marines landed their Chinook at the football stadium near Nuffara point just outside Victoria. They quickly disembarked and headed up the minor road that ironically Edward Sophia had brought his prisoners from Nadur along a few hours earlier.

“Are you sure you know where the Police Station is?” Ahmed, turned to the Lieutenant at his side, “I do not like to waste my time.”

"Absolutely Admiral, we did a Sat Scan and I have the direction finder with us; it's just as you go into the town, about ten minutes walk sir."

When they did finally arrive Ahmed sent his marines in first and when the building was 'safe' he went inside, instructing his Lieutenant to remain outside to 'keep watch'.

Ahmed found the station empty and silent. "Where are the policemen?" He asked a marine who was walking from the direction of the cells; he came directly to attention. "Sir I think you should follow me."

He followed the marine until he saw locked behind the bars of the numerous cells, several policemen, one of them had the rank flashes of a high ranking policeman.

"Chief Superintendent Sophie I presume." Ahmad spoke with a slight smile on his face.

Edward felt embarrassed. "They tricked us Admiral; I had them all here, up till two hours ago."

"And where are they now then?"

"I don't know."

Ahmed turned to go but stopped when Edward interrupted him again, "Aren't you going to let us out?"

The Admiral spoke to his nearest marine loudly so that the imprisoned police could hear him. "Marine, ensure this building is 'cleansed' before you leave." Then he walked calmly out of the station ignoring the pleadings of the Chief Superintendent.

"Lieutenant!" Ahmed shouted, ducking slightly as two grenades exploded dully within the inner reaches of the Police Station, "Our spies have left."

"Sir I have been asking around and there are some people here who claim they were forced off a bus by a group of British men a gunpoint."

"Did they give you any idea where they might have gone?"

Yes. Sir…they are headed towards Mgarr."

Ahmed thought for a moment, *"Why would they want to go to Mgarr?"* "Lieutenant; good work, take six men and get down to Mgarr as quickly as you can, I will take the Chinook back to Malta and we will wait at Marfa just in case they manage to escape you; they cannot get far…what ever they are up to." Ahmed was about to leave, but stopped when he had an after thought. "Oh, Lieutenant, these people are spies; we do not take spies as prisoners….is that clear?"

"Aye…. Aye, Sir." The lieutenant saluted and then turned, his face had suddenly drained of its blood as the seriousness of the situation impacted his mind.

Chapter Nineteen

"The first thing we need," Angelina pointed out as though she were about to go on a shopping trip, "Is weapons and then some training on how to use them."

They were all sitting together in a house in Gzira around a wooden table where a woman had offered them cooled water when they arrived but had said nothing to the group; she was now nowhere to be seen.

Zammud looked around the walls of the house they were in and noticed signs of dampness; with much of the paint now falling into little piles of flakes on the skirting. Through a partly open door he could see a young boy fully absorbed and apparently unaware of their presence, playing on a TV video game. Zammud felt confused with the speed of events that were now overtaking his life, from the shock of finding himself in one of the ancient inner rooms of the Tarxien Temples, where his 'interrogation' had taken place, to the now almost ordinary settings of someone's living room, he wondered if he had agreed too easily or whether his reasons for agreeing were transparent to the other two men sitting opposite him and Angelina; it made him feel weak and foolish.

He tried to change his train of thought. "How many men and woman do we have?" He asked in an almost professional military manner; but there was an uneasy quietness before one of the other two men at the table responded. "Major…there are only the three of us here."

Zammud thought he had misheard so cautiously asked the question again.

"There is only us three and yourself, there were others but most of them are now in prison or dead."

"If they are in Libyan prisons they are as good as dead," thought Zammud, reflecting on this new piece of information, he lowered his head onto his hands feeling exhaustion suddenly flush through his whole being.

"We have taken a vow to the death Major."

Angelina's voice seemed to bring Zammud out of the hypnotic weariness he was feeling, he lifted his head slowly with a feeling of regret. "That is what will probably happen to us all….what do you consider are your chances against the whole of the Libyan detachment here; there are now probably between nine and ten thousand professional and well trained soldiers scattered around the Island?" Zammud got up from his chair and flung his hands into the air almost mocking the small group and their intentions. He turned to face them, his face set in a fierce expression. "You have no chance at all."

"Then," Angelina was now standing up to face Zammud, her perfume causing him to soften his stance as the fragrance once more invaded his senses, she gazed directly into his eyes, "We will all die trying."

Zammud started to walk backward and forward in front of the others as they sat in silence; he was deep in thought as to what to do next.

"We need weapons and training Major." Angelina tried reminding him of the original plan before she sat down opposite the other two Maltese.

The next few moments passed in silence as Zammud continued pacing backwards and forwards trying to put together a safe and reasonable plan in his mind, but no matter how hard he looked at their position, he could not see any way of avoiding any suicidal actions. The he stopped and looked at the three eager faces in front of him. "There is one place where we can get weapons, if you are up to it?"

Angelina sprang from her seat full of enthusiasm, "I knew you could help," she said as she flung her arms around Zammud and kissed his cheek. Zammud didn't know what to do, he felt embarrassed by the outward show of Angelina's affection, but he also noticed that the other two didn't seem even to notice. As Angelina pulled away from him her perfume lingered around him, causing his legs to go weak and his head to swim. *"Dam that perfume."*

"Where is this place?" Asked one of the men at the table interrupting Zammud's thoughts; he had a familiar look about him that Zammud had recognized on occasion but couldn't place.

"Marfa Ridge!" The words had just left Zammud's mouth when he remembered who the familiar man was; a vision of a gentle stranger with a blue cross walking through the flames and the smoke of battle, flashed before him mind.

*

Gaz, Betty, Tony, Jerry and the others had parked their bus just beyond the point to the right of Mgarr Harbour; the last thing they wanted was to be seen by any more of the Gozo Police, they assumed that every policeman on the island would by now be looking for them, however they didn't know about Ahmed's visit to Victoria, or his ruthless way of dealing with 'apparent failure'. They were all casually stretching and checking their personal bits and pieces when Robbie shouted out in an obvious panic, he had walked few hundred yards in front of the group to do a 'point' guard with two of his men. "Libyans are coming!"

He had only just finished shouting when the first of the bullets from the Libyan's automatic weapons strafed the road to either side of him as he ran back towards the bus with his men. From behind Robbie came a scream and a groan as one of his men fell to the ground dying as the white hot metal found the first of its targets. Robbie continued to run as did the other diver, swaying from side to side to give the Libyan shooters less of a stable target and at the same time waving his arms to encourage the others to move quickly, when they arrived back at the bus, panting from the effort of the almost panic run, Gaz and Chris and the others where already firing back with the small police Glock pistols they had managed to 'commandeer' from the Station at Victoria. As they all cowered behind the old Gozo bus, they could hear the sound of hundred's of bullets tearing into the flimsy metal sides of the bus. Gaz and Chris continued to fire back and although it was enough to keep the cautious Libyans at bay, they all knew that sooner or later they would be beaten.

"So," Robbie was still hiding as he struggled to get his breath from the stress of having just cheated death by moments, "They must ken aboot us by now, why else would they have chased us and fired without any warning?"

Gaz leaned back into cover from the side of the bus where he has been firing from. "So what's your point Robbie….its hardly the time for analyzing?" Gaz glanced to see if Betty was ok as he talked to Robbie; she was behind the bus covering her ears from the noise; there was nothing else she could do as there was not enough small arms to go round.

"You, Betty, the Wing Commander, and the MP need to get going oot of here; dae ye ken whit I'm saying?"

"Were not leaving anyone Robbie." Gaz was shocked at even the suggestion.

Robbie grabbed Gaz by his collar and flung him against the side of the bus. "Noo look here wee man, we dinni hae time fur a debate, the Libyans will kill us all anyway, so you need to get these Scuds oot of action for us all or this will be a waste….understand?"

"But!" Gaz realized the terrible truth that was now facing them.

"Git goin Gaz, I widdni like to see whit the Libyan's might do wi your Betty; there's nae time fur arguing, just get oot of here."

Without saying another word Gaz pushed Robbie to the side and went to get Betty, Tony, and Jerry together. After a few moments he turned, looked at Robbie, then the four of them left, heading for the harbour and one of the many abandoned boats there.

Robbie stood watching them for a short time as the blitz of bullets continued to noisily rattle the bus; soon it would be so badly damaged that it would offer no cover for them. He signaled to Chris, and after offering to cover him and his men's retreat, he turned his attention to the fire fight once more.

"Were getting low on ammo, Chief," one of the divers to his side shouted just a moment before he was struck instantly dead by a Libyan bullet that passed cleanly through his head. Robbie knew it was near the end of his 'mission'; he turned to see if Gaz and the others were out of danger, but he couldn't see for the rocky cliffs behind him, he was however surprised to see Chris and his men still with him and his divers. He shouted across, "I thought I told you to go Captain?"

"Now come on Chief, since when did rankers give orders to Captains?" He smiled cheerily as he replied.

Robbie half saluted before he returned to the job in hand; then he noticed to his dismay three or four Libyan's running forward with grenades in their hands. "Shoot those - ," was the last order Master Diver McMaster gave as a series of explosions rocked the entire area and the fragmenting grenades did their gory work..

When the young Libyan Lieutenant and his men arrived at what remained of the bus, they were surprised to see a Priest kneeling over the bodies of the fallen Maltese soldiers. One of the Libyan soldiers; a sergeant, raised his pistol to 'finish the job' but the Lieutenant pushed the mussel of the weapon down.

"Were finished here," he said, looking at the weeping Priest placing a strange coloured scarf around his neck and kissing it.

"But sir the Admiral said there were to be no survivors."

The Lieutenant glanced threateningly at the soldier, "I said; we are finished here soldier."

"Yes **sir**." The sergeant decided it would be prudent not to push the point.

As he and the other Libyan's walked away from their handiwork, the Lieutenant looked at the priest for a moment longer; he came to attention, saluted, then smartly turned and left the only survivor; Father Dominique Caruana, to his religious duties.

*

Admiral Ahmed was standing at the ferry terminal at Marfa Point; he had moved down from the ridge when he was told of firing coming from Mgarr across the channel. There was no doubt in his mind that the young Lieutenant, he had tasked with finding the divers, had not only found them but was now removing the nuisance they would have become. Still he felt uneasy about the whole scenario; there was the nagging question of why they were here in the first place, and why they would take the huge risk of coming across to the mainland of Malta. To try to alleviate some of his fears, he had ordered a small Libyan Navy Corvette to patrol the channel south of Comino; just in case. His years as a naval Officer had trained him to always check out doubts or hunches. Precaution often revealed pitfalls in time; or in this case possible mistakes or incompetence, Ahmed trusted no one. As he watched from the point, he saw with some satisfaction the Corvette coming slowly round the sea ward side of Malta in a 'search and rescue' approach; or in this particular case 'search and destroy'. Ahmed wasn't sure what they were looking for and there were still plenty of small boats in the water either returning or fleeing from Malta, although they had decreased in number as time had gone on, but his troubled doubts were strong enough to command the search anyway. "If in doubt," he had told the Lieutenant in charge of the Corvette over the radio, "Blow them all out of the water." He knew that even that approach could never be guaranteed to be one hundred percent effective, but it would certainly reduce the odds. However, he didn't even know at this time if there was any reason to; it was just a 'feeling' that would not go away. There was something else on his mind but he couldn't draw it out from his memory, there were too many things going on for him to concentrate properly.

*

Captain Ross Morgan was becoming impatient with his role as a submarine commander; he was not the sort of man to be impressed with the latent power he had control of; he wanted to use it occasionally. He was itching for 'action' and felt that while others were fully engaged with the present crisis, he and his crew were languishing on the bottom of the sea off the coast of Gozo. The pilot they had surfaced for and rescued, had involved some danger and Ross had thrived in the adrenalin rush it provided, but now as he lay on his bunk he could hear the mundane sounds of the subs routine and the inactivity was starting to frustrate his eagerness. He turned onto his side and tried to sleep it off, but he was far too on edge to relax, so instead he got up and walked along to the sub's control centre to chat with the duty officer.

Chief Roland turned his swivel chair to acknowledge Ross as he arrived at the centre, then he returned to the task he was performing with a sonar scope. Other than the occasional sound of men talking, everything was running in a well rehearsed routine.

"How's the shift?" Ross asked, speaking to the Duty Officer in an attempt at generating some sort of conversation.

"Quiet sir," he sounded as bored as Ross felt.

"Go get yourself a coffee or something lad, I'll take over here."

"Aye, aye sir." The Junior Officer made no attempt to hide his joy.

After the young officer left, Chief Roland turned to face Ross in his swivel chair. "Couldn't sleep again sir?"

"No chief I feel a bit unsettled today."

"No change there sir."

Ross ignored his Chief's comment. "What are you up to Chief?"

"Oh, this, just doing a bit of fine tuning on the sonar, sir…no big deal really."

"Oh!" Ross commented, disappointment once more returning. *"Things don't even break in this can."* "If you need anything Chief, just let me know."

"Aye, Aye, sir."

Chief Roland had just turned his chair to face the consol again when he noticed a faint sonar pulse appear on his 'un-tuned' consol. "Sir…something is showing on the surface."

"What is it Chief?"

"It's hard to tell sir. I have had the equipment 'offline' for servicing so we are a bit off tune; we are lucky to hear this one, what ever it is."

Roland worked franticly to restore the sonar to its full working state and when he had finished the familiar sonic tone was echoing loud in the control room. "It's a Corvette sir or something of that type."

Ross felt the excitement rise within him. "Get me periscope Chief."

"Aye aye sir….it's all yours." Even as he spoke the periscope rose through the control room decks and Ross placed the eye rubbers to his face.

"It's a Corvette alright Chief, Libyan by the looks of it doing search and rescue sweeps - good lord they are firing at small boats, down scope."

"What's going on sir?" The Chief was looking with concern at Ross.

"They must be looking for something, but firing on suspicious looking boats…maybe….just in case. Give me periscope again Chief."

Once more the scope rose up from the metal decking of the sub and into Ross's arms. He swung round looking in every direction then refocused on the Libyan Corvette. "Ah it looks like what we said Chief, he's looking for something or……" Ross stopped talking as he fumbled with the focus controls of the periscope; he was peering hard into the eye sockets of the equipment. "Chief come, have a look at this small Maltese fishing boat."

Roland had never known his Captain ask for an opinion of a periscope view before so he hesitated briefly.

"Come on man, hurry or we may miss this."

Intrigued, Roland got to his feet and looked into the viewer. "No…it can't be!" He said stepping back from the periscope.

"That's what I thought," said Ross.

"So that's why the Corvette is doing the sweeps, its looking for Gaz and Betty our two agents, what are you going to do?" The Chief's voice was now full of concern.

"I noticed they had two other men in their boat and both had helicopter flying overalls on…hmmm…..Chief contact CNC we need permission to intervene on this one."

While the Chief was away from the control centre sending off their finding to CNC Norfolk, Ross paced the floor; it would only take an instance to send the message, but Ross knew that CNC sometimes took their time in replying, and that was why he was taken by surprise when the Roland returned with a piece of paper in his hand only a few moments later; Ross noticed a large smile on his face.

MESSAGE ADMIRALTY CNC NORFOLK STOP
TREAT ANY LIBYAN ACTIVITY IN YOU AREA AS HOSTILE STOP
TWO HELICOPTER PERSONEL AS FOLLOWS
WING COMMANDER SHOTTS OC BRITISH BASE IN SICILY - AND
EURO MP ANTONY DAVIDSON STOP
IMPERATIVE THEY ARE PICKED UP STOP
WHEN OPERATION COMPLETE YOUR POSITION WILL BE
COMPROMISED MOVE TO ....

Ross didn't read the rest; he too was now smiling at the prospect of some action at last. "Chief Roland, prepare to surface, prime tubes one and two for firing...oh and while your at it, we better sound 'action stations', keeps the troops on their toes eh Chief?"

"Aye, Aye, Captain, it does seem appropriate sir."

Roland smiled; the atmosphere in the Submarine suddenly felt 'lighter'.

*

Gaz, Betty, Jerry and Tony had managed to slip away unnoticed from Mgarr harbour, as they started the outboard motor on the small boat they had found, they could still hear the sounds of firing from not so far behind them. Each was lost in their own thoughts as they silently pushed the boat out to sea. They were still in silence when they heard four explosions behind them, and then the awful quietness that always seems to hang heavily in the air after a battle. Betty started to weep as Gaz said, "Grenades have finished it." The others were numbed. Nothing more was said as Gaz piloted the small unstable fishing boat out to sea and in the general direction of Malta. Gaz had hoped to land around the top side of Malta in the bay at Mellieha, but these hopes were suddenly dashed. They heard a large gun being fired somewhere to their front and as they continued on, a Libyan Corvette suddenly came into view; it had just fired at, and sunk, an innocent Maltese refugee boat, similar to the one they were now in.

They now realized that only a miracle could save them and Gaz looked in sadness at Betty whose eyes said everything that needed to be said between them.

*

Admiral Ahmed was now following the progress of his Corvette with satisfaction. He made a mental note to get the name of the Corvettes commander; he needed more men like him who were prepared to be ruthless in carrying out his orders. He watched without feeling as another Maltese fishing boat started to sink as a result of the Corvettes search, but there had still not been any report of anything out of place from the normal. Then he saw the Corvette turn and head towards another boat that was heading out to sea to pass the headland to the north. He raised his powerful navy binoculars once more to bring the scene closer, and then something inside of him began to sink. Just behind the Corvette, still unnoticed, was a large area of water bubbling as though it was suddenly boiling; and he knew right away it had to be the 'as yet unconfirmed' British Submarine.

Ahmed knew there was nothing he could do, even as he watched, the first of the two spearfish torpedoes hit the Corvette with an eye blinding explosion that shook the ground he was standing on. Then he watched as the black shape of the Vanguard Class submarine broke through the surface of the sea, the same question still running around his mind unanswered; *"Why, and who are these people, what are they here for?"* The Admiral had guessed that the sub was responding to the four people in the small boat coming from the direction of Gozo, and that could only mean one thing; his Lieutenant had failed to eliminate all the suspects that were in the Chief Superintendent's custody. *"I'll have his commission,"* he thought to himself as he turned to leave Marfa Point; the sound of another Spearfish torpedo now finding its target.

*

When Captain Morgan gave the order to surface, he also broke all his tactical training by ordering tubes one and two to be fired as the sub was on its way to the surface. As his 'ship' broke the surface of the Mediterranean he heard the explosion caused by the first torpedo hitting its target. It must have hit the ammunition store of the Corvette because the explosion was fiercer that he had expected. That was followed by a second lesser explosion that confirmed his first assessment of the situation. When he and the duty officer climbed into the look-out part of the sub's 'sail' all they could see was debris all over the surface of the sea, but no sign of a Corvette.

Ross buzzed down to where Roland was waiting with some of the men. "Chief, no sign of the Corvette, we must have hit the ammo store, but I can see the fishing boat....get the lads ready to receive it, and be quick Chief, we don't want to attract any unwelcome Libyan aircraft ."

"Aye, aye Boss."

Chief Roland passed out SA.80's before he took his men out onto the deck of the now fully surfaced submarine, then they waited until they could see the small boat start to head towards them.

*

Gaz, Betty, Jerry and Tony had expected the worst when they saw the Libyan Corvette turn in their direction;

they all thought that 'it was over' and had resigned themselves to an uncertain future when the Corvette suddenly and without any warning bust into a bright fireball of flying debris. Gaz flung himself onto the floor and pulled Betty down with him, the other two automatically followed suit and they lay there still as they heard another smaller explosion. The small boat they were in was rocking violently from the aftershock of the first explosion and at one point Gaz wondered if the boat would capsize. He held Betty down trying to protect her with his own body until the noises they were hearing around them changed to a familiar and very loud sea churning sound that Gaz couldn't place.

Jerry heard the same noise and decided to lift his head out of curiosity, fully expecting someone to try to take it off, but when he did, he understood. He reached over to Gaz without saying anything and indicated that he should look up as well. Gaz looked up and so did Betty. "It's our miracle Gaz," she said as she pulled herself fully back onto the small boats seat.

There was a feeling of excited elation as Gaz once more maneuvered the fishing boat, this time towards the waiting sub. When they reached the side of the huge underwater 'mammoth' Gaz looked up to see Ross high in the sail.

"We meet again Blue job, how come we always have to rescue you fellows?"

Gaz waved as he helped Betty and the others off the fishing boat, then, when he himself was eventually pulled up by the Chief's men, the Chief reached out and shook Gaz's hand. "Welcome on board sir…its good to see you again."

"Come on ladies," shouted Ross. "We can't hang about while you two renew your acquaintances…..Mohammed might want to join in."

"He's right sir," Roland said to Gaz. "We better get going….the Libyans aren't going to like what we did to their nice boat."

As Gaz slipped through a hatch at the bottom of the 'sail' he could here Ross shouting into the internal communications system a relaxed but none-the-less urgent order. "Dive, Dive, and lets not hang about gentlemen."

Within minutes the submarine had disappeared under the deep dark waters, the only indication that it had been there were the scattered fragments of the decimated Corvette and an empty Maltese fishing boat. Moments later a lone Libyan 'Foxbat' reconnaissance fighter flew over the area scrambled from Tripoli, but by then the Vanguard Class Submarine was well on its way to its new co-ordinates, south of Malta.

Chapter Twenty

News of the massacre of the Policemen in Gozo became CNN's top story and spread world wide bringing instant condemnation from all the Western nations, and in particular the European Union. From that came allegations of atrocities against the Maltese people and a strong demand from America that all Libyan forces withdraw from Malta. Libya retaliated by claiming that Britain had committed an act of escalation by allowing one of its submarines to operate and sink a Libyan vessel on legitimate patrol duties in the Mediterranean. What they didn't mention was what those duties were. Once more there seemed to be an impasse and in response a British Naval blockade was positioned off the coast of Libya to prevent further supplying of their garrison in Malta. Libya countered by firing another Scud missile into Sicily and threatening more should the blockade remain. The European War Council were tempted to fire a Trident in retaliation at Tripoli from Captain Ross's Submarine well within range, but the Americans intervened and applied pressure to hold for the moment; all hope seemed to rest on destroying the Scud launchers on the ground in Malta; everything possible was being tried to prevent full 'out and out' war in the Med.

*

Major Zammud and the other three resistance members decided to wait until it was dark, before heading out of their 'safe house' in Gzira. They all quietly slipped into an old grey Mercedes that had lost its comfort appeal years earlier and set off towards Marfa Ridge. Zammud was now dressed in typical Maltese civilian clothes as were the others; mostly tea shirts and shorts but they all carried a hand gun each which Zammud had warned must only to be used in an absolute emergency. It wasn't that he felt any compassion for his fellow Libyans; it was purely a logistical matter of a limited amount of ammo.

They decided to avoid the coast road as it had become the favoured route of the Libyan heavy artillery, and transport supplies for the build up of its Forces at the North East of the Island; taking instead the route through Mosta then on to Zebbieh to catch the track that would take through Manikata. They were all aware that sooner or later they would have to drive the main road from Mellieha to get to Marfa Ridge, but they had no choice, from Manikata onward, they would be in considerable danger, but they all accepted the risks. In fact, apart from the holes in the surface of the road from Manikata, the journey proved to be without incident and as the four entered Mellieha town, they were surprised to see the streets free and empty of any sign of Libyan forces.

Angelina was sitting beside Zammud in the rear seats of the Mercedes as the others drove on through the quiet centre of the town. He could see the rows of tourists shops that had now been boarded up by their owners, perhaps hoping for better days to come again, but that wasn't his main concern, as the car started to take the steep and winding road out of Mellieha, Zammud had become conscious of Angelina's closeness; her leg was touching his leg and he was feeling very uncomfortable. He looked at her in the darkness and saw her smile briefly before she turned her head to look out of her window; Zammud realized he was sweating heavily and it wasn't the night heat of the late summer. Then there was the perfume! He found it hard to concentrate when he was near to her. He was still in a trance when the Mercedes came screeching to a stop. "What the…..?"

The male nurse who had rescued him from the battle field turned from his front seat and pointed ahead "Libyan check point."

Zammud looked forward towards the bottom of the winding road they were on and saw a roundabout, where, sure enough, there were two Libyan guards.

"What will we do now?" One of the Male nurses asked.

"Drive on," Angelina said before Zammud could say anything, "I know how to handle these two soldiers."

As the car moved forward towards the roundabout one of the guard's waived at them to stop.

"What are you going to do?" Zammud asked Angelina.

Angelina smiled, "Same as I do to you my handsome Major." There was an impish look in her eyes.

Before Zammud could stop her, when he realized what she intended, Angelina was already out of the car and walking sensually towards the two guards.

Zammud felt a pinch of jealousy as he watched Angelina flirting with the Libyan guards; he wondered what she was telling them as she kept on pointing towards the car and the soldiers laughed with her. Then, unexpectedly, Angelina walked back towards the Merc on Zammud's side and opened the door. "Get out Major, and do exactly as I tell you."

Zammud puzzled by the command in Angelina's voice slipped out of the car, he was only just out of his seat when Angelina grabbed him and said, "Kiss me Major and make sure its convincing."

He glanced at the two guards who seemed to be waiting expectantly, then without saying anything he kissed Angelina but he didn't need to act as though he meant it.

Angelina had to push Zammud back slightly. “Steady Major,” she said looking into his eyes, I’m your ‘escort’, not your girlfriend.”

“What have you told them?” Zammud asked in a breathless whisper.

“The truth; you are a Libyan Major going to examine the battle at the ridge, I’m just your ‘pick-up’ going along for the fun of it.” She looked into Zammud’s eyes as though looking for something, “You did mean the kiss, didn’t you…you weren’t pretending?”

Zammud didn’t answer.

“Oh no,” said Angelina, suddenly serious, “This can’t be….you better go and talk to your men, have a rude joke with them about me.” She pushed Zammud from her and turned him towards the guards, giving him a gentle push in their direction. “Zammud,” she said as he started to walk towards the two guards, “Be careful.” As the Major walked towards the check point the others prepared their hand guns; Angelina had just sat into her seat in the Merc when the male nurse turned round, “I told you it could get complicated.”

Angelina blushed but said nothing as she ‘readied’ her pistol with cold determination.

*

Gaz and the others waited in the Ward Room inside the massive submarine; a young sailor had brought them tea and coffee along with some hurried sandwiches and a few freshly baked cakes, which they devoured hungrily; the sight of the food reminding them that it had been a long time since they had eaten anything. Now with most of the food gone and the tea and coffee consumed, they waited patiently on Captain Ross’s arrival. There wasn’t much to say but Gaz felt unsettled and paced the floor of the Ward

Room; the only sound he could hear was the low gentle hum of the submarines nuclear powered engines.

"You might as well sit down Gaz, and relax," said Tony watching him pace the floor. "It could take a while before Captain Ross has re – sited the submarine."

"Gaz isn't the type to hang around and do nothing Sir," Betty commented. "Besides that, the last meeting with Captain Ross was a bit of a 'testosterone' event for them both."

Jerry laughed. "Well let's hope things have moved on; there's been a lot of water passed under the bridge since then, young lady."

Gaz said nothing he was thinking back in response to the Wing Commanders words. *"He's right, so much had happened in such a short time; so many friends gone forever, and now married?"* He felt a tear forming in his eyes and Betty noticed it.

"Gaz come and sit down with me; I'm sure it won't be long now."

Jerry and Tony also noticed Gaz's tears but said nothing; they realized he had been through more that any of them had. As Gaz sat down heavily beside Betty on one of the soft 'E plan' sofa's that lined the Ward Room walls; they heard Captain Morgan's foot steps coming towards them.

Everyone stood up when he eventually entered the ward Room, with the exception of Gaz; he wasn't being deliberately rude, although he might not have stood up under other circumstances, but he felt heavy with grief and weariness which for the moment held him in a sort of paralyses.

"Welcome gentlemen…..and ladies. I trust you have been well looked after by my crew…please take your seats." Ross glanced at Gaz but said nothing.

"Accommodation has been prepared for you all in my officer's area towards the front of the ship; I am waiting on CNC at Norfolk giving me instructions as to what we should do with you all."

Gaz looked up at Ross his voice shaky but determined. "Captain we already have our orders."

"Orders, that I am not aware of….. Mr. Seymour."

Tony now felt an obvious unhealthy tension between the two men. "Captain Morgan."

"Ross. Please call me Ross."

"Ross," Tony continued. "You obviously know who we are; I am EMP Tony Davidson British Ambassador to the European Parliament, and this is Wing Commander Shotts. Commander of the British Forces in Sicily, we do indeed have our orders as Gaz has pointed out, now I ……."

Ross didn't allow Tony to finish. "Sir on this boat I am the senior Officer and you are my guests until I hear from CNC."

"Then," answered Jerry. "I suggest you get on with your communications Captain, it is important that we are put back on Malta."

"Look Wing Commander, I have lost the whole team of divers that we sent to find Mr. Seymour, and I still haven't heard from Robbie, so until I have clear instructions from CNC I cannot take any more chances; this is after all a Nuclear Sub and we have already risked being compromised twice on account of Gaz, Betty and the American…." Ross stopped for a moment and looked at Gaz, "Where is the American flyer?"

Betty looked at Gaz who was staring at the floor, she knew he couldn't answer so she spoke through quavering lips, "James, I'm afraid, is dead." Betty kept her face set firm so as not to give into the grief she felt.

"I'm so sorry," Ross replied genuinely shocked at the news.

"There's more Captain," Betty added. "Robbie and the other divers; they also died defending our escape so we could continue with our mission, that's why it is important that we get back to the Mainland."

Ross sat down when he heard about Robbie and the other divers. "I'm so sorry," continued Betty. "They didn't stand a hope of defeating the Libyan soldiers who chased us, it was an act of bravery; they were great men, we shall miss them all very, very much."

When Betty had finished speaking Gaz burst into a full show of grief; he groaned loudly as the tears ran down his face, and as Betty pulled him into the comfort of her shoulder, he wept openly; his whole body trembling with intermittent spasms. Captain Ross rose from his seat and quietly left followed by Tony and Jerry, leaving Betty and Gaz alone to share their grief privately.

*

Admiral Ahmed had become a man obsessed with a single purpose; find the 'spies' who had been rescued by the British Submarine. As a tactical genius he had reasoned that whatever it was they were on their way to Malta to do, the chances are they would still be planning to carry it out. He also came to the conclusion that if a Nuclear submarine operating in the area was prepared to compromise its position, then it had to be important and that could mean only one thing; the Scuds. At the back of his mind he also remembered that Major Zammud was still missing, and it was niggling at him for some reason he could not work out.

When he arrived back at San Anton Palace that evening, without wasting any time, he walked into the communications centre and ordered an immediate build up of all coastal patrols; as yet they had not any reconnaissance aircraft, such as the Foxbat that had returned to Libya, but he did have several Corvettes and a lot of men and vehicles. The order was simple, "If anyone tries to land from the sea into Malta; shoot to kill ….with no exceptions;" from that point on, the Island became isolated from the outside world.

Ahmed knew now that all he had to do now was wait on the 'spies' making the next move, so he walked back along to his Palacial Office, shouting for his secretary; but there was not response. Once in his office he picked up his phone and shouted at the sergeant who answered from the communications centre. "Where is my secretary?"

"Sir," came a shaky answer in reply. "She hasn't been seen since….after…the….em…!"

Ahmed growled at the sergeant before slamming the phone back down on its receiver. He was growing impatient with what he considered to be gross incompetence among his men when his phone buzzed again.

"Yes!" He growled again.

"Admiral we think we have news of Major Zammud sir."

"You think, isn't good enough, I want facts"

"Sir two guards at Mellieha are sure he was the missing Major. He was dressed in civvies and accompanied by two Maltese men and one woman, but they said he even claimed to be the Major, sir."

"Any idea what he was doing there?"

"Yes sir, the guards said he was going to inspect the battle site at Marfa point, but they didn't finish the report….the line went dead sir."

Ahmed ignored the latter part of message; guards were easily replaced but something didn't make sense. "Why would he……?" He stopped in mid sentence, the shocking answer forming in his mind.

"Sir?" The voice on the other end of the phone sounded puzzled.

"By Allah….its the weapons; he must be after the discarded weapons."

"Sir?"

"Stop saying sir and get me a good armed gun ship….it seems that our Major Zammud may have changed sides."

When Ahmed had put the phone down he began to pace backwards and forwards across the floor of his office; he knew that getting a gun ship armed and ready would take a while and all he could do now was wait.

*

Zammud had felt uneasy talking to the two guards about the fictitious relationship he was having with Angelina. Although it seemed to work, and the guards let them pass, Zammud had a feeling it had been too easy, and as they drove away past the bay on their right he turned in his seat to glance back; to his horror he saw one of the guards on a field telephone.

"Stop the car." He shouted, his sudden command causing the driver to automatically slam his foot on the brake pedal.

"Zammud…what are you doing?" Angelina asked, gripping hold of the seat in front, but Zammud was already out of the Mercedes and running towards the two Libyan guards. They saw him coming and tried to reach their AK-47's which were lying at the side of the road, but their apathy towards their duties was their downfall. As he ran Zammud fired his pistol without stopping until he heard his weapon click and his ammo run out; by that time the two soldiers were lying still at the roundabout in a large pool of their own blood. Angelina was out of breath when she and the other two Maltese caught up with him.

"What are you doing…are you mad?" Angelina was annoyed at the brutal and seemingly unnecessary waste of life.

"I knew it was too easy; they knew who we are."

"How is that possible?" The driver of the Mercedes was bending over the two bodies to check if they were dead; he nodded to confirm that they were.

"The Admiral has probably primed the guards to look out for me."

"Why not arrest us then?" The other Maltese man asked as he picked up the AK-47's. "These might be handy," he added.

"I don't know," Zammud replied, but we better get out of here quickly. "The guards managed to phone before I brought them down, so we can be sure they will be looking for us soon."

The four turned quickly and ran back to the waiting Mercedes. Once they were all in, the driver slammed the throttle to the floor and the car sped off to the shrill sound of screeching tires burning on the uneven road surface with a strong acrid smell coming from the friction stressed rubber wheels. If anyone in the local houses near to the roundabout saw anything, there was no indication from the darkened windows.

*

Admiral Ahmed was almost bursting with violent anger by the time he received word that a helicopter had been sent from Luqa, as he had requested, and that it would be with them within minutes. He had wanted to shout at the sailor who had brought the message but decided that it would be a waste of time; especially when he saw how frightened the sailor was. *"I wonder how he drew the short straw,"* went through Ahmed's mind, but when he noticed the sailors rank badge he guessed the reason. After dismissing the young rating he glanced at his watch; it had taken over an hour to get the helicopter ready and as far as Ahmed was concerned, that was far too long. He decided to have a little chat to the pilot about 'readiness'. Ahmed put on his ‘berry’ and walked back down the long corridor towards the Palace courtyard. He kept his eyes to the tiled floor to avoid looking at anyone; he was saving his frustration for the pilot, but when he looked at the helicopter as he arrived at the courtyard, he face lit up and he immediately forgot about his anger over the perceived delay: There in the orange bathed light of the courtyard’s sodium lamps, stood one of Libya’s latest reconnaissance and ground attack ‘chopper’s; the Ka-52 Alligator a Russian build gun-ship based on the Kamov Ka-50 Black Shark.

Ahmed turned towards the young pilot his face transformed from anger to wonder. “When did these arrive on the island?” As he spoke he reached out his hand to touch the cold surface of the aircraft.

“Three came four days ago Sir; but this is the first to be put together and ready for duty.”

“What have we got for this mission Airman?”

“Sir, at the moment all we have is the 2A42 30-mm rapid fire gun; but for the brief I have, it should do the trick nicely.”

“I’m sure it will Airman, I’m sure it will.” Ahmed was still lost in admiration for the deadly machine.

“Well; can we go then?” Asked Ahmed; pulling himself out of the momentary idolatry.

“Yes sir.”

They both climbed into the cramped cockpit of the Alligator and after putting on the ‘HUD’ helmets, the pilot primed the two turbo shaft engines; the coaxial rotors blades that give the Ka-52 its amazing maneuverability, slowly came to life. Within minutes they were off the ground and ‘dipping’ towards Marfa.

“Now you are in for a very big surprise Major Zammud,” thought Ahmed as he ran his hand gently over the Alligators internal computer consoles and switches. “There is only one thing you need to know, Admiral;” the

pilot said as they took off, "How to work the ejection seat, however unlikely that might be."

*

"I'm coming with you." Captain Morgan insisted; he had called the four together after receiving instructions from CNC.

"What were your instructions Captain?" Jerry was pouring himself a coffee but curious as to why Ross should want to leave the submarine.

Captain Ross handed Jerry a piece of paper which he read and then passed to Tony. "Captain, it say's in your signal that we are to be dropped discretely at a place called Ghar Lapsi if judged to be safe; I can see no reference to you coming with us." Jerry sipped the hot coffee gratefully.

By now Gaz had the piece of paper and was reading it with Betty; he wondered what the Captain was up to.

"You will note gentlemen….and ladies." Ross smiled at Betty who frowned in reply. "The signal say's we are to assist you as much as possible; so I will come to assist you."

"Absolutely no way," Betty said. "We are not here to pander to your action man fantasies."

"I will remind you CPO Williams that I am a Navy Captain and you are a lowly Chief Petty officer."

Gaz stood up aggressively, his face angry at the way Betty has been spoke down to, but Tony stepped in between Gaz and the Captain. "Captain, up till now I would say you have been very courteous and the hospitality you have shown us old boy has been exemplary; it would be a shame if I had to write a report to my friend the Prime Minister about your lack of, shall we say, respect for His Majesties agents working directly under his personal instruction……don't you think?"

Ross, however, didn't even flinch for a moment. "Mr. Davidson."

"I prefer to be called Tony, thank you."

"What?"

"You will address me as Tony, Captain; I outrank you."

"That might be the case…er…Tony, but at sea I am the sole commander and if I decide it is 'safe' to drop you at Ghar Lapsi; then I will be coming with you."

"What is this?" Betty said under her breath.

"Ross." Gaz spoke to get the captains attention.

"Captain Morgan to you," interrupted Ross with a show of how much he disliked Gaz.

"Ross," asserted Gaz ignoring the Captain's extreme snobbery. "If we do allow you to come with us, and that's only 'if', you do realize that you will be under my direct command."

Ross looked at Jerry and then at Tony; they both nodded in agreement. For the moment he found himself speechless and as he was re-assessing the situation, he noticed that Betty was smiling.

There was a period of quiet as everyone waited on a reaction from Ross, but Jerry broke the silence. "Gaz, what is the problem anyway if the Captain wants to come with us, we could do with another person?"

Gaz looked at Betty but she gave no indication about how she felt. "Only on one condition." He was now looking directly at the Captain. "From now on there will be no reference to rank; only first names to be used between us….even on ship, and when it comes to matters of the mission, you must be absolutely clear in your mind that I 'call the shots'…..Ross."

They all looked at Ross waiting on his reply; he was about to argue about something, but changed his mind, as he did, he held out his hand to Gaz, "I agree."

"Then," Gaz accepted the handshake and looked at his watch. "We have two hours to rest, get our stuff together and get off this sub before it gets light."

As they left to get ready, Betty looked at Gaz, "Is it wise to take him with us?"

"Probably not," Gaz replied, stretching himself out for a short rest along one of the couches. "But we shall see."

Betty smiled and joined him; the thought of the coming mission blanking out their grief of friends lost forever.

Chapter Twenty One

The scene at Marfa Ridge was just the same as when Zammud had left; there had been no attempt by the Libyans on the island to 'clean up' the debris. The bodies of the dead had been removed though, but Zammud could not get the horror of the butchered regiment from his mind. The others with him, including Angelina, seemed to be unmoved as they searched among the debris for serviceable weapons.

Zammud joined Angelina with the search. "Found anything worthwhile yet?"

"No. - One of the others has found a couple of serviceable weapons, but I'm afraid that most are too badly damaged to be of any use to us." Angelina sounded disappointed, but Zammud felt it as well. Then they spotted something that made their hearts leap. "That will do nicely," Angelina smiled as she lifted it heavily from the ground. "Heavy thing isn't it?"

Zammud gave her a hand to lift the long tubular weapon. "A hand held SAM," he said with satisfaction. "We could take out one of the transport aircraft with this."

"Or even a ship," Angelina said cheekily. As she laughed at her own joke she saw Zammud's face go serious.

"Angelina, you said it wouldn't be possible earlier at the check point, what did you mean?"

"Major, this is hardly the time or place to be….."

"I've never met a woman like you before." He had interrupted Angelina but spoke as though he were slightly embarrassed.

"Look Zammud, I felt it the first time I met you in hospital, but we could never be."

"Why?"

"You are a Muslim and a Libyan." Angelina was getting upset. "I am a Catholic, it would not be allowed, not after all this….even before all this."

Zammud was going to protest but one of the other Maltese came over. "You two ok?" He was looking between them both as though he sensed some form of tension. "Anyway, we've picked up pretty much most of what we can find……well look at that beauty!" His eyes caught sight of the SAM launcher. Angelina looked at Zammud for a moment before turning to speak to the others and discuss their 'finds', or lack of them.

Afterwards, when they had managed to load their disappointing cargo aboard the Mercedes, Zammud jumped into the rear seat again beside Angelina but they both said nothing more.

"Are we going back to Tarxien?" The driver was smiling; he was happy they had found a SAM.

Angelina nodded and the car drove back towards Mellieha.

*

"That could be them Admiral." The pilot was pointing to the FLIR (Forward-looking Infrared indicator). Ahmed could clearly see the marker that his pilot was pointing to on the terrain following radar console. It was the only movement at this side of the island and he was in no doubt it was his quarry.

"Let's go Airman; you will give me control of the cannon - please."

"Yes sir what type of ammo shall I program."

"You mean I have a choice?"

"Yes sir. You can have High-fragmentation and explosive incendiary rounds, or armour-piercing."

"Oh in that case we will have the incendiary if you please." Ahmed answered with a note of pleasure. *"This is going to be a real piece of fun."*

As the pilot quickly explained how the gun worked, the Ka-52 banked to its left and dipped as it dropped into its attack mode just north of Mellieha Ridge.

*

The Maltese driver was the first to notice the helicopter as it banked in the darkened sky; he had seen the glint on its metal sides as it came into the line of the moon light which was casting silver like shadows over the whole of the Island. He wasn't sure at first what it was but rather than take a chance with anything he turned slightly and told the others what he thought he had seen. Zammud, unaware of the threat, thought it was probably a 'spotter' looking for them, so not to worry as they would be well gone by the time the information was passed along the various military channels: He had no idea that the Russian made Alligators had been brought to Malta.

The first point at which Zammud knew he had underestimated the threat was when the Ka-52 opened fire with its fragmenting incendiaries. There was a serious of loud explosions, and then an infinitesimal moment later, the body of the Mercedes shook as the shells riddled its metallic body.

Zammud heard himself shouting, "Get down," but there was no way to escape the continuing blitz of the helicopter now hovering above them. As the glass and metal of the 'Merc' buckled and smashed, the two Maltese in the front died as they were literally shredded apart.

Zammud, still cowering under the explosive hail of phosphorous fire and fragments, had no idea how he managed to get out of the car, but he was aware that he was lying by the road side and from the corner of his eye he could see the SAM lying just within his reach.

*

Ahmed saw the Mercedes just in front of him and without even warning his pilot he opened up the Alligators gun and watched with amusement as the 'Merc' disintegrated under the impact of the four hundred or so shells the gun was carrying. He was considering, *"just for the experience,"* changing over to the armour piercing shells, when he saw a movement on the ground below them and slightly to his front.

Pointing to his front, he nudged the pilot, "What is that?"

The pilot looked hard for a moment as he kept his aircraft steady. "Looks like a........" His calm voice suddenly changed to a panic of shouting. "Get out, eject, eject.....get....." He never finish his message, the SAM that hit his Ka-52 entered the cockpit and moments before it exploded; took his head clean off.

As Ahmed flew into the dark at a breathtaking speed on his ejection seat, he saw the bright orange flash of the exploding Alligator; its rotors separated and twisting through the darkness. He then felt the intense heat on his body before the shock wave hit and rendered him unconscious.

*

After Zammud fired the SAM, and the explosion of noise suddenly ceased with the exception of the burning Ka-52 now lying a few hundred meters away; the night was plunged into a deafening silence. Zammud's head was ringing with the impact trauma but he managed to crawl toward wreck of the Mercedes. "Angelina, how are you?" He listened hard through the noise in his head but heard nothing. "Angelina where are you?" This time he spoke louder, and after listening for a few moments, he thought he heard a weak groan from the other side of the car. He crawled around, fighting to keep his mind conscious and just as he felt the darkness of unconsciousness pull him under, he saw Angelina lying in a ditch at the road side. He tried to shout but it was lost in the darkness that flooded his mind.

*

"Sir." The Duty Communications officer said as he stepped into the Control Room of the Vanguard Submarine preparing to surface. "The satellite has picked up a large explosion towards Mellieha Ridge."

"Any ideas?" Ross spoke calmly; his mind stayed on other things.

"No sir, it just came out of the blue sir, although an aircraft was traced in the area; most probable a helicopter."

Ross turned to Jerry. "What do you think; a crash?"

"Or resistance, fighting back," suggested Gaz.

"Good thinking old boy, could be the lead we need." Tony added.

"Ok….we will head for Mellieha when we go land side?" Betty suggested attentively.

"Probably as good a place as any," Jerry said.

"Prepare to surface." Ross made no comment; he had a sub to drive. "Up periscope Chief."

"Aye, aye, Boss."

*

When Gaz and his team landed at Ghar Lapsi, the dawn light was just starting to cast its morning haze across the surface of the sea, and they were grateful for its cover as they made their way from the small fishing huts that lined the quay and up the steep cliff face road. They were carrying a lot of ’kit’ with them so the walk up the steep incline was hard work, but eventually they reached the small junction at the top.

“Which way now Gaz?” Ross asked while looking out to sea, he was making sure the sub was already out of sight, and relaxed when he saw it had disappeared into the black depths.

“We can’t go via Dingli; the transmitter station will be crawling with Libyans.”

“So will Siggiewi, young man, there’s one there as well, you know.” Tony was familiar with the communication sites on the Island.

“Yes that’s true but we could get transport there, we need to get mobile.”

“I’m with you Gaz,” said Jerry. “But it might be a good idea if only two of us go into the town.”

“Ok.” Gaz opened his map. “You and a volunteer go into Siggiewi, the rest of us will wait here.” Gaz pointed to the ‘Underground Chapel’ known as the Laferia Cross. “Who wants to go with Jerry?”

“I’ll go,” Ross said cheerily. “We can’t leave the Air force to get all the glory.”

They all walked towards Siggiewi until they came level with the Chapel, then Ross and Jerry walked on towards the town. As they left Gaz shouted after them “Make sure it has ‘Aircon’ guys, it’s getting too hot to drive!”

Jerry and Ross waved while Gaz, Betty and Tony headed west along the track that would take them to the cover of the underground Chapel.

*

Admiral Ahmed was relieved to see one of his Libyan Coast Guard Corvettes heading towards the area that he was manipulating his chute into. He had recovered from the initial shock of being fired upon, but had no doubts in his mind that the perpetrator of the incident was the one and only Major Zammud, and he was now more determined that ever to track him down. As Ahmed hung suspended in the air above Malta, he could see the cliffs that surrounded 'Golden Bay' just beyond Bajda Ridge and started to pull on the Parachute's control cords so as to land in the shallow waters off the Bay. Ahmed felt an air of satisfaction as he watched the Corvette maneuver into a rescue position, but what the Admiral didn't know was that the Corvettes detour into Golden Bay, had allowed Ross's submarine to offload its 'cargo', and slip silently back into the depths off Ghar Lapsi without being detected.

Once on the Libyan boat, Ahmed lost no time in radioing his Communications Centre and ordered a search party into the area of the crashed 'Alligator', adding, as he shouted down the head set, "Major Zammud has become a very dangerous man…he must be caught." He paused and then added, as the Corvette revved and swung round to head back to Wied-Zurrieq where he was to be landed and drove back to Luqa to pick up another chopper, "He may be injured but if he resists arrest - kill him."

*

As Ross and Jerry entered Siggiewi the misty haze was starting to lift and the sun's orange morning glow was casting its blanket of warmth over the ground. There was no sign of any life except the barking of dogs and the morning sounds of the cockerels welcoming the day, but Jerry and Ross entered the town cautiously anyway. It paid off, as they randomly turned into a road that led to the Town's main roundabout, they almost walked into a group of Libyan soldiers who were changing their guard at a curfew post.

Jerry was the first to see the soldiers and reacted by pushing Ross against the side of a house they were near; without saying anything he 'mouthed' the words "Libyans," then nodded in the general direction. They both pushed themselves against the house wall and wondered what to do next.

Ross took the lead and nudged Jerry gentle, when he had his attention, he indicate with his eyes and Jerry saw the half open door in a house opposite, and understood. They both made a mad dash for the door and pushed it open as they 'dived' inside. Still without saying anything they lay against the hallway wall and rested, getting their breaths back from the adrenalin fueled dash. They were only inside the house for minutes when Jerry nudged Ross to get his attention; as Ross looked up from the floor he saw at once Jerry's apparent concern. In front of them stood an older Maltese couple and the man had a shot gun pointed threateningly at Jerry and him.

*

Father Dominique Caruana had found it easy to cross back into Malta, the Libyans, he discovered, had a lot of respect for Holy Men regardless of their ethnic/religious identity, he even at one point had been offered a lift by a group of friendly Libyan soldiers heading from Marfa point to Mellieha, which he accepted gratefully. As he chatted and joked with the soldiers he started to feel sorry that the circumstances undoubtedly made them enemies, but for a moment in time, he was able to see them purely as men with needs and his heart went out to them in compassion. The spell of equality was shattered however, as he rested in an abandoned café near the edge of the town in the early dark hours of the morning. First he heard the noise of a helicopter hovering nearby, then the sound of its heavy cannon firing. *"Why would the Libyans be firing over by the ridge?"* His first thought was that it was purely an exercise, but that thought was shattered by the night being lit up with an enormous explosion, as the helicopter was hit by what seemed to Dominique like a 'shooting star', and although he didn't know why, an inner sense told him he would be needed. It took Father Dominique only ten minutes to reach the crash site; as he looked around at the scene of devastation, he saw the burning Helicopter and immediately assumed that nothing could have survived the holocaust. While he was still considering the fate of the pilot, his hearing caught the faintest sounds of life coming from a badly shot up Mercedes. Praying into himself, he crossed his chest and then ran towards the wreckage of the car, to its rear he saw a man and a woman lying still but holding hands tightly. "*Dear Lord!"* He said to himself. *"These two are alive, and they look like Maltese."*

Father Dominique bent over the two casualties and started to examine them for injuries, but apart from some very heavy bruising, they both seemed otherwise OK.

"Who are you?" He asked hoping for an explanation more than pushing for one.

"I am Major Zammud, and the woman is Angelina, a nurse from Mtarfa."

"You are Libyan?" The Father asked, puzzled as to why a Libyan helicopter would want to be shooting at Libyans.

"I am a Libyan deserter and Angelina is all that is left of the resistance." Zammud's voice was by now very weak and faint. "You must help us Holy Man."

"Can you both walk?" Father Dominique had already decided to help them, even before Zammud had mentioned the resistance.

Zammud asked Angelina if she was able to move, but she only groaned.

"I think I can." Zammud said straining to get up.

"There is an old tower near hear," said Dominique. "You can rest and hide there....but you will need to be quick, the Libyan soldiers once organized, will be looking for you."

Zammud managed, with the Father's help, to get on his feet. Although he was shaky and weak, they both managed to help Angelina, still groaning and semi-conscious to her feet, and they almost dragged her across the rough terrain towards Ghajn Znuber Tower. By the time the Libyan search parties reached the site on Ahmed's orders; the trio were well clear and hidden.

*

"Who are you, and what do you want?" The elderly Maltese man asked, as his wife gripped his arm hard; she looked frightened but the man, in spite if his age and obvious frailty stood his ground fearlessly.

"Just take it easy with the hardware." Ross was raising his hand in caution.

"You are British?" The man was surprised and lowered his shotgun slightly.

"Yes," Ross decided to trust him.

"I used to work for the British Forces; RAFM, I was a 'snowdrop' way back in the seventies....you know an RAF policeman."

Jerry felt himself relax as Ross continued to explain who they were.

"Well I am Captain Ross Morgan of the Royal Navy and this is Wing Commander Jerry Shotts." Jerry smiled on his introduction.

"Wow!" The old man said, "And I was only a corporal." He turned to his wife, "Quick Rosie these men look as though they could do with a drink, its not often we get a full blown Wing Commander for breakfast my dear."

"Tea for me," Jerry added as the old woman turned and walked down a corridor into a room at the end.

The old man lowered his shot gun. "Tea eh - you must be Brits after all?"

As they all followed the woman down the corridor the old man turned and asked, "Why have you come here then?"

"That's a 'need to know' question," said Jerry not willing to get this couple involved in any trouble.

The old man laughed. "The military never changes eh….well I'll put it another way; how can I help you?"

"We need a car," said Ross almost as though it might be a totally impossible request.

"With Aircon." Jerry added humorously.

The old man stopped, then shook his head before slowly walking into his kitchen where his wife had already put Maltese bread and goats cheese out on a large wooden table.

"The car is not a problem; I'm too old to drive it anymore….but with Aircon…sorry, I can't help you there. Anyway sit, you must eat, and then I will show you my car."

Ross and Jerry had forgotten how hungry they were so they gratefully sat down to eat, however before they did they noticed that the old couple started to pray, so they lowered there heads and waited until they had finished.

"Amen," said the old man. "Now you can eat - my two friends."

*

When Ross and Jerry had finished the breakfast, enjoying the down to earth conversation of the old couple; they were led outside to the rear of the house and a broken down shed that seemed to second as a garage. As they opened the door, chickens came fluttering out of the dark interior, and Ross and Jerry started to wonder what type of broken down car would be inside; they were taken aback when the old man pulled off a cover that was protecting his car. It was old, there was no doubt about that, but it was still in an immaculate condition, the Mark.iii Ford Cortina looked as though it had never been driven.

"This has to be an antique," Jerry said admiring the smooth blue paintwork, and pointed wings.

"Aye." The old man was reminiscing. "This is my pride and joy."

"We couldn't possible take this car," Ross explained, "it's priceless."

"No…you must" replied the old man. "Whatever you are here for, I feel it's important, and let's face it, if I can help in some way to liberate the Maltese people….I will be contented."

"But….." Ross, however was cut off sharply.

"Let's be honest, if you take my car it will not be reported stolen and no one will be looking for you; you know it makes sense."

Ross looked at Jerry but he just shrugged. "Gaz isn't going to like it not having Aircon."

"He can walk then." Ross was smiling at the old man. "We have a lot to thank you and your wife for."

"Just do your work well lads; that's all I ask."

"We will not forget your kindness," Jerry said as the keys were put in his hand.

*

Ahmed had just been informed that there was no sign of Zammud at the crash site, as he was being taxied in a Westland Gazelle towards Mellieha. He was finding it almost unbelievable that anyone could have survived the terrible onslaught of the 'Alligator', and even though he guessed that the SAM had been launched by Zammud; he had to assume that it must have been a desperate fluke that he managed to hit the chopper. *"He must be there!"*

Ahmed spoke into his Comms helmet. "I want a thorough search made of the area; he cannot be far; I will be with you soon ETA ten minutes....find the treacherous deserter."

*

Betty was the first to see the blue Ford Cortina coming along the narrow track towards the underground Chapel where they were hiding.

"Gaz...Tony...you better come and see this....I really do not believe what I am seeing....talk about sending boys to do a man's work!"

Gaz and Tony came stood beside Betty at the front entrance to the Chapel; in the not to far distance they could see the Blue Ford coming towards them and Ross was frantically waving from the passenger side.

"My word," said Tony in surprise, "it's an antique Cortina....well I never."

Moments later the car came to a gravely sounding stop raising dust from the track where the cars brakes had locked the front wheels on the loose surface.

"What do you think guys?" Jerry and Ross climbed out of the driver's seat, both their faces lit with large grins.

"What can I say lads?" Gaz was trying to keep a straight face. "Its....well....I'm speechless"

Betty however was not so stuck for words. "There are two things men loose their common sense over and one of them is cars; I ask you, what on earth are we going to do with that old piece of Junk?"

"You said there were two things; what's the other?" Ross asked intrigued.

"What?" Betty's mind was filled with what she perceived as a significant problem.

"Two things Betty, you said?"

"Work it out for yourself, car boy"

"Ooooh.....touchy aren't we?" Ross was using the situation for his own fun, but Betty was well used to sailors banter and contemptuously ignored the comment.

"Ok lads that's enough....was this the best you could do?" Gaz was now looking inside at the old yet immaculate interior. "Nice though!" He caught a glimpse of a frown from Betty as he spoke.

"You cannot look a gift horse in the mouth," Jerry pointed out, "but we can explain on our way to the top of the Island, if we must."

"You must." Betty said sharply sarcastic. "I'm sure it will be very interesting to hear, after all it isn't every day one finds such a wonderful 'toy for the boy'."

"Let's get going." Gaz was beginning to feel protective towards his secret wife. "There's some serious work to be done.

"I'll drive." Jerry said as they all squeezed into the Cortina; Ross and Jerry in the front and Betty, Gaz and Tony in the back.

*

They had no choice but to follow the rough track road from Siggiewi to the North side of Rabat; there was a lot of Libyan troop movement at the Rabat/ Hamrun junction as well as a high concentration of Maltese workers trying to go about their own businesses, but the shear volume of traffic appeared to be working to their advantage. There were road side checks and barriers from time to time, but they were mostly waved through these to avoid holding up the Libyan military traffic. From there they followed the road past Mdina that took them to the outer roundabout on the edge of Mosta, then veering left they followed the sign posts to Zebbieh; by the time they reached the tiny village of Zebbieh, Ross and Jerry had told the others about the old couples kindness at Siggiewi.

"I take it all back boys." Betty interrupted, still sounding sarcastic, as the Cortina pulled up at a small Maltese café opposite the Skorba Temples. There was no sign of any Maltese locals or Libyan soldiers in the area so Jerry ran out of the car, and moments later reappeared with cool drinks for everyone. After a brief stop to refresh, Jerry started up the Cortina again and they then followed the road to Manikata where they unexpectedly found themselves caught up with large numbers of Libyan soldiers being drafted into the area.

Chapter Twenty Two

Zammud and Angelina rested from their wounds oblivious to the world around them. As soon as Father Dominique had settled them inside the Ghajn Znuber Tower, they had fallen into a deep sleep, partly due to exhaustion but also because of the heat, blast, shock and minor shrapnel wounds they had sustained in the fight with the Alligator; Father Dominique was worried that they may need water and food when they came round, so he decided to leave them alone and go on a search for the things he may require. Manikata was the nearest place where he knew to get what he needed, so after praying for his two dependents, he made the sign of the cross, and then left.

It didn't take the Priest long to reach the road that led into the village and, as before, he found the Libyan soldiers friendly, often waving to him as they headed into the search area where the Libyan 'Alligator' had crashed. When he eventually arrived at the outskirts of Manikata, he saw a village full of soldiers with very few Maltese venturing out into the streets, and that's why the Blue Cortina caught his attention. It was parked outside of a small local café on the edge of the village and for some unknown reason; he felt it looked out of place. *"Most people in their right mind wouldn't leave a precious antique like that in full view of the Libyans!"* He decided to investigate, conscious that something deeper was urging him other than pure curiosity. Walking up to the narrow door of the café, he stopped and peered in, but the dark interior made it impossible to see inside until his eyes adjusted after the effect of bright morning sunlight.

"Father Dominique…no it can't be?"

The Priest tried to re-focus his vision; he thought he recognized the woman's voice.

"It is." The same disembodied voice spoke again with a sense of excitement coming from the still dark interior. "Gaz…. its Father Dominique and he is safe and well."

The Priest then heard a shuffle of chairs and then moments later two people stood in front of him, their faces lit up with sheer joy. When Gaz and Betty flung their arms around Father Dominique he felt his spirit rise in new hope for the future.

"Gaz….Betty my dear children…I thought you were both missing…even dead." As the three old friends stood at the door of the small café embracing each other, the Maltese Priest wept away all his grief and held on to Gaz and Betty as though everything in his world depended on these two people.

*

Zammud was still in a semi-conscious state of exhaustion when he heard the sounds of a small helicopter flying over the tower they were in. He had a vague memory of the friendly Priest who had helped him and Angelina find shelter but his ability to make sense of the whole event was cloudy and unordered in his mind. As he lay unmoving on the hard floor of the ancient tower - a memorial to a time when the Knights of St John once ruled and protected Malta against a previous Islamic invasion - he laughed inwardly to himself of the irony of his situation: For some reason unknown to him at this time, he found it funny that he a Muslim should be protected by a Christian Priest and then an ancient Christian sect.

As he tried in his mind to make sense of everything around him, he heard the small helicopter pass over head, and instinctively knew that the sound meant danger to him and Angelina. Zammud turned his head; he had almost forgotten about Angelina, she was lying close to him and groaning as she was coming out of her unconsciousness. Then he heard voices, they were quite far away but he had no doubt they were getting closer, and they were Libyan. He crawled over to where Angelina was now stirring and placed his hand over her mouth to silence the increasing volume of her groans. When Angelina felt the sudden restraint on her mouth, she panicked and started to scream and struggle, but Zammud held her tight and at the same time tried to calm her down.

"Angelina…it's me…Zammud….you need to keep quiet and lie very still." As he spoke he nodded with his head towards the door of the tower where the sound of the Libyan voices was getting louder.

Angelina nodded, her recognition of Zammud becoming clearer, and Zammud lifted his hand from her mouth; as they lay in the dark interior of the tower, they could hear the helicopter hovering above them and the shouting Libyan NCOs giving out their orders to their men, as though trying to out shout the noise of the Helicopter's rotors. Zammud and Angelina felt trapped, there was nowhere to hide and nothing they could do except wait on the inevitable.

Zammud took hold of Angelina's hand and was surprised that she didn't try to with draw it, he did notice however that she was trembling uncontrollably, so he lifted his arm and placed it around her shoulders drawing her close; there was nothing else he could do to help her as the Libyans started to kick the tower's door off of it's hinges.

*

Admiral Ahmed was hovering above Ghajn Znuber Tower in the Westland helicopter when he saw the two weak people being carried from its interior. He felt a sudden excitement fill his whole being as he recognized one of the now struggling captives. *"At last my wayward Major, justice has been served after all....we have along overdue appointment."* He turned to the Westland's Pilot. "Put me down as near as you can to those traitors," at the same time pointing to a spot just ahead of the two fugitives and their now gathering captives. Once landed, Ahmed removed his Comms helmet, stepped out of the helicopter, and straightened his uniform before walking deliberately casually towards the group of excited men in front of him; he was determined to get maximum 'mileage' out of the situation.

After shoving his men aside to make a way into the presence of Zammud and Angelina; Ahmed now stood glowering at them both with a look if total contempt on his face. He reached forward and lifted Zammud's face up to his, so he could look him directly in the eyes.

"Well Major Zammud, we meet at last; you didn't think I would ever forget you, did you? After all you were one of my....er....better officers." He let go of Zammud's face feeling slightly annoyed that he saw no sign of any fear in his eyes.

"And who is your lovely accomplice?" Ahmed now turned his attention to Angelina, who was being held on her feet by two Libyan soldiers.

"You leave her out of this; she has nothing to do with you." Zammud said it with such anger and passion that his words came out like a serious threat; Ahmed smiled menacingly.

"So Major, it would seem you have more than a passing interest in this young Maltese lady." Ahmed walked around Angelina looking her over. "She will, I'm quite sure, give me some.... What shall we call it……entertainment later." He grabbed her dark hair and pulled it violently causing her head to whip backwards.

Zammud struggled to get loose but he was too tightly held by the Libyan soldiers around him. "You lay a finger on her Ahmed, and I will kill you."

"Take these traitors away," the Admiral shouted. "I will expect them at my palace quarters in San Anton within the hour."

As both Zammud and Angelina were taken away struggling and forced into the back of a large truck, Ahmed watched silently for a minute or two, then he casually walked to the waiting Gazelle and within minutes he was airborne and heading back towards Luqa, ignoring the antique blue Ford Cortina pass below him; he still had a British Submarine to find.

*

"We must hurry," Father Dominique said, after being introduced to Tony, Ross, and Jerry. "That helicopter seemed awful close to where I left the Libyan Major and the girl from the resistance." He had taken only a few moments to explain why he was in the village in the first place.

"The Major would be a handy man to have on our side." Ross was in agreement of moving quickly; he was already on his feet with his back pack half flung over his left shoulder.

"That's assuming he has defected?" Tony felt an element of doubt.

"We go with the Priest," said Gaz, placing his hand on Father Dominique's shoulder. "I would trust this man with my life."

"Me too." Betty answered in support of Gaz.

"You're the Boss," said Jerry, "let's go."

“Bless you all.” The Priest added as they picked up their personal back packs and headed out into the bright sunlight of a new day. As they drove down the narrow track towards the Ghajn Znuber tower, they saw a military vehicle convoy that passed them and then turned towards Mellieha. A moment later a Libyan Naval Westland flew overhead and banked before heading in the direction of Luqa.

When Gaz and the others arrived at the tower, Father Dominique jumped out of the rear door of the Ford and ran towards the shattered doors; the others sat in the car, Ross breaking the silence of the disappointment they shared with the Priest by stating the obvious. “Looks like we are too late guys.”

“Looks very much that way old boy.” Tony had just stepped out of the hot interior of the Ford; the others following his lead.

Gaz walked towards the Father; he was still looking at the spot where Angelina and Zammud had last been seen, but sensed Gaz’s nearness.

“We must go after them Gaz.”

“Look Father, I know you are feeling bad about this; we all are, but we have a mission….we can’t go running around looking for a Libyan Major who may or may not be a defector.”

The Priest looked at Gaz directly. “After all we have been through, you owe me this much Gaz.”

Gaz felt shocked, unable to reply, but the Priest continued. “Look Gaz there is virtually no resistance left on the Island, but the two people who were here…..they were trying to do something for Malta…..It must mean something that they shot down a Libyan helicopter and that a whole army of soldiers came looking for them, I’m not sure why you are hear Gaz but I do know you need these two people.” He grabbed Gaz by the shoulders and looked him directly in his eyes, “You owe me Gaz.”

Gaz was still undecided about what the Priest was insisting on when Betty came up beside them; she put her arm through Gaz's arm and drew him gently close in affection, and kissed his cheek. "What's up lover?"

Gaz was about to say something when Father Dominique interrupted. "Speak to this 'bone head' Betty; maybe you can get some sense into his ungrateful head."

"Dominique, that's unfair." Gaz expressed his disappointment as the priest walked away from them and the others still waiting by the Ford.

"Father, where are you going?" Betty was both concerned and mad. "What were you taking about Gaz?"

"He said we should go after the Libyan and the Maltese girl….and that I owe him!"

Betty ran after he Priest but shouted as she ran. "We do owe him Gaz….he married us, remember?"

Gaz felt uncomfortable as the others heard Betty shout; Tony thought he had misheard. "Jerry, did she say they were married, old boy?"

"They kept that a national secret," Ross remarked smiling, then he shouted over to Gaz, "you owe him Gaz Seymour, and it looks like pay back time."

As Betty spoke to the Priest, her pleadings were obvious, Gaz walked back to the Ford Cortina. "You heard right…we were married by the Father just prior to being arrested in Gozo by the police." Gaz paused when he remembered James's death at the hand of the Chief Superintendent. "And I do owe him, we all do….but I cannot ask any of you to go chasing after a renegade Libyan Major on the whim of the priest; we have a mission; the Scuds……"

Jerry interrupted Gaz before he could finish what he was saying. "Look Gaz, it strikes me that if we are to find the Scuds in the first place; the Libyan Major would be the ideal way of doing it."

"But we have the 'Satnav' kit from the submarine and the......"

"No good," Ross interrupted smiling, "unless they fire them again, and even then we will only get a fix on where they fired from; by then they will have moved on."

"So you are all suggesting we go after the Major?"

"Your call old bean," replied Tony as Betty returned with the priest.

Gaz turned and shook Father Dominique's hand as he and Betty waited on a decision. "We do owe you Father."

"Then we should head for San Anton Gardens," Father Dominique shouted to the others, "that's where they will be taken; the head quarters for Naval Communications and the office of Admiral Ahmed, but we must be very careful, I am told he is a very violent man."

"So the Navy is heading up the invasion then?" Ross spoke rhetorically, "seems they do get some things right then."

"Get away with you," said Jerry slapping his back.

Gaz smiled at Betty as they squeezed into the hot interior of the Ford. "No he might be right Jerry, the navy got at least one thing right that I know about."

"You're biased," replied Jerry.

"Or hen pecked old boy." Tony joked.

As they turned back towards Manikata, Father Dominique, Tony, Betty and Gaz laughed as Ross and Jerry made exaggerated hen sounds from the front. The Ford engines revved and it churned up a dust cloud before moving off, as its tyres spun, searching for a grip on the hard stony surface.

*

For Ahmed every thing was about power, even down to obsessive things like making sure he would be at

San Anton ahead of Major Zammud. In his mind it would not look right if he was not there to receive his prisoners; he realized that on this occasion he could not afford to miss the expectant rush of sheer 'domination' that he would experience. He had done it so many times in the past and relished the fear he saw in his captives eyes as he stood in his best uniform to 'welcome' them, but he knew that all these would pale into insignificance compared to the sheer delight of seeing his Major beg for the Maltese girl.

Ahmed knew that Major Zammud had shown no fear of him at the tower, and normally that would have worried him; junior officers who didn't fear there superiors were a threat, he knew that because he was once the same, a junior officer full of ideals and ambitions; it was important to get Zammud to beg, there was nothing else for it. Ahmed was pleased that Zammud had been captured alive, especially with the girl, her presence would make the whole affair profitable and for Ahmed; enjoyable.

He was dropped by chopper at the palace square and as was his usual practice, checked with his 'Comcen' in the Palace next to his Palacial office. "What's the word on the convoy with the prisoners?" As he shouted, the whole room stood to attention.

"ETA fifteen minutes, Sir," an anonymous voice shouted out.

Without replying Ahmed walked from the 'Comcen' and took the short walk towards his office. *"Only fifteen minutes to get ready; better hurry, I must look my best for the Major and his woman."* Once in he closed his door and prepared for the 'moment'

*

Zammud and Angelina sat for most of the journey in quietness; it wasn't that they didn't want to speak to each other, every time Zammud attempted, he received a heavy slap by one of the guards. He tried on one occasion to loose the tie-wraps around Angelina's and his wrists, but that also apparently warranted a slap by one particularly over zealous Libyan. Zammud tried to ask the soldier if he was in the habit of striking commissioned officers, but the slaps got harder, so Zammud decided that the soldier was relishing the excuse for violence; it was best they sat still and didn't speak.

Eventually, however, Angelina noticed the familiar streets of San Anton and nudged Zammud. As they entered the Gardens the lorry they were in grinded to a halt and the overzealous guard kicked them to their feet. "Come on get up and get out...**move**!" Jumping awkwardly out of the lorry to the ground, they saw the immaculately dressed shape of Admiral Ahmed only a short distance to their front.

"Welcome Major Zammud, I hope my guards have treated you well."

"Go stuff yourself," replied Zammud standing fully erect.

"Now, now Major, is that the type of language you usually use in front of attractive ladies?"

"Go stuff yourself," Angelina's voice was shaking but none the less determined.

Ahmed was unperturbed; he was totally in control of the situation and enjoying it immensely. He walked towards Angelina and sniffed the air near to her, speaking quietly. "You have a beautiful smell young lady; I think we will have a lot of fun together."

"You dare touch her and I will personally….." Zammud didn't finish his sentence, he had forgotten about the overzealous guard, and was sorely reminded with the wooden butt of an AK in his back.

As Zammud fell in pain to the ground Ahmed, still smiling, leaned close to Angelina intent on whispering something in her ear; but he never managed it. He doubled up in pain almost at the same time Zammud fell to the ground; Angelina being a nurse, knew exactly where to bring up her knee for the best effect, and the Admiral fell to the ground in agony beside Zammud.

Zammud saw Angelina standing upright and proud moments before the keen guard knocked her unconscious with the back of his hand.

Chapter Twenty Three

As Europe continued to increase the number of its forces along the whole length of the Mediterranean from Spain to the Greek Islands, Islamic nations from Turkey and North Africa started to build up their forces, mostly supplied by the wealthy states of Saudi. America sent a delegation to Saudi to protest about the supply of Arms and equipment to North Africa and other nations around Israel, but no agreement was reached because the Americans refused to withdraw its Navy from the coast of Israel. Libya sent a protest to the European Parliament about the illegal presence of British ships blockading off their coast, demanding that they stay within International boundaries, but this was refused until Libya agreed to withdraw its forces from Malta. The Libyan government, in turn, maintained that they were legally defending Malta from foreign interference as agreed by treaty. It seemed nothing could stop the threat of a full blown Mediterranean war. As if to remind Europe of its responsibility to withdraw its forces; another Scud was fired at Sicily from Malta; however, in Captain Ross's absence, the British Nuclear Submarine patrolling of the south of Malta received orders from CNC Norfolk to fire a single Trident Missile into the Libyan Military Air base outside of Tripoli, fitted with a conventional warhead. Although the damage was limited, it was enough to send a signal to Libya from the European Parliament that said in effect; "We are seriously committed to this." No retaliatory order was given by the Libyan government; they were prepared to wait until pressure from their Muslim Allies brought recognition of their sovereign right to rule Malta and establish a forward Islamic front. Meanwhile, in Gozo, relief agencies were starting to get supplies through to the thousands of refugees stranded there and the small sister Island was fast becoming a massive refugee camp.

*

It had taken Gaz and the others almost two hours to get near to San Anton due to the heavy traffic that was continually negotiating the narrow streets around Hamrun. The Military vehicles were the worst, they found getting around the tight streets extremely difficult, and Ross 'lost it' on a few occasions with holdups and the standard of driving which had him continually swerving to avoid a crash. At one point Jerry pointed out that the same 'hold ups' they were experiencing now, could be a good thing if they were on the run, that seemed to work for at least a few minutes, then Ross was back again to Ross's private version of what a good 'road rage' should sound like, and this continued until they reached San Anton..

They waited until it was dark; walking around the area in two's to pass the time. No one questioned them; why they were there or what they were up to, and when the sun started to set they met up again to plan their next move.

By the time early darkness in Malta arrived; they had already decided on a plan. Gaz, Jerry and Father Dominique would try to gain access to the Palace and search for the two captives. "It isn't much of a plan." Betty had commented, but when pressed, she conceded that she probably couldn't come up with a better one.

"Just be careful," she said to Gaz as they each removed a small revolver from their personal back packs before they left to climb over the wall that surrounded the

Gardens where the Presidential Palace stood. "I'll be here when you get back - lover."

As Jerry helped the Priest over the wall and then disappeared himself, Gaz turned, waved to Betty and the others, then he too went over the wall and into the darkness.

*

Gaz, Jerry and the Priest crouched low in the flower beds at the other side of the wall, where they decided to wait a few moments to see if they had been spotted by anyone. As they crouched together peering into the eerie moon lit scene in front if them, Gaz could see the well attended flower beds, bushes and trees, that gave the gardens their famous name; a short distance to his front was the dark outline of the silhouetted Palace. He was meditating on the peacefulness of the silvery scene when Jerry nudged him, and motioned him to look to his right: Someone was moving among the dark bushes.

Gaz indicted that Father Dominique should stay where he was and that Jerry should come with him; when it was understood, Gaz and Jerry crept away to surprise the lone figure who seemed to also be trying to keep out of sight. When they were in striking distance, they both jumped from the cover of the bushes and grabbed the stranger, pulling him into the bushes struggling. It didn't take the two men long to realize that the person they were now trying to restrain was a girl, and although she wasn't very strong, she was feisty. Gaz held on tightly to her mouth while Jerry held her down with his arms fully wrapped around her slim body.

"Hold still," Gaz said struggling to hold her squirming body, "and we will let you go."

When she heard his voice the girl went still, but Gaz noticed a puzzled look in her eyes.

"We are...if we let you go you must promise not to scream...ok"

The girl nodded her head in agreement and although Jerry was shaking his head against the idea, Gaz slowly released his hold of her mouth.

"You are British?" She asked in a quizzing voice.

"Yes," Gaz replied. Jerry let go of the girls arms and shrugged as though resigned to the disaster that could follow a bad decision.

"Why are you here in the Admiral's Gardens?"

"Oh that's just great!" Jerry humped. "What are you going to do now Gaz....shoot her?"

"No one is going to shout anyone," said Father Dominique suddenly appearing.

"Geees Father!" Jerry got a fright from the Father's sudden appearance.

Father Dominique kneeled down with the young girl and spoke to her in Maltese for a short time. Gaz was worried about the outcome of their 'break in' now and so was Jerry, but they both sat in silence until the Priest was finished.

"I have some good news for you both." Father Dominique wasn't smiling. "This young lady is called Agnes and she was the Personal Assistant to the Admiral who now governs Malta."

"You said 'was'?" Jerry was now curious.

"He...lets say...abused his authority."

"What?" Gaz said, not really expecting a repeat.

"The point is," continued the Priest, "she will help us get inside; she knows everything about the Palace; she was working here before the invasion, for two years."

"Why would she do that?" Jerry asked, still doubting that such good fortune happened in real life.

"Oh that's simple Jerry, she hates the Admirals guts....that's all I am prepared to say for now."

"Can we trust her….how do we know it's not a trap?" Jerry was looking at Gaz with a measure of concern.

"If Father Dominique trusts her…then so can we. Let's get on with this job."

*

Major Zammud was dragged along a long corridor inside the Presidential Palace; he had been in the Palace before but this corridor was new to him. He could hear the ranting threats of the Admiral a short distance behind him but he was more concerned about Angelina. He twisted his head to the side as his feet scrambled to find a grip on the stone tiles floors, but the force of the two strong soldiers holding him by his bound arms was too great. Zammud was in agony with the plastic tie-wraps around his wrist but still he struggled as he attempted to get a view behind himself. Then out of the corner of his eye he saw Angelina being dragged, still unconscious, between another two soldiers close behind him so he stopped struggling and let the two Libyan soldiers drag him to where it was they were taking them; he was sure that Angelina was being taken to the same place.

They soon arrived at their destination; it wasn't a cell or anything like Zammud had expected. Once the soldiers had opened the large wooden doors, Zammud and Angelina were roughly flung into a small room beyond, where they both landed heavily causing Zammud to groan. When the soldiers left, Zammud heard the locks being secured and he knew that wherever they were, whether it is a cell or the small but well furnished reception they were now in; they were still the Admirals prisoners and there was nothing he could think of to get them away to a place of safety.

He heard Angelina groan.

"Angelina; are you alright?" Zammud slid across the floor until he had her head resting on his lap, then he stroked her hair gently.

Angelina came round slowly at first, but it didn't take her long to work out where they were when the memory of Ahmed doubled up I agony came back into her mind. "I'm ok Major....did I do the wrong thing?"

"Well it certainly put an end to the Admirals dignity."

They sat for a moment in silence but then Angelina started to giggle under her breath.

"What's funny?" Zammud didn't see the funny side of anything at the moment.

Angelina made no attempt to lift her head from Zammud's lap instead she replied, "The Admirals face, my sweet Major, you should have seen it from where I was standing."

Zammud felt his face start to smile at the thought, but when he looked at Angelina and her apparent delight at the memory, they both bust out into peals of heavy laughter that echoed down the empty Palace corridor where they were imprisoned.

*

Admiral Ahmed was so inflamed with anger when he picked himself up from the ground, that he ordered the three Libyan soldiers who had responsibility for Angelina, locked up for disobeying a direct order. Then he turned on an unfortunate soldier who had seen the funny side of his Admirals discomfort and ordered him to be shot. As he walked angrily back into the Palace, intent on dealing directly with Zammud, the soldier's NCO pleaded with the Admiral to withdraw his order. "Ok," Ahmed snapped a response to the NCOs annoying determination, "I will shoot you instead." Then he stepped into the cool interior of the Palace leaving a silent and stunned Libyan Corporal.

Once inside the Palace Ahmed was met by a young navy signals officer. "Sir you have a message from Tripoli…and it's very urgent."

Ahmed stood as though he was being pulled in different direction, after a moment or two of silence he responded to the officer, "Ok bring the message to my office." *"Zammud and his Maltese vixen will have to wait for the moment."*

Once in his office he sat down slowly and rested, the blow to his groin had sapped his strength but he knew he couldn't show it. The young officer followed moments later with a paper informing him that the military airbase at Tripoli was temporality out of action and that there would be no more supplies by air until further notice. The message also added that the Scuds and their associated launchers had to be moved and hid somewhere were they could not be found; any more firing of the Scuds was also temporality suspended.

"This will take hours," thought Ahmed. He stood up, slammed the table with the message still in his hand and shouted, "Get me the Scud commanders." *"Zammud I haven't forgotten you."*

*

Gaz and Jerry followed the priest and the Maltese girl Agnes, through the Gardens until they came to the main gate that opened into the Garden side of the Palace.

"I don't like this." Jerry was still not convinced of the Maltese girl's authenticity.

"I don't like it much either," Gaz replied, but I still think we can trust the priest judgment.

Agnes ran ahead of the other three and then approached the guard at the gate and started to talk to him like an old friend.

"What's she saying Father?" Jerry asked quietly.

"They think she is still the Admirals PA; it's a very simple plan Jerry; we are just going to walk through the gate."

"I wish you had discussed this 'simple' plan with us first." Jerry was by now full of deep concern.

"Look," Gaz said quietly, "she is waving us through."

Gaz, Jerry and Father Dominique walked up the steps to the gate and fully expected to be arrested, but the Libyan guards waved them through laughing as they passed. Once through they headed towards the Palace Archways that would take them inside.

"Agnes, what did you tell them?" Jerry was puzzled that they were allowed in so easily. Agnes smiled but didn't answer him. She turned and said something in Maltese to Father Dominique. "Gaz - Agnes says the guard told her that a man and a woman were taken to one of the guest receptions at the end of the corridor here….and something else which I didn't understand….something about a 'Full Monty' show at the officers mess….what ever that means."

Jerry smiled at Agnes and she smiled back before they ran along the corridor that led to the reception room. Once there, Agnes knocked on the door and said something quietly in Maltese; as they all waited, the moments seemed like hours. Jerry and Gaz held their SIG pistols ready, both fitted with silencers, just in case they were interrupted by any Libyans. Then suddenly, but very quietly, they all heard a faint knock from the other side of the door; they had found Angelina and Zammud.

*

“We haven’t got much time.” Father Dominique’s voice sounded urgent as he tried to force the door with his shoulder.

“Wait Father!” Gaz stepped forward and gently pushed the priest to the side. “It will need a lot more that good intentions to get this thing open.” Gaz cocked his pistol pulling back on the main body of the weapon as he spoke, then turning his head slightly to avoid any shrapnel that could come from the splintering lock on the door, he fired two shots. The noise though muffled seemed to explode in the corridor and echo along its dull walls; for a moment they all stood still as though expecting a group of Libynas to come running. However, nothing happened and Jerry, the first to move, kicked hard at the door and it flew open under the impact. Inside the reception room they saw Zammud and Angelina huddled in a corner, holding on to each other I fear.

Father Dominique ran inside the room and went straight to the couple. “Oh my children, my dear children…..what have they done to you?”

“Were alright.” Zammud replied lifting his arms to get assistance to rise; they were both still dazed from the encounter with the over zealous guard and the Admiral.

Jerry ran to help the priest while Gaz stayed at the doorway keeping an eye on the long corridor. “Quickly!” he said without turning to face the others, “we need to get going.”

Jerry, Father Dominique and Agnes struggled to get Angelina and Zammud up, but once up, they were both able to stand, even though they looked a bit shaky on their feet.

“I don’t know who you all are,” Zammud said passing Gaz at the door still supported by Jerry, “but we owe you.”

“Enough time for that later,” Gaz replied. “First - lets see if can get back out alive.”

Father Dominique and Agnes passed moments later with Angelina; Gaz noticed there was blood on the nape of her neck and wondered what she had done to deserve the Libyan's anger.

"What's the plan Gaz?" Jerry was now standing a short distance from Gaz still supporting Zammud; his arm around the Libyan Major's waist.

Gaz shrugged but before he could say anything, Agnes interrupted. "Come, follow me…I know a way to get out."

Jerry looked at Gaz as though to say, "Should we?"

Gaz nodded and when Jerry looked perplexed he asked, "Have you got a better idea at the moment mate?"

"We are wasting time." Agnes said irritated by the lack of trust they were demonstrating in her.

"Lead on." Gaz said, indicating the way forward with his pistol still in his hand.

Agnes smiled at Jerry as though she had won some sort of contest and then she and the priest dragged Angelina into the darkness of the corridor.

"I think she likes you." Gaz said to Jerry smiling, as he took hold of Zammud's arm, placing it over his shoulder to help carry him. Jerry didn't reply; he seemed detached from what was going on around him for the moment. "I guess the feeling mutual then?" Gaz asked casually as they followed the other three into the darkness. Jerry still said nothing.

*

Agnes took them on a maze like journey through a seemingly endless amount of corridors; although in reality the whole trip through the Palace took only a short time. They all felt the tension build up expecting at any moment to 'run' into Libyan soldiers, but the palace, to all intensive purposes, seemed deserted. At one point they stopped as

Agnes warned them to get out of sight; she had seen a man dressed in the uniform of the Libyan Navy hurriedly pass in front, but he didn't see them and within moments they were on the move again.

Eventually they reached the outside perimeter fencing of the Palace, where they could go no further. "We have to go through the guard once more to get back to the Gardens." Agnes pointed with her face in the direction of the gate they had come through earlier.

"Not much chance of a.... 'Full Monty'.... with two more people than we arrived with." Jerry noticed Agnes blush as he deliberately emphasized the 'Full Monty'.

"We will have to rush them," Gaz said reloading his SIG. "It's me and you Jerry, but we have the element of surprise."

"With you buddy." Jerry replied coming along side Gaz and tapping his shoulder. He then felt a kiss on his cheek and when he turned he was looking directly at Agnes who had moved close to him and Gaz.

"Be careful."

"Er....ok...I...er...will." Jerry felt his face flush where the wetness of Agnes's kiss seemed to linger.

"After three - Casanova?" Gaz asked, smiling at Jerry's obvious embarrassment.

"Get on with it man." Jerry sharply replied, attempting to remain as 'manly' as possible as he perceived he should under the circumstances.

*

Gaz and Jerry approached the two Libyan sentries across the small court yard where the gate to the Gardens was situated. The Libyans saw the two strangers walking directly towards them and immediately, threateningly lowered their AK's.

“Halt!” One of the guards shouted, but Jerry and Gaz kept walking towards them.

“Halt…my weapon is ready to fire.” The Libyan guard challenged once more.

Both Jerry and Gaz felt a measure of comfort with these challenges, recognizing that the Libyan was going through his official challenge procedure; they had one more challenge before the guard would fire, and that gave Gaz and Jerry enough time to get close enough to ensure a ‘kill’.

“Halt or we will…..” The rest of the guards words were lost to the sound of two dull thuds and the clatter of their weapons falling to the ground as they grasped at their hearts before collapsing; dead.

As they dragged the two guards out of sight and then turned to wave the others on, Jerry noticed that Agnes was not with them.

“Where’s Agnes?” Jerry asked Father Dominique who was busy crossing himself when he saw the two guards as he arrived at the gate.

“She was with us one minute, and the next she was gone….that’s all I have….like a ghost.”

“Well where ever she is, we owe her an awful lot.” Gaz was pushing open one of the large metal gates as he spoke. “Come on mate we need to go.”

Angelina and Zammud were by now able to stand themselves and as they all made their way into the dark shadows of San Anton Gardens; they could hear the heavy footsteps of several Libyan soldiers running across the Palace courtyard they had crossed moments earlier.

“They’ll not be shouting warnings when they discover the guards,” said Gaz trying to hurry them up.

“We’ve no chance now,” Zammud added, “it was a good attempt my friends, but……” His words were cut short by the first salvo of bullets hitting the earth and concrete path to their sides.

*

Betty and Ross had been standing by the wall next to the car park in front of the gardens chatting, trying to look as much as lovers as they could, while at the same time keeping their distance; Betty had no desire to get close to the Submarine Captain even if it was to save their lives or the lives of their friends. A Libyan soldier passed once or twice and glanced their way but other than that, the night seemed quite.

Ross had just finished looking at his watch concerned about the time the others were taking, when he heard shots being fired from within the Gardens walls.

"In the car Betty; that's our lot for sure."

Betty didn't argue, she had heard the dull sounds of the SIG's mingled with the harsher cracks of Kalashnikovs.

With the engine revving in the old Ford Cortina, and its wheels screeching to find grip on the tarmac beneath it, Ross and Betty raced towards the nearest locked metal gate that led into the garden. There was a loud thump as the front of the Ford hit the gate, followed by the sound of bending metal as the momentum of the car took the gate off it's hinges.

"Right sailor boy…turn right." Betty shouted; she had seen Gaz and the others dive for cover behind one of the several fountains in the Garden. Ross obeyed without thinking and within moments they were directly in the Libyans line of fire. Ignoring the well kept plant beds and bushes, Ross drove the Ford straight to where the others were sheltering; the bullets from the Libyans were hitting the car everywhere but Ross managed to keep the old Ford on course. Under a continued hail of bullets Ross stopped the car next to Gaz and Jerry. "Get in!" Ross shouted and Jerry, Gaz, Father Dominique, Angelina and Zammud unceremoniously piled into the back seat of the car. As Ross reversed the Ford to turn and escape, a Libyan soldier stepped in front of them and raised his AK menacingly. Ross wasted no time in revving the engine and as the car screeched forward once more; the careless soldier was hit, sending him spinning to the side of the car screaming in agony as he was left lying among the flowers.

As they left San Anton Gardens and swerved right towards Rabat, the back window of the Ford shattered when a hail of bullets found their mark, but Gaz and the others kept low, and soon they were out of sight and range from the place where Gaz and the others had been rescued. Betty sat in silence, staring ahead, her eyes fixed and unmoving.

*

Admiral Ahmed was returning from the task of directing the re-deployment of the Scuds, when he first heard the shots from the direction of the Palace. He tried to call ahead but there was no response to his calls, even from his personal mobile. He reached over from the back seat of the military green saloon and prodded the driver in the back. "Get a move on driver."

"Aye, aye. Sir," the driver said pushing his foot reluctantly to the floor.

As they turned the corner past the Corinthian Palace Hotel; now closed and used as a billet for officers, they saw a blue antique Ford Cortina speed away from the Palace gardens pursued by soldiers firing after it.

"Stop!" the Admiral shouted to his driver, and as the car stopped, he pushed the switch that lowered his electric window.

Ahmed leaned out of the saloon's window and caught the eye of the nearest soldier. "What is happening here?"

The soldier was out of breath when he answered but attempted to speak and stand to attention at the same time;

he was nervous when he saw the Admirals arm epaulets. "Sir some people shot the two guards at the Palace gate. We thought we had them cornered sir but that blue car drove in and rescued them…sir."

"Why would.....?" Ahmed got out of his car. "You and you….come with me; quickly."

The Admiral ran ahead of the two guards who were following him and led them down the corridor where Zammud and Angelina had been held. When they arrived Ahmed didn't bother to look inside the reception room; the splintered lock on the door told him all he needed to know.

"Who would risk.....?" Ahmed had no need to think further, his instinct told him the answer. *"The submarine, it must be them."* He turned to his guard, "Get me an armed combat chopper."

"But sir, I'm only a private soldier, I don't have that ……"

"You dare defy me?" Ahmed had no time for more perceived incompetence.

"Yes sir….I mean, no sir…I mean …er…."

"You're wasting my time."

The soldier said nothing in reply; he saluted and ran off into the night.

Chapter Twenty Four

The young girl sat still in the abandoned animal pens within the furthest corner of San Anton Gardens. She had made a very rudimentary home of the stable she was now in and had often thought about the pleasure she would have when the opportunity for revenge presented itself. That was until recently; prior to meeting Jerry. Getting the Admiral back for what he did to her, was all she thought about, but now there was a new focus in her mind. As she wept, Agnes half wished she had left with the others, but then, she had reasoned, her hated Admiral would escape her vengeance and she couldn't allow that for any reason. Agnes tried hard to re-focus her thoughts once more to images of Ahmed pleading for mercy, but they no longer came to her, instead she saw Jerry in her mind looking around with concern for her, and she started to cry heavily. *"I'm sorry Jerry, but I cannot leave here....not yet...not ever."*

*

Just before they reached Rabat, Ross swerved the old Ford off the main road and followed a very uneven and narrow road that had no sign posts to indicate where they were going. On either side of the narrow road were high loose rock walls that hid them from any chasing Libyans and Ross was able to slow the vehicle down so that the occasional holes in the surface of the road, that made the whole car shudder when hit, could be avoided. As he maneuvered the car along the track, he noticed a small brown tourist sign that was pointing south and read Verdala Palace and Busket Gardens so he took the left turn indicated and within minutes they found themselves surrounded by thick trees deep in a cool valley.

"Seems like a good place to rest Betty." Ross commented glancing at her. When she didn't reply he reached over to touch her but withdrew his hand quickly; it was wet and sticky. Ross shouted "Gaz" while at the same time slamming the brakes of the car so hard that it swerved off the narrow road and onto a wild grass verge at the side. When the car had stopped, ignoring the complaints from the back seat, he quickly moved out of the driver's seat and ran round the front of the car to where Betty was sitting.

"Gaz…you better get out….Betty has been hit, I think." As he spoke to Gaz, Ross was already pulling Betty out of the Ford and on to the hard dry road side dirt.

Gaz said nothing as he struggled to get out of the cramped back seat of the car. Once free of the others he knelt down beside Ross, lifting Betty's head onto his lap and 'cupping' her face with his hands. "Betty are you ok?" He asked quietly and gently, but there was no answer.

Father Dominique got out of the car and kneeled beside Ross and Gaz, placing one arm on Gaz's shoulder. "Let me have a look," he said, then placed his fingers on her neck to check for life. They all waited in silence as the Priest lifted her arms next and felt her wrists. "She's alive."

"Thank you!" Gaz said quiet prayer, looking up at the sky; he wasn't sure who he was talking too but he didn't care either; he just needed to say thank you to someone. "How bad is it Father?"

"Looks like she took a bullet in her side; it shouldn't be fatal, but she cannot be moved very far."

Angelina knelt down beside the Priest. "I'm a nurse Father, let me have a look."

As Angelina examined Betty's wound and Gaz continued to gently stroke her face, the others gathered around Father Dominique at his request. "You all must go on without me and Betty, I can find help. There are a few houses by the Verdala Palace gates; I will get help for her there."

Jerry pointed to Gaz. "We're with you on that one Padre, but will you be able to convince Gaz?"

"I will stay with her as well," Angelina said standing up, "she needs to have the bullet taken out."

"No," Zammud replied, fearful of loosing Angelina, "it's too dangerous…there will be Libyans swarming all over the place soon."

"I am staying Zammud, I am needed here."

Gaz was listening to the conversation and gently laid down Betty's head on the ground before standing up to face everyone. "I'm not leaving her."

"It's the best thing to do Gaz old man; she will be safe with the Priest and Angelina." Tony spoke for the first time with a hint of authority.

Gaz looked at the Priest and Angelina. "Look after her…she is very special."

"We will," Angelina replied.

"And you look after yourself," Zammud said, looking towards Angelina, "you are special too."

Angelina blushed but smiled.

"Come on then," said Ross, "we have an appointment with some Scud's."

As they squeezed back into the Ford, Father Dominique and Angelina looked on in silence. They still didn't speak as the Blue Ford sped off down into the green valley of trees and disappear as the narrow road took a left bend in the distance.

*

Admiral Ahmed was slightly disappointed when a Gazelle turned up at San Anton rather than an 'Alligator'; however he consoled himself when he saw that the Gazelle helicopter had been fitted with a 30mm GAIT gun. *"It'll have to do,"* he said to himself, as he picked up the comms helmet then lifted himself into the left hand seat next to the pilot. "Rabat," he said to the pilot, "then out from there….we are looking for an old Blue Ford Cortina."

The pilot nodded and within moments the rotors were 'chopping'. The Gazelle lifted from the tarmac in front of the Palace, hovered as the pilot checked directions, then dipped as it picked up speed and headed towards Rabat.

*

From Busket Gardens Ross took the road marked 'Clapham Junction' and when they arrived at a white Chapel on the cliff edge of 'Dingli Cliffs', they stopped, unsure what to do next. It was Zammud who spoke first. "Did I hear you right back at Busket; you are after the Scuds?"

"That's right," Gaz said cautiously. No one else spoke.

"I can help you."

"Why would you want to do that; aren't you a Libyan?"

"Yes my name is Major Zammud of the Libyan Infantry; but I am afraid my Country thinks I am a traitor."

"You will be if you help us," Ross said turning to face the others in the back seat of the Ford.

"My loyalty is to Libya, but Admiral Ahmed is a mad man; he needs to be stopped." Zammud spoke with anger when he mentioned Ahmed.

"And what about the Maltese Nurse, old boy," Tony asked? "How loyal will you be to her?"

Zammud was taken back by the new direction of questions. "If you do not trust me then let me go, I will return to the Priest and Angelina."

"What?" Jerry said sharply. "And allow you to tell every Libyan from here to Valletta what we are here for…..no way."

"I believe him," Gaz said now getting out of the hot interior of the car; with the others following suit. "He was locked up when we found him and this Admiral sounds to me to be a nasty piece of work, by all accounts."

Jerry raised his hands in protest but said nothing, instead he turned away and looked out to the vast sea in front of the cliffs.

"Ok Gaz." Ross was now standing beside Zammud. "It's your call on Zammud here; what now?"

Gaz looked at Zammud. "You said you could help?"

"The Scuds, when they are not in use, are stored at Kalafrana near Birzebbuga - its not too far from here."

"Good a place as any to start Old Boy," Tony said smiling at Gaz.

"We need to get rid of the car," Zammud said, "every Libyan on the island will be looking for it."

"What?" Ross was stunned by the sudden revelation.

"No way!" Jerry added.

"The car goes." Gaz replied firmly without any hesitation.

"But Gaz it's an antique; it's…."

"Going over the cliff." Gaz interrupted causing Tony to laugh into himself. "Come on everyone – and I mean everyone - help me push it over."

"Oh that's adding insult to injury," Jerry said as he leaned on the back of the Ford ready to push.

"Good bye beautiful." Ross kissed his hand and laid it on the bonnet of the car before joining the others.

"The British are strange," Zammud thought, as they all heaved the car over the edge of the cliff and watched it tumble down the few hundred feet, finally crashing in the green allotments below, sending parts flying in all directions. As the others turned to start walking along the cliff road, Ross stood looking down at the wreckage of the Ford. *"What a waste!"* Then he too turned and left.

*

They had only walked as far as Gebel Cantar when they heard the sound of a vehicle coming their way.

"Get out of sight," Gaz Shouted to the others, and they all scattered making the most of the sparse cover in that area. As they lay waiting a green Libyan thirteen seater van came down the narrow road; the driver oblivious to everything except the CD player he was attached to.

Suddenly the van came screeching to a stop in front of the Gaz's hidden men. "What is he doing?" Jerry asked, pointing across to the other side of the road.

Gaz looked in horror; Zammud had waved down the lone driver and was now talking to him. As they watched they all wondered what would happen next; they didn't have to wait long, as the Libyan soldier stepped out of the driver's seat, Zammud grabbed him from behind and forced his arms into a painful arm lock. While the soldier's face was being forced against the door of the van, Zammud waved frantically at the other to come out.

"Doubt him now Jerry?" Gaz asked as they stood up and ran towards the van; Jerry said nothing.

As they tied up the soldier with rope they had found in the back of the untidy vehicle, Ross slapped Zammud on the shoulder. "You had us worried for a moment there you know."

“What do you want done with your friend here Zammud?” Tony asked cheerily as they made sure the Libyan was securely disabled.

“We can drop him off at Wied Zurrieq; he might enjoy a trip to the Blue Grotto.”

“Hope he is a good swimmer old bean,” Tony added.

*

Ahmed and the pilot had searched all over the Rabat area and were now heading up towards Dingli Cliffs and the transmitter site that was situated by ‘Tal-Vecca’ on the edge of the cliffs. He was getting frustrated and found it hard to believe that an old blue Ford Cortina could move about the countryside unseen. They landed by the Transmitters and after speaking to the signals officer in charge of the site, took off again and headed towards the cross roads sign posted ‘Clapham Junction’. They had only just become airborne when the pilot nodded sea ward to get the Admiral’s attention.

“Sir, look over the cliff next to that Chapel.”

The pilot flew over the cliff edge and then took the Gazelle carefully down to the Allotments that perched on the cliff edge before dropping off towards the dark seas below. As the chopper came to a hover just above the ground Ahmed saw the remains of the blue Ford.

“Quickly pilot, take us up; without their transport they will not get very far.”

Once more the Gazelle rose above the cliff edge and started to sweep the area of Clapham junction, but they saw nothing. As they widened the search they flew over a Green Libyan army van missing it by a few meters, but there was no sign of the fugitives Ahmed was looking for.

“OK Pilot head back to Luqa we will have to think this through further; sooner or later they will show their hand, and we will have them; including our elusive Major Zammud."

*

It was heavy work for Father Dominique and Angelina carrying Betty uphill through the trees at Busket but they soon came to the houses that faced the Verdala Palace's main gates. They saw movement behind one of the shuttered windows of a house so the Priest knocked on the door.

"Please go away; we don't want any trouble here." The voice was that of Maltese man.

"My name is Father Dominique, and we have a seriously injured young woman here."

"Just leave us; we have no more to give you." The voice replied shakily.

"In the name of all that is holy; show us some mercy," Dominique pleaded. "If this British woman does not get treatment soon, she may die… do you want that on your conscious?"

Dominique could hear an argument between a man and a woman which seemed to go on for a long time.

"We have no where else to go," Angelina pleaded, "please help us."

The argument stopped at the sound of Angelina's pleading; then they heard a woman's voice reply. "We will help you…get the door….George, don't be so selfish."

Father Dominique and Angelina breathed a sigh of relief as they heard the locks being undone. When the door finally opened they were greeted by a large Maltese man, and his small wife pushing from behind him. "Come in please….let me help you….George… get some white sheets."

“God bless you both, “Father Dominique said helping to lift Betty, who was now groaning, through the open door way.

*

After dropping off their Libyan captive at Wied-Zurrieq, whom they tied to a concrete post at the bottom of the boat ramp, Gaz and the others then headed towards the port of Kalafrana taking the costal route past Hal Far industrial estate to the Ghar Hasan Cave, where they stopped to formulate their next move.

Chapter Twenty Five

Now aware of the stiff resolve of the European Countries facing the Islamic nations over the issue of Malta, many of them started to talk about 'peace' and 'compromise'. A delegate was sent to Brussels to discuss the many problems now facing both sides and after a lot of debate; both sides willing to meet the other part way, a treaty was signed and the world breathed a sigh of relief. There would be no war over Israel or any attempt to expand the Islamic territories. Libya protested to the Arab Council about being 'sold out', and they found themselves isolated with a growing threat of an invasion by British forces to retake the Maltese Islands.

Assurances were received from the Arab Council that no action would be taken against any attempt to invade Malta by a legitimate British force, but would rally if any other country attempted to support the British. It looked like a show down was inevitable between Britain and Libya over the rights to Malta; Libya refusing to retreat.

*

Admiral Ahmed knew his time was running out, he had received word from Tripoli that a British invasion was possible and that he would be expected to resist at all costs. He was presently at Luqa Airport waiting more information about an expected attack when an army Lieutenant approached him and saluted smartly.

"Yes Lieutenant?" Ahmed was pacing back and forward in a small office that was once a ticket collection point for tourists.

"Sir…thought you might be interested, we have just picked up a soldier from Wied-Zurriq. He was tied up to a concrete port there and mentioned something about some British and a Libyan Major…Sir."

"Take me to him," Ahmed said, then stopped and thought for a moment. "*Of course the green army van we flew over*." "Cancel that…Lieutenant. Get me the pilot who was with me when I flew in…we are going out again."

The Lieutenant came to attention; saluted the Admiral and then left.

Within a few hours the Admiral and his Gazelle were once more air borne and heading for the coast, their first stop would be Wied-Zurrieq and they were there in minutes. When the Admiral was convinced there was nothing to see that indicated what had happened to the green van, he told the pilot to follow the coast road down towards Birzebbuga; it was at that point he knew why the British from the submarine had landed. *"By Allah….They are after the Scuds."* He turned and shouted to the Pilot. "Get me the Scud commander at Kalafrana…quickly." He had just finished shouting when the Gazelle was rocked violently by a large explosion towards the Port at Kalafrana. Ahmed heard the Gazelle's warning tones and saw various lights flashing as the pilot struggled to keep control of the aircraft; he was just getting to grips with it when another explosion rocked the small chopper again, this time flinging it far of the coast line and out to sea. As it spun around over the water Ahmed started to pray, his mind filled with a real fear of dying, but just when he thought they would hit the surface of the sea, the chopper suddenly lifted under the pilots control, and Ahmed felt his stomach sink gratefully. As they flew on towards the Port a large black mushroom cloud was rising into the air partly blocking their vision from the total devastation on the ground below.

*

The plan was simple. Zammud would lead Gaz, Jerry, Tony and Ross into Kalafrana Port, pretending to be Maltese workers; Zammud's fluent Libyan would vouch for them at the gate. Then it was a case of finding the stored Scuds and, using the small explosive devises they had with them in their packs, damaging them beyond useful repair.

The whole plan even though simple, worked a treat and without any delay or hold ups, the team found themselves inside the Port, following Zammud to the storage containers where the Scuds launchers were kept.

Tony kept guard while the others packed their devises into various places on the launchers; it was guess work as none of them really knew much about Scuds. "We could have done with Betty being here now," Gaz said placing a device inside a launchers door, "she could have told us all the weak points……hope she is ok."

"She's tough is that one." Ross said placing his hand on Gaz's shoulder, "She'll be fine you'll see."

"That's it!" Zammud shouted. "Let's get out of here….the timers are set for fifteen minutes."

As they ran for the gate, a guard shouted for them to stop, but they kept going until they heard his AK being cocked.

"Geees," Jerry said flinging his hands in the air as they all slowed down to stop. Gaz looked at his watch as he raised his hands above his head. He was counting to himself as he did, but his lips were moving silently. "Twenty three, twenty two, twenty one……."

Zammud saw what he was doing and nodded to the rest to look at Gaz, by that time he was down to, "Fifteen, fourteen……."

They all stood for a moment as the guard walked towards them.

"Five, four, three, two, one……."

There was a pause that seemed to last for an eternity, as Gaz and the others flung themselves onto the hard concrete road. The guard was about to shout but the words never came. The explosion sent a huge fireball upwards and outwards from the Scud's location, the force behind the explosion sending anything within the immediate area into the air; including the Libyan guard.

Gaz felt the heat searing over his back but looked to see if the others were ok. One by one they lifted their hands heavily. Gaz got to his feet and started to run tapping the others as he passed; soon they were all running away from the scene of destruction, cheering, laughing and congratulating each other as they ran.

They saw a Libyan Gazelle in the sky above them as it passed over them and disappeared into the black cloud of smoke, but they paid little attention to it; the mission was complete, now they could go home.

*

Admiral Ahmed walked back along the long corridor towards his Palacial Office; he was weary and broken. He glanced at the Naval Communication Centre as he passed but had no strength to go and cause his usual mayhem. Once inside he pulled off his gun belt and flung it across a wooden chair in the corner of the large office. Then he gratefully sat on his luxury leather chair allowing his weight to relax and fill every contour. Ahmed thought he saw something move to his right so he gently swung his chair in that direction.

"Oh it's you....I thought you had gone......come back for some more then?"

There was no answer as the person he was addressing moved closer.

Ahmed thought he saw a glint from something in the person's hand. *"By Allah...it's a knife."*

"You're not serious are you? Come over here and help me with my boots."

Still no answer, but Ahmed began to feel sweat running from his brow into his eyes. He reached for his gun but then remembered he had flung it over the chair in the corner.

"Come now I'm sure we can work this out amicably....you cannot hope to get away with such a thing."

By now the person had moved so close to Ahmed, he could see her burning red eyes; red through nights of endless weeping.

"Plead for mercy....filth," Agnes said vehemently, now within stabbing distance of the Admiral. "Plead and beg like I did you monster....beg before I kill you."

Ahmed felt himself shaking, he tried to shout for help but the words wouldn't come. He felt a sharp pain as Agnes lunged forward and planted her knife into his chest.

Ahmed looked at her, his eyes full of hate and loathing, "I will never beg anything of you."

Then she thrust again.

He tried to stand up to protect himself, but his legs gave way and he fell to the floor, as he crawled away from Agnes, his blood left a thick red trail on the marble tiles. The last thing he knew was Agnes standing above him; she was weeping as she grabbed his hair and lifted his head to expose his neck. She died shortly afterwards under a hail of bullets, when a group of Libyan soldiers charged into the office and saw Agnes standing over the mess that had once been the Admiral.

Chapter Twenty Six

Shortly after the destruction of the Scuds and the other military equipment stored at Kalafrana, British troops landed at Marfa Ridge from Gozo where they had prepared for a long fight. However, with the Admirals death many of the Libyans simply gave up; there was no desire to fight in them. The British did come across the very occasional element of resistance but when that happened, the local Maltese rose up and defeated the opposition. Soon Maltese everywhere were following the example, and in a short time the Libyan forces were surrendering to the British Forces rather than fall into the hands of the revenging Maltese populace.

*

After being rescued by his submarine off the coast of Wied-Zurrieq with Gaz and the others, Ross locked himself in his cabin for several days. He was so upset about missing the firing of the Trident missile from his own ship; he couldn't face looking at his men, especially his junior officers who had been tasked with doing the job in his absence. He felt an air of superiority when ever he entered the ships mess, emanating from almost everyone around him; they knew and Ross knew they would probably never get another opportunity this side of their careers.

"Professional snobbery," was the only thought of consolation he could muster.

*

Jerry returned to Sicily and his desk at the British section of the base; it didn't take long for him to feel at home again, especially when 'Chops' his PA dropped his coffee all over Jerry's fleshly washed summer uniform.

"Sir," Chop's said wiping up the brown mess from Jerry's desk, "you have a signal from European Joint Command."

Jerry smiled as he wiped the brown coffee from the white piece of paper.

"It's good to be back Sergeant."

"Its good to have you back," Chops replied walking towards the office door quickly before his Wing Commander lost his sense of humour.

"Sergeant!" Jerry shouted, smiling as he saw the large man freeze.

"Sir?"

"Get the unit commanders to my office; looks like we may be going back to Malta."

"Sir?"

"Come on Chop's get a move on…I haven't got all day."

As he left and closed the door Jerry heard the phone drop onto the hard floor as it slipped out of 'Chops' padded hands.

Jerry leaned back on his chair and looked out of his window at the various aircraft sitting on the 'pans', *"It really is good to be back."*

*

Father Dominique Caruana was given the appointment of Bishop of Malta for his part in showing compassion to every side involved in the crisis, and he immediately set in motion reforms to the Islands religious community. His bravery was noted by the new British High Commission and he was asked to mediate between the European Government and his own government to re-establish a British Base on the Island; a job that he took on with joy.

*

Betty sat in the sun facing the Verdala Palace, she had been recovering from the wound to her thigh for six weeks and was still in some pain, but she was enjoying the peace and the warmth of the high noon Maltese sun when she heard a helicopter coming near.

"Angelina, quickly come out here." Betty shouted but didn't move, the wound to her leg was healing but as yet she was not able to stand.

Angelina came running along with Father Dominique to watch as the military helicopter hovered now just beyond the house they were at.

"Is it Libyan," Betty asked unsure of what would happen next?

"I'm not sure," said Angelina as the aircraft settled on the area in front of the Palace gates.

"Father, what do you…?" Angelina had turned around to speak with the Priest, but he was walking slowly back towards the house, with a smile on his face, and muttering something to himself.

Angelina turned her head back, just as she heard Betty fall onto the ground; she had tried to get up from her wheel chair. "Betty what are you doing?"

Betty pointed at the Helicopter from the grassy patch she was lying in, her face lit up in intense joy.

Angelina looked up from where Betty was lying and tears started to fill her eyes as Gaz and Zammud ran towards them, shouting their names above the 'chopping' drone of the helicopter as it lifted back off the ground, dipped, and flew directly over them before banking and disappearing over the tree tops of Busket Gardens below.